THE FOURTH REICH

MITCHELL PARKER CRIME THRILLERS BOOK 3

HELEN GOLTZ

For my two wonderful aunties—
Pamela Westwood and Fay Wardell

1

MITCHELL PARKER STOOD ALERT, WATCHING AND listening. At six-foot-two with dark hair and an athletic build, he was ready for this, trained and attuned. He squinted and his blue eyes scanned the area. He had just downed one suspect at close range but he saw a movement, a shadow in the window of a building opposite. He dropped low, loaded two rounds into his handgun and ran in the shadows towards the building. He was feeling good, fit again; time had ensured his injuries from the last mission were more mental than physical now.

There it was again; the same movement. He raced to the building, easily taking the two flights of stairs and bracing as the figure emerged from the top stair. In a split second he assessed the enemy and fired. A noise behind made him wheel around, gun at the ready, but he stopped just in time as the picture of a child appeared.

In his earpiece he heard the command to stand down. Mitch unloaded his weapon and holstered it. He moved down the stairs back to the command center where Joseph Nabor, the training instructor, waited. He stood a foot shorter than Mitch and a foot wider, most of it muscle.

"Not bad, not bad at all, Mitch," he said, taking the gun from Mitch and checking it.

Mitch grabbed a bottle of water while he waited for the report. He followed Joseph to his desk and dropped into a chair opposite.

"How did you feel?" Joseph asked, taking a seat.

Mitch shrugged. "Fine."

"And the point-blank range shots?"

"No problem. It is closer to what we've experienced in the real world lately."

Joseph nodded and looked at Mitch's score sheet, made a few notes, and signed it. "Out of the sixty rounds, you did pretty well. You did better at the two-handed shooting after stage one, but most agents do. Fifteen yards was your best, but all up you got fifty-two out of the sixty. A good result. That's Hogan's Alley and your VirtSim both done now," Joseph said, referring to the Virtual Simulator Tactical Training system that Mitch had recently undertaken.

Mitch thanked him and while looking over the sheet, finished the bottle of water. "What did Ellie get?" he asked after his team member Ellen Beetson.

"Fifty-eight," Joseph said with a smile. "Don't need to look that one up, she's a crack shot."

"Damn, she's done it again," he sighed.

"If it's any consolation, you're ahead of the rest of your team ... Nicholas and Adam," Joseph said.

"Nope," Mitch rose, "the only consolation, Joe, is that she's on my team." Mitch smiled and departed with a wave.

2

THE FILM FLICKERS ON THE BARE WHITE WALL OF THE museum ... black and white, grainy. In the dark, the museum guests watch, their faces lit by the light that spills from the haunting images. On the white wall screen, a line of people shuffle in rows of two through the Auschwitz arch and into the bleak surrounds. Some glance around, their faces masks of confusion. At the gate, dressed in striped pants and tops resembling pajamas, some in striped coats, are gaunt prisoners watching the new arrivals. The new arrivals are hurried by German guards—officious men with weapons. One woman, a mother, clutches the hand of a teenage girl as she looks directly at the camera—a look, a plea for help.

The camera pans to the end of the line where people are being herded off a train freight carriage, clutching their luggage and each other's hands. A dog breaks away from the guard and rushes towards the row of marchers, and many scream in fright, pushing the people in front of them to move faster. Soon the platform is empty except for a pile of suit-cases, several guards and their dogs, and a number of bodies. The train moves slowly away.

The film cuts to another scene—a long line of people are being marched out of the camp. They are painfully thin and trundle along. Nearer to the gates a small group of prisoners look out with trepidation. The camera closes in on one man then the film flickers and disappears.

There is a sense of relief from the audience that it is over. Suddenly the screen comes to life again. A message appears in large red handwriting, written across the last frame of the film ... *Nazi, Jew hater, fake!* It flashes for five seconds before the film frame goes to white, then crackles and stops; the room re-turns to complete darkness.

Guests at the presentation gasp, some look em-barrassed and look away; some appear angry that the guest of honor should be humiliated in this way ... one person claps.

3

MITCHELL PARKER, WEARING A DARK NAVY SUIT, CRISP white shirt and blue and gold patterned tie, paced around his office reading a file. He went in one direction, past the back of his desk, past the meeting table, across the glass windows and entrance door, and back to where he started. Occasionally he stopped, looked up to think, and then continued his path. From the office opposite, John Windsor watched him.

It was early Tuesday morning at the FBI offices in Washington D.C. and only a couple of staff had arrived. John Windsor, the Executive Director for the Trans-National Crime Unit and Mitch's manager, sat across the room, directly opposite Mitch's office. In his gray suit, almost the same color as his well-groomed hair, he sipped his tea, waiting for

Mitch to finish the file and react. Seeing Mitch close the file, John rose and walked over to his office.

"What do you think?" John asked.

Mitch exhaled. "I think you need to get *Ghostbusters* on this one."

John laughed. "But really."

"I mean, really." He dropped the file on the desk and it opened, showing a black and white photo of a man with a shaved head, wearing a faded jacket with the Jewish star on it, the Star of David. "Got anything else?" Mitch asked.

"I've sent you some CCTV footage. I'll give a full briefing to the team at eight this morning if you want to check it out before then."

"What do you think?" Mitch asked, stopping John as the doorway.

John exhaled. "I'd say there's something in it."

———

"Welcome Adam," John said when the team had taken their seats in his office.

"Thanks, John." The new member of the team raised his take-away cappuccino in acknowledgement.

John looked at the faces in front of him. Last assignment, Mitch had let one of his agents go, transferring Samantha Moore into Computer Forensics,

7

where she was more suited. Ellen Beetson, an original team member—small, fit, a crack shot and diver with shoulder-length blond hair—remained second-in-charge.

The two other male team members were Nicholas Everett—tall, blond, a childhood friend of Mitch's and ex-Air Force pilot—who had come into the team through the backdoor as an informer, but had earned his stripes to stay, and Adam Forster—a tall, wiry, dark-haired agent who had just returned from a long UK stint—who was newly assigned to Mitch's team. They had worked together on a job in London only six months earlier and Mitch had full faith in his abilities, maybe less in his attitude. Mitch was prepared to take that risk to have Adam Forster's skills on board ... Adam was ex-MI5 and MI6, had served in Northern Ireland, Germany, Bosnia, Russia and China and undertaken counter-espionage work for the British foreign intelligence service. Being fluent in four languages was also handy.

"I have a case which is a little unconventional," John began.

"Is it a case yet?" Mitch asked. "I still think it is one for *Ghostbusters*."

"Hold that thought," John said. "There's been a series of incidents at the Holocaust Memorial Museum. Last night an honored Jewish guest, Benjamin

Hoefer, was delivering a speech at the museum to launch his father's biography; his father survived a Nazi death camp. At the end of his talk he showed a film which featured his father in the last frame. It starts with Jewish citizens being marched into Auschwitz and ends with the camp inhabitants being marched out just before the Soviets arrived. Now watch what happens."

John played a file on his computer, projecting it onto the wall opposite. The team turned to watch as the footage of the Jewish prisoners being pushed out of the train onto the platform played across the screen. It cut to the columns of prisoners being marched out of the camp. The film narrowed in on a small group of prisoners at the Auschwitz gates, closing in on one man before fading out. "Keep watching now," John said. The screen flickered alive again and the bold, red words reading *Nazi, Jew hater, fake!* flashed across the screen.

"Wow," Ellen exhaled.

"So why are we getting the case?" Mitch asked.

"There's been a number of incidents at the museum late at night when it is closed, things missing, items defaced—but more importantly the Jewish guest speaker Benjamin Hoefer has had death threats," John said. "He just began a book tour. I won't say it is an easy case, the file is light on."

Mitch nodded his agreement. "Has Benjamin Hoefer got security appointed to him?"

"Yes, but you'll want to chat to him and the museum staff, maybe do a bit of surveillance and digging, you know the drill," John said. He glanced at his watch. "I've got a meeting in five minutes, any questions?"

"So someone thinks Benjamin Hoefer is a fake but fake what? Fake Jew, fake sympathizer or was his father a fake?" Adam asked.

"Pretty hard to fake being deported to Auschwitz when you're in the film frame, unless the footage is a fake," Nick said.

"How's your German, Adam?" Mitch asked.

"Gut genug," Adam answered. "Good enough!" he translated.

"Okay, let's get copies of the file, everyone have a read and meet in my office in twenty minutes. We'll strategize." Mitch rose to leave.

Ellen Beetson cleared her throat. "Mitch, John, before we go, I want to say something if that's okay?"

"Sure," Mitch said.

"I know that I am the only girl in the team now," Ellen began, "but I don't need to be protected, carried, or pampered. I expect that you will acknowledge my skills, respect that I am Mitch's right-hand person and can hold my own in a fight, with a gun and underwater. Yes?"

"Absolutely," Mitch said.

Nick and Adam nodded.

Ellen reached out for the file. "I'll do three copies." She walked out to the copier.

Mitch watched her leave. "She's five-foot-four and scares the hell out of you, doesn't she?"

———

Twenty minutes later, with fresh cups of coffee, the team gathered in Mitch's office. As Adam entered, John walked past and called out. "Adam, get a haircut."

Mitch looked at Adam's short ponytail that clipped the back of his suit jacket.

"Seriously?" Adam dropped into a seat opposite Mitch.

Mitch shrugged. "See how long you can get away with it."

"Yeah, Mitch has been able to get out of counseling for years by pretending he doesn't hear John," Nick told him. "Worth a try."

"It's not that I'm ignoring John," Mitch started, "it's just that every time you turn around there's someone wanting to know what's going on in your head."

"And you don't want to know what's going on up

there," Ellen finished for Mitch as she flicked through the copy of the file.

"Thanks Ellie," he smirked. "By the way congrats on still being the best shooter in our team."

Ellen grinned. "Ah, you've done your test."

"I have, and full credit to you. Glad you're on my team."

Ellen nodded her thanks. "Good of you, Mitch. A lot of managers and team members, especially male team members," she said with a glance to Nick and Adam, "wouldn't be such good sports."

Mitch frowned. "Yeah well I'm pissed off and I still want to beat you, but well done anyway."

Ellen laughed.

"That's because you're usually the best at everything, Mitch, so this is out of character," Nick said, loosening his tie and sitting back on the chair.

"No I'm not," Mitch answered defensively. "Ellie is a better shooter and diver, you're better at navigation and math, and Adam ... well I don't know yet."

"Driving," Adam said.

"No, I doubt that," Mitch smiled, "but there'll be something. Hopefully we'll find out before you leave in a year's time."

"I'll do my best to find something," Adam joked.

"Okay, let's get to this case," Mitch began. "Aside from what you read in your notes, this is what I can tell you about the guest speaker, Benjamin Hoefer."

He looked to his notes. "He was born in 1939, he's now seventy-four; his father was Eli Hoefer, born in Berlin on 22 September, 1920 and died here in the US in 2005 of heart failure, aged 85. Eli was a law student when he was taken to Auschwitz with his wife, Yetta in 1941. Benjamin was two years old. He was taken in by the neighbors, a childless couple." Mitch showed Adam the file and the couple's name.

"Gynther and Antje Bäcker," Adam pronounced the names in their German dialect, "or as we might say, Ginter and Ancha Baker."

Mitch continued. "Yetta, Benjamin's mother, died in the camp, Eli survived and returned to collect Benjamin who was seven when he returned in 1946."

"Benjamin wouldn't have recognized his father," Ellen said.

"No, wouldn't have known him," Mitch agreed.

The group looked at the photos of the family.

"Amazing there are any family photos," Nick said. "So why did Benjamin wait almost a decade after his father's death before putting out his father's story and his own memoir?"

"Good question. Worth asking, as well as how the photos survived," Mitch agreed. "Eli brought his son Benjamin to the States in 1948. Benjamin was schooled locally and graduated as a teacher of languages and literature and has taught all his life. Two months ago, Benjamin released the memoirs and has been touring with the publisher to promote them. They tell the story of his father's life and what he recalls about his own time with the German family," Mitch continued. He picked up Benjamin Hoefer's book. "I'll speed read it tonight and pass it around."

"I've already read it," Adam said.

"When? It's only been out a month," Nick said.

Adam shrugged. "I bought it a few weeks ago. I like to read, it helps me sleep at night."

"And?' Mitch asked.

"Well sex helps too," Adam joked.

Mitch gave him a wry look. "And what did you make of the book, I meant."

"Ah," Adam grinned, "the book. Benjamin paints his father as a hero; surviving the camp, helping others, doing the long march. But what's interesting, more so now that I've heard about this incident at the museum, is that Benjamin doesn't get anyone to validate his father's version of the story. He then elaborates about his own childhood, living with a German family and how he was passed off as a German child."

"What about Yetta?" Mitch asked.

"He talks about the loss of his mother, but again there is no investigation into her, how and when she died in the camp or any accounts from survivors who remember her ... if there are any still alive—they'd have to be in their mid-nineties by now. He recites what he was told about his mother by his father."

"Odd, there's a line of investigation there too." Mitch added a note to his list. "So as well as that, we need to find out why Benjamin is being threatened, why he is being called a fake or why his father is being called a fake, who has access to the museum after hours, what groups Benjamin belongs to or represents, who was at the function, who might have access to that film and see where the original is if that is not it, and get anything we can find about their history."

"Anyone got any Jewish connections?" Ellen asked.

The three men shook their heads.

"Mm, bad luck," Mitch agreed. "Okay, Adam and Ellie, start with the author Benjamin Hoefer, then move onto the book." He handed it over to them. "Validate what you can and talk to whoever can give you insights...whoever might still be alive. Nick and I will head to the Holocaust Museum."

"You're not sold on this one are you?" Nick asked.

Mitch frowned. "From what we know to date, I don't know why they'd put FBI agents on it. Unless there's something they're not telling us, again."

4

A HUSH DESCENDED AS THE CHIEF EXECUTIVE OF THE
New Aryan Order (NAO), Dirk Schmid, strode down
the long aisle in the middle of the packed room. A self-
assured man in his forties, six-foot-two, with broad
shoulders, athletic, tanned with thinning blond hair
and sharp blue eyes, he wore the Nazi uniform like the
model of the perfect Aryan man. Two men followed
him on stage, his brother Thorsten, the organization's
financial controller—a slimmer version of Dirk but
with fearful eyes—and the operating officer, Michael
Krupp, a respectable looking man in his sixties.

Close to three hundred men and women rose to
their feet, and as Dirk turned at the podium to address the audience, he saluted them. In unison, the
members responded with 'Heil Hitler' salutes. Be-

hind him large banners featuring the swastika hung from the ceiling. A large framed photo of Adolph Hitler took pride of place on center stage.

This was no normal party; no skinheads or thugs looking for a fight or somewhere to belong. Admission was by birthright and achievement only: German ancestry, a degree qualification and an investment of half a million dollars each. They were the educated, wealthy elite; and dangerous. Together they prepared for the Nazis' return to power but Dirk Schmid had another agenda—a very personal one involving Benjamin Hoefer.

He took a deep breath and looked out over the audience; his colleagues resplendent in their uniforms. He drew strength and pride from what he saw. He began his address using the words of Adolf Hitler:

"My German countrymen and women ..."

The audience burst into applause and shouted, "Heil Hitler."

Dirk Schmid continued. "Every month we gain in strength. I look around and I see so many great minds sharing a vision. The Führer said in his speech at the Berlin Sports Palace on January 30, 1941, that *'changes of government have occurred frequently in history, and in the history of our people. It is certain, however, that never was a change of govern-*

ment attended with such far-reaching results'." The audience murmured their agreement.

Dirk continued, talking over them. "The Führer says the Reich was desperate and he was called upon to take over the leadership at a time when it did not seem that they could ever rise to power. I quote 'We were given power in circumstances of the greatest conceivable pressure, the pressure of the knowledge that, by itself, everything was lost, and that, in the eyes of the noblest minds, this represented a last attempt'." Dirk looked up for effect. Like Adolf Hitler, Dirk's oratory skills were his best assets. Seeing he had the audience in his hands, he continued.

"The Führer said, 'unless the German nation could be saved, by a miracle, the situation was bound to end in disaster.' When he started the Movement, he had but one thousand members. Can you imagine that? How that changed once the Führer came to power! In his words, 'here are 85,000,000 Germans looking into the future with pride and confidence. They are heirs of a great history.' We are now heirs of a great history and this is but the beginning."

Every person in the room rose to their feet and cheered.

"Sieg Heil," Dirk Schmid led the crowd.

"Sieg Heil, Sieg Heil, Sieg Heil!"

5

MITCH DROVE PAST THE AUSTERE BUILDINGS OF THE Holocaust Memorial Museum. Out the front, a bus pulled up and tourists piled out. He indicated and turned left into D Street and pulled his black Audi into the parking station.

"Mind if I stay in the car?" Nick said, tapping his fingers on the armrest between them.

Mitch looked over at him. "Why, what's wrong?"

Nick sighed. "Nothing." He opened the car door and got out. Mitch did the same and locked up.

"Are you serious?" Mitch asked falling into stride beside him as they left the parking station.

"No, yes ... this place freaks me out." Nick looked around uncomfortably.

"We're not even inside yet. You should have said, you could have partnered Ellie or Adam."

"What? And missed out on the chance to spend some quality time together?" Nick said.

Mitch grinned. "Yeah, figured you've been missing me, given you and Sam spent so much time together last case."

"Alas poor Samantha, I knew her, Horatio." Nick shook his head.

Mitch grimaced. "I still believe it's the right thing, she was out of control and—"

"Don't start, she had to go," Nick agreed before Mitch began his guilt trip on moving agent Samantha Moore out of his team.

"Yeah, she had to go." He self-consciously rubbed his arm where a burn, now healed, had been as a result of Samantha's maverick behavior.

The two men entered the museum. The same height but mirror opposites—Mitch dark hair with blue eyes to Nick's blond appearance and green eyes —they looked out of place in their suits amongst the museum-goers.

Mitch went to the information desk while Nick stood against a wall out of the way of a tour group heading to the museum lifts. Mitch waited until he had the receptionist's attention. She was a well-groomed, middle-aged woman in a black suit with a sensible haircut.

"Mitchell Parker and Nick Everett to see Hanna Berkman please," he announced.

She nodded, scribbled down the names and picked up the phone handset.

Mitch stood back and waited. Hanging up she caught his attention as a continuous flow of people gathered around her desk taking the information sheets. "She'll be with you in a moment Mr. Parker, if you care to take a seat." She pointed to a bench seat against the side wall.

"Thank you." Mitch nodded and moved to join Nick. "Been here?"

"Yeah, we had the tour when we were recruits," Nick said.

"Oh yeah, I forgot that they still do that," Mitch said, having gone through the training a few years before Nick.

Mitch saw a slim woman in her late-fifties, or possibly early-sixties, approach him. He stood up and introduced himself and Nick.

"Come through to the exhibition room and I'll tell you what I know," Hanna Berkman said.

Mitch summed her up as he followed. She looked kind, but in-charge, sensible and knowledgeable.

The two men followed her through the crowd and into a special room that was sealed off from the public.

Hanna turned to face the men. "Benjamin Hoefer's exhibition of his book and special artifacts was due to open today. Last night was the launch and that is when the incident took place. So as you can understand we're delaying the opening until we have the all-clear from either yourselves or the police that there's no evidence in the room that will be destroyed," she said.

Mitch and Nick moved further into the room as Hanna closed and locked the door behind them.

"This exhibition tells the story of the last evacuees from Auschwitz from January 17 to 21," Hanna explained as Mitch and Nick looked at the images and displays. "The Germans marched more than fifty-six thousand prisoners out of Auschwitz and its sub-camps. Many of them had survived the camp but would die on the march, just before liberation. They marched them in columns in bitterly cold conditions with little or no water, food or rest. Those that were too weak to continue were shot along the way."

Mitch nodded, listening. "Death marches."

"Yes, that's what they were," Hanna agreed.

"Why did they evacuate them then?" Nick asked.

"The German military force was collapsing, the Allies were closing in—the Soviets from the east, and the British, French, and Americans from the west. They began to panic, to move prisoners out of the camps near the front," she said. "Benjamin Hoefer's memoir begins here because it is when his father returns home to him. His father survives the death march. In his book, Benjamin does go back into the past to tell his father's story of his time in Auschwitz, but the most moving image is this one." She pointed to a large black and white photo featuring a long line of people being marched out of the camp by the Germans. Close up in the right hand side of the shot was a number of prisoners standing near the gate. One man was circled; Benjamin's father.

"And the film reel that is shown is the film footage of this shot?" Mitch asked.

"Exactly," Hanna said. "But the next frame has been desecrated. We were mortified, as you can image. Would you like to see it?"

"Yes, please," Mitch said.

Hanna went to a wall phone, pressed an extension and requested that the film be shown. Within a few minutes the footage flickered on the same blank wall as on the night before.

Mitch and Nick watched the railway scene then the next frames as the prisoners were herded out of the Auschwitz gates bearing the words "work will set us free." Eventually, the film flickered and disappeared before the message appeared in large red handwriting ... *Nazi, Jew hater, fake!* A few seconds later, the film frame went to white, then crackled and stopped.

Hanna turned to Mitch and Nick.

"Can Nick speak with the projectionist?" Mitch asked.

"Of course," Hanna said. Again she went to the phone and within moments a small door opened at the back of the room and a young man appeared. He beckoned Nick to enter the projection room.

"I have some routine questions if I may?" Mitch began.

"Of course, Mr. Parker, let's sit." Hanna moved to a bench seat in the corner.

"Mitch, please." Mitch sat and leaned forward, his hands clasped. "Why?"

"Yes, I've been wondering that as well. This is the first time we have had anything of this kind happen here." She sighed. "I've read Benjamin's book; it's an important work for Jewish history."

"Have you or the museum been threatened?" Mitch asked.

"Not at all."

"Do you know of any party—a group, an individual, who would have cause to do this?"

"There's always someone who thinks the Holocaust was a Jewish invention or thinks we should forget about it."

"But this is personal," Mitch said.

"Yes, so it would seem. This is the first time I've met Benjamin, so I can't claim to have an inside knowledge of his life or that of his father, but we've never had anything like this happen before and we've had many themed exhibitions, book launches and speakers from survivors and descendents."

"How would someone get access to that film to put that last frame in?" Mitch continued.

"They would have to have a security key to get up to the projection room. We've run our CCTV footage and our computer checks. We can't find anything. And no, we don't believe anyone on staff did it."

Mitch frowned. "I assume the film was viewed and run to the end before being shown publicly?"

"I'm not sure what you mean," Hanna said.

"It didn't arrive with the last frame already on it?"

"I see. No, we had a run-through before the launch. It wasn't there then."

"Right. Tell me about the strange screenings at all hours," Mitch said.

"Well Mitch, I'm not one for ghost stories, but the security guard reported on three consecutive nights that the film started by itself and froze on that last frame. The first night it was at ten p.m., the second night at eleven p.m. and last night at midnight. He went upstairs to see who was in the projection room, and there was no one there. I mean obviously there was someone, someone had to start the film, but he hasn't caught anyone."

"Any significance with the timing?"

"Not that I've worked out yet," Hanna said.

"Is it film or on computer? Could someone log in or set it on a timer for it to start and finish?" Mitch asked.

Hanna considered the question. "It is film, but best you ask the projectionist that sort of question."

Mitch nodded. "Thank you. I'll come back to you if we have any further questions." He rose.

Hanna stood. "This is an amazing exhibition," she said. "A dignified and honorable exhibition and I want it to be seen and remembered as such. While I would love big numbers through the door, I don't want a ghost story attracting people here."

"I understand," Mitch said.

Nick re-entered the room through the same door.

"Well, thank you for your time," Mitch said.

Hanna pulled a business card from her pocket. "No doubt you'll have more questions," she said. "It would be lovely if we could open the exhibition tomorrow..."

"I don't think we are going to need to seal the room, but I'll get back to you today on that one." Mitch followed her out of the room. On the way to the car he turned to Nick. "What did the projectionist say?"

"What didn't he say!" Nick lit a cigarette as they walked to the car. "Ronald, Ron to his friends, is a little excited about the history of film and assumed I would be too. In a nutshell, the writing definitely wasn't on the film when it was delivered to the museum. Someone has put it on since. Only Ron, the cleaner and Hanna have access to the projection room as far as he knows and as we saw, it can't be entered without a key. There is a part-time projectionist but he only works on-call if Ron is unavailable. He's a college kid and doesn't have access; the security officer lets him in and out."

"Did he say if it was film, disc or CD? Could it start on a timer?" Mitch asked.

Nick shook his head. "It's a reel of film and has to be laced onto the projector to start."

They arrived at the car and Nick stubbed the remains of his cigarette out.

"Prints?" Mitch asked.

"Worth a try, given only Ron has, in theory, handled the film."

Mitch unlocked the car and dialed John as they pulled out of the parking lot.

6

ADAM FORSTER AND ELLEN BEETSON SAT IN THE foyer of the five-star hotel waiting for Benjamin Hoefer to join them. Many of the tables and chairs in the foyer were taken by business people, networking, waiting to lunch or waiting on airport transfers. In their suits, Adam and Ellen blended in with the business crowd; on the weekend, the hotel was taken over by families and couples on romantic escapes.

"Coffee?" Adam asked.

"Yes please, but I can wait until Benjamin joins us," Ellen said, looking around.

"I can't. He's ten minutes late, he's got five minutes more and then I'm ordering. What's he doing up in his room besides keeping us waiting?"

"He might be on the phone or—"

"Being a star," Adam said. "We're not the media or his fan club."

Ellen frowned at him.

"Sorry, I'm not patient by nature." He watched the elevators. His light gray suit seemed too large on his frame and he had permanent stubble on his face which John Windsor had noted and mentioned to Mitch earlier.

"Clearly. So ..." she sat back in the plush cream foyer chairs, "can I ask why you decided to come to the US?"

"You just did," he teased her. "I was bored."

"Yes, I can see how that would happen, Mr. Impatient."

Adam smiled and breathed in deeply. "Right, yes, relax." He joined Ellen in sitting back in the chair and glanced around to scope the room.

"Worked out the best exits?" she asked.

"If we're attacked through the front, there are two exits to my right ... one behind the bar and one through the restrooms. If the attack is from the lifts, then the front is the most obvious, but there's also a door behind the concierge desk. We can easily be concealed behind a number of objects so that's not an issue if we need to defend the area." He stopped, realizing she was joking. "Sorry, security habits die hard."

"So I hear."

"Mitch?" Adam asked.

"He's the scoping king, never sits with his back to the door and profiles everyone in the room before his coffee has arrived. So you didn't come back for Samantha?"

Adam pushed up the sleeve of his coat suit, glanced at his watch and at the elevator. "No, Sam was just a fling. Fun, but not life changing, although I'm having dinner with her Friday night."

"You know she's keen on Mitch?" Ellen said.

Adam grinned. "Come on, me or Mitch? As if," he teased. "Mitch is so uptight, he'd be talking work in bed. Besides hasn't he got a girl? He did when we were on the UK mission."

"He broke up with her. Said she was too uptight."

Adam laughed. "Right."

"Besides, he's not uptight socially, just during working hours because his head is always in multiple places," she defended Mitch.

Adam looked at Ellen. "So Samantha's keen on him, huh?"

Ellen grimaced. "I'm not playing your game."

The elevator doors opened and Benjamin Hoefer appeared. He looked around the foyer and Adam rose and approached him. He introduced himself and brought him over to Ellen to do introductions. Adam signaled the waitress and the three ordered coffee.

"Forgive me for keeping you waiting, my daughter was on the phone and she's worried for me, so I couldn't rush her off," he said. Benjamin, a large man with a full-facial beard, sank into the chair. He wore a loose white cotton shirt over black pants.

"That's no problem," Adam said.

Ellen shot him a look.

"Awful business, most distressing," Benjamin shook his head.

"Let's start at the beginning. Are the death threats, in your opinion, related to the release of the book?" Ellen asked.

"Absolutely," Benjamin said.

"So prior to that, you were not threatened in any capacity—through your work, through your networks, clubs or in your personal circle?" she clarified.

"No, never. And my father died over a decade ago, so it's a long grudge if someone has been waiting for this long to get him," Benjamin said.

"When did you receive the first threat?" Adam asked.

"When the book was released, I received the first one. It was an email sent to the book's website. No name, no location."

"What did it say?" Adam asked.

"It said exactly what was on the last slide of the film shown on the launch night—*Nazi, Jew hater, fake*—except it also said, *tell the truth.*"

"Do you know what that means?" Ellen asked.

Benjamin raised his hands in frustration and shook his head. "I don't, I honestly don't. The book is the truth; my truth as I know it. The stories my father told me and his notes, the life I remember."

"I've read the book and it is a very personal tale; but you don't substantiate any of the incidents with other accounts from witnesses," Adam said.

Benjamin Hoefer looked surprised.

"You have read it then?" he said.

They waited as the waiter placed their coffees in front of them, before Benjamin continued.

"No, I don't substantiate stories for a number of reasons. It is my story and my father's. Read any autobiography and it is in the first person, it's not usually substantiated. Secondly, there are very few people still alive who could testify or support our truths and those that are, have settled all over the world. My account is not unique, there are many good voices that have told similar stories—it is just my story."

"So, the Bäckers, the family that took you in, are they still alive?" Adam asked.

"I don't know."

"You didn't stay in touch?" Ellen said leaning forward. "Were they not your rescuers?"

Benjamin pursed his lips. "It's hard to explain. Yes, they saved me and of course how could I not be grateful, as was my father. But I was a child when I was taken from them and it's complex and hard to understand. They looked after me but they also were intent on 'Germanising' me."

"Wouldn't that be for your own protection?" Adam asked.

"Perhaps," Benjamin said. He stopped to sample his coffee. Ellen and Adam waited. "You must remember that after the war the world was displaced. In 1948, following intense lobbying by the American Jewish community, the US Congress passed legislation to admit four hundred thousand displaced persons here in the States. My father and I were amongst them."

"So you were how old when you moved to the US?" Ellen confirmed.

"Nine, not an age where I would stay in touch with adults. I don't know if my father ever contacted them again in all honesty and we are talking about a time when mail was unreliable. We were writing to the other side of the world with a world full of displaced people."

"Did you ask him?" Adam asked.

"Of course, but it was so hard to get him to talk

about those years. That's why this book is released after his death; he would never have agreed to it," Benjamin said.

"How old were the Bäckers when you lived with them?" Ellen asked.

Benjamin sipped his coffee and put his cup back into the saucer. "They seemed old to me then of course, but they were only in their early twenties I think."

Adam did the mental calculations. "So if they were alive, they would be in their nineties now."

Benjamin nodded. "When my father returned I didn't know him, but I was always treated like an alien, never like their child, so I wasn't unhappy to go with him. Putting it in perspective ... I spent five years with them, from the age of two to seven years of age. Then I haven't seen them for sixty-eight years. I can't see how they could possibly be connected to the threats I'm receiving."

"It's a long bow," Adam agreed, "but we're just trying to cover off everything. So from your teaching days, did you have any enemies, competitors or anyone who disliked you?"

"Well not that anyone told me to my face. And again, I retired from teaching when I was sixty, fifteen years ago. Why wait this long to vent at me? No, I think it is related to the book and it is connected to something that has been said in the book, or it is one of those Holocaust-denial groups."

"Are you an only child? No siblings, stepbrothers or sisters?" Ellen asked.

"No, my father had many women companions but he never married again. I don't know why. He said he loved my mother and would stay married to her forever even if she was gone, but their life together was so short really, seven years. They met at church when my mother was fifteen; she died when she was twenty-two. He then spent the next fifty or so years a widower," Benjamin shrugged. "I've never known love like that."

"I imagine few do," Ellen agreed.

"I'm sorry, but I must go." Benjamin glanced at his watch. "Have I answered your queries sufficiently?"

"Yes, but just one quick question please," Adam said. "You had the email threat, but any other threats?"

"We started the book tour here in Washington at the Holocaust Museum. That was always our plan and it has only been during the launch and a few days before that we've had the strange late screenings of the film and that message. That's it so far."

Adam and Ellen rose and thanked Benjamin Hoefer. They headed to the concierge and waited while Adam's Porsche was brought to the front of the hotel. Ellen watched Benjamin Hoefer as he made his way to the elevator. She felt saddened for the elderly man.

"What do you think?" Ellen lowered her voice.

Adam also spoke quietly. "He doesn't seem frightened, does he? I'm not sure whether that means at his age or given his background he's resigned to whatever will be. Or maybe he doesn't think it will amount to much or it's a publicity hoax and he's in on it."

Adam smiled as he saw his car being driven towards him.

Ellen shook her head. "Men and their cars."

"Want to drive?" he asked.

Ellen's eyes lit up. "You bet."

7

THE WAITRESS SMILED A DIFFERENT SMILE FOR DIRK Schmid—attentive and longing—as she placed his German potato pancakes in front of him. He returned her smile with cool confidence. He waited until his brother Thorsten's mushroom schnitzel arrived moments later and then tried his meal. It was his favorite restaurant, a German place in downtown Washington D.C., and he habitually ordered the pancakes served with apple sauce and sour cream.

"Always good here," Thorsten said after his first mouthful. "So are you pleased?"

Dirk smiled. "Delighted little brother, delighted. Every meeting more and more members and even more signing up that can't get to meetings. How are our coffers looking?"

"On the books as of today, twenty three hundred full-paid members." Thorsten glanced around and leaned closer to his brother. "That gives us a bank balance of ..."

"I know," Dirk cut him off. "More revenue than almost half of the world's countries and no deficit."

Thorsten nodded, his eyes shining in admiration of his brother.

"You are such a natural leader, Dirk, our father would be so proud if he knew of your work. Our grandfather on the other hand ..." Thorsten let the words hang.

Dirk's eyes narrowed. "Our father is a true German, we are lucky. Unlike our grandfather; weak, a stain on the family history."

"I know I have asked you this once before ... but are you sure Dirk? Expose Eli Hoefer and we risk being exposed and us becoming associated with him," Thorsten said.

"If we do the job right we won't be associated. I don't care if he comes out as a traitor, only interested in self-preservation, because his descendents have made up for that. Besides, I want what is rightfully ours and I want Benjamin and his book of fiction shut down."

. . .

Later that evening, Ellen and Nick walked through the Holocaust museum. Nick glanced at his watch.

"Eight now. If the ghost is true to form, he'll start the film at one a.m.," he said.

"Or, at ten p.m. again and start the cycle over. Either way, we've got a few hours to kill before we have to get out of sight," Ellen agreed. "So eliminating the only people who know we are here—the Director Hanna Berkman, the projectionist because he had to give us the key and the security officer in the foyer—there should be another presence in the building if that film is to roll."

"In theory," Nick agreed.

They walked along the backlit displays. The overhead lights were off; the venue silent.

Nick shuddered. "Creeps me out."

Ellen stopped and looked up at the display of clothes worn in the concentration camps that hung above her. She moved through the exhibition; Nick reluctantly followed. The lighting was too dim now to read the personal accounts, but no words were needed for the rail car, the bunks and the piles of hundreds of shoes. She moved across the levels from floor to floor, stopping to look at the family photos. It was eerily quiet.

Nick's phone rang and he jumped. Ellen smiled at him as he rolled his eyes.

"Mitch," he answered. "I'm whispering because

it is so quiet in here. We're both fine … uh huh … okay … bye."

"What's up?" Ellen asked, also in a hushed voice.

"He wants us in position now in case the ghost projectionist arrives early."

"Probably best," Ellen agreed.

She followed Nick back down to the foyer and entered the room where Benjamin Hoefer's exhibition was displayed. As Nick entered behind Ellen, the room filled with light and a film began to flicker on the white walls … the trail of Jewish people could be seen walking out of the camp, looking bewildered, painfully thin and lost.

"Crap," Nick hissed as he hit the panel in the wall, springing open the projection room door, and bolting up the stairs. Ellen drew her gun and remained on the floor.

The security guard raced into the room and Ellen pointed upstairs. He took the stairs up after Nick. The film came to an end a few minutes later, with Benjamin's Hoefer father in frame … the last screen flickered up with the red writing reading *Nazi, Jew hater, fake!* The room faded to black.

Nick and the security guard returned from the projection room and stood with Ellen.

"There's not a soul up there. No way in, no way out," Nick panted.

"And no one came down the stairs," Ellen confirmed. "Are you sure no one is hiding, no window?"

"Absolutely positive," the guard said. "We searched the cupboard and under desk space and there are no windows. It's just a small dark room with a light."

"They must be hacking in to do it somehow," Ellen said.

"It's film," Nick said. "It's not a computer. The film is on a reel and someone had to roll the projector for it to start. But no one did."

"Someone did," Ellen corrected him. We just don't know how they did. There's no man hole?"

"We're going back up. Can you watch this door?" Nick asked the guard.

"Sure."

Nick entered the stairwell and Ellen followed. They explored all surfaces on the way up and into the room.

"Good grief, it is just a tiny room!" Ellen exclaimed as she entered the small projection room.

Nick turned on the light and also ran his torch light around all surfaces.

"I think we can safely say, no one came or left this room," he said.

"I think you're right," Ellen agreed. She looked at the projector with the film sitting in it. "Want to break it to Mitch?"

———

Mitch shared an end balcony table and a bottle of wine in an Italian café in Georgetown with an attractive red-haired woman. They had finished their mains when his phone vibrated, again. She frowned at him.

"Sorry, it's work again, I really have to take this." He gave her an apologetic look and began to move away from their table.

She held up her hand. "You stay, I'm going to the ladies' room."

He stood and waited for her to leave before speaking, turning his back to the restaurant and keeping his voice down. "Nick?"

"Over already and before you say anything, no we weren't too late, well we weren't in the actual projector room but we've scoped everything ... no one came in or out."

"Damn. Well I guess it's an early night for you two then." He glanced at his watch. "Thanks for taking the shift."

"No problem. How's the date going?" Nick asked.

"Who said I was on a date?"

"You did. You said you had a commitment."

"I could be at ... at ... football training."

"What's she like?" Nick asked.

"Are you alone?"

"Of course. Ellie's with the security guard. Your secret's safe with me!"

"It's a set-up. A favor to get Henri and Ann off my back—there's no such thing as free board," Mitch said referring to his stepfather, who was also the head of the FBI's science division, and his wife, Ann.

"So what's she like?" Nick asked.

"She's ... I don't think she's coming back from the ladies'... anyway, see you tomorrow." Mitch hung up.

8

HENRI SPALTER, HEAD OF THE FBI'S SCIENCE AND
Technology Branch, professor of science and
Mitchell Parker's stepdad during his teen years after
Mitch's father disappeared, hadn't seen much of
Mitch himself since he moved out of Henri's guest
wing last month. Henri's wife, Ann, was missing
having Mitch to fuss over, but it was only ever a
short stop for Mitch between moving out from his
ex-girlfriend Charlotte's house and finding somewhere new to live.

Henri had already heard from Ann; last night's
date with Mitch and Melissa was a disaster. Henri
had warned her, but she thought they would be perfectly suited; the daughter of a work colleague and
Mitch, who clearly needed a new love distraction—
according to the women who know best in these

matters. Still, Henri thought as he printed out some test results, Mitch could have turned the phone off during dinner.

"Lads, I'm going upstairs to drop off some results and get a briefing," Henri said to his two young lab assistants.

"Want me to take them up?" Jared asked.

"Thanks Jared, but it's good to keep the circulation going. Now listen up lads, Mitch is coming down sometime in the next half hour to pick up that envelope on the desk." Henri pointed to a large envelope that included some of Mitch's personal mail. "If he asks, let him know I'm very cranky about last night." Henri smiled.

"What happened last night?" Tom asked.

"The wife set him up on a blind date and Mitch spent more time on the phone than on the date."

"Poor guy." Jared shook his head. "My mother is always setting me up with daughters of her friends. I had to invent a girlfriend to get her off my case."

"Should have told her you were gay," Tom said.

"No, then she'd try and convert me."

Henri laughed and departed with a wave of the papers in his hands.

———

Mitch paced around his office.

"Adam and I met with Benjamin late yesterday." Ellen gave Mitch an overview of what little they had learnt as she sat perched on the corner of the office couch. "And of course we had no luck last night ... the film showed but no one was there to show it."

"That drives me crazy," Mitch said.

"Perhaps there is a ghost," Adam said.

Mitch looked at him. "Well you've just volunteered for the next shift there, Casper. But before you do that, Adam, can you start working on the ancient history? I'd like you to look into the backgrounds of everyone connected with Benjamin Hoefer and his father, Eli, dead or alive."

"On it," Adam said.

"We've got a legat in Berlin if you need help," Mitch said referring to the FBI's Legal Attaché Office, "but with your German language skills you should be okay to do a bit by phone initially."

"Ja," Adam agreed in German.

Mitch turned to Nick. "Nick can you cover modern history? Take the guest list from the book launch at the museum and work your way through them. Can you also find out who was the benefactor of Eli's will—I'm guessing it's Benjamin—and what he was worth?"

"Got it," Nick agreed.

"Ellie, follow up on the prints on the film, check out the projectionist's background and get to Benjamin's speaking engagement this afternoon ... he's talking at the Jewish Community Centre at two p.m."

Mitch continued. "I'm going to investigate the neo-Nazi and Holocaust denial groups and see if they have any interest in Benjamin and his book."

"You can't do that alone," Nick said. "I'm coming with you."

"Thanks, but it's okay," Mitch said. "I'm only sussing them out at this stage. I'm starting with the Anti-Defamation League and Human Rights Law Center—they report upon local neo-Nazi activities. But I'll partner up once I know who to visit. Check in regularly."

Mitch watched his team leave, then, with a quick glance at the clock, grabbed his car keys and decided to drop in to catch Henri on his way out. He took the stairs down, flashing his pass on the security scans to push open the glass doors. He could see Tom and Jared at work but no sign of Henri.

"Hey Mitch," Jared greeted him with a glance to Tom.

"Hi Jared, Tom." Mitch glanced past them into Henri's office. "Henri not around?"

Tom grimaced. "No, I think he wanted to be out when you arrived."

Mitch turned to look at Tom.

Jared continued. "He left an envelope on his desk for you; said it was mail you were expecting."

Mitch walked past them into Henri's office and grabbed the envelope with his name on it. When he came back out Tom and Jared were watching him.

"Did he say anything else?" Mitch asked, looking from one to the other.

"Not really." Jared rose and came around the desk to grab a document from the printer. "He's been cranky today though, don't you think, Tom?"

"Yeah," Tom nodded, "didn't even improve after his coffee. Said the wife was giving him a hard time about a date last night or something."

Mitch sighed. "Great. Well, tell him ... no it's cool, I'll catch him later. Thanks guys." Mitch left feeling that they weren't quite telling him everything. *Damn, Ann's cheesed off and Henri's getting the roll-on effects. Why set it up in the first place? I didn't want it,* he stewed on his way to the car. *I'll get some flowers and take them to Ann. Women!*

9

ADAM FORSTER PLACED HIS LATTE ON HIS DESK, removed his jacket and sat down. He looked around; John Windsor and Mitch's offices were empty, Nick and Ellen were out but at the far end of the office, another group of employees was hard at it. He logged into the computer and checked his emails. For a moment he sat back and drummed his fingers, then leaned forward, logged into another screen and opened his personal emails. Six emails; one from his lawyer and none from her. He opened the lawyer's email and clicked on the attachment. It was official, he was divorced.

Adam sighed and logged out. His wife, *no, as of yesterday ex-wife*, was really gone from his life. He rubbed his hands over his face. He hadn't told Mitch he was married when they were on the UK mission together, no need to: they were separated then for the second time and Samantha was an amusing distraction. No need to tell him now, either, I guess, he thought. *Impossible woman.* He closed his email account.

Adam came back to the now with a thud as Nick appeared and dropped down in the chair at the desk opposite him.

"Thought you had the place to yourself, huh?" Nick asked.

"All good, I'm not one for my own company," Adam said. He took a deep breath and opened his notes. *Right, Benjamin Hoefer, let's look into your history.* He logged into jewishgen.org to begin, typed in the family names he knew and began there.

———

Mitch glanced at his watch: he would just make it to his appointment with the Director of the Anti-Defamation League and Southern Poverty Law Center if the traffic kept moving. It stalled to a crawl again and he sighed. Spotting a street park, he swung the car in, alighted, paid the meter and decided to walk the few blocks. As he raced along, his phone rang; he glanced at the screen—it was his new housemate, Lyn.

"Lyn," he answered. "All okay?"

"Yeah, just letting you know I was going to have a few girls over for dinner if that's okay? About five or six...you're welcome to join us of course and bring a friend."

"Ah, thanks for letting me know. I'll be working late so I probably won't be there until after ten or so."

"Okay, but don't be shy, they won't bite. Are you running or have I caught you in the middle of something exciting?" she asked.

"No, just running. I had to park two miles from my meeting."

"Okay, over and out," she said.

Mitch looked at his phone—she was gone. He liked a straight-to-the-point person. He arrived at the gray ten-story building and, straightening his tie, he ran up the stairs to the reception area. Within five minutes, he was in the Director's office.

"Thanks for seeing me," Mitch said.

"Always happy to work with the FBI," Allan Butler said. He pointed Mitch towards a couch, poured two glasses of water and sat on the couch opposite.

Mitch studied him; he must have been close to seventy years of age, tall and wiry, dressed in a brown suit.

"Been doing this for a while?" Mitch asked.

Allan smiled. "Do I look old and tired?"

"It would take its toll," Mitch said. He noted the room also looked tired; tired cream curtains, old framed photos and a desk that looked like it came off the Ark.

"Yes, it can get to you. So from what you said on the phone, I understand you are looking for possible groups or individuals who could be threatening the book tour or Benjamin Hoefer personally."

"Yes, except they are not accusing Benjamin Hoefer of being a Jew or Holocaust supporter, they're accusing him of being a Jew hater and a Nazi." Mitch handed over the photo of the last frame of the film reading: *Nazi, Jew hater, fake!*

"Yes I understand. So they are accusing him of making a name or money out of misery that he or his father didn't suffer," Allan said. "So he's one of them ..."

"In theory yes," Mitch said.

Allan sat back and exhaled. "I think you have to talk to some of the local groups and see what they know about Benjamin, if anything, and they may have a lead for you—if they'll talk to you."

"Have you got a starting place for me? Some local contacts?" Mitch asked.

"Indeed I have." Allan leaned back and grabbed several pieces of paper from his desk. "There are currently over eighty active neo-Nazi groups across the States."

Mitch's eyes widened. "You're kidding me?"

"I wish," Allan said.

"I had no idea," Mitch said.

"Yes. Believe it or not, neo-Nazi groups still share a love for Adolf Hitler and Nazi Germany and a hatred for Jews. But they don't just hate Jews, they're open to hating any minorities, you know, like gays and lesbians."

Mitch thought of his new housemate and wondered why anyone would choose to hate Lyn and her girlfriend, Sandy. He shook his head.

Allan continued. "They blame the Jews for all our social problems and believe there is a conspiracy and that Jews really control the government, banks and media."

"So Benjamin Hoefer's book would offend them because he's reminding us that the Holocaust happened, except for the fact that they think he or his father is a German traitor who'll sell his name and country to associate with the Jews and take a slice of monetary pie."

"Sounds like it at face value," Allan said. He handed the list to Mitch. "There are two in this area so that's where I'd start—the UNP which stands for the United Nazi Party and the NAO or New Aryan

Order—but assuming Benjamin is on tour, it could be any number of groups."

"From your experience, does the crime so far have any hallmark traits?" Mitch asked.

"Not really. I can't say I've seen anything like this. But whatever you do, don't go alone."

———

On his way back to the car, Mitch spotted a florist and grabbed a bouquet for Ann. He spun by her and Henri's house on his way back to the office and found her at home.

She answered the door in her tennis outfit, her graying hair neatly tied back.

"Mitch, what a lovely surprise and good timing; ten minutes earlier and I wouldn't have been home. Come in."

Mitch followed her into the palatial home where he had been recently staying for a few months between housemates.

"You should have told me you were coming and I would have made you lunch," she continued, as he followed her into the kitchen.

"That's okay, I've got to get back to the office anyway."

"I was just about to make a sandwich, let me make you one for the road," she said, starting to prepare. She stopped and looked up at his face. "You boys never eat properly. Are you okay in your new home?"

"Fine. I just wanted to say sorry about stuffing up the date last night. I hope it doesn't put you in a bad place with your friend." He handed over the flowers.

"Mitch, they're lovely," she said, taking the flowers and inhaling their perfume. "Just lovely." Ann unwrapped the clear cellophane from the bunch of vibrant orange lilies and white roses and reached up into a cupboard for a crystal vase. "Orange is such a cheerful color. You shouldn't be wasting your money on me, really, I don't care if the date works out or not, it's just worth a try to see you happy."

Mitch frowned. "Oh, I thought you might have been upset."

"No, I thought she was rude for leaving. Goodness, you've got an important job. If she can't handle a few calls on the first date, she'll never be right for you."

Mitch's eyes narrowed. *I think I've been had by Henri.*

———

On his way back to the office, Mitch rang Henri.

"Hello Mitch, Ann just rang and said you dropped in the most beautiful bouquet, how thoughtful," Henri teased.

"Henri, you and your conspirators ... when you least expect it!"

Henri laughed. "Sure son, I'll put the boys on notice, do your best. So did you get to finish your meal last night?"

"Only the main. At least she left before I had to buy her dessert," Mitch said. "Anyway, I was just ringing to let you know that I'm eating the best chicken and salad sandwich I've ever had. Ann made it, and I noticed you left your lunch at home."

"Did you bring it with you?" Henri asked.

"You're joking aren't you?" Mitch said, and hung up with a grin.

10

THE BOOK LAUNCH AT THE JEWISH REGIONAL
Community Centre was a sell-out with all of the two
hundred seats taken. Ellen Beetson stood at the
back of the room watching the proceedings. She
studied the faces and took in the exits, staging and
balcony. There was still ten minutes until the talk
began. She glanced at her phone, *no messages*. She
sent a quick text message to Mitch to update him. *At
book launch, nothing untoward yet. Crowded House.*

He texted back within minutes—*just heading
back to office, need back up?*

Ellen looked around; all seemed in order. *Hard
to say but all looking under control,* she texted back,
then grabbed a seat on the aisle where she could
make a quick exit.

Five minutes later a young man came on the

stage and the audience broke into applause. Ellen put her phone on silent vibrate and put it back in her coat jacket. The young man thanked the audience and spoke of the guest of honor.

After a few minutes, he introduced Benjamin Hoefer. Audience members rose to their feet and applauded the elderly man as he made his way to the microphone. Ellen noted that he seemed genuinely touched. He waited until the audience settled and began.

"This is my father's story," he said with a glance to the screen behind him featuring his father's photo on the book cover. "Can you imagine for a moment what it was like? We see the images in black and white and don't connect, but my father was a man of color, of flesh and blood. We lived as a family. Father went to work each weekday morning to teach literature to the fresh young minds at university, and my mother stayed home to care for me and to look after the household. At the end of his day, he returned home and we ate together. My parents, like your parents before you, like you, shared the stories of their day and put the children, me, to bed." He stopped to draw a deep breath; the room was silent.

"Then imagine tonight there was a knock at your door and your family was told to pack only a few necessities and be on the street in fifteen minutes. What would you do?" Benjamin Hoefer asked.

Ellen looked around; the audience members were transfixed by his words, imagining themselves on this journey. Several women were emotional, dabbing their eyes.

Benjamin continued. "I was two, and remember nothing of the night, but I have the picture that was painted in my mind from the retelling of the story so often. I was told our neighbor, a kindly young lady, entered via the back door and my mother bundled me into her arms. My mother and father hurriedly packed some clothing and took their suitcase and went outside. They joined with other neighbors and were pushed up onto the back of trucks. I would never see my mother again. My father would not return for another five years, a stranger to me. I am grateful to have this opportunity to tell his story of life in the camps and to tell of how we became a family again."

It was then it happened. The audience gasped, and several members screamed. Behind Benjamin Hoefer, two large banner strips unfurled and fell behind him, each featuring the Nazi swastika. Ellen ran down the side aisle and behind the stage. She raced up the stairs to the balcony where the banners had been unfurled and saw a figure in black running down the opposite stairwell. She ran across the back of the stage in pursuit. As she opened the stage door and raced out onto the street, she saw the figure in black leap into a car, and slam the door. The driver took off. The plates were obscured.

Ellen returned to the theater as the audience was being evacuated and Benjamin Hoefer led away by his own security team. She sought out the theater manager.

———

"Six girls coming around for dinner!" Nick shook his head. "What a waste, a real shame."

Mitch sighed and dropped down into the chair at Ellen's desk next to Adam and Nick.

"It suits me fine," Mitch assured him. "Anyway you should be pleased that I want to get out of the house tonight, I'll do the museum shift Adam, and you can go have a life."

"Nick's right," Adam agreed. "What's the point of having a roommate if she and all her friends are gay? She's got six babes coming round for dinner and not one you can hit on or who might sleep over."

"Just because Lyn's gay doesn't mean all her girl-friends will be," Mitch said.

"So there's some hope for you yet." Nick brightened. "Just when your mother and I had given up."

Mitch looked from one to the other. "When did you guys launch your dating agency? What have you found?"

Just as Adam began to answer, Mitch's phone rang.

"Ellie," Mitch answered. He listened to the account of the incident at the book launch. "Okay, we need to get witness statements and see what CCTV footage we can get. Stay put and I'll send back-up." Mitch hung up. "Let's go. There's been another incident, I'll update you on the way."

———

Ellen had gathered statements from the staff and any guests who came forward claiming to have seen something. She had secured the list of attendees. She spotted Mitch coming through the foyer in his dark suit, his eyes scanning the area, and she waved to get his attention.

"Hey Ellie, any insights?"

"I and three witnesses saw a man, with dark hair, slim, agile which would suggest young, wearing all black—jeans and a long sleeved shirt. No one saw him from the front or enough to be able to identify or describe him. I saw him get into a black van, no visible registration and he was driven off."

"So there were two of them working the scene then," Mitch said. "Nick's hitting up the neighboring buildings for CCTV footage and Adam's organizing to get the banners removed to see if we can lift any prints but it's unlikely. Run me through what Benjamin was doing and saying just before the banners unfurled."

Ellen frowned. "He was creating the picture of what it would be like to get that knock on the door and to be told to leave your home and family. I can't remember the last thing he said, but there were people filming his speech on their phones. And the center was filming it to upload online."

"Okay, point me towards the manager and I'll check that out. You keep going with statements."

Ellen pointed to the bearded, middle-aged man talking to reporters.

"Great," Mitch muttered and headed towards him.

———

"Joseph Belkind," the center manager introduced himself to Mitch, and the men shook hands. "Josh was filming it," he answered Mitch's query. "Come this way, I'll take you to him. Who would do this?"

"Good question," Mitch said. "And why."

"I have to deal with a few things, so can I leave

you with Josh?" Joseph asked, indicating the young man. "I'll be around if you need me after."

"No problem," Mitch said. He waited for Josh to rewind the footage and then watched it right through. The last line before the banners unfurled was Benjamin Hoefer saying, "I am grateful to have this opportunity to tell his story of life in the camps and to tell of how we became a family again." Mitch asked for the footage to be sent to his phone. *So is someone upset about Benjamin Hoefer telling the story of his father's life in the camp or is it because they had a chance for a life again and someone else didn't?*

———

An hour later, Mitch gathered his team in a nearby coffee shop for an exchange of information. He looked up and realized it was counter service.

"Right," he said as he rose. "What will it be?"

"A half-strength soy latte, please," Ellen said.

"Cappuccino with a double shot thanks," Adam added.

"An espresso, but can you ask them to make it fresh so it's hot?" Nick asked.

Mitch rolled his eyes. "Four cappuccinos then." He went to the counter, placed the correct orders and returned.

"Adam, what have you got from this morning and the book launch?"

"I'm just warming up, but I've had a few interesting discussions this morning. Gynther and Antje Bäcker, the family that 'adopted' Benjamin and according to him tried to Germanize him, are both now dead. But they have a son Ives who is seventy-two and a grandson, Dieter, forty-five years of age. I had a chat with Ives and he has given me Dieter's number so I'll try that later." He stopped as the coffees arrived.

Ellen brightened. "You did get my soy latte!"

"Are you kidding? I wouldn't be game not to," Mitch teased, stirring his cappuccino. "So what did Ives have to say?"

Adam continued. "Not surprisingly, he had no idea what I was talking about, but eventually he remembered Benjamin. He was four when Benjamin was seven so we're not talking about any memory that is really going to help the case here. He said though that he always thought Benjamin was his brother so he was surprised when this man came to take him away."

"Mm, so his parents never told him that Benjamin was not related. I wonder if they thought that would protect both boys or if they assumed Benjamin's parents wouldn't come back alive," Mitch thought out loud.

"Any point talking to the grandson, then?" Nick asked.

"Yeah, well I thought the same thing," Adam continued, "but Ives told me that Dieter had done quite a lot of work on the family history and family tree, so you never know. Benjamin might feature in it. As for here," Adam looked across the road to the Jewish Community Centre. "The boys dusted for prints around the banner and found none, as you would expect. I'll check with local printers, but I suspect whoever has done this print job is not going to own up to it."

"Anyone printing Nazi swastikas is probably in on it," Ellen agreed.

"Nick?" Mitch turned to him.

"As you suspected, Benjamin is the sole bene-factor of his father's will, but Eli is worth a reasonable sum according to the solicitor. Eli and Yetta might have been newly married and starting their careers when their life was interrupted, but Eli was from wealthy stock. He managed to have a number of German confiscated artworks returned to him in the mid-1990s, and a Swiss bank account established by his father, who clearly had some foresight, was also resurrected."

"So roughly what was he worth at the time of his death?" Mitch asked.

"In 2005, about $2.5 million according to his so-licitor."

"That's nice," Adam said. "Could be a relative or two now coming out of the woodwork to make a claim on that."

"They've taken their time," Mitch said. "But the book launch might have brought it to light."

"Yes, not small change, especially as my research indicated that less than twenty per cent of the value of Jewish assets stolen by the Nazis and their collab-orators had been restored at the time of Eli's death. So he did well," Nick said. "Moving on from that, I've checked every name on the guest list from the Holocaust Museum book launch and found no one shady, or with a criminal record or strange alle-giances that are in our database anyway. Now I'll start on the guest list for today's book launch and run the model van to see how many thousand there might be on the streets."

Mitch nodded. "Thanks. Ellie?"

"No prints on the film at the Holocaust Museum as expected. I checked out the projectionist's back-ground and he's Jewish through and through. He's doing a Bachelor of Arts in Jewish Studies at the uni and supporting himself with the projectionist work. His ancestors are Jewish and he lost a number of family members in the Holocaust," she said. "If he has a reason to be angry at Benjamin Hoefer I don't know what it is because he seems to be a big fan and has an autographed copy of the book on his desk. As for this book launch, everything was normal until the banners unfurled."

Mitch glanced at his watch. "Call it a day. I'm heading to the Holocaust Memorial Museum for the night."

"I'm coming with you," Adam said. "I was looking forward to having a private wander through."

11

———————

BENJAMIN HOEFER SCURRIED THROUGH THE FOYER OF the hotel building where he was staying during the book tour. He kept his head down, avoiding eye contact and reached for the lift button. It arrived moments later and he entered, relieved to see it empty. He pressed his floor number and stood back. He was feeling his age; weary from the stress of the book launch and the continued attacks.

As the door began to close a male figure jumped into the lift. He pressed a button for the eighth floor and moved to the back. The door closed and the lift began to rise. Benjamin glanced towards the man; he wore a dark suit, long black coat, a pale blue wool scarf and a black fedora. The man moved to the lift buttons again and pressed the stop button.

The lift jerked to a halt. He turned to Benjamin Hoefer.

Benjamin took a step back, pressing himself into the corner of the lift.

"I have a message for you," the man said.

Benjamin inhaled sharply, waiting for the blow or a weapon to appear. The young man smirked, enjoying his power.

"You have until the end of the week to deliver. Should you fail to do so, we will take the appropriate action. I hope not to have to return, Herr Hoefer."

The man turned, restarted the lift and exited on the eighth floor.

Benjamin stood shaking. He knew ... he would have to agree to their terms or risk his life and tell the police. Either way, he was dead.

———

Nick gave Ellen a lift home in the borrowed company car as Mitch and Adam headed to the museum.

"Never thought I'd see that," he said.

"What?" Ellen asked.

"Adam volunteering for a night of surveillance over a night off. I thought the ladies' man would find someone to hang with."

Ellen smiled. "We don't really know much about Adam though, other than he took a minute to get Samantha into bed in London and he has picked up where he left off here."

"If I was to profile him, I'd say he likes everything fast—fast cars, fast relationships and fast jobs. But happy to be wrong." Nick shrugged.

"Unless it is all a front and he's secretly longing to settle down and be domestic," Ellen said.

They looked at each other and laughed. Nick returned his eyes to the road.

"Yeah, not that," Ellen agreed. "Sam's pretty upset though. She thought once she left our team Mitch would ask her out."

"She's too high maintenance for Mitch. She needs someone who adores her and tells her all the time. Mitch would struggle with the right answer to 'does my butt look big in this?'"

Ellen laughed. "Marcus used to adore her but clearly that wasn't enough," Ellen recalled, thinking of the Caribbean Casanova from their laboratories at work. "You are too hard on Mitch."

"I'm not hard on Mitch, I just know him. I wouldn't want him to go out with Sam; she'd eat him alive. I've had to take him out and get him drunk several times since he broke up with the psychologist; I've got his back."

"So why aren't you interested in Sam?" Ellen asked.

"Because I want someone who adores me and tells me so all the time," he teased with a flick of his hair.

Ellen smiled and shook her head. "Men."

They drove in silence for a short while.

"There's something niggling me about Benjamin Hoefer," Ellen mused. "I feel like he knows something that he's not telling us."

"The whole thing is weird," Nick agreed. "If you thought Benjamin or his father were fakes, why not just sell your story to the media, like everyone does these days. Why go about this clandestine operation of shaming Benjamin?"

"Exactly," Ellen said. "Which is why I think Benjamin knows why or who is doing it but is not revealing all. Why would this start as soon as the book was launched? If you had suspicions about Benjamin or his father, Eli, surely you would have confronted Benjamin before this."

"Unless there's someone else in the book that is incriminated or could be. Has Mitch given it to you yet?"

"Yes, but I only started it last night. There's nothing in the first five chapters."

Nick pulled into the driveway of Ellen's small white townhome.

"Want to come in for a coffee?" she asked.

"Are you going to show me your etchings?" Nick asked.

"You should be so lucky. But I do need a jar opened."

"Right, duty first then." Nick turned off the ignition and followed her in.

———

John Windsor glanced at the clock; it was nearly six-thirty. He was going through his emails for the last time before heading home when he came across an email from the Head of the Employee Wellness team. He was suggesting mandatory counseling for Mitch and his team given the trauma witnessed on the recent Cape Hatteras case. He was recommending six sessions each.

John scoffed, *good luck with that.*

He fired back an email saying he agreed in principle but suggested they aim for two and that he would put it in action immediately.

John looked at Mitch's record. He and his team had notched up a good track record for closing cases and seem to have transitioned well with the swap of Samantha and Adam. *A bit of counseling won't hurt him given the break up with Charlotte and the body count from the last job. He's impossible to read, could be traumatized or blissfully happy, who knows, except Henri maybe,* John mused. He placed a quick call and just when he thought he must have missed him, Henri answered.

"No, I was in the fridge putting samples away," Henri said.

"I was just calling to see how Mitch is going," John said.

Henri laughed. "Yes, no point asking him I guess. Ann and I were just discussing this last night. He seems to be good actually. Since coming back from Cape Hatteras and finding his own place, he seems a bit lighter."

"Might have put Charlotte behind him," John said.

"Yes, she was completely wrong for him. He caught up with Ann yesterday and she said he seemed back to his old self. Why do you ask, is something wrong?"

"No, not at all," John assured him. "I've just got to send his team for mandatory counseling so it got me thinking."

"Oh. He'll hate that. Good luck getting him there. How many sessions?"

"Six."

"Good Lord!" Henri exclaimed.

"I'll take two but don't tell him that, I need some bargaining room," John said.

12

THE SECURITY GUARD LET MITCH AND ADAM INTO the Holocaust Museum and the three men went straight to the projection room. All was in order.

Mitch glanced at his watch. "Not sure what time we might be treated to a ghost screening tonight but I'll stay here if you want to wander around."

"Thanks, yeah I'd like that," Adam said. "Yell if you need back-up. I'm sure I'll hear you, it's like a tomb in here."

Mitch turned to the security guard. "Are the screenings still continuing?"

"Every night without fail."

"What time last night?"

"I wasn't on last night but the other guard wrote it up at eleven p.m. The latest one we've had was midnight and the earliest at six p.m. I'm glad you're back, it creeps me out." The sturdy young man shuddered.

Mitch assessed him. The security guard would not have been a day over twenty-five years old and was built as if he spent all day doing weights. "Is this your full-time job?"

"No. I'm studying physical health at college. This is my part-time job. It pays well and I can study at night while I'm here," he said.

"Any theories on how they are doing the screening?" Mitch asked.

The young man shook his head. "So you don't think it is ... like spiritual?" he asked.

"Uh, no, I definitely don't. I just want to work out how they are doing it," Mitch said, turning on the lights of the small room and running his hand along the panels of each wall.

"Well, I'll leave you to it." The guard backed out.

"No one else is in the building? No other security or the projectionist or cleaners?" Mitch asked.

"No, just me and you two." The security guard departed.

Mitch looked down below and watched him leave the room. He pulled a torch out of his pack and began to survey the room inch by inch. After an hour, Adam entered the room.

"Wow, well that's sobering," he said.

"You can say that again," Mitch agreed.

"Nothing?"

Mitch shook his head. "Not that I can see. I've checked all the wall and ceiling panels, checked the projector, checked the window outside the room, the pantry in the nearby hallway, you name it."

"Want to get a pizza delivered?" Adam asked. "I'm starved."

Mitch glanced at his watch. "Yeah good idea. It's nearly eight-thirty, so assuming the latest screening is eleven p.m., we've got a bit of time to kill. You go if you want."

"And miss out on dinner and a show!" Adam exclaimed. "No way. I'll go see what the security lad wants and order. Pepperoni and olives?"

Mitch looked surprised. "You remember that from London?"

"Yeah, I'm good on small details."

"That's scary. Yeah, thanks. Leave the door open." Mitch slid down the wall onto the floor. Unbeknownst to him, he was sitting on a trapdoor that led to a small room—a shrine, prepared by a member of a sinister organization, The New Aryan Order.

———

Lyn Williamson, her girlfriend, Sandy, and five friends sat on the floor drinking tea. On the coffee table in front of them sat four large platters dotted with the remnants of tapas and sushi. Wine glasses were emptied and a large tiramisu was almost gone. In her late twenties, slim with a bob haircut and premature gray strands already appearing, Lyn glanced to the clock. It was nearing ten p.m.

"So we're not going to meet the new housemate tonight," Alice said. "We probably scared him off."

Julie, her partner, laughed. "Yeah he probably thinks six lezzies have moved in with hairy armpits and all able to beat him in an arm wrestle."

"Well only four lezzies," Karen corrected them. She nodded to Sarah opposite. "We haven't seen the light yet."

Lyn laughed. "No, Mitch is all right, he's pretty laidback. I'd say he was the ideal housemate. He's never here and pays in advance."

"So what is he like?" Sarah asked.

"Tall, dark and handsome," Sandy filled in. "I could almost change sides for him," she teased with a wink to Lyn.

"Baggage?" Alice asked, reaching for another small piece of tiramisu.

"Probably," Lyn said, "but who knows. He doesn't say much. I had a glass of wine with him the other night on the deck after work and we talked football for a while. Then we discussed work and he said he was an investigator, and moved in here because he broke up with his girlfriend and they were living in her house."

"Seen any of his friends?" Karen asked.

Lyn smiled. "No but if he invites any of his eligible pals here, I'll text you and Sarah immediately."

"Good," Karen said, "that's the least you could do since I introduced you and Sandy."

"And that was a match made in heaven." Lyn smiled at Sandy.

———

Adam yawned. "That it?"

Mitch nodded. "Midnight and no ghost screening. I think we can safely assume that there's no screening because we're in here, someone was tipped off and there's no ghost but a very real projectionist."

Adam got to his feet, extended his hand, and pulled Mitch up. He grabbed the empty pizza boxes and soft drink cans, stuffed them in the plastic bag they came in and led the way downstairs. Mitch checked the room and closed the door behind him on departure. They checked out with the young security guard.

"Thanks for doing the shift," Mitch said as they walked towards their cars. "Don't come in early tomorrow."

"I've got a call to make to Germany tomorrow, so I want to make it about nine or ten a.m. That's about three to four p.m. in Germany which should catch Dieter at work. Failing that, if I'm still up at three a.m., I'll catch him at nine a.m. at his work. So if you don't see me ..."

"Gotcha," Mitch said with a wave as he got into his Audi.

At one a.m., the security guard heard a noise. With his hand on his holster, he hesitantly walked into the room with Benjamin Hoefer's exhibition and book on display.

Flickering on the walls was the footage of Jewish people shuffling along. Several seemed to look directly at him, and then the film closed in on survivors at the Auschwitz entrance gates.

He raced out of the room, closing the door behind him, and locked himself into the security office. He logged the screening time as an incident in the security book. He sat back, nervous, and watched and waited. The next morning, he resigned.

13

"THANKS FOR MAKING THE TIME TO TALK WITH ME, Herr Bäcker." Adam Forster made the call to Germany at three a.m. local time and spoke in his best German dialect.

"Dieter, please call me Dieter," the forty-five-year-old grandson of the family that once cared for Benjamin Hoefer said.

"Thank you. I understand that you have no direct memory of Benjamin Hoefer as he was long gone before you were born, but I understand you have been putting together the family history. Did the Hoefer family feature in it ever so briefly?"

"Briefly, yes," Dieter Bäcker confirmed. "I'm not sure what will interest you so shall I tell you the little I know? Perhaps you will steer me if there is something of relevance."

"That would be great," Adam agreed.

"My grandparents, Gynther and Antje, were close friends of Eli and Yetta. They were all around the same age, recently married, and often had dinner parties at each other's houses. It was only when the tension began to rise around the Jewish population that Eli suggested it might be better for my grandparents to distance themselves a little from him and Yetta. I was told that story by my father. It was generous of Eli."

"And safer for your grandparents," Adam said.

"In hindsight, we know that is the truth," Dieter continued. "They had a plan in place however, that if anything should happen Gynther and Antje would take in Benjamin. So that night when the trucks arrived, they met at the back door as planned, Yetta gave Antje Benjamin's small bag of goods and the young man himself and then Eli and Yetta were taken away. Are you a father, Adam?"

"No, I can't imagine the anguish of leaving behind that little boy," Adam answered.

"I know. My wife and I married quite late, in our mid-thirties, so I have two sons aged seven and two, the age Benjamin was when Eli and Yetta left. I can't conceive of having to do that." He sighed and, gathering himself, continued. "You know of course that Benjamin was with my grandparents from the age of two to seven before he was collected by his father, Eli, who survived Auschwitz."

"Your father, Ives, whom I spoke with yesterday, said he didn't know Benjamin wasn't his brother. What did you make of that?" Adam asked.

"Yes, I know where you are going with that. Did my grandparents perhaps hand over Eli and Yetta to the party, assuming that they would never return and Benjamin was going to be part of their family."

"Benjamin says he was Germanised by them," Adam added.

Dieter sighed. "Yes, interesting. Addressing the first assumption, I don't know if they handed Eli and Yetta over, but I doubt it. They were close friends and they took a risk taking that little boy. They could have let him go with Eli and Yetta but they passed him off as their own. Over 1.5 million Jewish children died in the Holocaust, Adam, and a two-year-old, which Benjamin was at the time, would have been put to death quickly."

"Yes, very true," Adam said.

"Which is why I believe they Germanised Benjamin," Dieter continued. "For his benefit, and for their safety. While it sounds like wires are applied to the head to Germanise, it's not that drastic. It just means they ensured Benjamin spoke and reflected the German language and customs."

"So what happened when Eli returned from the camps?" Adam asked.

"Well that's an interesting story and there's not much to it," Dieter said. "My grandparents were both out when they returned home to find my father Ives alone with the nanny. She had a note scribbled by Eli. He had returned while they were absent and taken Benjamin. I have the note still. Off the top of my head, it says that he was free, but could not stay to see them; they would be too shocked by his appearance. He thanked them for protecting Benjamin, who he described as all he had left in the world and the only reason he rose every day. That was it."

"So they never saw Eli then or again?" Adam asked.

"They never saw or heard from him or Benjamin again." Dieter said.

"Dieter, would you or your father have any mementos? An old photo, clothing, hairbrush, anything at all that belonged to Eli or Benjamin? We would get it back to you of course."

"You're trying to establish if they're related?" Dieter asked.

"We're trying to establish he is Eli Hoefer," Adam said, noting Dieter didn't miss a trick.

"My father has a lot of old chests and junk in his attic. Given he believed he was Benjamin's brother, he's more likely to have something of his. But you never know, perhaps my grandparents stashed some sentimental items for Eli and Yetta. Can you leave it with me?"

"Of course, thank you," Adam said.

"I have a busy work week but give me the weekend. If you would like to call me this time next Monday, I'll let you know. But don't expect too much," Dieter said.

"I really appreciate it. Danke sehr, Dieter, danke."

————

Mitch was the first of his team to arrive at the office as usual and he looked around for John Windsor. His office lights were on but he must have been somewhere else in the building. Mitch turned to his office, entered, hung his jacket on the back of his seat and sitting, logged into his computer. Today, he intended to visit the first of the neo-Nazi groups and have another go at talking with Benjamin Hoefer. *He knows more than he's saying*, Mitch mused. He saw the email from the museum and opened it; the film showed at one a.m. *Damn! So someone entered after we left or else was already in the building.* He shook his head.

"What's up?" John Windsor entered his office.

Mitch looked up.

"Morning. We staked out the Holocaust Memorial Museum until after midnight and the film didn't run ..."

"Just when you leave, it shows?" John finished his sentence as he sank into a seat opposite Mitch.

"Yes. Which means someone got into the building after we left or was already in it, hiding. If they are trying to create fear around the exhibition, they're doing a good job. The young security guard resigned after that incident according to the Director Hanna Berkman who emailed me this morning."

"Might help tickets sales though," John said. "On another matter, I have some news that is not going to please you."

Mitch groaned. "Is it Samantha?"

John looked confused. "No, I think she's settled in okay."

"Budget?"

John shook his head. "Worse. Counseling."

Mitch pushed back from his desk. "No. Who?"

"All of you. Well, not Adam. The Head of the Employee Wellness team wants you, Nick, Ellie and Samantha to attend mandatory counseling. He read the report on the Cape Hatteras case and thinks it was fairly traumatic. He's recommending six sessions each."

Mitch shot out of his seat. "Impossible. No, no way."

John held up his hands motioning Mitch to calm down.

"Is it really mandatory?" Mitch strode to the window.

"Yes."

"Six is ridiculous, I can't do six, I haven't got time."

"Mitch, sit down," John ordered. "For crying out loud the counseling has to be easier than the assignment."

"No, it's not," Mitch said, as he remained standing. "You know I think counseling is bullshit. They'll go back over all this past stuff that has nothing to do with the case, or work."

"Okay, take a breath, I'll negotiate. How many can you do?" John began his bargaining.

"None."

John frowned at him. "Do I have to remind you that you are a team leader and—"

"One then."

"Three," John suggested.

"Two," Mitch said. "Two for each team member."

"Right, leave it with me." John rose.

Mitch blocked him at the door. His eyes narrowed. "How many sessions did they really want us to attend?"

"Six, on my word," John said.

Mitch moved aside and let John pass but he was sure he saw him smile ever so slightly. He returned to his desk, sent his team an email suggesting an afternoon catch-up at two and then rang Nick.

"I'm about fifteen minutes away," Nick answered.

"So you haven't left home?" Mitch asked.

"Uh, no."

"Good, I'll pick you up in ten." Mitch hung up, grabbed his car keys and departed.

14

MITCH PULLED UP OUTSIDE NICK'S APARTMENT AND beeped the horn. Nick came to the front stairs and frowned. Mitch put the window down.

"My dates usually come to the door!" Nick joked.

Mitch laughed. "You're an idiot. Get in the car."

Nick locked the front door and ran down the stairs. He opened the car door.

"You brought the Audi?"

"I've only got the one car," Mitch said.

"Funny. You'll have a swastika carved into the bonnet when we return," Nick said.

Mitch shrugged. "I was going to get a pool car but we're going to a private address in the suburbs, not a party meeting. It just happens to be the home of the leader of the United Nazi Party. I figured it would probably be okay," he said, turning the car out of Nick's driveway. "Where's Amy?" Mitch asked after Nick's housemate who worked in the library at the FBI offices.

"In the shower, getting ready for work," Nick said. "Hoping she'd come out and wave you off?"

"Yeah, I was actually," Mitch said.

"Why don't you ask her out again? She's still keen even if you did blow her off for Charlotte the first time," Nick said.

He shrugged. "I'm taking some time out."

"Yeah I get that," Nick said. "So who are we seeing?"

"Jonathan Charles Wickham, J.C., to his friends. He's the head of the UNP which stands for the United Nazi Party, or the Commander as he calls himself," Mitch explained.

"Good of Commander Wickham to deign to see us," Nick said.

"He asked our nationality first—he might even try and recruit us. There's two main Nazi-sympathizer groups in the district and this is one of them. Wickham's got a rap sheet a mile long, most of them for public nuisance."

The men drove for fifteen minutes, discussing aspects of the case.

"What do they stand for?" Nick asked.

Mitch exhaled. "They've got a doctrine—all the things you would expect, like America for whites only, non-citizens can live here as guests and subject to laws for aliens, no Jew or homosexual may reside in America ... you get the idea. They are five thousand members strong."

"Wow," Nick said.

Eventually, Mitch turned off the highway and into a small, tree-lined street. The apartments were small and presentable. He scanned for number eighty-two.

Finding it, Mitch pulled up and the two men got out of the car. Mitch took his jacket off and threw it in the back seat next to Nick's. He locked the car and followed Nick up the path to the small brick block of four apartments. He saw the curtain move on a bottom floor window. Before they knocked, a tall, wiry man with hair shaved close to his scalp opened the door.

"Are you the cop that called?" he asked.

"Not a cop, but yeah I called and this is—" Mitch said.

"Brought back-up hey?" the Commander cut him off and stood aside to let them in.

"We always travel in packs," Mitch said. He observed the room. It was neat but old; worn brown carpet, a tired tweed couch and wall-to-wall photos of Wickham and fellow UNP members in Nazi uniforms, marching and protesting.

Wickham pointed to the couch and the two men

sat while he yelled out to a woman who was out of sight. He came and sat opposite them.

Mitch took in Wickham's black t-shirt displaying the organization's logo, three stud piercings on his face and the parade of tattoos on his arm.

A large woman entered the room. Her long hair was tied back and a printed dress stretched across her body.

"I could do with a coffee, love," Wickham told her. "You two?"

"Just had one, but thanks," Mitch said, noting the wedding rings on their fingers.

Nick shook his head and gave her a smile.

"I wanted to know if you had any interest or any information on who might be disrupting Benjamin Hoefer's book tour," Mitch began.

"Yeah," Wickham said, clasping his hands between his legs. "Benjamin Hoefer. Haven't read the book, but it should be in the fiction section."

"Would any of your members be keen to close his book tour down?" Mitch asked.

"Sure, yeah, but we don't do that, it's not our style. That's not what we're about." He took the coffee from his wife and thanked her. "But the protest, it sort of works for us ... raises awareness of what we're all about. So great, we'll ride on that."

"Do you have an idea whose style it might be?" Nick asked.

Wickham shrugged. "Not really. You've got to pick your fights, you know what I mean? I don't want to waste our members' time protesting about another Holocaust story. Whatever. We're looking at the big picture stuff ... you know immigration, education, aliens. You guys should come to one of our meetings ... you'll agree with what we're about. We stand for ..."

———

"What did you think?" Nick asked on their drive back to the office.

"I think his I.Q. is less than the national average and that was a waste of time, but at least we can eliminate the UNP," Mitch said.

"I got the feeling he couldn't organize a one-man parade," Nick added. "This Benjamin Hoefer case seems too sophisticated for his lot."

"I'm with you there. We cheesed him off though, not taking those membership papers; he's militant about their beliefs."

"Yeah, that was an ear bashing," Nick agreed. "But there was no way I was taking those papers."

"I thought he was going to burst a blood vessel," Mitch agreed. "There's another group I want to check out—The New Aryan Order. I've just got to get a contact."

As they neared their office, Nick said, "I've got to get some cash, can you let me off on the corner? Want a coffee?"

Mitch pulled over. "Yeah, thanks." He let Nick out and turned off into the FBI headquarters parking lot.

————

Mitch exited his car in the parking lot and locked it. As he put the keys in his coat pocket, he saw a shadow in his peripheral vision and whirled around. The punch was hard and unexpected, a hit straight to his eye. He reeled back only to be hit from the other side directly in the face. His assailants were two men, wearing dark masks. He felt blood pouring from his nose. The second punch knocked him down; he hit the concrete of the parking lot floor.

Reflexes kicked in. He shot up and delivered a quick, hard punch to the first assailant's throat. He ducked a swing to his head and landed several sharp blows to the second man's ribs, dropping him to the garage floor. They hurt his hand as much as the assailant, who doubled over in pain.

Mitch finished off the now wheezing first man with one sharp hit to the face. As both men lay crouched on the ground, Mitch saw the two security guards running towards him.

"Thanks guys," he muttered as he straightened his jacket. As he turned to wipe a mark off the Audi, he saw the UNP symbol on one of the men's pockets.

Yeah, he was angry; angry enough to send his storm troopers, Mitch thought. We should have just taken the registration papers and binned them later.

———

By the time Mitch spoke with the security officers, Nick had arrived back in the office with the two coffees. He looked up as Mitch walked past. Mitch's nose was bleeding, dripping onto his collar and the front of his white shirt, his suit was covered in dirt from the parking lot floor.

"What the hell? I just left you five minutes ago and you get into trouble. How did that happen?" Nick asked.

John came out of his office, hearing Nick.

"Christ, Mitch, what happened?" He followed Mitch into his office. Nick joined them.

"It's nothing, no big deal," he said looking around for something to block his nose bleed. John gave him a clean handkerchief.

"I just got jumped in the parking lot. Why are

you always carrying a clean handkerchief?" Mitch asked.

"Our parking lot? How does that happen? Where's security?" John demanded.

"They came, eventually."

"For crying out loud. Go and see the medic while I go and see security."

"It's okay." Mitch dropped into his chair.

"Now, Mitch!" John said.

"Right." Mitch got up again.

"Seriously, we're getting mugged in our own parking lot now," John continued to mutter as he left the office and headed to the stairwell. "What's the point of security?"

Nick followed Mitch out of his office. "Look on the bright side, he hasn't sent you for counseling yet."

"Oh yeah, about that ..."

15

Mitch sat in his office, his team around him. His shirt was stained with blood and his eye bruised. He listened to Adam Forster's report with disbelief.

"So the family never saw Eli Hoefer," Mitch reiterated. "He came to pick up Benjamin, left a note and took the kid?"

"Precisely," said Adam.

"The German mother ..." Ellen looked to Adam.

"Antje," he filled in the blanks.

"Yes, Antje," Ellen continued, "she must have been worried sick. She's looked after this little boy from the age of two to seven and suddenly he's gone with no goodbye, no ensuring he has all he needs. It's appallingly cruel."

"Maybe he genuinely didn't want them to see

him like that, but I would have been so grateful to them for looking after Benjamin I'd want to thank them," Nick said.

"It's definitely odd," Mitch agreed, "and it means no one can really verify that Eli Hoefer was the man who collected Benjamin Hoefer. Great work Adam, keep digging. Nick, want to fill them in on our visit to the first neo-Nazi group?" He instinctively touched his bruised face.

"You should put some ice or a steak on your eye," Ellen said.

"I'd love a steak right now," Nick said.

"Me too," Adam agreed with a side serve of ..." he saw Mitch's expression. "Never mind."

"Onto more important matters," Nick continued. "We paid a visit to the UNP—United Nazi Party ..."

While Nick filled the team in, Mitch glanced at Benjamin Hoefer's schedule for the rest of the book launch. Benjamin had two days rest before his next speaking engagement. *Excellent, I want to speak with him again.*

Nick cleared his throat. "Finished here," he said as Mitch continued to read.

"Oh right." Mitch looked up. "Thanks."

"Ellie, what have you got?"

"The case breaker," she said.

Mitch looked up. "Really?"

"No, I just wanted your undivided attention." She smiled.

"Funny." Mitch smirked, closed the file he was reading and sat back.

"The CCTV footage from the Jewish Community Centre and neighboring buildings all feature the black van taking off but the plates have been blacked out. Every ticket holder was validated and none of the staff noticed anyone suspicious entering the building before the event to put the banners up," she said.

"Which means they could be on staff," Adam added.

"Except I checked out all the staff and no one stands out, or to be honest is young or slim enough to match the person I saw running away." Ellen held up her hand. "Yes, they could have been a friend, ally or relative, but that's casting a wide net. Also I ran checks against the Jewish Community Centre staff and the Holocaust Memorial Museum staff and ..." she dragged the suspense out ..."no connections," Ellen finished.

"Damn," Mitch sighed. "Okay, I've got to go and give John an update, so Adam can you stick to the ancestry line ... are you okay doing that solo?"

"Sure," Adam said, "happy to."

Mitch continued, "Nick try and get us a meeting

with The New Aryan Order tomorrow then, swing by Henri and ask what we would need if we wanted to do genetic testing on Benjamin Hoefer and his deceased father and how we can go about legally getting what we need."

"Done," Nick said.

"I'm on that track too—that they might not be related," Adam interrupted, "I've got Dieter looking through his father's attic to see if he can find any mementos from Eli, Yetta or Benjamin."

"It's a possibility; I want to put that question to Benjamin Hoefer and see his reaction. Ellie, can you try and get an audience with Benjamin this afternoon in an hour or so? You and I can swing by and see him."

"Got a clean shirt?" she asked.

He looked down at the blood stains. "Good point, allow enough time for us to drop by my place, thanks. Then can you help Nick with research...run background checks on the key identities in The New Aryan Order and find out whatever you can about them and their platform."

Mitch rose and headed to John's office, and his team dispersed.

———

"So what have you got?" John Windsor pushed back from the desk and gave his attention to Mitch.

"I've got a ghost projectionist who is still screening the film nightly at Benjamin Hoefer's memorabilia display at the Holocaust Memorial Museum; a slim person wearing black and driving around in a black van with no plates who unfurled banners at Benjamin Hoefer's last book launch; a possibility that Eli Hoefer was not Benjamin Hoefer's father which begs the question of who was he and could he have been a Nazi or fake as the ghost proclaims? I don't think Benjamin Hoefer is being completely upfront with us; I've got another neo-Nazi group to see today and the one I have seen doesn't have the smarts to pull off what is currently going on."

"Okay, do you want back-up when you see the other Nazi group?" John asked.

"No. I want to know why we are on this case."

John looked surprised. "What do you mean?"

"I don't know why we are on this case. Seriously, John, an author is getting a few threats, so what? We're wasting our time."

John exhaled.

Mitch leaned across the desk. "I'm handing this case back to you John unless you tell me why we're on it. Who has requested it?"

"Close the door," John said.

Mitch leaned over and swung the door closed.

"You don't get to hand back cases, Mitch."

"Then why give us something then tie our hands? I've got about three months of annual leave owing, and now seems a good time to take it if you don't need me on the job."

John's eyes narrowed with annoyance. "It's classified, Mitch, but we need to persist with this case."

"It's rubbish. We're chasing our tails doing something the local police could be doing."

John tapped his fingers on the desk and studied Mitch.

"Get security clearance for us, John. We're 'need-to-know' if we're running the case and it's bullshit that they should expect anything less."

"Leave it with me," John said, "and close the door on your way out."

Mitch left as John picked up the phone to make a call. He walked past his team and returned to his office. He glanced back towards John's office and saw him rub his hand across his forehead while talking on the phone. Mitch logged in with his password and checked his email. There was a video sent to select staff titled *How to take out two baddies.* He opened the file to find CCTV footage of himself knocking out the two parking lot assailants in four moves. As it finished, he watched as he turned and wiped a mark off the Audi. The words flashed up,

'WARNING: don't touch the Audi'. Mitch smirked and shook his head.

"Nick!" he called out and looked up just in time to see Nick disappearing down the stairs.

"Off to see Henri," Nick yelled.

"You'll keep," he called after him.

16

ANESTHETIST DR. DIRK SCHMID SAT IN HIS TASTEFUL office in the medical wing of the Fairchild Private Hospital; he was not required in surgery for another hour. In this role, there was nothing that connected Schmid to his other life as Chief Executive of The New Aryan Order. On his large timber desk sat a framed photo of his family; the perfect Aryan family. His glamorous blond wife, Steffi, stood with two fair and healthy looking sons aged six and ten and his beautiful teen daughter, now fourteen.

Logging onto his computer, he went to his personal screen, put in his password and logged in externally to his home email. There were several emails including one from his brother; a press clipping about the uproar at Benjamin Hoefer's last appearance at the Jewish Community Centre. *He should never have survived in the first place.* He thought about how his medical skills could have contributed towards the creation of Hitler's Aryan master race...and still could.

He clicked on a document and put in another password to open a strategy paper, the *Fountain of Life 2*. The original *Fountain of Life* program or *Lebensborn* launched by the Nazi Party involved men of the SS mating with blue-eyed, blond Nordic girls with no Jewish ancestry. Of the ten thousand children that were born in World War II as part of a Nazi genetic engineering plan to build an Aryan master-race, just over three thousand were still alive, all now in their sixties. Schmid and the NAO were working with their German allies to get their DNA, sort out who had mated with purity and produced offspring that could still be eligible for the program.

Schmid looked at his family portrait again; *Steffi was perfect on many levels and will be again when I find the next round of matches for her to mate with.* Like all members of the NAO, it was her duty to reproduce —same as that of the other members who were good specimens. His eyes strayed to the image of his teenage daughter in the family portrait. *Allie, just like her mother, and at fourteen, not long until she will be useful.*

———

"How's things in the nerd, I mean nerve center?" Nicholas Everett teased Henri's two assistants as he strode through the lab.

"Keeping the organization going," Jared said, and grinned.

"Thank God for you guys," Nick said.

"Hey funny video Nick, has Mitch seen it yet?" Tom asked with a nod to his email inbox.

"Yeah and I'm sure I'll pay for that later." Nick grinned. He rapped on Henri's door. "Can you spare me ten minutes, Henri?"

Henri looked up from his computer. "Nicholas! Good to see you. Yes, indeed...in fact you can save me for ten minutes. I'm preparing a paper to deliver to the executives next week and trying to put every-thing that might be too scientific in lay-terms. See, you're glazing over already."

Nick laughed. "Throw in some subliminal slides, like a photo of a plane or a Ducati, the latest Glock or adventure skiing. I hear that works."

"Good idea. Shall I make one of my organic coffees?"

"Thought you'd never ask," Nick said.

Henri called out to Jared and Tom who declined the offer of a coffee. "They'll have no internal organs left by the time they're thirty. All those high energy drinks. So how are you, Nicholas?"

Nick slid onto a stool and loosened his tie, as Henri made them both a coffee.

"Good."

"And your mom and dad?" Henri asked.

"Still going around the country in their Winnebago, discovering America."

Henri laughed. "Yes, Ann is keen to do that one day soon. I'm not so sure. I think I would rather fly to the location, experience it and fly back to base."

"Yeah, I'm with you on that one. The folks are like two peas in a pod though. They ring up and put the phone on speaker then finish each other's sentences for the length of the call."

"How lovely. You're very lucky, Nicholas."

Nick shrugged. "I'm lucky they're on the road and not giving me a hard time about getting a haircut and a girlfriend." He accepted the coffee and sugar sachet with thanks.

"So you want to talk genetic testing?" Henri sat opposite him.

"Are you psychic or is Mitch checking up on me?"

"Neither. I ran into Adam in the hallway and he said you'd be on your way. How's he settling in?"

"Got a place, got a woman, getting paid. Doing

better than Mitch and me, I'd say," Nick said. "So what did Adam tell you?"

"Not enough. What do you need to know?" Henri asked.

"We've got a case and we think Eli Hoefer who died close to two decades ago is not the biological father of Benjamin Hoefer."

"The writer of the Holocaust memoir that's attracting all the attention?" Henri asked.

"Precisely. So what would you need to prove a genetic connection? Love this coffee."

"Yes, it's a good blend; discovered it after years of taste testing. Any relatives alive?"

"At this stage, not that we know of. Benjamin's mother died in Auschwitz, he is an only child and if there is a relative of Benjamin's alive, it won't be in the US, given he and his father immigrated here after the war," Nick filled him in.

"Right. What we need to do DNA testing is a cheek swab, or blood. Obviously getting both from Benjamin Hoefer will be easy but from Eli ... impossible," Henri said. "If you can find a relative that you know for sure is related to Eli, not Benjamin, then this will work for the deceased alleged father, but a few relatives would be better."

Nick nodded and sipped his coffee.

"This is where it gets tricky, Nicholas. Ideally, you want to find the parents of the deceased which is impossible because they are long dead, any known siblings of Eli Hoefer, or any children of Eli's aside from Benjamin."

"He only had one child, Benjamin. But now that you say that, perhaps there was a reason he didn't continue to procreate," Nick said.

"Mm, maybe. It is possible to attempt a DNA paternal relatedness test using DNA from a known niece or nephew, but we can't guarantee conclusive results since aunts, uncles, nieces and nephews will share only about twenty-five per cent of Eli's DNA."

"What if Benjamin had his father's hairbrush still. Could we use hair to test DNA?" Nick asked.

"Good question. Yes and no...we require at least five to six hairs but given Eli was aged, well gray hair does not usually provide a good hair specimen so there's that challenge, but worth a try. You want the hair follicle, so it must be from the root, not a clipping," Henri informed him.

"So even if it is an old sample, say a decade or so, it is still useable—the DNA doesn't die so to speak?"

"It's useable," Henri said, "because you've got the resources of a lab that can do it. It's not easy or cheap. Of course you could exhume the body ... or was Eli cremated?"

Nick's eyes widened with the possibility. "I don't know. But there's no way we would get approval to do that at this stage; no real grounds to do so. So if he was buried ..."

"Then he could be exhumed and DNA tested against his son's DNA."

"But," Nick said, "if he was cremated?"

Henri shook his head. "Then that would not be good news. The high heat of the cremation process destroys DNA. However, one part of the body that is weakened but still intact to some degree following cremation is a person's teeth. But, virtually all properly performed cremations will ultimately pulverize the teeth, so there is little chance of intact DNA."

Nick nodded. "You're not giving me a lot of joy here, Henri."

"Sorry. Come down with an easier question next time." He smiled.

"Loved the video from Nick," Ellen teased Mitch.

"Yeah, hilarious," Mitch agreed.

"Good moves. What's the story with this car?" she asked as they headed to Mitch's house for a change of shirt. "Why do you love it so much?"

Mitch looked away from the road and over at Ellen.

"I don't, Nick just beats that up," he said, and returned his eyes to the road.

"Yeah, he does, but you still love it."

Mitch shrugged. "It's the first thing I've ever owned."

He felt Ellen staring at him.

"Really? But you own a house, even if it is rented out, you still own it."

"But I bought this first. Actually I always wanted a BMW but when I test drove both, I liked the Audi better." He ran his hand over the top of the steering wheel.

"But didn't you own a car or motorbike when you were in the Air Force?"

"No, you didn't really need to. You were always stationed somewhere and when you had an off-base pass, you'd usually taxi somewhere in a group because you were going to have a few beers anyway. You just didn't need wheels."

Ellen persisted. "But what about when you were a kid ... didn't you own a bike?"

"Nope," Mitch fidgeted. "Are we meeting Benjamin at his hotel?"

"No, but nearby; a coffee shop around the corner. He requested we meet him there. Really, no bike?"

Mitch sighed. "No, I didn't own a bike."

"What kid doesn't own a bike? A train set? A scooter? Even poor kids get hand-me downs or 'find' them."

Mitch pulled at his tie, loosening it. He was getting into dangerous territory; territory he didn't talk about, least of all with his team. He felt Ellen looking at him, waiting for an answer.

"You and Nick must have biked around when you were kids. You know, have wheels will travel," Ellen persisted.

"Yeah, I had a bike sometimes, but Dad owned it. He owned everything."

He saw Ellen turn and look straight ahead at the road, processing what he said.

He cleared his throat. "Sometimes he would give it to me, sometimes he would take it and lock it up, or get rid of it, just to remind me that everything we had was his or because of him."

"I see," she said.

"But Nick had a few bikes so it wasn't a big deal. I'd just go to his place and we'd take off from there."

"Did you get birthday and Christmas presents?" Ellen asked.

"Of course," Mitch said. "I'm not Oliver the orphan."

Ellen laughed. "So you got to keep those then?"

Mitch shook his head. "Only if Dad didn't see or find them. We owned nothing. I remember one Christmas, Mom bought my brother Dylan and me the most fantastic train set. She worked part-time and saved up to buy it. You had to build it, you know, assemble the train and the whole city and landscape. We loved it. We spent about two weeks putting it together, painting the village and the landscape, the whole thing."

"That's cool."

"It was," Mitch agreed. "Then one night Dad came home drunk as usual, took a baseball bat to it and smashed it completely."

Ellen gasped. "What did you do?"

Mitch looked at her. "Nothing." He turned his eyes back to the road, indicated and turned off at the street entrance to his and Lyn's residence. "A ten-year-old and a seven-year-old don't take on a drunk man wielding a baseball bat. We cleaned it up and threw it in the bin the next morning like we were told."

Ellen ran her hand along the window ledge of the car. "No wonder you love this car." She sighed. "I had so much when I was a kid."

Mitch grimaced, ready for the inevitable comparisons.

Ellen continued. "But I was adorable," she teased.

Mitch laughed. He glanced at her, shook his head, surprised and pleased she had not gotten heavy. "Yes ... I bet you were."

Mitch's phone rang and he answered it hands-free. "John, I've got Ellie with me, we're on our way to talk to Benjamin Hoefer."

"Right. I have clearance to give you that information you wanted. I suggest we talk and then you can brief Ellie and the lads. How long will you be?"

"An hour tops. Do I need to know before we talk with Benjamin?"

John thought for a moment. "What angle are you taking?"

Mitch nodded to Ellen.

"We'll grill him some more on who he thinks is pulling these stunts," Ellen answered, "we believe he knows but is frightened to say, and we're going to cut to the chase and ask if he really thought Eli was his biological father and then ask for a genetic sample," she said.

"Okay." John thought again. "No, it can wait. I'll see you in an hour." He hung up.

Ellen turned to Mitch. "What was all that about?"

"I gave the case back to him, said it was a mission for the local police unless he told us the full story about who commissioned the investigation and why we're on it."

"Yeah, I did think it was an over-reaction, giving us this case," Ellen agreed. "How did John take that?"

"He understood and said he'd get us clearance, which he has, but I suspect I'll get a lecture later. I want to know who is behind this brief. It's information that we should have had from the start."

Mitch swung the Audi into his driveway and turned the car off. "Come in while I change. You can meet Lyn, she works from home."

Ellen's eyes widened in surprise. In the years she had worked with Mitch she had never met anyone from his inner sanctum except Henri and that was only because he worked at the FBI. She took her seat belt off and hurried to catch up with him before he changed his mind.

17

Mitch glanced at his watch; it was nearly midday but felt like it should be five p.m. already. He could see Benjamin Hoefer sitting in a window seat of the coffee house waiting for them. Mitch shook his head.

"Why doesn't he put a name tag on? Given he's in danger, the least he could do is move inside out of sight," Mitch said.

"He wouldn't think of that I suspect," Ellen said. "Not everyone thinks like us."

"Really?" Mitch looked at her, surprised. "That explains a lot." His phone rang and he saw Nick's number come up. He quickly answered.

"Hey what's up?"

"We need a hairbrush or comb that belonged to his father or something that might have some DNA on it," Nick said. "He might have kept them out of sentimentality."

"I'll ask the question," Mitch said.

"Yeah, good luck with that. Otherwise I'm looking for long-lost relatives," Nick said.

"Okay. Did you get John's note re the briefing this afternoon?"

"No, I'll check emails now," Nick said.

"Check Adam has got it too will you? See you then." Mitch hung up and joined Ellen, and they entered the coffee shop.

Benjamin rose to greet the two agents and they shook hands. Mitch took in the area and sat facing the door. The three ordered tea and coffee.

Ellen asked after his health as Mitch watched Benjamin's reactions.

"Mr. Hoefer, I need to ask you some questions which won't be pleasant, but they're important if we are to protect you and find whoever is threatening you," Mitch said.

"Of course," Benjamin said.

They waited as the waitress placed their order in front of them.

Mitch began. "To give you some context, I'm trying to establish why someone might have a vendetta against your father, not you. Clearly you would not have recognized your father when he returned to collect you post war."

"That's true. I was two when he and my mother were taken away and seven when my father returned alone," Benjamin said.

Mitch nodded. "Have you ever doubted he was your father?"

Benjamin looked surprised. "No. Why would I doubt that?" He looked from Mitch to Ellen. "What man would come out of a concentration camp and return to collect a child that wasn't his own? How would he know to do that? I don't understand why you would ask that."

Ellen stepped in. "The banners and wording on the video have included the word 'fake'. We're trying to establish what that means and we're looking at a lot of angles. Perhaps your father has been mistaken for someone else or the perpetrator has taken umbrage with some of your research or facts."

Benjamin nodded. "He's the only father I have ever known since I was seven."

"But you thought Gynther Bäcker was your father until Eli arrived?" Mitch continued.

"Yes, that's true. It was traumatic but I know they did that for my safety."

"Why didn't your father ever remarry?" Mitch asked, turning to watch two men who passed close by their coffee table.

"I wondered the same." Benjamin sighed. "He

had lady friends, many—and many long term girl-friends, but he did not want to marry or have any more children."

"Could he have children after what he suffered in the camp?" Ellen asked.

"Again I don't know." Benjamin looked from one to the other. "Maybe some medical records exist somewhere. That generation and mine for that matter don't air the family laundry. Do you know if your parents could conceive or had difficulties?"

"No, true," Ellen said, "but most only children do ask their parents for a sibling at some point in time."

"I never did that because there was no mother in the house," Benjamin explained.

"Did your father ever mention any surviving brothers, sisters, cousins, aunts or uncles?" Mitch persisted.

"I am sure there were surviving relatives but you have to remember what the world was like post war. There were millions of displaced people. My father never wanted to speak of the war; he came to America to forget that life and to start again. He would shut down any questions I had."

"One last question please," Mitch said, noting the elderly gentleman was getting tired. "Have you had any direct experience or contact with any neo-Nazi groups, at any point in your life?"

"Never. That's why this is so strange. Why bother causing a storm about an old man's memories when there are so many Holocaust stories out there?"

"So, no direct letters or threats to you?" Ellen asked.

"Nothing." He shook his head vehemently, but avoided eye contact with the two agents.

Mitch frowned, sensing Benjamin Hoefer wasn't telling the truth and wasn't going to any time soon. He offered to walk Benjamin back to his hotel but he insisted on going alone. Mitch watched him walk down the street and into the hotel before he and Ellen returned to the car.

"What did you think?" Ellen asked Mitch as they drove back to the office.

"I think he's a bad liar and he's afraid," Mitch said. "I'm not sure if he is afraid of repercussions from whoever is threatening him or afraid of what he might find out about his past. The problem is it is too late, he's started the ball rolling. I need to get Nick to interview him."

"Why?" Ellen asked, surprised.

"He's good at reading people. He's always been good at that," Mitch said.

"And we're not?"

"Not as good as he is. I think Adam is like me, we don't trust anyone until they've proved themselves to be trustworthy; you on the other hand think everyone is well-intentioned until they prove themselves not to be; and Nick nails it most times. I need to get his read on Benjamin Hoefer. Speaking of Nick, since you are second-in-charge and have a fair bit on your plate, you could hand over the team medic role to Nick. He was in search-and-rescue in the Air Force. He's qualified."

Ellen looked impressed. "So you did take on board my little speech about respecting my skill and roles, Mitch."

Mitch smiled. "I do think of the team's career satisfaction sometimes."

"So John's idea?" Ellen asked.

"Yep."

18

JOHN WINDSOR WAITED UNTIL MITCH AND HIS TEAM had sat down and closed the door before he gave them the classified information which formed the background of the case. He gave the necessary precautions in relation to the information he was about to share. Mitch tapped impatiently.

"There is an American-born citizen by the name of Ulric Adler." John spelt the name out as the team jotted it down. "He is of German descent and has come to the attention of the FBI through one of our Hate Crimes Working Groups. An investigation has been launched by that team."

"What's his connection?" Mitch pushed.

"That's the catch and why this information wasn't revealed to you yet. Adler is a socialist and a local independent candidate who has expressed interest in running for the office of President in the next elections. Alder has a formidable support team and our insider information tells us that his campaign funds are unprecedented. Some may say his party has neo-Nazi tendencies. We are still in the process of understanding who he and his party are and more importantly what they stand for," John said. "Hate itself is not an offence as you know, so at this stage, you are not to approach him directly, as he is under surveillance. If we were to get this wrong, it would be a disaster."

"So there's a chance that the Benjamin Hoefer incidents are linked to Adler?" Mitch frowned.

"It may have nothing to do with Adler, but with someone in his party. We don't have evidence of this yet, but Adler was seen in security footage at the Holocaust Memorial Museum book launch and just as quickly disappearing out of sight."

"And we're just hearing this now?" Mitch asked.

"Mitch, your job is to exhaust all other avenues connected to Benjamin Hoefer as the Adler angle is already being investigated. The Hate Crime Investigation Team is watching him. If both teams connect the dots, so be it, but we have to play this very carefully and there can't be any possible risk of a public or media leak, given his connection."

Mitch nodded. "So we need to continue investigating why Eli or Benjamin Hoefer might be targeted and ..."

"Yes, you need to continue exactly as you are," John stepped in. "Continue your investigations to find out if Eli Hoefer was really Eli Hoefer, why Benjamin is being targeted, and what it is about that book that is causing these hate incidents, but under no circumstances approach Adler or his office."

"Benjamin didn't mention anything about Adler when Mitch and I spoke to him just now," Ellen said, "but clearly he knew Adler or was possibly being threatened by him if he was at that first book launch."

"He'd be too terrified to mention it I imagine," Mitch said. "Anything else we need to know?"

"That's it, but I will be getting updates from the other team and I will feed your reports to them, Mitch, so I'll keep you updated."

Mitch, Adam, Nick and Ellen rose to leave.

"Mitch, stay a minute," John said.

Mitch's team left and John closed the door. Mitch sat back down in front of John's desk.

"You understand your orders here don't you?" John said, rising and moving to the same side of the desk. He leaned against it.

"Of course," Mitch said. "We won't be going anywhere near that side of the investigation."

"Good." John crossed his arms in front of his

body. "Mitch, don't pull that annual leave bullshit on me again or you'll be answering to Ellen, understood?"

"John, if we get to the stage where you need to demote me, I'll do us both a favor and leave. Why couldn't you just tell me there was more information but it was classified? At least then I'd have gotten the idea that there's a bigger picture and just kept drilling away."

John thought for a moment. "And you don't think you would keep at me for it?"

Mitch frowned and didn't answer.

"I give you what I can when I brief you. It's in my interest to make sure you have the best brief you can get for your safety and effectiveness. So don't second-guess me," John said and before Mitch could respond, he continued. "I'd let me have the last word on this too."

Mitch nodded and said nothing.

"Okay, you can go," John said. "And don't forget you have your first counseling session in thirty minutes."

Mitch rose and left John's office.

19

ADAM FORSTER WENT UP THE PATH OF THE AGED CARE home. Sitting in the garden was an old man dressed in a three-piece suit, sharing a pot of tea with a younger man. They raised their hands in a wave and Adam responded. He followed the signs to the reception area and found a young woman in the office. Dressed in a knitted sweater like something one of the patients would have made, she looked up and greeted him. She was older than he'd realized, probably late forties. He read her name badge—Andrea Kotery.

"Hi Andrea, I'm Adam Forster, here to see Betty Lang please."

"Ah yes, Mr. Forster." She rose.

"Adam, please."

"She's been so excited all morning in anticipation of your visit," Andrea said.

"Even for a visitor she doesn't know?" Adam asked.

"It can be a lonely place, Adam. Some of our residents never receive a visitor. You'll be a good distraction and she can show you off," Andrea teased. "Come through, she's in the sitting room and you can have tea in the atrium."

"Thank you." Adam followed Andrea down a hallway into a sitting room where different groups of elderly people gathered—some knitting, playing board games, watching television or reading. Some just sat and stared.

"Mrs. Lang, Adam is here for you."

Adam looked around wondering which lady it would be, but then Betty Lang clapped her hands together in pleasure.

"Adam, delighted." She pulled herself out of a blue lounge chair and offered Adam her hand. She was tiny, just over five-feet, and frail. She wore a floral dress and a white cardigan and had short, curled hair almost as white as her cardigan.

"Why don't you take Adam through to the atrium, Mrs. Lang, and I'll get some tea sent to you both."

"Thank you dear," she said to Andrea. She

looped her arm through Adam's and looking up at his over six-foot frame, she led the way.

"She's a delight our Andrea; we all love her."

"I can see why," Adam agreed.

They walked out into the garden and into an atrium with small tables and chairs. A few other family members and friends were catching up in the area. He saw her safely to a chair and sat opposite.

"It was good of you to see me, Mrs. Lang," Adam said.

"Please call me Betty, it's short for Elizabeth you know. My parents were staunch monarchists. My sister is Margaret and my brothers William and George. Now, you want to speak to me about an old beau of mine."

"I do. Eli Hoefer," Adam said.

"Ah Eli," she sighed, "such a dear, dear man and we wrote right up until his death. We went out for nearly a decade you know."

"But he didn't want to commit?" Adam asked.

"He was married, even though she had departed. That is what he always said, and I understood that, Adam. I lost my first husband too. We were married thirty years and raised three beautiful children."

"I'm sorry, Betty."

"Oh don't be. Many people don't get thirty wonderful years. I was blessed. Then Eli and I met and we shared another decade of happiness in our six-ties; what luck."

"Can I ask why you parted?" Adam said.

"My sister fell ill and I moved away for six months to nurse her. I wasn't sure if I would return and so we freed each other to move on."

Andrea reappeared with another employee and they delivered tea and a plate of biscuits.

"So kind dears, thank you," Betty said.

Adam nodded his thanks. Betty poured the tea.

"So did Eli meet someone else while you were away?" Adam continued.

"No dear, I did." Betty Lang giggled like a schoolgirl. "I met Brian and we married and were together until death did us part. Well he departed, but we did have twelve splendid years, and here I am now. Nearly ninety-two might I add. It's a funny life, Adam, people come and go; you've got to grab what you can when you can."

Adam smiled at her. "Yes, that is a good lesson to remember, thank you Betty. So will you get one more marriage under the belt do you think?" Adam looked around for suitable partners. "I saw a distin-guished-looking chap on the way in."

Betty laughed. "Oh you terrible boy. Well, there is a lovely gentleman ... no, I'm only being silly. You young people think you will love once, but you will love all your life."

Adam smiled and raised his eyebrows.

"You don't believe me. One day you'll say 'that Betty, she was right'!" She reached for a biscuit.

"I hope so," Adam said. "Can you tell me what Eli and his son Benjamin were like together?"

"Oh yes. Very close, but Benjamin was an adult when I met them both of course. He was in his forties. He doted on his father and seemed to want to know as much as he could about him, but Eli was a closed book. He was one of the few people I know who could actually live day to day."

"Did he ever mention a relative or friend to you, or anything about his past life?" Adam said.

"Not intentionally. Once he slipped and referred to his brother. I told him he had never mentioned he had a brother and he was quick to say that it was just a term he used for a close childhood friend. He reminded me he was an only child like his son but I wasn't convinced ... something happened later that made me think he was lying. Why are you asking, Adam, is Benjamin in trouble?"

"No, nothing like that. It's just that Benjamin has released a book about his father's story and some people don't like it. He's been threatened. We're trying to work out why."

"Hmm." Betty sat back and thought about it. "Maybe Benjamin's cousin can shed some light on it."

Adam nearly dropped his tea cup. "Cousin? What cousin?"

"Oh yes, that's what made me think Eli was lying. Eli's nephew, that would be Benjamin's cousin, arrived from Germany one day out of the blue. Eli introduced us without explaining who he was and was quick to hustle me out of the room, but not before this young man told me he was the grandson of Eli's brother—let me think, Eli's brother's name began with an 'H', like Herbert or Herman, not Harry—anyway the nephew was only a young man, about half the age of Benjamin. I called Eli to task on this because he told me he was an only child. He still insisted he was and gave me this elaborate story about his father having a stepfamily and this young man was a step-nephew if such a thing existed; he succeeded in confusing me. But the young man was gone the next day; Eli said his nephew couldn't stay, he was on a tight schedule. I can't remember his name now, or can I ..."

Adam's heart raced as he waited patiently.

"Eli made short work of him," Betty continued. "I didn't really understand that because I thought if Eli loved his brother or step-brother he would have clutched at any memory. But Eli was insistent that he had to put distance between that part of his life for his and Benjamin's sake. The nephew and Eli looked a lot alike; could have been his own grandson, but he looked nothing like Benjamin." She frowned and closed her eyes.

Adam waited, not breathing, not moving.

Betty opened her eyes. "I'm sorry my dear, I can't remember—but I will. These things come to me like a bolt out of the blue these days. Shall I get a message to you if I remember?"

"Betty, that would make me the happiest detective on the squad," Adam said.

Betty giggled again. After they had finished another round of tea, Adam saw himself out. He looked back at her and she waved.

Suddenly she called out a name. "Schmid! That was it, Adam."

Adam raced back to her side.

"Schmid was his surname. I only remember because I had a piano teacher by the same name when I was a child. Can't remember his first name though."

"Betty, if I was ten years older I would propose," he teased.

"Away with you." She giggled again.

20

MITCH TOOK A DEEP BREATH AND RAPPED ON THE door. He heard a voice inside instruct him to enter. Reluctantly he entered and closed the door behind him.

Dan Tarrow, counselor, rose from the couch and met him halfway across the room. He was Mitch's height, with a shaved head, tanned and fit. Mitch noticed on the desk behind was a framed photo of Dan finishing a marathon.

"Mitchell Parker, the hardest man to get to counseling I hear," Dan smiled and indicated the green leather couch. "Have a seat, Mitchell."

"Mitch is fine," Mitch said and moved to the couch. He sat forward on the edge.

"You're here for an hour so make yourself comfortable. Want a tea, coffee or water?" Dan asked.

"No, I'm okay, thanks," Mitch said.

Dan looked surprised. "Really? Because that would have taken up to at least ten minutes of interview time."

Mitch smiled and shook his head. "Okay, got any filter coffee that drips really slowly?"

"Bound to." Dan rose and went to make them both coffee. "How do you take it?"

"White, thanks," Mitch said, studying the room.

"Why the aversion to counseling?" Dan asked as he found two clean mugs.

"I don't believe it helps." Mitch turned to face him. "You spill all this stuff and when you leave, it's still with you. What is the counseling supposed to achieve?"

"C'mon, surely somewhere along the line just talking with someone impartial has helped you put things in order in your head. Sometimes it is just hearing yourself say it out loud that makes you consider the validity. No? Never experienced that?"

"Can't say I have. You know, in the past, it was considered shameful to show a weak side and to say you're not coping. Several generations came back from the war and never spoke about it. They didn't self-combust," Mitch said, watching Dan.

"You don't know that though." Dan stirred sugar into his own cup. "Maybe they took it out on their wife or kids or drank too much. Maybe they led a shorter life due to stress and bottling it up."

Mitch sniffed with disbelief.

Dan returned and placed the coffee in front of him. He sat opposite with his own cup and sipped from it.

"Thanks," Mitch said.

"So you're telling me it has never helped you?" Dan pushed.

"I guess once it might have helped me sort some stuff into categories," Mitch conceded. "But I would have got there myself eventually."

Dan smiled. "Well let me try and earn my living." He picked up Mitch's file.

Immediately Mitch stiffened. He began to fidget, realized he was fidgeting and sat perfectly still. While Dan looked at the file, he continued to look around the room. It was stark, a clock on the wall ... *forty-five minutes to go ... white walls, white blinds ... three exit points—a door and two windows.* He turned back to find Dan looking at him.

"Your last case was a tough one," Dan said. "Multiple dead bodies including fellow law officers; you were tortured; you had a staff member who let you down; and all but one of the villains was killed. It was a high body count."

"It was, but not by our hand," Mitch agreed.

"Does that make a difference?" Dan sat back and put his arm on the back of the couch. He rested Mitch's file on his legs.

"Of course. No one wants to take a life."

"Not even if they deserve it?" Dan asked.

"No, not even then. But it is easier to justify it in your head if that's the case," Mitch said.

Dan nodded. He tapped on Mitch's file. "You have a fairly dark history here, Mitch, from a pretty young age," he said.

Mitch looked at the clock. "Took you eighteen minutes to get there; others have done better."

Dan laughed. "Yeah well it's not relevant to the case you just came off unless something major happened that threw you back into your childhood and you reacted accordingly?"

"Uh, no," Mitch said.

"Right, well let's stay in the present for now, but if you do ever need to talk about your history ... I've had a lot of experience in that."

Mitch nodded.

"I'll take that as you won't be seeing me anytime soon," Dan said.

Mitch smiled and sat back. "So, Cape Hatteras."

Dan rose, and adjusted the blinds to cut the light streaming into the room. Reflected in the glass window he saw Mitchell Parker run his hand over his face, glance to the clock, then restrain himself. Dan noted Mitch knew all the cues to look in control. He turned and sat back on the couch opposite him.

"You did a good job on the case, the bosses were happy. In fact your track record for closing cases is impressive," Dan said.

Mitch shrugged. "You do the best you can; I've got a good team which helps."

"Let's talk about the torture."

Mitch straightened.

"You were missing for close to forty-eight hours, during which time you were restrained, blindfolded, beaten, burnt and kept dehydrated. Did you want to walk through what happened?" Dan asked.

"You just did."

Dan nodded. He had read the incident report from Mitch's last case, and knew the extent of his injuries.

"What was going through your head?"

"The drill."

"Mitch ..." Dan frowned.

Mitch looked towards the window, and locked his jaw. "I thought I'd never get out of there alive."

Dan waited.

Mitch turned to look at him. "I've had a lot of close calls, but I thought that was it."

"Why that time?" Dan asked.

"Because we didn't know the underground cell existed, we hadn't found it in our survey of the property, so no one knew where I was. Plus they took my watch that had the tracker from me and at that stage I knew they had killed the four police officers—I figured killing another person would be no big deal to them."

Dan nodded but said nothing.

Mitch sat forward on the couch and rubbed his arm which had been burnt during the torture. "What a stupid way to go though—because Sam screwed up. Who walks into their lair like that?" He stopped rubbing and talking, bit his lip and sat back.

"So you're still harboring a lot of hostility towards Samantha," Dan stated.

Mitch sighed. "Everyone makes errors on a case, but willful disobedience of orders and plain stupidity just pisses me off."

Dan smiled.

"Too blunt?" Mitch exhaled and smiled back.

"Nope, I get it. I served for ten years before I became a psychologist. If you can't follow an order you shouldn't be in the field. Have you spoken with Samantha about it?"

"At the time."

"But when you're in pain or have a flashback, it's her fault?" Dan asked.

Mitch looked to his right, to the window again. "I'm not in pain and I'm not having flashbacks about it."

"Okay," Dan said. "So look at me and say that."

Mitch frowned and looked at Dan. He spoke the words again. "I'm not in pain and I'm not having flashbacks."

"Very good," Dan said. "So you sleep well, no night sweats? Honestly, Mitch?"

Mitch hesitated.

Dan waited. After some time he realized Mitch wasn't going to answer. "Tell me about the vault?"

"What vault?"

"When you and ..." Dan turned to his notes, "... Nicholas, when you and Nicholas went to open the storage vault."

"Oh, that," Mitch said. "We expected to find some missing police officers dead in there and we were right. Shook Nick up a bit, but he had some counseling as you know. All better!" Mitch smiled at Dan.

"Didn't shake you up though, huh? How come you held it together?"

"Training," Mitch said. "Part of the job."

Dan reached to the water jug in the middle of

the table between them and filled both of their glasses. Mitch drank it within minutes.

Dan noticed as Mitch glance at the clock again.

"Surely seeing something like that is a rarity on a job?" Dan asked.

"I was telling Ellie, it was one of the first things I encountered when I started the job. You know how it works, Dan. You go there expecting and preparing for what you'll see and it minimizes the trauma. It's when you don't know what to expect that you can get affected."

Dan refilled Mitch's water and he drank it again.

"Time's up. One more to go, see you then." Mitch rose.

"See you Mitch." Dan watched him leave. He sighed, shook his head and made some notes on Mitch's file.

———

Seeing Mitch return to his desk, John Windsor put in a call to Dan Tarrow.

"Dan, John Windsor," he introduced himself. "I know your session with Mitch was private, but tell me, did he respond to it?" he asked, looking across the office at Mitch seated back at his computer.

"Well, it's safe to say he's the master of masking," Dan said.

"Mm," John agreed. "So was it of any value?"

"For me more than him," Dan said. "He's an interesting study. Never lets his guard down while you're watching. But I caught him out a couple of times in the window reflection."

"So he's not saying how he's dealing with things?"

"Oh, he's not lying about anything," Dan said. "He simply doesn't answer if he doesn't want to. Great self-control. I'm looking forward to the next session."

"Thanks Dan," John hung up and walked over to Mitch's office. He rapped on the glass door, entered, and sat in the chair in front of Mitch's desk. "How did the session go; was it any help?"

"For what? I wasn't looking for help."

John sighed. "Right. So was it of any use?"

"No, but I knew that before I went. Nice guy Dan, a bit different."

"How?"

"He doesn't really prod."

"That's good that you connected with him, because he wants you to have the full six sessions," John said.

"What? No!"

"Just joking," John said.

"On what planet would that ever be funny?" Mitch shook his head.

"Oh, lighten up," John glanced at his watch. "Late lunch. Want to get a sandwich?"

"Sure." Mitch rose.

John followed him out of the office. *Yes, the master of masking.*

21

THE TWO MEN GRASPED HANDS. TALL, BLOND AND striking, Ulric Adler, candidate for President, looked into a mirror image of himself in Dirk Schmid, anesthetist and head of The New Aryan Order.

The maître d' arrived. "Gentlemen, as always, good to see you. Your regular table is ready," he said, and led the way.

"Thank you Franz." Adler followed. They heard the day's specials, and ordered lunch and wine.

Adler sat back, laced his fingers and looked at Dirk. "It's all happening."

Dirk grinned. "It's so close, I can taste it. With you as President, and the support of our Order, no one in modern history has ever been as close to saving America as we are now."

They stopped talking as the waiter brought an expensive bottle of wine, Dirk tasted it, gave the waiter a nod and two glasses were poured.

Adler lifted his glass. "To making history."

"To making history," Dirk agreed and touched his glass to Adler's. "Let's talk business before we relax."

Adler nodded.

"The latest figures from Thorsten." Dirk pulled a sealed envelope from his leather bag and handed it over.

"How is your brother?" Adler asked.

"In good health. But you know Thorsten, he worries if he hasn't got something to worry about." Dirk sighed. "We've refined the campaign messages, plus we've got our next fertilization round about to begin."

"Purity," Adler said sipping his wine. "Well done Dirk, well done. And you're balancing all this with your medical work?"

"It is my duty and my honor."

"Do you ever think what it must have been like to have served with him?" Adler said, loosening his tie.

"Yes. It's the reason I became an anesthetist ... I imagine the work I could have done then, what I could have contributed."

"And you will, now, in the Fourth Reich," Adler said.

———

Mitch arrived in the kitchen in dark track pants and a light gray pullover. He smiled at Lyn who was wearing a panda-print onesie with matching slippers.

"Cute," he said. "If only I'd kept my tiger print pajamas."

"Really?" she asked, wide-eyed.

"No."

Lyn laughed. "You know this is the first night we've actually been home together to cook for weeks; how exciting!" She grinned at him.

"Yeah, well hope you're not relying on me to help create a culinary masterpiece. I'm good with pasta though," Mitch said.

Lyn sighed. "Yes, that's what all men say. Okay your pasta, my Bolognese sauce, we'll be fine."

"Just issue orders and I'll comply. Red?" Mitch asked, reaching for two wine glasses.

"Please," Lyn said, grabbing some tomatoes and herbs from the refrigerator. She set them up on a chopping board and pulled a sharp knife from the drawer.

"No Sandy tonight?" Mitch asked, placing the glass of red wine in front of her.

"No, we don't catch up every night. And that wouldn't be fair on you either to have her always here."

Mitch shrugged. "I'm not fazed, I'm not around much."

"I noticed. Will you chop the tomatoes into small cubes and finely dice the parsley and basil? I'll put the pasta on, oil the pan and set the ... shall we eat here at the bench?"

"Sounds good." Mitch took the knife and began to dice.

Lyn moved to the ceramic glass top, selected the heat, grabbed a pan, and lightly poured in some olive oil. "I see Sandy here three nights a week, go to her place two nights a week and we have two nights apart," she continued. "When you get a girlfriend, we can work out the nights if you like so you have the place to yourself. Ellen was very nice and very cute."

Mitch looked up at Lyn and smiled.

"Yes, she's lovely."

"You would be good together; you have similar features and characteristics," Lyn said. "You know they say good couples look alike?"

"Do they?" Mitch asked. "What's in the water

this month? Everyone's trying to partner up. Do you want this straight in the pan?"

"Yes please," Lyn said, grabbing a wooden spoon.

"Aside from the fact that Ellie and I work together and I'm her boss, we're too alike to make it work. We both don't need to socialize, don't like big groups, think too much for our own good, can drive along for hours without a word ... we'd end up being a little old couple on the couch with matching slippers drinking sherry."

Lyn sighed. "Sounds divine. I don't believe in opposites attract. I think it is good to have a partner who is like you. I was married once."

"Really?" Mitch said, as he started dicing the onions and olives. He glanced at Lyn in her onesie and tied back hair and tried to picture her with a man.

"So you didn't know you were gay?" he asked, swiping his watering eyes as a result of the onion.

"I think I always knew. But my father was an Episcopalian minister; I would never have been able to come out."

Mitch frowned. "I thought they were okay with that, even had ordained gay ministers or am I thinking of the wrong crowd?"

"No you are thinking of the right 'crowd'," she grinned at him. "But my father was much more black and white in his views. He's probably rolling over in his grave now. He was happy when I married Sebastian and it was good for a few years, but neither of us was really happy. Seb's remarried now with kids."

"Are you friends?"

"Yes, I love him, he's one of my dearest friends and I love his wife and kids too. But we were opposites and so was the boyfriend I had before him. Both very social people and I struggled with being around people and having people over all the time. I thought there was something wrong with me, so I tried and tried, but I love my own company. Sandy and I like small groups and our downtime. So I think you and Ellen would be most suited."

"Hmm," Mitch said.

"That wasn't actually a word."

Mitch laughed. "Yeah, not going to happen."

"Do you like her?"

"Of course, what's not to like," Mitch said pushing onions and olives off the chopping board into Lyn's tomato mix.

"You know what I mean," she grilled him.

"I've had better interrogators than you so that's not going to work."

"Well, I do have two single friends who have grilled me about you—Karen and Sarah—or maybe if you have some single male friends?"

"And if that doesn't work out ... at this rate, I'll be moving every six months won't I?" He reached for his wine and returned to the kitchen stool.

"But think on the upside. What if it did work out?" she asked.

22

NICHOLAS EVERETT'S COUNSELING SESSION WAS scheduled for eight a.m. He preferred to get it out of the way early and get on with the day. He also didn't want to go home heavy after a session of baring his soul and being analyzed.

"You had a few sessions after the last case," counselor Dan Tarrow said as he sat on the couch opposite Nick reading his file. "I hope it helped."

Nick nodded and inhaled. "I went through my whole career in the Air Force without encountering any dead bodies. Then I saw a lifetime's quota I think in one month."

"From what Mitch tells me, though, that body count is fairly unusual for your team. Are you happy in this role?"

"I love it. Best thing that happened to me in a

long time was meeting up with Mitch again," Nick said, "and getting this placement."

"Yeah, you've been nearly a year in the job now. It has to be good for Mitch to have you and Henri around—a support network," Dan said.

"Works both ways."

Dan waited a few moments before moving on.

"Are you dealing with what happened last time? Finding the four police officers' bodies and the elderly couple on the boat ... any flashbacks, night sweats, nightmares?"

"To be honest, once I spoke about it after the event, I guess you could say I released it. Does that make sense?" Nick said.

"A lot of sense. So nothing you want to discuss or work through in regard to the last case?" Dan studied him.

Nick shook his head. "Nope."

"Nick, since we have time," Dan looked at the clock, "let's talk about the passing of your fiancée."

Nick shuffled in his seat. "I really don't want to go there."

"And that's why we should." Dan looked at the file again. "Ana."

Nick winced as Dan said her name.

"It's been two years since Ana was killed in a car accident."

"I'm well aware of that," Nick snapped. He rose

and went to the window. "Dan, find something else to grill me on. If I knew you were going to fill the session this way, I would have come up with some nightmares and flashbacks."

Dan leaned back in the couch and looked at Nick. "You're sounding like Mitchell now. Come on, Nick, let's cross this hurdle."

"Why? Why is it relevant?" Nick asked, turning to face Dan.

"It's relevant. I just don't pull things out of the file because I'm nosy. Come back, sit down."

Nick wandered over and sat down.

Dan continued. "I'm bringing this up because in here," he waved the manila folder at Nick, "there are three separate reports filed throughout your training and work over the past year which indicate that your actions—brave or foolhardy—show your willingness to rush in and help a colleague or test a weapon for example, may be because you have no concern for your own safety. To me, this says that if you were killed tomorrow, you wouldn't care."

Nick laughed. "So?"

"Well that worries me a little."

"Why, in case I drag someone along with me?" Nick asked. "I would never do that."

"I know, Nick," Dan said. "No, it worries me because you're a young man. You may think you won't love again, feel great again or commit again, but you will."

Nick shook his head. "I'm not interested."

"Of course you're not. But it's been two years now ... where are you at, in your head space I mean? Are you angry, depressed, reflective?"

"Is this where you pull out the stages of grief chart?" Nick rose again and began to pace. "I'm well past the shock, I should be past the anger ..."

Dan Tarrow held up his hands in resignation. "Okay, time out, time out." He rose and went to the coffee machine. "How do you take it?"

Nick shook his head.

"Nick, have a coffee with me. How do you take it?"

"Black and strong."

The two men did not speak until the coffee was made and they sat down again, the coffees on the table between them.

"There's no timeline for grief; I'm not saying you need to get over it, move on, find someone tomorrow," Dan continued. "But I am saying you can't carry the guilt around forever."

"Yeah, so if you were driving and killed someone—especially someone you had committed your life to—when would you let that go?" Nick asked.

Dan inhaled. This wasn't going as well as he had

hoped. He was about to try another tack when Nick started to speak.

"It was my first loss."

Dan nodded, encouraging him by not interrupting.

"I wanted it to be me. I still want it to be me."

Nick stopped and they sat in silence for a few minutes. Dan waited.

"I was off the planet for a few months after," Nick said. "My family helped me a lot but I could only be around people who really understood; who had been through something similar. That helped, but sympathy and comments like 'sorry for your loss' drove me crazy. She wasn't a loss, she was my life." He struggled to keep his composure.

Dan didn't move, letting him talk freely.

"I didn't wash the sheets or anything that she had touched. I could smell her and I wanted to keep that for as long as I could. You know what's the hardest part? It's all the firsts ... the first night without her, the first weekend, the anniversary of the first week of her death, the first birthday and Christmas without her ... I didn't go out with friends because when I was home, I was close to her. Everyone insisted that I should get out more, that it would be good for me; but it drove me insane." He stopped, reached for the glass of water and drank from it.

"Why didn't you contact Mitchell since you were once so close?" Dan asked.

Nick scoffed. "And say what? Hey, we haven't caught up for years, I'm miserable, thought I'd ring."

Dan watched him. "So what did you do?"

Nick inhaled. "I left the Air Force, got drunk every night, got drunk every day. It was Ana's sister, Maria, who helped me get through it. She came around about three months after to see me and I think she got a bit of a shock at the state I was in. She cleaned me up; we sort of helped each other. Then I'd feel guilty that I felt okay and the pain would return. It was this mixture of guilt and relief if I had a break from the pain or slept well at night." Nick stopped. "Then I'd have days where I would start to feel okay for longer periods of time or if I was distracted I didn't think about it sometimes for a few hours, even a half day, and I'd feel guilty."

"Understandable and normal," Dan said. "What happened next?"

"I found work flying for a Nevada company that did the gold route collections; being busy was good I realized, so I did every shift I could and more. I did what Maria told me to do ... to go on living until I'm alive again. So I'm living; then I caught up with Mitch. Here I am." He wiped a hand over his eyes. "Happy now?"

Dan closed Nick's file. Time was up.

"What would make me happy, Nick," he said, "is if you go away and think about the fact that we all will die in some way. Fatalists might say that is determined from the start of our life; I'm not saying that, but what I want you to do is think about the fact that if Ana was given twenty-eight years to live, how lucky were you to be given some of those years to share with her. It wasn't a malicious act; but yet you're imprisoning yourself. You don't know how many years you are going to have but you could bring some happiness into someone else's life and vice versa."

Nick looked skeptical. "Yeah and she might have been given eighty years until she met me."

"Have you had sex since?" Dan asked.

"Jesus Christ," Nick muttered.

"Have you?"

"Yes."

"Did you make a connection?" Dan asked.

"Just one night stands. They were meaningless."

"For you maybe," Dan said. "It's okay if it is not meaningless you know."

Nick bit his lip before speaking. "I'm managing my exposure to grief."

"What does that mean?"

"Exactly what I said." Nick looked at him.

"It's a nice idea but I'm not sure life works that way. You have to be open to connecting again."

"I have my family, my friends and my work. I'm busy and 'connected' as you say. That's enough." Nick looked at the clock.

"Yes, time is up. Nick, I know you have heard it all before, or so your expression says," Dan said. "And you'll have heard what I'm going to say to you next as well. But if Ana had been driving and you died, how long could you stand to see her left behind suffering?"

Nick looked to the window.

"It's a serious question and I'm after an answer. If not today, next session. How long could you stand to see her punish herself? Think about that and remember, it works both ways."

23

Mid-morning, the team sat around the large rectangular table in Mitch's office for a catch-up session. Mitch kicked it off.

"The Holocaust Memorial Museum has reported that the screening of the film continues every night at random times. They've gone through three security guards since the exhibition started. I'm not sure at this stage we have the resources to spend any more time there, but I'll pick a random night and get down there."

"I'll come with you," Adam offered.

The team looked at him.

Adam shrugged. "I'm new in town, no friends, no family, nothing to do. Take advantage of it. In a few months, you'll have to make an appointment to see me."

Mitch smiled. "Lucky me, thanks. Also, I'm putting further discussion with Benjamin Hoefer on ice. We know now that he's not telling us the whole story but I don't see any point pushing that with him. He's clearly scared and has been warned off talking to us, so we'll come at it from a different angle. Nick what have you got?" Mitch asked.

"The good news is that Eli Hoefer was buried, not cremated ... fortunately the Jewish faith frowns upon cremation, although more Jews are doing it these days. But unless you can think of a reason to exhume Eli Hoefer's body, we're going to struggle to get some DNA."

"And Benjamin doesn't have a comb, brush or anything of his father's that he can give us, but I suspect he wouldn't tell us even if he did," Ellen said.

"Yeah, well no reason to exhume him at this stage. I'd never get that across the line," Mitch agreed.

"There may be hope yet," Adam jumped in. "You know I've been talking with the members of the original family that adopted Benjamin for those five years while Eli was in a concentration camp. Gynther and Antje Bäcker are both dead, but their grandson, Dieter who is forty-five has been doing the family tree. I mentioned to Mitch that Dieter's going to go through some memorabilia chests at his father's house. They may have something or nothing, but he vaguely remembers seeing some of Eli and Yetta's possessions amongst them."

"So Gynther and Antje kept them all those years?" Ellen asked.

"They were close, remember? And then overnight they were taken away. Perhaps they just wanted to keep some things for them but of course they never came back. Well Eli did but didn't stick around to say hello or thanks," Adam said.

"Let's hope something they kept might have some DNA, but we won't hold our breaths on that one," Mitch said. "Done, Nick?"

"Done." Nick sat back.

"Ellie?" Mitch called for her report.

"Nick and I have been doing some research on The New Aryan Order. They'll see us tomorrow if we want to come thirty minutes before their monthly meeting."

"Good of them to spare us thirty minutes." Mitch frowned.

"Indeed." Ellen passed around several pages of notes. "This is a summary of their structure and platform. Let me just clarify though that this is their published profile and platform. These organizations often publish what is palatable but share more with members."

Mitch glanced over the notes.

"That's all," Ellen said.

Mitch looked up. "Adam, you're on a winning streak, what else?"

"You'll love this." Adam grinned at the group. "Yesterday I had a date at the aged home with Betty Lang."

"Buddy, if I had known you were that desperate I would have set you up," Nick cut in.

"Betty was worth it. She dated Eli Hoefer for ten years."

"Ah, she was one of the women that he wouldn't marry," Mitch said.

"Exactly." Adam leaned forward enthusiastically. "Anyway, get this, Betty said on one occasion Eli slipped and referred to his brother. She questioned him on it because he had told her he was an only child and he was quick to say that it was just a term he used for a close childhood friend."

"This is good," Nick said. "So Eli might not be Eli."

"It gets better, Betty was on fire," Adam continued, playing the storyteller. "Just as I'm about to leave, Betty says that maybe Benjamin's cousin can shed some light on Eli."

"Benjamin's cousin?" Ellen chipped in.

"Yes," Adam continued. "According to Betty, Benjamin's cousin, Eli's great-nephew, arrived from Germany one day out of the blue. He claimed to be Eli's brother's grandson."

"So he'd be a lot younger than Benjamin?" Mitch asked.

"Yes, sounds like he was only just legal age when he visited, and Benjamin was well into his forties when Betty and Eli were dating in their sixties," Adam said. "Anyway, Betty asked Eli how it was possible for him to have a brother now if Eli was an only child, and he spun her a story about his father having a stepfamily. She said he was there one day, gone the next and looked a lot like Eli. Betty remembered the cousin's name because she had a piano teacher by the same name ... Schmid."

"Wait, I know that name," Nick said, rustling through his and Ellen's research notes. He pushed a sheet of paper towards Mitch. "The head of The New Aryan Order is a man by the name of Dirk Schmid."

"There's a happy coincidence," Mitch said, looking down the list of the organization's key staff. "And the treasurer of The New Aryan Order is Thorsten Schmid. This changes everything." Mitch looked at his team. "Adam, can you find out what Schmids entered the country around the time Betty is referring to?"

"Already did," Adam said. He looked to his notes. "A Julian Schmid fits the bill. He was in the country for three weeks at that time visiting from Germany on business according to his visa, and spent one of those days visiting Eli Hoefer. I can't find any connection with him and Eli other than Betty saying they were related, but it's a red flag again that maybe Eli Hoefer is not the Eli Hoefer that Benjamin Hoefer thinks he is ... if you know what I mean?"

Mitch agreed. "It's looking that way. You and I, Adam, will meet with The New Aryan Order before their meeting and if we get to talk to one of their Schmids, we can find out if they know a Julian."

"I can come with you," Ellen interrupted. "It might diffuse tension to have a female there."

"I couldn't agree more," Mitch said. "But you and Nick look Aryan and that might come in handy. Especially Nick."

"Tall, blond, handsome," Nick cut in, "so true."

"How do you feel about joining the party?" Mitch asked.

"I do look good in a uniform," Nick said.

24

"I STRONGLY RECOMMEND AGAINST IT," DAN TARROW said as he paced in John Windsor's office. He had heard of Mitch's plan to use Nicholas Everett to infiltrate the neo-Nazi party, The New Aryan Order.

John leaned over to his desk phone, dialed Mitch's number and called him in.

They waited for him to enter.

"What's up?" Mitch asked, closing the door of John's office behind him.

Dan Tarrow dropped into one of the chairs in front of John's desk. "Mitch, I think it would be an error to send Nick in to infiltrate the party."

"How did you know?" Mitch looked from Dan to John. He sat on the edge of John's timber drawers leveled against the window.

"Nick mentioned it to me when I caught up with

him briefly this morning...he had to cancel one of our sessions to go to the meeting tonight."

Mitch looked frustrated. "Okay, tell me what your concern is?"

"Mitch you know Nick better than anyone, and you know he doesn't have any real concern for his own safety; I have a few reports that have high-lighted that," Dan said.

Mitch looked to John. "Not from me. He's not going to be in any real danger here," Mitch pointed out. "We're not at war and it's not the real Nazi party, just a group of like-minded people with a desire to have an Aryan race."

"True, but Nick is, in my opinion, really vulner-able at the moment to being swayed."

"So you think he'll get amongst this strong-minded group and may be persuaded to join them for real?" John asked.

"For a guy that doesn't have a racist bone in his body, you think he'll decide he wants to live in an Aryan America?" Mitch asked.

"It's more subtle than that," Dan told them. "It's like people who join cults. Often they're a bit lost, they're loners or—"

"Nick's not a loner—he has me, the team, his work, his family, his housemate, Amy," Mitch said.

Dan held up his hand asking both men to wait. "I'm not saying he's not supported and connected.

That's different from what's going on in his head. You can be surrounded by people and be lonely, Mitch. He's disengaged, going through the motions with no real purpose and you're sending him into a group where he'll be admired, valued and given purpose."

Mitch breathed in deeply and thought about it. He turned to John.

"What do you think, John?"

John frowned. "I understand Dan's concerns and agree they're valid, but Nick is a trained agent, you're a small team with limited resources and I'm wondering if we can tell Nick these concerns and open his eyes to it."

Dan nodded. "I could make him aware of it or you could Mitch—you two are close. I don't mind if you say the concerns came from me."

"I can send Ellie in with him, as husband and wife. If I did that and I also debriefed with him after every meeting, can we stay on top of it?" Mitch asked.

"Yes I think so. To be honest, I'm pleased that you even entertained the idea, Mitch," Dan said.

Mitch looked surprised. "Just because I don't like counseling doesn't mean I wouldn't do whatever it takes to protect my team. There's plenty of psychology I do believe in, like brainwashing, profiling and mindfulness. I'll talk to him."

Mitch rose and left.

Dan Tarrow looked to John Windsor. "Who was that?"

Ellen sat with Amy Callaghan, the team's allocated contact in the Criminal Justice Information Services Division. The two petite blonds focused on the screen of data in front of Amy.

"Dirk Schmid," Amy said, squinting at the screen. "Interesting. Dirk was a bit of a radical in his university days; arrested a number of times for demonstrating unlawfully. Nothing more than that though. Has legally purchased two weapons that are registered. His brother, Thorsten, appears to be much more conservative; no fines, arrests or even a speeding ticket, and no gun ownership."

Ellen made notes. "What was Dirk protesting against?"

Amy opened another file. "Hmm, the usual—raising university fees, proposed cuts, brain drain protest—that's educating international students and letting them leave the country with a head full of knowledge while depriving local students."

"Makes sense given who we think he is," Ellen muttered.

"And he was very vocal at a protest against increasing the quota of international non-American students at American colleges and universities."

"Nothing since he graduated?" Ellen asked.

"Nope, he's the ideal citizen. An anesthetist, married to Stephanie, three children, and lives in a very nice part of town. His brother, Thorsten, is an accountant, married with two children—twin boys."

"Oh well, nothing to explore there really." Ellen closed her pad. "How's life living with Nick?"

"He's a good tenant. Not there much, leaves early, home late. Keeps his mess in his room—you should see it, it's a disaster—but he's good in the other rooms. How's Mitch? I haven't seen him for ages," Amy asked.

"He's Mitch ... work, gym, running, work, gym, running. He's got a new place though and a house-mate, Lyn. It's good he finally found somewhere to live, although I think Ann, Henri's wife, was hoping he'd stay. She was feeding him up and fussing over him."

"What's Lyn like?" Amy asked.

Ellen gave Amy the answer she most wanted to hear besides 'married'.

"Gay."

25

"Your housemate was asking after Mitch when I was just with her," Ellen said as she sat at her desk, opposite Nick.

He looked over at Mitch's office and observed him pacing. "What is it with chicks and Mitch? He does nothing and shows no interest but they all want to make him pot roast," Nick said.

"It's the quiet, moody type with a dark nature," Ellen shrugged.

"Yeah?" Nick said. "Maybe I should be more like that."

"Nah, you're warm, friendly and energetic. You would attract a girl who wants a fast ride and a fun time. Mitch, well, he needs to be loved."

Nick shook his head. "He's doing just fine."

Ellen glanced at her watch and closed her laptop.

"Where are you going?" he asked.

"To get coffee. A girl cannot live on research alone. Want one?"

"Sure. Hang on, I'll see if Mitch wants one." He glanced at Ellen. "Don't say it, I'm just thinking he might be thirsty."

———

John passed Mitch's office, backtracked and stuck his head in. "You've got authorization for Nick and Ellie to go undercover. Stan's on the case."

"Great, thanks." Mitch rose. "I'll go pick up the paperwork."

"Before you do," John moved into his office, "when are you having your second session with Dan?"

"My last session," Mitch clarified, "is next week sometime. Why?"

John shook his head. "Just holding you to it."

"Yeah, thanks." He moved past John out of the office and to the stairs. He arrived at Stan's office, catching him on the phone. Stan beckoned him over and gave him a sealed envelope. Mitch mouthed the word thanks and headed back upstairs. As he arrived Nick and Ellen were returning with coffees.

"Ah, good timing, come in and let's check out your aliases," Mitch said.

Nick put the three coffees on the table, sliding one in front of Mitch.

"Thanks." He sat and opened the folder. "Mr. and Mrs. Bauer." Mitch passed them their new drivers' licenses and a fact sheet. "Same first names, that's safe."

"That's Ms. Bauer, thanks." Ellen grinned, as she took the license.

"Come on, you told me your goal in life was to be Mrs. Bauer," Nick ribbed her.

"Yeah, dream on hubby. We've been married two years and are trying for a family now, that's nice," she read off the sheet. "I'm a private tutor in English and French."

"And I'm a charter pilot for hire, that's safe," Nick said.

"Yeah, at least you can both deliver on those careers. So let's go through what your brief is," Mitch said, reaching for his coffee. He ran the pair through their role, expectations and limits. They established a covert word for use if both or either felt they were being exposed. Then Mitch began his drill.

"So what made you want to join?" he asked Nick.

Nick inhaled. "My wife and I are starting a

family and that process made us begin to look at the society we're bringing our child into. Our child deserves to have all the advantages of birth and pedigree."

Ellen nodded her agreement. "Plus, we want to be part of creating a future society that respects our Aryan blood ... our pure bloodlines. I don't want my child mixing with ... well just anyone," she said, her words laced with meaning.

Mitch nodded. "What do you think about immigration?"

Ellen answered. "All non-white immigration must be stopped and the sooner the better. I hope that's not too outspoken." She smiled sweetly.

"And all non-whites living here should be returned to their land of origin," Nick said, placing his hand on Ellen's shoulder. "We're very black and white on that, pardon the pun."

Mitch smiled. "You two will do. You have a lovely home at 14 Lilac Avenue." He pushed the address and a set of keys to both of them. "Leave from there and return there before and after every meeting in case you are followed. You'll need to stay there for at least an hour after each meeting and just check it's all clear before taking off."

"Done," Nick agreed. "We could start procreating in an hour."

"True," Ellen said, "to stay in-character."

Mitch rolled his eyes and continued. "The monthly meeting is at five-thirty tomorrow. Adam and I are seeing someone, Lord knows who, at five. New attendees are asked to arrive at five o'clock too so obviously we'll all ignore each other."

"Yeah, try not to get bashed up after this meeting," Nick said.

"With luck they'll go for Adam this time," Mitch agreed with a grin.

"Speaking of Adam, where is he?" Ellen asked, looking out to their desks.

"He's trying to get DNA from Benjamin Hoefer so he can be eliminated from the DNA we have. If we meet a Schmid at The New Aryan Order meeting I can try and get DNA from a cup, cigarette butt, whatever, to see if they are related to each other, and see if the cousin Betty mentioned is not a Jew but a German or related to a German in the party."

Nick exhaled. "You can't pick your family."

"We're done," Mitch said. The three agents rose. Mitch called Nick back. "What are you doing tonight?"

"Want me to come to the museum with you?" Nick asked.

"No. I thought we could get a drink and dinner."

"I can see if Amy will cook something for the

three of us. I know she'd be keen to see you even if it meant cooking."

Mitch shook his head. "It's no wonder you're single."

"Yeah, and what's your excuse?" Nick asked.

"I'm clueless," Mitch said.

Nick laughed. "Yeah, the pub's good."

26

Mitch and Nick found a table and sat down with their beers.

"I have to talk to you about something and I could say it diplomatically, but I'm just going to lay it on the line," Mitch started.

Nick held up his hand for Mitch to stop. He removed his jacket, loosened his tie, had a huge swallow of beer and then nodded for him to proceed.

Mitch laughed. "It's not that bad. Dan is worried that because you're disconnected from the world at the moment that if I send you in undercover, you could be swayed by the group and become a Nazi. So will you promise me you won't?"

Nick's jaw dropped open. He thought for a moment and then he laughed. "For fuck's sake! Well there's no guarantees; I don't agree with anything they stand for and I'll be working hard at not punching any of them out, but since I'm such a loose cannon ... is that really his opinion of my head space at the moment?"

Mitch nodded. "Yeah, clearly you're screwed."

"Shut up," Nick said with a grin. "So you're sending Ellie in with me to keep an eye on me?"

"No, I need Ellie to be a set of eyes and ears and a confidante amongst the women. I told Dan I was going to share his concerns with you. I'm telling you so that you go in with your head in the right place. I'll be pissed if you leave my family to go to the other side. Even more so because a psychologist will have been right."

Nick leaned forward and sighed. "Dan's wrong. Just trust me on that."

They drank and thought in silence. Eventually Mitch asked, "So what did you say to him that made him think that?"

"What did you say to him?" Nick asked.

"Me? About you?" Mitch shrugged. "Nothing."

"He said he had reports that said I was too willing to rush in and put myself in the line of fire."

Mitch finished his beer and frowned. "Nuh, can't remember putting any comments like that in your file, mainly because I don't think you are. Samantha yes, but you, no. It might have been during your training."

"Yeah he mentioned there were a few reports from then."

"He's probably embellished a bit to get a reaction." Mitch's phone beeped with a text message and he quickly checked it.

"My round, another light?" Nick rose. "Or have we been summoned?"

"No we're good, just an extra beer, Adam's on his way. He's got a crash course for you in *Mein Kampf*."

"Oh terrific, just what I need. I'm changing from beer to scotch."

———

Dirk Schmid closed the book he was reading and watched as his wife disrobed. In her small white satin slip she paused in front of the mirror, picked up the brush from the antique set he had bought her and ran it through her shoulder-length blond hair. She placed it on the dresser and rubbed moisturizer into her hands. She saw him watching, turned and smiled. Even after fifteen years of marriage, he never tired of watching her prepare for bed. She was as glamorous at thirty-five as she was when he met her at eighteen and married her at twenty. Allie was born one year after.

"Marry me, Steph?" he asked.

Stephanie laughed. She flashed the large diamond ring on her left hand and walked towards the bed.

"I'm already married." She lowered herself into bed beside him. "You see when I was young and wild I met this dashing man. He was tall, blond and handsome and he took my breath away." She leaned in to kiss him. "I couldn't say no and to this day, I only have eyes for him."

He returned her kiss and pulled her towards him. Slowly he slid his hand under her slip and he heard her groan with expectation. When they had finished making love, she sighed with contentment and rolled over to lean on his chest.

"Darling, when can I stop the program?"

Dirk inhaled.

"You know I will do anything you want me to do and you know how loyal I am to our vision and country, but ..." she chose her words carefully, "I'm physically, emotionally and mentally yours. I always have been and being partnered with other men in the program, well ... "

He smiled and stroked her hair as he looked down into her blue eyes.

She cleared her throat and continued. "Could you not take my eggs and transfer them, rather than me having to do the act?"

Dirk moved her gently off his chest and pulled himself up to lean against the bed head. He crossed his arms across his chest.

"You know I would love to do that, but that would be more painful for you and..." he held up his hand to continue as she began to protest, "I'm the leader. How would it look if all the other wives did their duty and mine received special dispensation?"

She nodded and gave him a feeble smile.

"But when you are with the other women ..."

"No." He stopped her. "Don't go there, Steph. It's not love and it's not attraction. I am focused purely on creating the *Fountain of Life 2* program. While I am in the act, I am thinking of our vision, values, our strengths. Sometimes I can't distinguish one woman from another. It will never be what we have."

She nodded, content with his words and needing to hear them.

"You are the love of my life, Steph, all I've ever wanted and as beautiful as ever. There is no one who can fill your shoes. As for doing your duty, you can retire at forty; it's only five more years and look at the beautiful offspring we have both produced."

"But they'll never know who are their real mothers or their real fathers," she said.

"The foster parents are their real parents as far

as they are concerned and they are being brought up with the right values and beliefs. That's all they need, Steph. You need to be strong."

"I hate being away for the months in hiding." She sensed his anger and looked up quickly. "But don't doubt for a minute my conviction, darling. I am completely behind you and the vision. I am the first lady after all." She smiled.

"That you are." He stroked her hair. "And no one could do it with as much style and sophistication. Has Allie started her period yet?"

Stephanie bristled. "No."

"As soon as she has, we need to prepare her for the program."

"Yes," Stephanie agreed, feeling fear gripping her heart like a vice.

———

Mitch glanced at his watch. It was nearing ten p.m. He had dropped Nick home earlier and was now at the Holocaust Memorial Museum with Adam. He walked around the small, enclosed space, shining his torch along every surface. Adam did the same, but crawling along feeling the crevices of the floor in the small projector room. Adam turned around and collapsed back against the wall.

"Nothing?" Mitch asked.

"No loose panels, no wires, no cameras, no idea how that movie shows every night."

Mitch frowned. "Could there be another area it is projected from, like back projection, and we're looking in the wrong area?"

Adam raised his eyebrows in thought. "Could be. I'll go look around the wall the film is screened on." He opened the door, letting in the hallway light for a moment before it went to black again.

Mitch stood, waiting for his eyes to readjust to the dim room. "C'mon, there must be a way," he said out loud. He rocked back and forth on his heels and that's when he heard it—a slight creaking noise. He stopped and dropped to the floor. Feeling around the black carpeted floor, he found no obvious gap or break. He pushed until he heard the creaking noise again and found the area it came from. He ran his fingers along the area. *Nothing.* Then he had a thought. *What if it is some kind of trapdoor that is opened from underneath and my weight is bearing down on it, preventing it from opening? So the ghost projectionist has not been able to start the film until we've gone and gotten off the floor?*

Mitch rose. He had to get off the floor but be able to reach it to see if it was sprung. He started with the desk. If he could lie along the desk and press along the floor at certain points, it might just work. He moved to the end of the desk and crouched on what was left of the surface area, getting completely off the floor. *This is when I need someone small like Ellie here.* He leaned down, and pressed hard along the floor, hoping it would spring open. *Nothing.* He got off the desk, moved it along a few feet, lay on it again and repeated the pattern. This time it worked.

Mitch gasped with surprise and delight. A panel of the floor completely covered in black felt suddenly sprang up an inch at one end. Mitch dropped to the floor on the opposite side of the square panel and lifted it up. It was hinged. Running from the edge of the trapdoor was an iron ladder, the rungs padded with black felt to reduce noise, Mitch guessed. He shone his torch into the area; it was a small tunnel wide enough for him to fit in. The tunnel diverted sharply showing only a few feet in front of him.

Mitch pushed the desk and projector back in place. He stepped down onto the ladder and from the top rung could easily reach to push the film on. He started the film, knowing Adam would race to join him. In minutes, Adam came through the door. He looked at the projector and then to Mitch halfway into a hole in the floor.

"Damn, so it's not a ghost," he said, disappointed.

Mitch grinned. "Want to stay here and keep watch?"

"I'd rather come with you." Adam looked past Mitch into the tunnel. "Security's on its way."

"Okay, let's go." Mitch dropped down the ladder into the tunnel and Adam followed, leaving the trapdoor open. The security officer ran into the room to see if they had caught the projectionist only to see them disappearing into the tunnel.

———

Mitch led the way down the narrow tunnel. It was paved with bricks on the floor, walls and ceiling.

"I bet there are a hundred of these little tunnels in old buildings like this," he said.

"Let's see where it comes out, although if it was a bomb shelter or an escape, there should be some-where wide enough to huddle," Adam said.

"Here it is," Mitch saw a small entrance to the right. He pushed open a door and stood, his eyes wide and mouth open.

Adam arrived next to him. "What on earth?" He took in the small room.

It was a shrine to the Nazis; wall-to-wall photos of Hitler, the Nazi party, Nazi youth and swastikas, a mannequin featuring a full Nazi dress uniform and flags.

"Well we can safely assume we have the den of our protestor." Mitch moved into the room and looked around. "Let's bag something, see if we can lift prints and find him or her."

Adam moved his torch along the wall. "Man, this is creepy."

"You said it," Mitch agreed. He took piece of paper from the desk, wrapped it around a couple of photos and a pen and pocketed them. "That might do it. Let's see where the tunnel comes out."

Adam led the way and the two men walked another fifteen yards before coming to a heavy iron door. There were no cobwebs and it had been opened recently. Adam put his shoulder into it but it swung easily. They came out in the garden on 14th Street at the side of the museum. The door was obscured by two trees.

"Well, that solves that riddle." Mitch looked around the exit.

"Still disappointed there wasn't a ghost," Adam said.

27

Ellen did not sleep well Wednesday night and by about four on Thursday morning, she gave up and rose. For hours into the night she had read the philosophy and vision of The New Aryan Order and speed read *Mein Kempf* supported by numerous cups of coffee and diet cola. She studied her alias and Nick's and created safe answers in her head for any questions she might get asked.

Ellen wanted this assignment. She hadn't told Mitch or the team but this was very personal to her and it was something she could do to help, to make a difference. Beetson, her name, was Scottish from her grandfather's line, but her grandmother was a Rosenberg. Ellen's grandmother, as a young woman of twenty, was deported by the Germans; her two sisters, three brothers and parents died in concentration camps. Ellen remembered hearing her mother tell the stories passed down; when her grandmother was liberated, still a young woman in her mid-twenties, she had nowhere to go, no family left and no house to return to. She followed the stream of displaced people for years searching for cousins, aunts or uncles but with no success. Then she realized she had to begin a new life or she would never live. Ellen's grandmother emigrated to England but within six months of arriving in London met a Scottish gentleman, married him and the Beetson clan continued even if the Rosenberg family did not.

Ellen had tossed and turned, deciding whether to declare to Mitch that she had a vested interest. She decided not to; she had to do this and he might prevent her.

———

Mitch and Adam waited in a small room at the headquarters of The New Aryan Order.

Adam looked around. "Nothing that says national socialist order here. We could be waiting to see the bank manager." He drummed his fingers on the chair, then straightened his tie.

"Making you nervous?" Mitch asked.

"Well yeah actually. I'm not big on idiots."

Mitch laughed. He glanced at his watch. They had been offered only a thirty-minute meeting and whoever was to meet them was already five minutes late. The door opened and Mitch rose as Thorsten Schmid entered the room. Mitch introduced himself and Adam and the men shook hands.

"Please take a seat," Thorsten said.

Mitch sized him up. He was thin and wiry, which was accentuated by a slim-line fitted navy suit. He had to be about a foot smaller than Mitch and Adam, with thinning blond hair and prominent cheekbones.

"Thanks for seeing us," Mitch started. "We're investigating the sabotage of Benjamin Hoefer's book launches at the Holocaust Memorial Museum and the Jewish Community Center."

"The FBI is doing that these days?" Thorsten raised his eyebrows.

"It's a bit more complex than just the sabotage, but that's one element," Mitch said.

"And you think because we want an America for Americans that it must be us?" Thorsten asked.

Mitch noticed Thorsten's leg was shaking slightly. He was more bravado than confidence.

"No, not at all," Mitch said.

Thorsten looked surprised and Mitch leaned forward. "But we thought if anyone knew who might be in the market to shake up Benjamin

Hoefer or move him along, this was as good a place as any to start."

Thorsten nodded. "Yes. I imagine so. I know of Benjamin Hoefer of course, I saw the publicity around the book launch."

"Have you read the book?" Adam asked.

"Yes, I have," Thorsten said. "I read widely, especially propaganda."

Mitch saw the hardening of Thorsten's eyes.

"As for who might be trying to scare him or shut down the promotion, that's more likely a nutter than our organization. You would be amazed how many people out there think the Holocaust was a hoax," Thorsten said. "Plus we get our share of punks and rebels trying to join. That's not who we are. We're not outspoken, uneducated and out of control. We're structured, affluent and wanting a good future for our children and our country. What Benjamin Hoefer is doing is of little interest to us."

"But enough interest to read his book?" Mitch asked.

"I like to gather different perspectives on history."

Mitch nodded.

"So any names, organizations or contacts that you think might help us?" Adam asked.

Thorsten shook his head. "Not really, it's not like

we monitor or keep records of other groups or applicants we reject. Will that be all?"

"Just one more question," Mitch said. "Did you have a relative visit from Germany about ten years ago by the name of Julian Schmid, who might have had a reason to see Eli Hoefer while he was alive?"

"We have many relatives who visit from all over the world. Julian might well be one although the name doesn't ring a bell. I'd have to ask Dirk. I can assure you however, none of our relatives would have any reason to speak to a Jew."

Nick and Ellen waited in the foyer. It was their first meeting of The New Aryan Order and they looked the part. They saw Mitch and Adam leave the building and studied them with cool observation; no one would guess they knew each other.

Nick reached for Ellen's hand. "Okay?" he asked.

She looked up at him and smiled like the loving wife. "Of course."

An attractive woman in her thirties arrived in the foyer and greeted them. "Mr. and Mrs. Bauer?"

Nick smiled. "Nicholas," he said, offering his hand, "and this is my wife Ellen."

Stephanie Schmid shook both of their hands. "I'm so delighted you have taken an interest in joining us. Please come through and meet our CEO, my husband Dirk, and we can talk about formalities."

She opened a side door off the foyer and showed them through to a palatial office. As they entered, Dirk Schmid rose. His eyes widened at the sight of Nicholas Everett—tall, blond, and athletic. Perfect. A version of himself a decade younger and next to him was his little blond wife. *I'll have her*, he thought with satisfaction.

28

THE NEXT MORNING JOHN WAS IN THE OFFICE EARLY. Time got away on him and before he knew it, it was time for Mitch's team meeting as the agents filed into his office. John drummed his fingers on the desk and looked out into the office. The clock read ten past eight. John looked at his watch again and then up at the faces of Mitch's team that were assembled in his office. "Where is he?"

Nicholas Everett rose. "I'll try his phone again."

"I'll see if he's emailed through a message." Ellen followed him.

Adam looked at John. "Well, I'll get lost I guess."

John smiled. "No, this is a good chance to catch up. How are you going Adam? Feel like you are settling in okay?"

"I am. I'm enjoying it. Mitch is a good leader—doesn't get in your face and calls it straight. Ellie and Nick work hard and have been really welcoming," Adam answered.

"Are you challenged enough?"

Adam smiled. "Mitch asked the same thing. I'm not always seeking the big thrills that are on my CV."

"I understand. He's pretty pleased with you though, I know he wouldn't want to lose you in a hurry. How's that haircut coming along?" John teased.

Adam automatically tugged at his short ponytail. "Ah yes, must find a good hairdresser."

Mitch raced into John's office, doing up his tie. Nick and Ellen followed him in.

"Sorry John, everyone," he muttered, and sat down. "Damn." He rose again, raced over to his office and grabbed his notes and diary. He came back in and sat down, conscious of everyone's eyes on him.

"Are you all right?" John asked.

"Fine. Okay, where were we?" Mitch said.

John frowned at him. "We were waiting for you. I don't start team meetings without the team leader. Did you sleep in?"

"I don't think I've slept past six a.m. since school.

Okay Ellie, want to fill us in on your audition last night?" Mitch continued.

"Nick and I—as Mr. and Mrs. Bauer—were warmly accepted into The New Aryan Order last night. However, there's a catch, the joining fee is half a million."

"You're kidding me?" John said. "Half a million dollars?"

"They do offer what they call 'scholarships' for members they feel might not be in the position to pay that membership but who would be an asset to the organization. They offer ten scholarships a year and we were offered one as a couple," Ellen said.

"Because we're perfect specimens," Nick confirmed. "It was a freaky thing though, sitting in this room of a couple of hundred look-alikes.

"Hold on," Mitch said. "Just back up here ... this is a worry. How many members do they have?"

"There were only a couple of hundred there last night but Dirk boasted they had over two thousand members," Ellen said.

Mitch looked at John. "Let's exclude a hundred of those as scholarships. That's nineteen hundred members contributing half a million ..."

"That's nine hundred and fifty million," Nick said.

"You're a freak with numbers," Mitch said. "Even

half of that is a frightening amount of funds for any organization to have; even the Democrats don't come close. So what exactly are they doing with that much money?"

John rose. "I'll have to pass this up the line if they don't already know. Are you sure that is what they told you the membership fee was?"

Ellen rose. "I have the membership papers." She went to her desk.

"They did tell Mitch and me that they were an educated, affluent group," Adam added.

Ellen returned and handed the papers to John, pointing to the paragraph where the fees were listed.

"John, we'd better accelerate this right now. That kind of money can buy votes, weapons, power," Mitch said.

"I agree. Give me the abridged version of everything else that's happening in case they ask questions," John said.

"We've accepted membership. Last night was meet-and-greet," Ellen said. "Our first official meeting is this Friday night and I imagine we will be more exposed to the inner workings then."

Mitch nodded. "Adam, want to fill them in on our adventure?"

"Yes. Mitch and I had a pointless meeting with

Thorsten Schmid from The New Aryan Order last night," Adam said. "He denied any interest or knowledge in the threats against Benjamin Hoefer and wasn't as keen as the last group we visited to suggest names. Also, fingerprints have come back from the projectionist lair and we have our culprit. He's a student of history, part-time projectionist and no surprise, of German descent. He's got a DUI recorded as a minor but nothing else, so he'll probably just get a warning."

"How did he get a job at the Holocaust Memorial Museum?" Nick asked.

"According to the HR manager whom I managed to reach about nine last night, projectionists are hard to find and he applied, seemed a good fit, was studying at a good college and his references checked out. I guess they weren't expecting a Nazi-sympathizer to apply for the job."

"Being a history student probably helped with discovering some of the old tunnels in the building too," Ellen suggested. "Does Benjamin Hoefer know him?"

Adam turned to Mitch. "Mitch is following that one up."

"I am and I don't know. I called on Benjamin this morning, thought I'd catch him early at breakfast, but he was gone," Mitch said.

"As in checked out of the hotel?" John asked.

"No, his luggage is still in the room. He didn't sleep in the bed last night and no one has seen him. I've got the hotel sending over a copy of the CCTV footage for the last forty-eight hours."

Mitch felt the blood begin pouring from his nose. He quickly put his hand to his face.

"Damn." He accepted the tissue which Ellen pulled from her coat pocket.

"Don't tell me; that's why you're late?" John rolled his eyes. "You went to the hotel room and someone was there?"

"Did you get roughed up again?" Nick asked.

"Someone was on his way out," Mitch confirmed. "I had to go home and change shirts, again."

"Just leave some in the office and save time," Adam suggested.

"Poor Mitch," Ellen said.

"You're the most expensive asset this department has," John said. "If you are going to go missing or put yourself at risk by investigating alone, can you tell me first?"

"So touching," Mitch said.

John smiled. "Go and see the medic."

"It's just a nose bleed."

"Want me to call him?" John reached for the phone. "Go now while I take this information upstairs."

"Fine, I should just move my desk there." Mitch rose.

"Need me to come with you?" Nick teased.

"What do you think he's worth?" Ellen asked with a smile to John.

"Priceless," Mitch rolled his eyes and walked out, and his team followed.

29

ON THE MONDAY AFTERNOON ADAM FORSTER
checked he had calculated the time difference cor-
rectly and placed a call to Germany to Dieter Bäcker
as promised. Dieter had offered to go through the
memorabilia chests at his father's house to look for
items from their former neighbors, Eli and Yetta
Hoefer, before they were taken away to the concentration camp and Eli returned, never to collect his
possessions.

Adam hoped for anything that might have a fingerprint, a strand of DNA, any item that could identify the Eli Hoefer who lived next door to Dieter's
grandparents was the Eli Hoefer who claimed to be
the same man who raised his son Benjamin in
the USA.

"I've been looking forward to your call," Dieter said after Adam announced himself. "It took some time, but it was most fascinating."

"That sounds promising," Adam said. "I really appreciate you taking the time to do this."

"There was one chest that was full of Eli and Yetta's items. I can't believe my parents kept it. I can understand my grandparents keeping it because they probably thought Eli might come back for it one day but my mother and father must have just forgotten it was up in the attic."

Adam waited patiently.

"It has wedding photos, a lock of hair from each of them, baby photos of Benjamin, a diary of Yetta's, baby clothes probably saved for the next little one they were hoping to have, and an item that I thought would really excite you."

"What?" Adam asked.

"A man's comb and brush set with hair in it and root hair as well. Will it still be useable?" Dieter asked.

"Definitely worth a try, we should be able to lift a print and maybe DNA. Well that's more than I hoped for, thanks Dieter, I really appreciate the effort you went to."

"Anything to help. So how shall I get this to you?" he asked.

"I'll come back to you about that; just be sure not to let anyone touch it. Keep it dry and preferably in the chest you found it in and I'll organize collection. I'll let you know the details," Adam said.

————

Dirk Schmid paced around his office at The New Aryan Order. He turned as the door opened.

"Ah, Lukas, come in and close the door," Dirk said.

The young student, thin, blond and tall, entered the room. He closed the door with a glance to the hallway.

"Uncle Dirk, I'm really sorry," he said.

Dirk held up his hand for silence and indicated the couch.

They sat on the expensive olive green Chesterfield couch.

"How's your mother?" Dirk asked, crossing his legs and draping his arm along the back of the couch.

"She's well, thank you, very busy with her charity work."

Dirk looked at the young man's face. He could see his own resemblance in the boy; he was just one of many young people that called him uncle.

"Young man, what you did for the cause was wonderful," Dirk said.

Lukas exhaled and visibly relaxed.

"Getting that projectionist job at the Holocaust Museum, working out how you could hijack the book launch and put the fear of God into them ... It was great work, son."

Lukas smiled. "It was my honor to serve."

Dirk smiled back, impressed by the young man's dedication.

"I'm just sorry I got caught," Lukas continued, leaning forward on the couch.

"It happens, it's not a big deal, but you must be very careful now. When they interview you, and they will, you must remember not to give away your association to our organization or to myself or Thorsten."

"Of course, I understand," Lukas said.

"I'll have the best lawyer I can get for you and we'll get it dropped—it was an act of misguided youth." Dirk waved his hand in the air. "We've got people in the right places to make this disappear."

"Thank you Uncle Dirk," Lukas said.

"Well done, Lukas, you are going to be a leader in our organization one day, a very valuable leader."

———

Adam ran into Mitch in the stairwell.

"You look happy, what's up?" Mitch asked.

Adam filled him in as they went back up to their floor.

"Great," Mitch said. "We'll soon know if Eli Hoefer was the real Eli Hoefer and if not, then we have motive. With luck that CCTV footage has come in from the hotel. I'm a little worried about the whereabouts of Benjamin Hoefer."

"I'm going down to get the profile on our projectionist from Amy," Adam said, returning to the stairs.

Mitch entered his office. He opened his emails to find the CCTV footage had arrived. Watching it, he rubbed his face.

Not good, this is not good.

On a hunch he picked up the phone and dialed Marcus. He asked him to check out if Benjamin Hoefer had left the country. He waited for the answer, thanked Marcus and hung up. Mitch rose and paced around the office, taking in the information he just received: Benjamin Hoefer had left the country—or been taken out—for Germany.

He exited the office and went to see John. He paced outside impatiently watching him on the phone.

John beckoned him in. "I'll call you back Dan,

Mitch is going to explode if I keep him waiting," he said, and hung up.

"Do you have to tell the counselor that?" Mitch asked. "We've got a problem. Benjamin Hoefer's left the country, he's on his way to Germany and I don't think it is by choice."

30

ADAM FORSTER FOLLOWED THE SIGNS AND FOUND THE library. There was only one person at the desk; a small blond with hair to her shoulders. She looked up as he approached.

"Adam Forster!" she said.

Adam looked surprised. "Amy Callaghan?"

"Yes!" She smiled. "I picked you in one. Nick's description was very good."

Adam's eyes narrowed. "Yes, I can only imagine. Anyway, thanks for digging for me, and what did you find on our young projectionist?" Adam leaned over the counter as Amy opened the file and placed it between them.

He looked up at her and then back at the file and picked up the one sheet of paper within it. "Hardly worth creating a file was it?"

Amy laughed. "We like our procedures. He's a college kid with no priors."

"I see." Adam looked at the color image of Lukas Goetz printed on the page. "Nice German-looking lad isn't he?" He read the information out loud. "Aged nineteen, history student, no priors, parents have nothing more than a speeding fine. Right then, thanks Amy."

"Anytime." She smiled.

He walked away and turned back at the door to find her watching him.

"How did Nick describe me?"

Amy cocked her head on the side, choosing her words. "Tall, ponytail and ... "

"And?" Adam prompted.

"Never mind."

———

Mitch gathered his team in his office. John joined them.

"We've got a few problems," Mitch began, "so let's chart this and see how it comes together."

"Want me to be the whiteboard scribe?" Nick rose.

"No one can read your writing, Nick, you should have been a doctor," Ellen said. "I'll do it."

Nick sighed and sat back down. Mitch paced as Ellen waited at the board.

"Okay, so we've got Benjamin Hoefer who seems to be the real deal connected to Eli Hoefer who may not be."

Ellen wrote the names on the whiteboard with an arrow between them.

"I've just found out that Benjamin's left the country and gone to Germany."

His team reacted and Mitch continued pacing.

"It looks like the man behind him in the CCTV footage is travelling with him but I'm waiting on identification of him."

Ellen drew a face with a question mark next to Benjamin Hoefer and connected them with an arrow.

Mitch stopped to look at a file on his desk and then continued. "We saw on the CCTV footage that Ulric Adler was at Benjamin Hoefer's first book launch at the Holocaust Memorial Museum. He's the socialist independent candidate, but we're not allowed to investigate that line." Mitch glanced to John. "So we don't know if he was threatening Benjamin or is a fan of his work, or there on some other business."

Ellen wrote Ulric Adler's initials and drew the connection with another question mark.

"We have The New Aryan Order ... unconnected

to Benjamin supposedly, except by the fact that they are a local neo-Nazi group and he has an anti-Nazi book out now. From that organization, Dirk and Thorsten Schmid knew of Benjamin, have read his book and have too much money invested in their organization to not be of concern to us. They may also be related to Julian Schmid who visited Eli Hoefer and claimed to be his great-nephew."

Ellen wrote up the names, separating them on each side of the board.

"If I could just connect them," Mitch thought out loud. "We know Benjamin was being threatened by someone ... but wouldn't tell us. Maybe it was Adler, maybe the young projectionist. What's his name Adam?"

Adam opened the file to look at the one-page with the photo.

"Lukas Goetz, college student, nineteen years old, no priors," Adam said.

He waited until Ellen added the projectionist's name to Benjamin Hoefer's side of the board.

Nick grabbed the file just as Adam was closing it.

"Hold on, we know this kid." He slid the page over to Ellen. "Wasn't he at the welcoming party the other night with all the newbies at The New Aryan Order?"

Ellen walked to the table and looked at the

photo. "He was. I even spoke to him for a minute or two."

Mitch's eyes lit up. "I love it when it comes together."

He watched as Ellen entered Lukas Goetz's name on The New Aryan Order side and linked the two sides of the board with an arrow.

"So they organized young Lukas to scare the hell out of Benjamin Hoefer, but why?" Mitch rocked back on the heels of his shoes, hands in pockets as he studied the board. "And we have Betty Lang." Mitch looked to Adam.

"Yes," Adam picked up the thread. "Betty who dated Eli for a decade and remembers his nephew, Julian Schmid, arriving from Germany out of the blue. Eli Hoefer also slipped up and said he had a brother, then denied it, then claimed he was a step-brother."

Ellen marked up both the brother and step-brother next to Eli's name on the board. She drew in another circle and marked it Julian Schmid, nephew to Eli, cousin to Benjamin.

"And Thorsten Schmid denied any knowledge of Julian Schmid when Mitch and I asked the question at our interview," Adam added.

Mitch stood back and studied the board. "Did I miss anything?"

They turned at a knock at the door. Marcus, the

team's Caribbean I.T. expert from the labs stood there with a file in his hands.

"Thought you might like to know who was travelling with Benjamin." Marcus handed the file to John, who handed it to Mitch. "The facial recognition software has found your man and I've confirmed he left the country on the same flight as Benjamin," he said.

Mitch took the file. He read the name and looked up at Marcus. "No doubt?"

"No doubt at all."

"Thanks, Marcus." He turned back to his team. "Julian Schmid has taken a trip to Germany with Benjamin Hoefer, his supposed cousin." Mitch walked to the nearest free chair, sank into it and studied the board.

"I hear Berlin is nice this time of year, a bit colder than here." John turned to him.

"Yeah, I'll take my translator." He nodded towards Adam. "Nick, Ellie, you need to continue as Mr. and Mrs. Bauer but report in to John and me each time. You're in very dangerous territory now."

31

"WOW, YOUR JOB IS AMAZING," LYN SAID FROM THE doorway of Mitch's bedroom as she watched him throw a week's worth of clothes into a travelling bag. "You really can't make any long-term plans can you? And how do you keep a relationship?" she asked.

"Yeah, well that's the tricky part."

"You know I have a good friend who is really independent and likes her own space," Lyn said. "She has always said she would love to live next door to the guy she marries—that's after they marry. I could introduce you."

Mitch looked at Lyn and smiled. "Thanks. But I'm kind of keen on a finding a woman who wants to be with me, but can cope with me being away if I have to travel regularly."

Lyn came in and dropped onto his bed. "Well

then you're going to have to go out with someone you work with who gets it."

"Yeah I've heard that suggestion before too," Mitch said.

"So have you? Been out with someone you work with?" she asked.

Mitch shook his head. "Not really. I took a girl from our library out to dinner one night but that was a bit of a disaster."

"But there must be good-looking females there; someone like Ellen?" Lyn said.

Mitch grinned. He zipped up his duffel bag. "I knew you'd get there eventually. I think you're a bit keen on her. Should I warn Sandy?"

Lyn laughed. "Not likely. I think Sandy might be the one." Lyn rose and hearing a car pull up, she pulled open his bedroom curtain.

"Your taxi is here. There's someone in the back seat already."

"That's Adam."

Lyn waved and Adam waved back. She dropped the curtain and followed Mitch out of his room to the front door.

"I'll see you in a week," he said. "Behave."

"Always."

She locked the screen door behind him as he started down the stairs.

He turned halfway on the front stairs to look

back up at her. "You've locked the back door haven't you?"

"Yes and this front screen too," She assured him.

"Good. You've got my number if there are any dramas. Even if I'm not in the country, I've got friends who are."

She smiled. "Mitch, you're so sweet. You know I've been living here for a year before you moved in. I'm okay."

"Yeah, but I didn't know you then," he said. "Now I have to worry about you."

She opened the screen door, raced down the stairs and gave him a hug. "Thank you for caring."

He rolled his eyes. "Now the door is unlocked again. Get up there."

She smiled and ran back up, closing the screen door and locking it.

He smiled. "See you in about a week, maybe."

He walked to the taxi and greeted the driver and Adam.

"Damn waste." Adam shook his head.

———

Nick took his tie off and threw it over into the back seat of the car.

"Ready?" he asked Ellen.

She took a deep breath and nodded.

"You look lovely dear." He smiled at her, appreciating the fitted red wool dress and boots she was wearing.

"Thank you, hubby, I know this is one of your favorites." She smiled at him sweetly. "Shame we're an old married couple or you might have ripped it off me later."

"Yes, shame," he agreed. "Let's get it over with."

They exited the car for the Friday night meeting of The New Aryan Order and entered the building. They looked around the foyer. To their right was a large room with chairs set up theater style. Around the edges of the room, close to a hundred people were milling, with coffee cups in-hand.

They saw Stephanie Schmid coming towards them.

"So glad you are both here tonight," she said warmly. "After the presentation, we'll have time to socialize and you can get to know some of our other members better. But for now, help yourself to tea or coffee. We'll open the bar after the meeting. Excuse me."

She was gone just as quickly to greet another couple that had entered behind them.

Nick looked to Ellen. "Coffee or tea?"

"Tea, make it a double," she said.

"Is this your first meeting?" a young woman asked Ellen. She was at least a foot taller, glamorous in leather pants and a pink sweater. Ellen noticed the huge diamond ring on her finger.

Bet she didn't need a scholarship.

"Our second meeting if you count the induction night," Ellen said. "I'm Ellen Bauer and this is my husband Nicholas."

"Sophie," the supermodel said, shaking both of their hands. "My husband Eric is over there." She pointed to a tall, athletic man also in his twenties. "This is our last meeting here."

"Are you leaving the group?" Nick asked.

"No!" she exclaimed dramatically. "We're moving into the next group."

Ellen looked surprised.

"Oh, you don't know yet. There are levels, five altogether, and you progress through them when you are ready, or earlier if Dirk thinks you should progress sooner." She looked over and smiled at her partner. "We've been accelerated early."

"Bravo," Nick said. "So what is this group about?"

"You learn the ideology of the group here, what we stand for and how we can make a difference. In the next group, you begin to contribute," Sophie said.

"I'm keen to contribute," Ellen said, looking up at her. "How can we do more?"

Sophie smiled. "Dirk will love you guys. I'm sure you'll be accelerated too if you feel like that. We do."

Sophie was about to continue when Thorsten Schmid took to the microphone and invited everyone to take a seat. With a wave she went to join her husband.

"How long is it going to take us to work up five levels?" Nick whispered in Ellen's ear.

"Too long," she mouthed back. They took seats near the door, training kicking in.

"Dirk must be in one of the other meeting groups," Ellen said.

"Yes, we've got to work our way up to him. I think we need to be expressing our desire to do more sooner rather than later."

Thorsten Schmid cleared his throat and welcomed everyone. He didn't have the confidence or presence of his brother and looked uncomfortable in the limelight.

"Welcome everyone, it is great to be together again, where we belong."

The room broke into enthusiastic support. Nick and Ellen joined in.

"Today's subject is our belief in the importance of motherhood and family. I look around the room and see so many noble and beautiful women here with their husbands, some with their children. To The New Aryan Order, the family unit is the backbone of a healthy Aryan society. Adolf Hitler recognized and valued the role of motherhood. Our Führer's mother died at forty-seven years of age when he was only eighteen. You will have read the beautiful poem he wrote about motherhood. The NAO believes motherhood is the noblest position to which any Aryan woman can aspire."

Again the room broke into applause. Ellen sat up and applauded enthusiastically, her movement catching Thorsten Schmid's eye. He smiled at her. Nick placed his hand on Ellen's back and she turned to smile warmly at him.

Thorsten Schmid continued. "A stable family unit is very important to the NAO. We do not tolerate divorce. Both the Aryan man and Aryan woman have clear roles to play as role models for the children. The woman is tender, looks after the home, is the nurturer and carer; the man must provide for and protect his family. Ladies, you are the carriers of our next Aryan generation, you can instill their values. We do not encourage women to work and abandon the most important role you have once your children are born; allow your man to succeed in his career so he can ensure you and the children want for nothing."

The members rose to their feet. Schmid held up his hands. "Please join me now to meet and greet one another, get to know each other and talk about the great nation we can create."

———

Mitch and Adam made their way onto the plane.

"Did you bring a good jacket?" Adam asked, eyeing Mitch's light-weight pullover and jeans.

"Yes thanks, Dad," Mitch answered.

Adam grinned. "And your toothbrush?"

"I was going to use yours." Mitch found their seat number, stuffed a small bag in the overhead locker and looked to Adam. "Window seat or aisle?"

"Aisle."

"Me too," Mitch said. "I'll take the window seat there, you take it on the way back."

"Deal," Adam agreed.

Mitch dropped into the seat and stretched out. John always booked the emergency exit row for his agents so there was plenty of leg room.

"I haven't told Dieter we're coming to collect the items in the chest in person," Adam said in a quiet voice.

Mitch looked around to see who was sitting around them. He returned his attention to Adam. "Good, let's not. Just in case Dieter or the items go missing. We're not really sure what's going on with Benjamin or Julian Schmid so let's just keep our cards close to our chest," Mitch said. "Why would Benjamin go with Julian? What has Julian got over him?"

"Unless he went willingly," Adam said. "Although the body language on the footage wasn't chummy."

"Benjamin's in the middle of a successful book tour and his agent has two more cities booked after D.C. A stop to Berlin wasn't amongst them," Mitch said.

"What's the Schmid connection? There's got to be something we don't know about Benjamin or his father, otherwise, like Thorsten said, there would be no reason to bother with a Jew like Benjamin," Adam said.

"Unless they're in the habit of bullying Jews who speak up. But taking them out of the country is a bit extreme," Mitch agreed. He tapped his fingers impatiently. "C'mon, let's get this plane up and get moving."

Adam smiled. "This is a nine-hour flight. Are you going to make it?"

Mitch looked over at him. "Do you sleep on flights?"

"Every time," Adam said.

Mitch shook his head. "I need a drink."

———

Ellen and Nick entered the home at 14 Lilac Avenue where they were to remain for an hour in case they were followed.

"I'm thinking we should redecorate," Nick said, looking around at the neutral living room.

Ellen laughed. "Can we afford to dear? After all you are the provider—how's the money supply?"

Nick shook his head. "I thought that was a performance worthy of an Academy Award nomination," he said to Ellen, dropping onto the couch. "When you leaned forward and caught his eye, just beautiful."

"And see the look I gave you." she fluttered her eyelids. "It was saying 'get me knocked up now and go out and kill the beast for dinner'."

"Speaking of which..." Nick looked to his watch. "It's after eight and I'm starving."

"Those canapés didn't fill you up? Want to call a pizza?" Ellen asked.

"No. If anyone is watching that wouldn't be very good homemaking behavior on your behalf. Can't you whip up something?"

Ellen's eyes narrowed. "Mm, I'll see if they've actually supplied anything." She opened the fridge to find it stocked with long-life milk and condiments. The freezer had a number of frozen meals in it, bread rolls and a loaf of bread. Ellen looked at the use-by date and everything was still safe. She moved to the pantry to find tinned soup and spaghetti sauce.

"You're in luck." She smiled at him. "I'm sure I can rustle up something. That should kill an hour or so before we can leave."

"I'd help, but I've got to conserve my strength to go to work and provide for you," Nick said.

"You've got one minute to get your butt in here."

Nick leapt from the couch and headed for the kitchen.

32

MITCH TURNED FROM THE WINDOW TO LOOK AT ADAM sleeping beside him. He slid down in his seat, closed his eyes and tried to relax. Ten minutes later, he opened his eyes again.

Right then, forget that. He reached for his iPad, read the report from Ellen on last night's NAO meeting and fired back a response. He updated his budget on the spreadsheet John had emailed through and sent that back. An hour had passed; he looked to his right, and still Adam slept.

Unbelievable. Dan Tarrow had sent through a note trying to pin him down for his second and final counseling session. He emailed back that he was overseas for an indefinite time. *Maybe forever where you're concerned Dan.* He smiled.

"What are you smiling about?" Adam asked, sitting up straight beside him.

"Dan's chasing me for another session. Good to be out of the country."

"He'll hunt you down. They're good at that."

Mitch turned to Adam. "Where did you learn German?"

"I started it at high school and spent a year on one of those exchange programs; best way to learn the language is to live there."

"Where, in Berlin?" Mitch asked.

"Yes. I studied it at university as well and..." Adam stopped and then continued, "my wife—ex-wife—is German."

"That makes it easier when you've got a practice partner. Is she in Germany now or the UK?"

"UK last time I heard from her."

Mitch looked away and then back at Adam. "I'm sorry it didn't work out. But you had a go at it, that's got to count for something."

Adam smiled. "Have you been married?"

"No. I've had one or two I thought I could have gone the distance with, but this job makes it pretty hard for any woman. She'd have to like me not around."

"And what woman would want that?" Adam asked just as the flight attendant arrived and offered them both coffee.

"Exactly," Mitch joked.

"You might need to get yourself a woman who works with us," Adam suggested.

Mitch looked over at him. "Did Nick tell you to push that? There's some sort of conspiracy going on with Nick, Ann and Henri to get me hitched. If I didn't know better I'd say Lyn my housemate was in on it too."

"It's people with partners; they love to match those of us without. Don't know what Nick's excuse is though." Adam thought about it.

"He's just taking the focus off himself. What is her name, your ex-wife?"

"Astrid. We met at school in Berlin when I was an exchange student. When I returned home, back to the States, we kept in touch and then my folks split, Mum stayed in the US and Dad moved to the UK. I went to university in the UK and I've been there for the last fifteen years. Astrid moved there for work after she graduated, and we married...and divorced."

"There's no formula, is there?" Mitch asked. "You can get married young, mid-life, old; no guarantees it will ever work."

"According to Betty, the guru of love, you have to fall in love as much as you can. But we had a bit working against us," Adam said. "I proposed when she first joined me in London, but she said she wasn't ready. So I waited. Then she wanted to know what she was missing, what else was out there. So I set her free."

"So if you set them free and they return, they're yours or some bullshit like that?" Mitch asked.

"Yeah and if they don't return, hunt them down and finish them off," Adam joked.

Mitch laughed. "Well clearly that didn't work since you got divorced and she's still alive."

"No she came back of her own accord. But then we had a bit of a crisis, so to speak."

"You don't have to tell me," Mitch said.

Adam shrugged. "Astrid was attacked. You wouldn't have heard of it in the US but she was one of the victims of the Essex rapist; kidnapped from a car park after she helped a man on crutches put his groceries in his car."

"Christ, that's horrendous," Mitch said.

Adam nodded. "After he was finished with her, he tried to strangle her and dumped her in bush land but she regained consciousness, got to help and could identify him from police shots. He was caught that same day but she was never really the same after that."

"How could you be?" Mitch agreed.

"We got married, but she was frightened to leave the house. Then she started disappearing for weeks at a time. She'd go to a friend's place or her parents or a women's shelter. I'd be sick with worry looking for her. I used up all my leave finding her several times. Then I'd bring her home and we'd talk through it, work through it and try and make her stronger."

Adam stopped talking as the flight attendant passed again with drinks.

"That's hell," Mitch said, and exhaled.

"The awful thing was that she couldn't believe I would find her attractive after what had happened and she wouldn't have sex. She wanted a divorce because she was convinced that she trapped me into marriage by making me feel sorry for her. She went back to Germany for a year." Adam sighed. "This went on for three years; disappearing, returning and disappearing again. Then she returned and began to work in a women's shelter. She studied psychology and the original Astrid was on the way back. Then one night she asked for a divorce because I reminded her too much of her past and she wanted to go forward."

"So you agreed. Is that why you wanted a stint back in the US?" Mitch asked.

"Yes." Adam looked to his watch.

Mitch nodded. They sat in silence for a few minutes.

"Only an hour until we land." Adam looked past Mitch out of the small window.

As if on cue the plane lights came on and the cabin crew began to move through the cabin collecting items.

"I'm almost afraid to ask, but how long have you been divorced?" Mitch asked, trying to ascertain Adam's state of mind.

Adam swallowed and thought before answering. "Just under a week."

Mitch exhaled. "Is your head on the job?"

"Every minute of the day; it's keeping me sane. You can trust me on that," Adam assured him.

Mitch nodded. "I get it."

———

Thorsten Schmid met with his brother Dirk after the NAO members left. They sat and shared a quiet drink.

"Who do you think has the most potential amongst the new lot?" Dirk Schmid asked. "Any stand-outs?"

"Yes, one by the name of Ellen Bauer who I get the feeling is keen to impress and another woman, Cecilia, who seems to have strong convictions." Thorsten puffed on a thin cigar and sat back on the leather Chesterfield.

"Ellen Bauer." Dirk nodded. He leaned over and topped up both of their glasses with scotch. "I've got my eye on her too; I'm keen to have her. Her husband Nicholas is an excellent specimen; he will be wonderful for procreation, just wonderful. Imagine him with Cecelia."

They heard a noise outside and Dirk rose, heading to the door. He opened it to find Ulric Adler letting himself in.

"Ulric, good to see you." Dirk shook hands with the Presidential candidate that the NAO was funding and showed him through. Thorsten rose and greeted him, grabbing another glass.

"I'm sorry I couldn't be here earlier for the new members' first meeting, crazy day." He undid his tie, put it in his pocket and took the opposite end of the couch from Thorsten. He faced Dirk, raised his glass and toasted.

"To the Führer our leader," the two men repeated the toast and they clinked glasses.

"Any news from Julian?" Adler asked.

"Yes, they have arrived in Berlin and are at the safe house," Dirk said.

"Are you sure it's worth it?" Thorsten asked.

"Over a million dollars? It's worth it, not just for the money but for the principle." Dirk bristled. "Shame on his treachery!" Dirk exhaled a plume of cigar smoke upwards. "Doesn't matter, we'll more than compensate for his weakness. But his son Benjamin will get a rude shock."

"Just don't let it infiltrate what we are trying to achieve. We have to stay focused—get nominated and get elected, then everything falls into place," Adler said.

"Don't worry Ulric," Dirk assured him, "my eyes are firmly on the prize. We've got some excellent new Aryan women too. There's a couple that we may be able to accelerate for the *Fountain of Life 2* program."

"I agree," Thorsten said, "it's a better intake than our last group I think."

Adler sighed. "I can see the future. I want it so badly I can taste it."

"Me too, Mr. President." Dirk raised his glass. "Now that sounds right."

33

—————

CLEARING CUSTOMS, MITCH AND ADAM WALKED OUT of the Berlin-Tegel Airport into a crisp evening.

"Holy crap, that's cold," Adam said, wrapping his scarf around his neck.

Mitch pulled his coat around him. "Let's get a taxi."

"There's a taxi queue," Adam said, walking towards the rank.

"Of course there is. I'd be disappointed if we didn't queue. We've queued all day; what's another queue." Mitch followed him.

Adam turned to look at him, laughed and kept walking.

"What?" Mitch smiled.

"You've had the patience of a saint all day while

I've been whining and now when we're almost there, you lose it."

"Must have been contagious," Mitch said.

"Or like me, you're tired, hungry and cold. I hope the hotel bar opens late."

They progressed quickly in the queue and found themselves in a taxi on the way to the hotel. In German, Adam gave the driver their hotel address, the Lux II. Mitch looked at his watch and calculated the time. It was eight p.m. in Berlin, two p.m. in Washington D.C. He put in a call to John and then to Ellen and Nick as he watched the Berlin scenery going by.

"All okay?" Adam asked when he hung up.

"Interesting. I'll tell you about Nick and Ellie's first meeting later. Are we there yet?" Mitch asked.

"Almost. You'll like the Lux II; one of the best locations. I'm a bit surprised John forked out for it. It's in the heart of the Mitte district, that's a bit of a hip area and good for public transport access," Adam explained. "It used to house the Russian secret service."

The taxi driver pulled up out the front and Mitch offered a credit card to fix up the bill. Both men grabbed their baggage.

"Nice," Mitch agreed. He looked up and down the street, "there's plenty open."

Adam did the talking as they checked in. They

took the elevator, and found the two-bedroom apartment.

"Wow," Mitch said, taking in the minimalist white room. Clean and modern, it included a small kitchenette and plenty of natural light. "John has excelled."

"Bedroom on the left or right of the door?" Adam asked.

"Left thanks," Mitch said, throwing his bag into the room. "Let's go eat."

————

Benjamin Hoefer was frightened. He was a man of peace who at seventy-five years of age was not in the best shape to be taking on an assailant let alone one almost thirty years younger. Julian Schmid bundled him into a small room and closed the door behind him. Schmid had picked the darkest part of the city and an obscure, tucked away apartment that could not be seen from the main street.

Benjamin had learned not to speak at the start of the journey; the threat of death didn't concern him as much as the threat of a violent death a long way from his home in the States. He wanted to be buried there, with his father Eli. He now knew he had done the wrong thing not taking the threats seriously. If only he hadn't released the book, he would be safe at home; he could have just written it for the museum instead of having it published.

"We will stay here tonight," Julian Schmid told him. "I'll order some food. Can't guarantee it will be kosher though."

"I don't understand what you want from me," Benjamin said again.

Schmid glared at him. "I told you, I am going to tell you the truth about who you are and who your father is and prove to you that your book is fiction."

"Why would I believe you?" Benjamin said, feeling braver.

"I don't care if you believe me or not, but tomorrow it will all be made clear to you and then you can share some of that inheritance that was never yours to have in the first place."

———

"Coffee?" Adam offered on their return to the room.

"Sure, thanks. I just want to go through our notes before tomorrow and what appointments we've got set up." Mitch grabbed his laptop and logged in, then ran quickly through his emails to see if any of them were urgent.

Adam joined him with the two coffees.

"Thanks," Mitch said without looking up. "John hasn't been able to trace Benjamin Hoefer and Julian Schmid's whereabouts yet. We've got footage of them arriving at Berlin airport and getting a taxi. They paid cash and were dropped in the city. They were tracked on CCTV for a few streets then disappeared and haven't checked in anywhere under either name, which is not surprising." Mitch looked up at Adam.

"Hmm, can you email me that report?" Adam rose, went to his room and came back with his iPad. "I'll have a look at the streets they were seen in and see if there is anything obvious."

"Done," Mitch said. "So tomorrow we start with Franz Schmid, father of Dirk and Thorsten, who doesn't know we're coming."

"That's right, and who may refuse to see us," Adam confirmed, looking at his own notes. "Franz is seventy-five years of age. His father was Hans Schmid, a German Auschwitz concentration camp guard who died not long after the war according to his grandson, Thorsten. I can't find any active records on his father or their history that substantiate Thorsten's claim, but that's the war for you."

"There is every chance Franz knows Julian Schmid, what he is up to and why Benjamin is here, so we're going to have to play this carefully. We're looking for Julian, not Benjamin," Mitch said. "I don't want to mention Benjamin until we've worked out what Franz knows."

"Got it. Plus we need to see if there is any evidence that the two men might be staying and hiding with Franz," Adam said.

"Depending on where that leads, we should split up," Mitch said.

"You'll need a translator," Adam said. "What are you thinking?"

"That after that meeting, we go to the other side of the clan so to speak and catch up with the family that looked after Benjamin while Eli was interned."

"Fine. Dieter, the grandson of Gynther and Antje Bäcker isn't expecting me as you requested, so I can drop in to his home and collect the items he has for me," Adam said.

"Good, let's stick to the unannounced visit—I don't want there to be any reason for those items to disappear. I want a fingerprint or a hair follicle from Eli Hoefer. Anyway, I'm thinking that you won't be in any danger going to collect that from Dieter so to save time, I'll go to the Berlin attaché office and meet our counterpart who I hear is fluent in English. I'll see if we can get some help with notifying local officers about Benjamin's disappearance and get his photo circulated."

"If she's a German babe and I'm stuck with Dieter and the old relics, I'm not translating for you for the rest of the trip," Adam said.

Mitch grinned. "It's a risk I'll take."

"When we're done on this case, we should visit the Auschwitz Museum before we leave. It's about five-and-a-half hours from here by car or train. Want to?" Foster asked.

"No. I don't think so, do you?"

"I've been there when I was living here. Everyone should see it," Adam said.

"Maybe if we have time before heading home," Mitch said reluctantly.

Adam drained his coffee. "I'm packing it in if we're done here?"

"We're done," Mitch said. "I'm just going to read through the updates, give Nick and Ellie a call and respond to emails, then I'll crash."

At midnight Adam came out of his room to go to the bathroom and found Mitch typing away on his laptop. At seven a.m. he found Mitch showered and dressed in jeans and a pullover, in the kitchen making coffee.

"Did you go to bed?" Adam glanced in Mitch's room.

"Yeah. I just have to be exhausted to sleep when I'm on a case."

"But that's every day," Adam said.

"True, but some cases require more thought than others. Drink that and we'll go." Mitch pushed a coffee towards him.

Adam opened the empty fridge in their kitchenette.

"Nothing sadder than an empty fridge. I'm stocking it today."

"With food?"

"Oh yeah, I'll get some food too," Adam joked.

34

Adam hailed a taxi out the front of the hotel and motioned to Mitch who was walking up and down the sidewalk talking on his phone to John.

Adam gave the driver the address for Franz Schmid's residence in Panke. Mitch finished his call and hung up.

"All okay?" Adam asked.

Mitch nodded. "John's just had a sighting of Julian called in by one of the local police here." Mitch was choosing his words carefully, not knowing if the driver spoke English. Dressed in jeans and pullovers, Mitch and Adam could have been tourists or men here on business and he didn't want to give the impression of being anything more threatening.

"Where?" Adam asked.

"It's a rented apartment; he's sending through

the address and has asked for local back-up to keep watch. I don't think we're going to get anything from Franz unless he's heard from his sons, Dirk and Thorsten."

"We can gauge whether he knows what his sons are up to back in the US," Adam said.

"And what he can tell us about his own father— Hans wasn't it?" Mitch asked.

Adam nodded. "But his father died when Franz was seven, so we may not turn up much there but where he served during the war."

"I wonder if Hans knew Eli," Mitch said. "That would be an interesting connection—Dirk and Thorsten's grandfather knowing Benjamin's father. They would have been of similar age and served at the same time." He gazed out the window, thinking. "Nice area, some beautiful old buildings."

"It's a very old part of the city, upper middle class," Adam said.

The taxi turned off a main road, went down a wide street with trees and parked down the middle of the road. Older, wall-to-wall-styled apartments lined both sides of the street. They pulled up in front of a six-story white building with ornate trimming around every level and window.

As Adam took charge of Mitch's credit card and paid, Mitch glanced up at the third floor and cast an eye along the windows. All had their curtains drawn.

Mitch thanked the driver and stepped out. Adam followed.

"Third floor, unit two," Adam said, looking at the panel on the ground floor. He pressed the unit bell.

The voice of an aged man answered in German. Adam replied and the door buzzed open.

"What did you say?" Mitch asked.

"We were visiting from the US and had just met Dirk and Thorsten. That was it, he opened up."

The two men entered the foyer. A dark timber staircase led upstairs and large windows streamed light into the building. They took the staircase to the third floor, found the unit and before Adam could knock the door was opened.

Adam introduced himself and Mitch. He asked if Franz spoke English and he shook his head. The older man seemed keen for the company. He offered tea and they accepted.

"He doesn't speak English," Adam said as Franz went to make tea.

"No problem," Mitch said to Adam, "I'll just observe. Ask him if he has a photo of his father, Hans, if you can work it in. Also when was the last time he heard from Julian, plus why he hasn't moved to the States with Dirk and Thorsten and ..."

"Yeah, I get it." Adam rolled his eyes.

"Sorry."

"I know this is hard for you because you're not able to control the situation, but you can watch his reactions when I drop names and see if they're genuine."

"Yes sir," Mitch said.

"Now that sounds good," Adam stirred him.

Mitch rose to help Franz as he re-entered with a tray of tea. He allowed Mitch to take it from him and pour as the two men talked in German. Mitch's eyes subtly scanned the room, and the faces in the framed photos along the ledges. He returned his attentions to Franz as he heard Adam mention Dirk and Thorsten. Franz seemed genuinely proud, his chest swelled and he glanced towards the photos of the boys as young men.

The conversation continued for another five minutes and then Franz rose, went to a cabinet and pulled out a shoe box. He sat back down and opened it, then sorted through the faded old photos. He pulled one out triumphantly and handed it to Adam.

"Mein vater," Franz pronounced.

Adam nodded. "Danke," he said taking the photo. He frowned and then smiled at Franz. He handed the photo to Mitch while telling Franz his father Hans was a most distinguished officer. Franz nodded proudly.

Mitch's eyes widened and then he made his expression neutral. He wanted to copy the photo and looked quickly to Adam who read his signal.

Then Adam mentioned the name Julian, and Franz smiled. He pulled out another photo of the same man he had called father with another young man. He spoke in German.

Adam handed the photo to Mitch and translated. "That is Franz's father Hans again, with Hans' brother, Herman. That would be Franz's uncle."

Then Franz explained Julian Schmid was Herman's grandson. Adam smiled and explained to Mitch. "So Julian is Franz's nephew and Dirk and Thorsten's cousin."

Adam informed Franz that they must take their leave but asked if he could trouble him for a glass of water.

"Natürlich," he responded and rose to get a glass.

"Unbelievable," Mitch whispered as he took a photo of the two old photographs with his iPhone. He hid the phone as Franz came back in the room.

Adam took the water with thanks, drank it quickly and they rose. Franz reached for the photographs and Mitch gave them back with a smile and a nod.

Franz saw them to the door and Adam expressed their thanks again.

The two men left the building and walked some distance before speaking.

"I can't believe it," Mitch said.

Adam pointed to a coffee shop where the tables out the front were empty. "We can have a coffee and talk without anyone hearing." They crossed the road, sat and ordered a coffee.

"I know it crossed our minds but I didn't think it was a reality," Mitch said. "That photo of Hans Schmid—Dirk and Thorsten's German grandfather, a Nazi elite, is Eli Hoefer. Hans Schmid is Eli Hoefer," he said it again taking it in. "Not hard to guess why he abandoned his son Franz and the rest of his family and pretended he was Benjamin's father."

"To save his own skin after the war," Adam said. "And Eli Hoefer had a brother Herman just like Betty said. Herman happens to be Julian's grandfather."

"Hans 'died' when Franz was seven, Eli was reborn... assuming the original Eli died," Mitch sat back, his eyes narrowed as he thought. "Tell me everything that Franz said," he directed Adam.

35

NICK AND ELLEN SAT WITH JOHN IN HIS OFFICE ON A conference call to Mitch and Adam in Berlin. It was eight a.m. in Washington D.C., two p.m. in Berlin.

"Go ahead Mitch, we're all here," John said.

"You've got the photo I sent you. It is a shot of Hans Schmid taken in 1945 when he was a soldier and member of the Nazi party. In this shot, he's about twenty-five years old. His son Franz, said Hans worked as one of the SS men assigned to guard duty at Auschwitz." Mitch continued, "The photographs that Benjamin Hoefer has in his book of himself with his father, Eli, show Hans Schmid and Eli Hoefer are the same man. Franz is two years older than Benjamin Hoefer. He was seven when he was told his father had died in the war and would not be returning home. Now we know his father

Hans didn't die, he sailed to the US and became Eli Hoefer and assumed the role of father to Benjamin."

Nick summarized, "So Hans Schmid threw away his family and country, and faked his own death straight after the war to save himself no doubt, and somehow he knew Eli Hoefer's story so could assume his life, what was left of it."

"And clearly brought great shame on his neo-Nazi descendants," Adam added.

"Precisely," Mitch said. "I don't know how he became acquainted with Eli in the concentration camp to know he had a son, but Adam's working on that."

"And it wouldn't have been too hard to ensure Eli's wife had died. Eli too for that matter," Adam said.

"How devastating for Benjamin when he learns his father and mother died in the camp and all his life he's been living with one of the men who killed them directly or by association," Ellen said.

"If he chooses to believe it," Mitch said. "Adam collected some original items of Eli and Yetta from Dieter, the grandson of their neighbors the Bäckers, this afternoon."

"They're on their way back to you now, John, for testing," Adam said.

"Thanks Adam. So why would the Schmid family bring Eli Hoefer into the light when Dirk and his brother seem like such die-hard neo-Nazis who don't want to be associated with a Jewish connection?" John asked.

"I don't think they want it to come to light, which is why they've got Benjamin Hoefer out of the US and tried to shut down the book launches with a fear campaign. But it is about money, I assume," Mitch said. "I imagine they wouldn't own up to the connection with Benjamin if there wasn't something in it for them. Eli left a huge sum in his will which will all go to Benjamin even if he turns out to not be his biological father."

"What now Mitch?" John asked.

"Now that we know Benjamin is in real trouble, we'll be staking out the hotel address you sent us. We'll move in as soon as we confirm he's there with Julian Schmid and it's safe to go in. So Nick, Ellie, what's your take so far on The New Aryan Order?" Mitch asked.

"The sooner we procreate the sooner we'll be accepted," Nick said matter-of-factly.

"Fine, I'll give up my career to have your babies and you can support me. Happy now?" Ellen said.

"Is that really the next step?" Mitch's voice came over the open speaker.

"It's going to get to that probably within a month or two if today's speech is anything to go by," Nick said.

"We'll have it wrapped up by then," Ellen said

confidently. "Otherwise we'll just have to tell them we're trying and expecting good news any minute now. Don't worry, Mitch, we've got a few levels to get through first I believe."

"When's the next NAO session?" Mitch asked.

"Tonight, lecture two and bonding with fellow Aryans," Ellen answered. "Lord knows what the subject will be."

"Well glean as much as you can, socialize, talk it up, listen, look supportive, whatever it takes," Mitch reminded them. "Despite what is going on here, I've a feeling there is something more sinister going on there. Anything more you can tell us, John?"

"Nothing you don't already know."

"No update on the candidate or his desire to be king, uh, Führer?" Mitch pushed.

"I'm taking the fifth, sorry," John said.

"Right. Talk later then." Mitch disconnected the call.

"Clearly not happy," Nick said.

"Yes, he's made that perfectly clear," John said.

36

Mitch disconnected the conference call in their hotel room.

"How often does that happen?" Adam asked.

"It's happening more and more. Pisses me off that we don't get a full brief," Mitch said. "It's like doing the job with one hand tied behind your back."

"You're going to have to swallow it better," Adam warned.

Mitch sighed and rose. "Yeah, I know."

He looked at his phone for a moment, then dialed John Windsor's number.

John answered on the first ring.

"Don't worry about it, Mitch, I get you're frustrated," he said.

"Thanks," Mitch answered and hung up. He

looked at the clock. "Let's move on this apartment lead. If we find Julian Schmid and Benjamin at their apartment location, we'll stake it out and all going well, close in."

"I'm good to go." Adam rose. His phone rang and he grabbed it. Recognizing the number, he answered: "Astrid?"

Mitch left the room. He sat on the edge of his bed and went through emails on his phone. A few minutes later he heard Adam calling out to him; he found him throwing clothes into a bag.

"I have to go right now, I'm sorry Mitch," Adam said, without looking up.

"Go where?"

"Home, UK. Can you get me a flight? I'll go to the airport and wait, any flight as soon as you can."

"Berlin to London?" Mitch grabbed his phone.

"Yes, I'll pay for it, can you just check flights?"

"It's okay, I'm doing it right now," Mitch said, calling up the team's travel agent. "Hi Rohan, yeah, good thanks. I need an urgent flight Berlin to London, now please." He looked at his watch. "Yeah he can be there in an hour no problem. Can you put it in Adam's name? Charge it to my account, I'll sort it later. Which terminal? Yeah, to Adam's phone. Thanks Rohan, appreciate it."

Adam ran into the bathroom, grabbed a few

items and came back into the bedroom, throwing them in the bag.

"Thanks Mitch, I'm sorry. What will you do for a translator?"

"Doesn't matter ... I'll go meet the local agent. You've got to be there in thirty minutes, flight leaves in an hour and Rohan is sending the e-ticket to your phone." As he said it, Adam's phone beeped that a message had arrived.

Adam threw his bag over his shoulder and looked at his phone as he headed to the door. "Got it thanks."

Mitch followed him to the elevator.

"Adam, what's happened?" Mitch asked.

"Astrid, she's tried to commit suicide. That was her mom. I've got to go to her."

"Sure, anything I can do?" Mitch waited with him until the elevator arrived.

"No, thanks for organizing the flight." The elevator arrived and Adam was gone.

Mitch went back inside and closed the door. "Right then." He looked around the large two-bedroom apartment of the hotel. Mitch's phone rang.

"Hi John," he answered.

"Mitch, what's happening? Rohan just called; why does Adam need a flight out?" John asked.

"Wow, word travels really fast. He has to fly to London, a family emergency."

"Is he okay?" John asked.

"He is, but his wife, ex-wife is not well."

"Right, Mitch, now listen to me. Do not go seeking out Julian Schmid on your own. Do you hear me?" John said.

"I'm just going to stake the area out, keep an eye on him and see if it is just the two of them."

"No, absolutely not, and that's an order. Stay put and I'll call the legat in Berlin and get you an introduction. If they are in the office, you can go straight there and with them go to Julian Schmid's location," John ordered.

"Benjamin could be in real danger. Why don't I just go and do surveillance and you can send the legat if he or she is available to meet me?" Mitch asked.

"Good idea, then you and Benjamin might be in danger. No, sit tight and don't move. I'll call you back in a few minutes." John hung up.

Mitch shook his head and began to pace around the room. He stopped, looked at the phone and went through the work emails to see what limited intelligence he had on Julian Schmid's location. *Not much.*

He tapped his foot impatiently and looked at his watch again. His phone rang; it was John.

"Okay, Eva Fuchs is the legat, but she's in Frankfurt today on business—back tonight. She's free tomorrow and can work with you then."

"Right. I'll go alone and stake it out."

"I don't like it. Call me when you get there," John ordered.

"I'll call you when I'm in position," Mitch said.

———

Nick knocked on the counselor's door and waited. There was no answer. He tried again and turned to go, almost bumping into Dan Tarrow.

"Sorry Nick, I was with a client off-site," Dan apologized.

"That's okay, I thought I'd escaped," Nick said as Dan unlocked his office door.

"You sound like Mitch now. And yes, I know it is your last session before you remind me. Come in." Dan led the way. He threw his coat over a chair and put his briefcase down beside his desk.

"I'm not against counseling," Nick said as he followed Dan in and closed the door behind him. "I just prefer to seek it when needed, not have it compulsorily. Sometimes you don't feel like talking and other times you need it."

"I understand," Dan said. "Have a seat. Tea or coffee? I'm going to have a tea."

"I'll have the same, black, thanks." Nick sat on the couch and loosened his tie.

Dan continued. "If we didn't have compulsory counseling though, people like Mitch for example would never come and then one day they implode, take a gun and wipe out half of their colleagues and everyone blames the company for not recognizing their stress."

"You've given this some thought then?" Nick joked.

Dan laughed. "Yeah, maybe. But seriously, I've seen it happen. I was actually involved in a case like that once. A young guy had a bad experience on a job and came back full of bravado." Dan carried the two mugs of tea to the table and placed one in front of Nick.

"Thanks, so what happened?" Nick asked.

"He knocked back the offer of counseling. It wasn't compulsory then. He went out on a few more jobs and in the end was taking pills and drinking a bottle of whiskey a night to get to sleep. Then, he missed out on a promotion and just snapped. Pulled his gun in the office and killed his immediate supervisor and three colleagues."

Nick shook his head. "Holy crap."

"I blamed myself for a long time; I saw the signs and I didn't act on them or request he be forced to come to counseling or be stood down for a short while."

"So what signs did you see?" Nick asked, reaching for his mug of tea.

"I'll tell you, but don't think I don't know that you're stalling," Dan said.

Nick laughed. "No, I'm genuinely interested."

"Yeah, it's not a bad thing for you to be aware of the signs anyway so you can keep an eye on your own team or recognize them in yourself. Mind you, it's not spying, it's care," Dan said. "The signs are sleep difficulties and nightmares; quick to anger or outbursts; depressed mood; being hyper-vigilant and not being able to unwind; decreased trust and intimacy; lack of self-care, you know like loss of self-esteem, lack of grooming, and difficulty concentrating at work ... just to name a few."

Nick nodded.

"Seen or experienced anything like that?" Dan asked, picking up his mug of tea.

"Well you'd know I'd be lying if I said no."

"I suspect you went through all of that and more when you lost your fiancée," Dan cut to the chase.

Nick drank his tea and put the mug down before speaking.

"All that and more," he agreed.

"How long did it take you to get through it, assuming after our last discussion your days are a bit brighter now?" Dan asked.

"Took ages. Even now there's things that tip me back there occasionally, but the acute pain is gone, it's just ... trying to find some motivation to carry on."

"The good thing about you Nick is that you can recognize it and talk about it. It can be very hard to help clients who don't want to admit to dealing with anything. Every single person deals with trauma and pain in life," Dan said. "It's part of having a healthy and fulfilled life, as weird as that might sound."

"I get it," Nick said. "If I had never felt that pain, then I would never have loved, and forming relationships is a major part of life."

"Exactly," Dan said. "And despite all the pain, wouldn't you do it all over again?"

Nick hesitated.

"You're hesitating because the agony was so overwhelming, but if you had the choice of never meeting ..." he glanced at his notes, "Ana, and not feeling pain, what would you choose?"

"Ana every time," Nick answered.

"And that, my friend, is healthy. Do you have any religious faith? For example do you take consolation in the thought that you will see each other again?" Dan said.

"I was raised a Catholic and while I'm not practicing, I believe we'll be reunited," Nick said and then sighed.

"But?" Dan asked, sensing there was more.

"You know what the hardest part of the whole experience has been?" Nick moved forward on the edge of the couch, put his mug of tea down and clasped his hands.

"What?" Dan urged him to continue.

"I could never feel her. Not once. I still can't." He rose and walked to the window. "It was like once she was gone, she was absolutely and completely gone. Some people say they feel their loved ones are around them or with them. I don't."

"Where is Ana buried?" Dan asked.

"She was cremated and her ashes put in a family plot. But no, I don't feel her there either."

"I have no answer for that," Dan said. "God and the next life are out of my scope but someone once said a similar thing to me. It wasn't until years after that they realized they were getting a sign, they just weren't open to seeing it. I'm not saying that's your situation, I'm just saying grieving is unique to every person."

"But yet we all go through it, how is it unique?" Nick asked.

"Because none of us are exactly the same. Those people I mentioned who were shot at work; one of them was a patient of mine. For a long time I grieved for her; not because I was in a relationship with her, but because her death was so futile. She was this young woman full of life and promise and then she was gone."

"Exactly, that's how I feel about Ana. Except I took that life." His voice raised in anger.

"No Nicholas, the accident took her life. You would have given yours in her place in a heartbeat if you could have. Does surrounding yourself with people and activity help?"

"Sure, but sometimes I just need to have time to think about her. When we were on our London assignment, sometimes I'd go out and jog in the early hours of the morning to get away from everyone and have time alone with her in my head."

Nick stayed positioned by the window, staring out. "Can we talk about something else for the last half hour?"

"Sure. Are you going to come back and sit down?"

"Nope."

"Okay." Dan watched him. "I've read your current work brief. How do you feel about being a Nazi?"

37

MITCH WENT TO THE FRONT OF THE HOTEL AND GOT into a waiting taxi. He read the address. The driver shook his head and Mitch showed him the address on paper. He said something again which Mitch didn't understand. He held up his hand to the driver to indicate for him to wait, opened the door and looked for a staff member. One of the reception staff who could speak English came to help.

Mitch showed the young man the address and the driver spoke to the staff member.

"Sir, he's saying this is not a good area, are you sure you have the correct address?"

Mitch nodded. "I see. Tell him thank you for his concern, but unfortunately it is correct."

The staff member translated and the driver shrugged.

"Thanks," Mitch said.

"No problem, sir."

The driver took off and Mitch closed his eyes, thinking about how he would handle the situation. They passed a sign that said Gesundbrunnen and Mitch checked his notes again. Eventually the driver pulled up, pointed to a small lane and wrote the total on a pad.

"Danke," Mitch said giving him a credit card. They completed the transaction and Mitch got out, immediately moving closer to the shops to blend in on the sidewalk.

He glanced down the laneway that the driver indicated. It was narrow and dark.

"Perfect," he mumbled to himself. There were three entrances on the left leading into two- storey industrial apartments—some appeared to be operated by businesses, others were residential. From the signs, Mitch could tell one was a tailor, and another did shoe repairs. It was going to be impossible to stake out the area with no light and nowhere to sit safely and observe. He moved out of the laneway and called John.

"Not ideal," Mitch answered his query. "Unless I sit at the bus stop there's nowhere to view the entrance or exit. If they don't come out I could be there all day."

"Abort then until the legat, Eva, can join you tomorrow."

"We can't risk that. They could move out tonight or Benjamin could be killed. I'm going to go in and see if there's somewhere I can lie low in the building. It's only two floors, so I'll try and stake it out."

"You don't know how many are in there," John said.

"Well the original sighting said it was just the two of them, didn't it?" Mitch asked.

"Yes, but there might be more staying with them. It's too risky."

Mitch sighed and looked down the alley. "Just let me stake it out and I'll come back to you. Any updates?"

"No," John said. "Check in as soon as you can."

"I will." Mitch hung up. He sat at the bus stop for a short period of time, taking in all of the windows and entrances. It was nearing five p.m. so the few businesses that were operating around the area would be closing soon. The tailor store attracted a few customers but the rest received little attention. Curtains on the windows of the apartments were open except for one room on the second floor to the right. Mitch counted the levels and estimated that could be the room where Julian Schmid and Benjamin Hoefer were. He rose, walked down the alley and found the offices and floor above shared a common stairway. He pushed on the outer door and it opened. The business on the lower floor had its door to the left with a sign that Mitch could not read. From a glance through the door it looked like a dentist.

Mitch looked around, felt the comfort of his gun in his jacket pocket and silently gave thanks its permit was accepted by customs and it wasn't confiscated. He quietly took the stairs halfway and glanced up to check the doors to the rooms above him were closed. He continued up and sidled next to a door with the word 'drei'—meaning three—marked on it. He checked the address again and confirmed it was correct. There was no sound from the room. He thought about his next move; to leave or to continue on. Checking his phone was on silent, he slowly tried the door; it was locked. Mitch lowered himself to look through the keyhole. He could see around the perimeters of the small room and it was empty.

With a glance around, he withdrew a small kit from his jacket pocket, found the right tool, and as silently as possible picked the lock. He rose, put the kit away, took hold of his gun and inched open the door. He scanned the room; no one in sight. He looked behind before slipping in and silently closing the door. Mitch stood and listened. *Nothing.* Staying close to the edge of the room, he moved down a small hallway and glanced into a room on the right. The office rooms had been converted to bedrooms with a single bed and cupboard against the wall. A suitcase lay open on the floor.

Mitch glanced to the mirror which reflected behind the door to check the room was empty. He moved to the next room—the bathroom. It was old with broken tiles and cracked grout. Several items belonging to a man were strewn around. He moved across the hall to what would normally be another office, to find a room with two single beds in it. One was made up, the other bed had a suitcase on top.

Mitch moved back to the kitchenette. A couple of paper ticket receipts from flights lay on the counter. He glanced at the names—Benjamin Hoefer and Julian Schmid. *Right room but where are you both?*

Mitch moved to the window, stood flush against the frame and glanced down the alley. No sign of anyone. He moved out of the door's line of sight and back down the hallway to call John, then changed his mind and sent a quick text instead.

"I've got the right room, but they're not in. Will wait."

Mitch entered the first bedroom again. He quickly searched through the luggage—Benjamin Hoefer's luggage. *Nothing telltale there.* He moved to the other room; to the small suitcase—just big enough for someone who lives in Berlin but may crash overnight to watch a held prisoner. Mitch waded through the case. He unzipped a section on top and found a couple of old receipts and a diary. Mitch leafed through it. He checked the current date and the coming weeks and read the entries. *This weekend, a convention at Nuremberg. Really?* He grabbed his phone and photographed the entry. He flipped more pages and photographed any pages with appointments. He went back to the opening page.

Bingo! Julian Schmid had written his address and email. Mitch photographed that page as well. He went through the rest of the diary and then returned to the case. He checked there wasn't a false bottom and opened all other compartments; *nothing else.*

Mitch returned to wait behind the entry door. If he could use the element of surprise and subdue Julian, then the local police could deal with it and Benjamin could return to the US then and there.

He waited.

————

Franz Schmid called his son Dirk in the United States. He checked his watch and worked it out to be around midday there.

"Father," Dirk Schmid answered. "Are you okay?"

"Fine my boy," Franz said.

"Hang up, it's expensive to call here, I'll call you straight back."

Franz Schmid hung up the phone. He thought about what a good man his son was even to consider such things with everything else he had on his mind. The phone rang and he picked it up quickly.

"Hallo sohn, wie geht es dir?"

"I'm good Father, thank you. Is everything all right?" Dirk asked.

"I have been trying to call you for a day, but I didn't want to leave a message with strangers."

"You can trust the people around me Father, they are good people," Dirk assured him.

"I learned a long time ago not to trust anyone my son. No one. I kept trying until I got you."

"That's fine, what did you want to tell me?" Dirk asked.

Franz could hear the impatience in his son's voice.

"I had two men visit me. They said they were friends of yours and were visiting Germany and came to pay their respects. Their names ... I can't recall now but they asked about the photo of my father."

"Did you show them Grandfather's photo?" Dirk asked, alarmed.

"Yes. I showed them my father as a young man in his uniform. I told them he never returned from the war."

There was a silence on the line.

"Are you there, Dirk?" Franz asked.

"Yes, yes, sorry Father, I was just thinking. What did they look like?"

"Both tall men, dark-haired. One had his hair tied back. That would never have been allowed at work in my day."

"No, indeed. Are they coming back?"

"They have no reason to and did not say they would return. I just thought you might like to know your friends dropped in."

"Thank you Father, look after yourself now. I'll call on the weekend."

———

Dirk Schmid placed a call to his brother Thorsten.

"We have a problem. Benjamin Hoefer's history is about to catch up with us. The two American agents are in Germany and they have been to see Father."

"What? Dirk, I told you to let it go, it wasn't

worth it. We really didn't need the money," Thorsten hissed down the line.

"It was the principle of the matter. I want Benjamin to know that he has spent his whole life living with a Nazi. Our hypocrite grandfather. That would stop him pedaling his fantasy book."

"Does Ulric know?" Thorsten asked.

"No, and I'm not keen to tell him. Get onto Julian, we need to tighten up this project," Dirk said.

"Leave it with me brother, I'll clean it up." Thorsten hung up.

38

It was now just after six, pitch black outside and dim in the room where Mitch waited. He had been there an hour, but given Julian Schmid and Benjamin Hoefer's luggage was still there, he knew they would have to return at some point in time. He sat on the floor, keenly listening and watching the hallway for a shadow from the opening of the front door. John had texted twice and Mitch confirmed he was still on watch. And then the door opened. He heard mutterings in German. Mitch rose, and pressed himself against the bedroom door of the room he believed was Benjamin Hoefer's.

In a matter of minutes, Benjamin entered the bedroom and took off his coat, which he threw over a chair.

Mitch could hear Julian Schmid talking. *Was there someone there?*

Mitch psyched himself and moved from the room to show himself to Benjamin Hoefer. He motioned for silence. The elderly man gasped and then nodded his understanding.

"Agent Parker," he whispered. "What are you doing here?"

"Bringing you home," Mitch said.

"Thank you, thank you." Tears welled in Benjamin Hoefer's eyes.

"How many out there?" Mitch nodded to the entry.

"Just one—Julian. He's on the phone."

Mitch nodded. "Are you okay?"

"I'm okay but I don't know what's going to happen; I want to go home," Benjamin said.

"I need you to stay here until I detain him, then I'll come and get you. Understand?"

"Yes, but how did you know I was here?"

"We've been tracking you since you left the country," Mitch told him.

"He forced me," Benjamin hissed.

"I know, but you should have come clean to us— that he had been threatening you. Don't leave this room, I'll come back for you."

Benjamin nodded and Mitch peered around the doorway. Julian Schmid was walking up and down the room talking on his phone. He was similar in build to Dirk Schmid, wiry and tall, and of similar age.

Mitch waited. His plan: when Julian Schmid hung up, he would pull his gun and close this whole exercise down. Within a minute, Julian pocketed his phone and turned to walk towards his room. He saw Mitchell Parker with a gun pointed at him.

He exclaimed something in German.

"FBI, I'm guessing you can speak English. Keep your hands up," Mitch ordered.

Julian kept his arms raised as Mitch frisked him. As Mitch moved back to face Julian he felt someone behind him. In his peripheral vision he saw Benjamin Hoefer before the heavy weight of an object hit the back of his skull.

———

Ellen stood with her glass of mineral water, casually observing her fellow New Aryan Order members at the early afternoon function. She was surprised so many people could attend an event at one p.m. It would be seven p.m. in Berlin and she momentarily thought of Mitch and wondered how he was going.

She watched Nick talking with a young male member whose suit alone, she surmised, would have cost more than her monthly salary. He was fit, blond, just on six-foot and keen to impress. As Ellen's gaze travelled around the room she found Thorsten Schmid looking at her. He smiled and nodded and in return, she gave him a flirtatious smile. *Good, got his attention.*

Thorsten broke off his gaze and headed to the stage. The room hushed as he approached the microphone.

"Good afternoon everyone, so good to see you and be together again." He favored Ellen with another look. This time Nick noticed and put his arm around her shoulder.

"Just a bit of housekeeping; the fire exits are at the back of the room, the restrooms are to the left of the entrance and it is non-smoking. It is great to see so many of you here for the early afternoon gathering. We mix up our times for security reasons—yes, there are those out there who don't understand our work or support our vision. We also like to change our meeting times to ensure those members who are shift workers or parents unable to get sitters can get along to the occasional meeting. Next meeting will be a lunch gathering on a Saturday; that's something to look forward to and we can spend the afternoon getting to know each other at leisure," he said. "The children are most welcome."

"Oh goody," Nick whispered in Ellen's ear. "I hate to have a Saturday with nothing planned."

Thorsten Schmid continued. "Today, my brother and our Chief Executive, Dirk Schmid, is able to join us and Dirk will talk to you about another one of our beliefs which I know you have endorsed and accepted into your lives by the very nature of being here. Please welcome him."

Thorsten stepped aside as Dirk Schmid came from a door at the side of the room to make a grand entrance. The room burst into loud and enthusiastic applause which Nick and Ellen joined in.

"Thank you and as my brother and our Financial Controller said, it is wonderful to see so many new faces taking up the pledge. Your passion and your commitment is so important; each and every one of you is the perfect Aryan citizen, and you are with us for that reason. We are proud to have you as members of The New Aryan Order," he said.

The clapping began again with gusto.

"He's as good an orator as Hitler," Ellen whispered to Nick as she smiled and clapped.

Dirk continued, "Tonight, I want to talk with you about the expression of our artistic soul. Art and education raises us above the masses; highlighting our history and culture. The beauty of art, whether it be graceful or brutal; the power of literature and music; the expression of our lives through drama, the importance of education for betterment and scientific inquiry—our creative genius must be fostered, but more importantly, protected from racial impurity."

Cries of agreement and "hear, hear," came from the floor.

Dirk raised his voice and level of passion and continued. "We must ensure our cultural heritage is not polluted by any alien influences, so that our heritage is constantly renewed and preserved and not debased!"

He spoke for another five minutes on the topic, working the audience to a level of high excitement. On finishing, the room erupted with cheering and Ellen and Nick yelled along with everyone else. Dirk looked around the room and settled on Ellen to grace with a parting smile. Thorsten watched him with narrowed eyes. He moved to the microphone again and thanked his brother.

"Please stay and mingle and share your thoughts and ideas. My brother Dirk and I look forward to talking with each and every one of you."

Dirk and Thorsten moved off the stage and moved amongst their enthusiastic supporters. Thorsten made his way to Ellen and Nick made himself scarce.

"You are impressive on stage," Ellen said quietly.

"I think you have me mixed up with my brother," Thorsten said, accepting a drink from one of the supporters.

"No. I think you might be the strong, silent communicator who doesn't mince words."

"Thank you," he said, flirting with her. "Perhaps if your husband is happy to mingle we could move into the lounge area and sit quietly for a chat. I'm not one for crowds and noise."

"Neither am I. That would be perfect," Ellen said, and with a glance to Nick who nodded his understanding, Ellen followed Thorsten out of the meeting room.

39

John Windsor swore under his breath. He glanced at the clock on the wall of his office; two p.m. in Washington D.C. meant it was seven p.m. in Berlin and he hadn't heard from Mitch for an hour. He tried Mitch's phone again and it rang out. He rang Nick to see if he had heard anything and it went to message bank. He tried Ellen's phone and couldn't reach her.

"For God's sake, three agents all out of reach, all in danger for all I know," he muttered. A cold feeling gripped his chest; a reminder of a team he had lost in duty many years ago.

He took a deep breath and rationalized. He knew where Nick and Ellen were and they would have their phones on silent during the NAO meeting. *They should be able to respond shortly given the meeting had now been going an hour. Mitch...he's there alone, in a country where he doesn't speak the language with no back-up.* He tried Mitch's phone again; no answer. He sent a text. "Text ASAP and confirm status." He waited.

John called Henri's office extension.

"Hi John," Henri answered.

"Henri, have you heard from Mitch in the last hour or so?"

"No, but let me check my phone in case I've missed a call or text," Henri said.

John waited. His phone beeped and he grabbed it, but it was a text from Ellen.

"We're fine, no word from Mitch, is all okay? Want us back?" she wrote.

Henri returned to the phone. "Not a word John. What's wrong?"

"Nothing yet. Adam's returned to London on a family emergency and Mitch is on stakeout alone; the legat wasn't available today. I'm probably over-reacting, just waiting for him to check in."

"Right. I'll keep trying too. Let me know if you hear from him, won't you?" Henri asked.

"Will do." John hung up. He texted Ellen back. "No stay there and finish NAO meeting, no problem." He didn't want Ellen and Nick distracted.

John breathed out. *I'll give Mitch thirty minutes more than I'll call the local Berlin police to raid the ad-*

dress. With Mitch's luck of late, he's probably been done over again!

———

Mitch woke up; his head ached and he lay still on his back staring at the ceiling. He felt the carpeted floor with his fingertips but couldn't push himself up. He looked around and had no idea where he was or why he was there. A dull ache thumped at the back of his head and after running his hand over the area he saw blood; he knew enough to know he had a concussion.

Mitch closed his eyes, trying to remember what happened and where he was. His thoughts were foggy. After some time he opened his eyes but nothing came to him. The room wasn't familiar. He listened; *definitely alone.* Panic began to rise within him; he tried to push himself up but dizziness forced him to lie back down.

His phone vibrated in silent mode, and he felt for it in his pocket. He answered with a groggy voice.

"Hello."

"Mitch! Thank God, why didn't you check in?"

Mitch closed his eyes and waited, letting the nausea pass.

"Mitch, can you hear me?" John persisted.

Mitch looked at his phone and put it back to his ear.

"Yes."

"Where are you?"

"On the floor," Mitch said. "In some room, somewhere."

"Good, well that narrows it down. Are you injured?" John asked.

"I think so."

"Are you shot?" John continued methodically.

"No, I don't think so, the pain is at the back of my head and there's some blood."

"Do you know who I am?" John asked.

"Yeah, John, I do."

"Do you know who you are?" John continued.

"Yes, Parker, FBI," and he rattled off his number.

"Okay, good, good. Can you remember what happened?"

Mitch closed his eyes again, then rolled on his side and let the vomit rise. He finished and slowly rolled back into horizontal position again.

"Mitch, do you know if you are in the same location you were at earlier?" John persisted.

Mitch looked around. "I don't know. I don't know where I was earlier or where I am at the moment. I'm on the floor. What was I doing here?"

John tried to keep his voice calm. "That's okay, we'll sort this out. Are you alone?"

"There's no one here," Mitch answered.

"Right, sounds like you've got a decent concussion. I want you to turn your watch tracker on for me. Can you do that?"

Mitch raised his arm, looked at his wrist and hit the tracker button.

"Done," he confirmed.

"Good. Now I'm going to send an ambulance for you and then I'll see if the legat, Eva, is in and if she can meet you at the hospital."

"If it's only a concussion. I'll be all right in ten minutes," Mitch said groggily. "I'll remember everything any minute now."

"Mitch I'm not asking you, I'm telling you. Stay on the line with me and don't get up. Do you hear me?"

"Yep."

"Mitch?"

"I hear you," Mitch said. "Stay on the floor."

"Don't hang up," John ordered him again.

"Don't hang up," Mitch repeated.

———

John shook his head. Using his other phone line he rang Marcus in the I.T. section and asked for an exact location from Mitch's tracker. While he waited, he spoke to Mitch again.

"Mitch are you there?"

"I'm here."

"Okay, don't hang up, stay with me. I'll be back in a minute." John went back to Marcus and got the exact address. He rang the legat, Eva, on her phone and found her at home. She took over, organizing the ambulance and planning to meet Mitch at the coordinates.

John hung up and rang Henri's extension to let him know Mitch was found and okay. He came back to Mitch. "I've got your location, an ambulance is on its way and Eva is on her way to meet you and the ambulance. Just stay put."

"I'm sitting up now, and it's okay," Mitch said. He lay back down again. "Maybe not."

"Mitch do not sit up. Do not move, do not leave the building. The people who are coming for you are on our side. Understand?"

"Got it."

"Stay on the phone with me until they arrive," John said.

"Sure. What do you want to talk about?" Mitch asked in a groggy voice.

John sighed. "How about how I'm getting too old for this."

"Are you? I hope there's no blood on my shirt," Mitch rambled on. "It'll be the third shirt this week. How do you get blood off a white shirt?"

"Mitch, you're killing me," John said.

———

Dirk Schmid poured two glasses of scotch and offered one to his brother. They sat opposite each other in Dirk's palatial office at the headquarters of the NAO and discussed the meeting as they often did after each session.

"You had them in the palm of your hand, again." Thorsten raised his glass to his brother.

Dirk nodded and sipped his scotch. "Isn't it amazing how many people believe in this message and yet the great unwashed and the powers-that-be continue to either ignore it or are oblivious."

"They're ignorant," Thorsten said. "That's why the educational campaign worked so well during the Führer's time; the films, the posters and cinema screenings of his speeches and the marches. Brilliant way to reach the population."

The men drank in silence for a while.

"You're getting very close to that new young woman, the Bauer woman," Dirk said.

"Yes, she's a perfect specimen."

"I've already ear-marked her," Dirk said.

"Perhaps you can give this one to me, since you always have first pick," Thorsten said with an edge of bitterness.

"Why can't you just have her after me?" Dirk shrugged.

"So she gets pregnant and then I wait a year to have her next? Thanks."

"I'll make you a deal. You can have her first and I have your wife."

Thorsten choked on his scotch. He stopped coughing and reached for a glass of water. "We had a pact that neither of us would have the other's partner. We have to think about our children."

"You just don't want me to be with your wife in case I'm better," Dirk laughed.

Thorsten rose.

"I'm just joking with you Thor, sit down."

"Sometimes, Dirk, your humor leaves a lot to be desired. In fact at the moment, your ego is so big, I hardly know you anymore." Thorsten put his glass down and opened the door to depart.

"Come on, don't be like that," Dirk called after him as the door closed behind his brother.

40

MITCH ATTEMPTED TO RISE AGAIN, AND THEN thought better of it. He could hear John speaking and raised the phone to his ear.

"I can hear the ambulance coming," John said. "That will be for you Mitch, so just stay put and let them do their job." As he finished talking Mitch saw two men in white uniforms and a large blond woman enter the room.

"Is that them?" John asked.

"I don't know, they're speaking German," Mitch answered.

The woman took the phone out of his hand and spoke in English. "Hello John, it's Eva here. We're with Mitchell now. I'll call you from the hospital."

"Thank you Eva, I'm very grateful."

"That's no problem." She hung up on Mitch's

phone and gave it back to him as the ambulance officers prepared a stretcher to lift him.

"Hello Mitchell, I'm Eva Fuchs, your legal attaché here in Berlin." She leaned over him. "Do you remember who did this to you?"

"I don't even know what I'm doing here." He closed his eyes as a wave of nausea passed over him.

An ambulance officer raised Mitch's head and waited. He said something in German and Eva translated.

"He said let him know when you are ready and they will move you onto the stretcher. Are you going to throw up?"

Mitch opened his eyes and waited a few seconds.

"It's passed," he said.

The ambulance officer shone a light in Mitch's eyes and studied his pupils. He said something in German and then they pushed Mitch on one side to put the stretcher under him.

Mitch woke in the hospital. He looked around at the sterile white room with a window that looked out onto another building. On the side of the bed was a table where his phone and hotel room key sat. Eva rose from a chair on the other side of the bed.

"You're okay," Eva told him. "Do you know who I am?"

"Eva," he said. "You shouldn't have stayed, I'm

sure you've got better things to do." He began to get up.

"It's my gym night but I'll catch up. Now stay put," she instructed.

"I'm fine, really," Mitch assured her.

"The doctor will tell us that. Wait and I will get him."

Mitch watched her walk to the door. She was an Amazon, easily six-foot-three or more, wide, solid but not fat and with short blond hair about an inch in length. She must bench press, he thought, looking at the size of her shoulders and arms. She had a presence, he decided, watching her confident stride.

Mitch touched the back of his head and felt an enormous bump and tender spot. He thought about what had happened. He remembered more now; Julian Schmid standing with his arms raised and then he remembered turning slightly to see Benjamin Hoefer about to strike. *That doesn't make sense. Why when I'm there to protect Benjamin, would he strike me down? Unless he's working with Julian on something or is too scared to have the mission interrupted. But what are they threatening him with?*

A bespectacled doctor in his late fifties entered with Eva and greeted Mitch in English.

"If you feel you are able to leave, then I will sign you out, Mitchell," the doctor said. "However, there are some symptoms you need to be aware of." The doctor moved to get his chart.

"That's all right, thanks Doctor, I've had concussions before," Mitch said.

The doctor ignored him. "Regardless, Eva will keep her eye on you. You may find yourself not able to think clearly or concentrate; have symptoms of nausea and vomiting; be a little short-tempered and unable to sleep; and you need to be careful because your balance might be off. Understand?"

"Yes," Mitch answered as the doctor shone a light in his eyes.

"Do as Eva says now for at least the next forty-eight hours. I'll discharge you and organize the paperwork if you want to finish getting dressed."

"Thank you," Mitch said. He swung his legs over the side of the bed, waited until he could see straight and stood up. He sat back down again.

"I'll get your shoes," Eva said.

"I'll be right," Mitch said.

"You heard the doctor, Mitchell, do as Eva says for the next forty-eight hours." She gave him a smile.

"It's going to be a long few days isn't it?" Mitch frowned.

"Oh yes," she teased.

"Eva, I appreciate you rescuing me but we have to move quickly. I'll get you up to speed but Benjamin Hoefer has been taken out of the US under threat. He's here, he's frightened and he knocked me out rather than be freed from his captor."

"What are they threatening him with?" Eva asked.

"I don't know but it must be major and I'm worried that once they get what they want, Benjamin will be superfluous."

Mitch rose, steadied himself, finished dressing and walked slowly out of the hospital room with Eva by his side.

"You can stay in my spare room tonight," Eva said.

"No that's okay, I can go back to the hotel," Mitch said as they left the hospital and she hailed a taxi.

"I have to watch you, just for the night, so you are coming home with me. If you are fine in the morning, I'll drop you back to the hotel to change before we begin work. I am all yours now for the next week if you need me."

Mitch wasn't sure whether to be worried or pleased.

41

"LET'S CALL MITCH AND SEE HOW HE'S DOING," NICK said, lying back on the couch in their fake marital home after the NAO meeting.

Ellen looked at her watch. "It's about two in the morning in Berlin. We can't call him."

"Oh yeah, I forgot about that. I hope the German legat makes the trip worthwhile. Speaking of sex ..."

"Were we?" Ellen asked. "Mitch wouldn't do the legat on a trip."

"You're probably right," Nick said. "He wouldn't be able to concentrate long enough to get—"

"—the motivation," Ellen cut him off.

"Yeah, that's what I was going to say. And while I think of it, I don't like you going off with Thorsten Schmid. How am I supposed to cover your back?"

"I'm perfectly capable of defending myself," Ellen reminded him.

"I've no doubt of that; you're probably better at it than I am. But that's not the point," Nick said. "We're not sure of what they're capable of. What did he say to you?"

Ellen pulled her legs up under her chin. "He's not a happy boy, our Thorsten. There's a lot of hostility and jealousy towards his brother. I suspect he's lived in his shadow for years."

"Well I don't appreciate him inviting my wife out for a private chat either. Well, I wouldn't if we were really married and I have to play that part."

"It was a bit strange wasn't it?" Ellen agreed. "It makes me wonder about this whole importance of the family, babies and the Aryan race. I know this is a bit out there, but did you notice there's a hell of a lot of flirting going on?"

"Yes. If there was a room available I'm pretty sure I could have gotten laid several times over with the married women there."

"You don't think ..." Ellen stopped. "No, it's a bit too out there."

"That everyone in that room is sharing the love to create a perfect Aryan race? If there's over two thousand members, that's a fair gene pool to access," Nick calculated. "I wonder how many of the women in the top tiers of the organization are pregnant, or are currently mothers and how many children they each have."

"If we can hack into the organization's records—and surely Marcus or Samantha can help us do that—we'll be able to find out a lot more about their identities and birth rates," Ellen said. She looked at her watch. "We can go in fifteen minutes."

"Want to get a drink out somewhere?" Nick asked.

"As long as we can eat too," Ellen said.

"Sure."

They sat thinking their own thoughts for a few minutes before Nick said, "I think the sooner you get pregnant the better. Because if your hunch about the procreating is right, I suspect Thorsten Schmid is ready to bed you."

"Ugh." Ellen put her hands to her ears. "Don't say that," she said as she put her hands down. "You've wrecked my appetite."

"You're talking to me, here," Nick scoffed. "I've seen you watch an autopsy and order a burger after. It would take a lot more than a roll in the hay with Thorsten Schmid to ruin your appetite."

———

"Well, I never saw that coming." Julian Schmid looked over at Benjamin Hoefer who looked every bit his age huddled in the corner of the car's passenger seat. "A Jew hitting an FBI agent who has come to rescue him in order to finish his work with a Nazi." Julian laughed.

Benjamin Hoefer pulled himself up in his seat and looked at the younger man opposite him.

"I did nothing for you and will never do anything for a Nazi. I did it for my father," he said, with anger in his voice.

"Your real father or the only father you've ever known?" Julian asked.

"What do you think?" Benjamin answered.

"I think it is a wonderful irony that a Jew has spent his lifetime loving a Nazi," Julian grinned.

"I don't believe a word you are saying." Benjamin looked out the window. He pulled his pale gray jacket tightly around him as he looked at the bleak day outside. Eventually he spoke. "You know what I think is a greater irony?"

"What?" Julian asked.

"That your relative, the elite Nazi serving the Führer, skulked out of his uniform and responsibility and was prepared to live his entire life as a Jew bringing up a Jewish boy because he was a coward and his own self-preservation was more important than returning to his own family."

"Shut up," Julian yelled and threw his arm across the car, hitting Benjamin in the face.

Blood poured from Benjamin's nose. The old man gasped in shock and scrambled in his coat for a handkerchief.

"If you ever say anything like that again, I will kill you before you ever meet your real father," Julian threatened. "He's dying, your real father, but if you like, you can beat him to it."

———

Mitch woke as Eva placed a mug of tea on the drawers beside his bed.

"How is your head feeling?" she asked.

Mitch looked around. "Where am I?" He took in the pristine white room with virtually no other colors except for a timber frame around a mirror and two cream-colored cushions.

"My place, remember?" she asked.

"It's so white, I thought I was in another hospital room, a much better one," Mitch said.

"I like white; it's clean," she explained.

"Looks good," he agreed. "I'm not one for trappings myself."

She pulled her white dressing gown tighter around her.

"We didn't ...?" he asked, watching her.

"No. You barely knew who you were let alone were in the mood to be sexy." She laughed a strong guttural laugh.

"Good, I mean, it's good that I didn't take advantage of you. I'll shut up."

Eva laughed again. Mitch propped himself up and thanked her for the tea. She sat on the end of the bed with her own tea. "You had a bad night I think. Some yelling and lots of turning. Is your head sore?"

He put his tea down and touched the spot where he received the blow from Benjamin Hoefer. "Yes, but no more than to be expected. What's the time?"

"Just past nine."

"What?" Mitch sat up suddenly and the pain roared up the back of the neck. He closed his eyes and gripped the side of the bed. "We have to get moving," he said, keeping his eyes closed. "I have a lead, a convention in Nuremberg we have to follow through, and I'm sure Julian Schmid will be there; but that might mean he gets rid of Benjamin beforehand. I've got to get the results of the DNA testing on Benjamin's father to confirm what the photo in Franz Schmid's house just told us...and get a report from my team back home ... "

"Mitchell, stop," Eva interrupted him. "It's about three in the morning there, so that will have to wait.

Let's get you up and then you can tell me what you know about the convention. Do you want a hand getting up?" she asked. "You could shower here and we can go back to your hotel later."

"That would save time, thanks. But no, I'll be right to get up. I just need to check if there's an email update from John in case any of your people have reported sightings of Julian Schmid and Benjamin overnight or he's scored any CCTV footage."

"Fine. I'll go get dressed. Come out when you are ready," she said.

Mitch watched her leave and reached for his phone. He waded through his emails and came across an email from Ellen. He read through her update on the meeting and authorized her to get the I.T. department to try and access the NAO's files and in particular, find the members and their maternity status. He replied to another half a dozen emails and then saw one from Adam. It was advising he would be bringing Astrid back to Germany to be with her parents and would see him in a few days. He fired back a response saying he was glad to hear it and he hoped Astrid was improving.

Mitch sighed, closed his eyes for a minute while he let the nausea pass and made a mental note to get some aspirin. He resumed his emails and saw a note from John to call him regardless of the hour.

He thought about it and decided a few more hours wouldn't make a big difference; he'd call John after six and let him sleep. He slowly rose, and headed to the bathroom. Invading Eva's bathroom drawers he found some aspirin and downed several before hitting the shower.

42

LOOKING EXPENSIVE, ULRIC ADLER STRETCHED BACK in business class on his flight from Washington D.C. to Nuremberg. He intended to catch up on paperwork on the nine hour flight and prepare his speech to give at the convention he would be attending. He was a strikingly handsome man in his late forties. Some of his party had described him as the blond J.F.K.—charismatic, charming, witty and insightful, and Adler knew exactly how and when to play those cards.

He put in the code to spring open the locks of his briefcase and pulled out an envelope. Ensuring no one was in reading distance of his work, he opened the envelope and pulled out a dossier about the convention he was attending. He found the particular paper he was after; a strategy paper prepared for him by the CEO of The New Aryan Order United States Chapter Dirk Schmid and the CEO of The New Aryan Order German Chapter Sebastian Graf. He flicked to the end of the document; the final blueprint. All parties had agreed and signed on it. The area waiting for his signature remained blank. His counterpart in Germany—Leon Voigt— was also running for the top office and if both men succeeded the alliance between the USA and Germany would create a new world force—the Fourth Reich.

He turned back to the front page and began to read. As he absorbed and agreed with the policies, he signed his initials next to those of Leon Voight at the end of each page. He read the executive summary again and felt a rush of excitement:

"When both men win their seats—Ulric Adler, President of the United States and Leon Voigt, Chancellor of Germany—the following actions and strategies will take effect immediately:

1. The immediate deportation of all non-citizens to their country of origin. The children of non-citizens who were born in the USA or Germany to non-citizens are deemed non-citizens;

2. Any further of non-citizens is to be stopped immediately;

3. Only those of Aryan blood are to be allowed to become citizens;

4. The establishment of Aryan nations in which Aryan children and grandchildren will associate only with each other; marry and procreate with each other;

5. Aryan couples will be given mortgage-free homes on land held by large corporate interests to reduce pressure on families and increase the opportunity for the procreation of large Aryan families;

6. Work will set us free. Honest work will be the cornerstone of the culture; a secure economy will serve the needs of the people, not the rich and the conglomerates;

7. Job creation will be guaranteed for citizens—men first who are supporting families;

8. The role of mother will be the most important job of married women;

9. Single women and empty-nesters may work to give back to society;

10. The best education will be offered to create a society of elite Aryans, both men and women. The syllabus will be chosen by the state;

11. Fitness of body is as important as fitness

of mind and the perfect Aryan race will be represented by the world's best athletes from our countries;

12. Aged family will be honored with provisions for their lifestyle and medical needs;

13. The nation will be violence-free. All acts of aggression will bring disrepute or shame to the family;

14. The establishment of a cleaner world, clean energy, clean land and progression towards a future society that respects nature and the environment and preserves it for future generations will be pursued;

15. Military forces will protect our values and not be distracted or stretched by interference in world disorder outside our borders;

16. The art and culture of our country will be preserved and patrons will be encouraged and acknowledged for their support and loyalty to country if they assist in the development and preservation of the arts."

Adler finished reading the document and proudly signed it with his very expensive Montblanc pen. "Ausgezeichnet," he said to himself, "excellent work." He would congratulate the two CEOs; the Fourth Reich document was outstanding. He looked at his Montblanc pen. Another example of German excellence, he thought. He put the document back in the envelope, fastened the envelope seal and placed it back in the briefcase he had been resting on his lap. He took a deep breath and willed himself to imagine his happy future.

————

Mitch and Eva sat in the car watching the home of Julian Schmid from the address found in Julian's diary from his luggage. A curtain had been opened in an upstairs window but there had been no other movement. In a few minutes, Mitch would receive a call from John Windsor for a conference call with his team and then Eva would go in and knock on Julian Schmid's door on the pretense of making a delivery to see who answered.

Mitch's phone rang and he put it on speaker phone. He glanced around to make sure all windows were up and there was no one nearby. Mitch introduced Eva to the team. It was seven in the morning in Washington D.C. and just on one p.m. in Berlin.

"What's the latest Mitch?" John asked.

"Okay." He exhaled. "Eva and I have been going through surveillance footage and CCTV most of the morning. We've got Julian Schmid with Benjamin Hoefer arriving here at his premises after midnight. Despite willingly escaping his own rescue, he appears to still be a prisoner of Julian's—we don't know what he has over him, but we're guessing that it is something to do with his real father. We're outside Julian's place now and there's been no one coming or going all morning but they are both in there."

"You don't want to move in and close it down?" John asked.

"Not yet," Mitch answered. "I want to see why Julian Schmid wants Benjamin Hoefer and why Benjamin is so terrified that he has to knock me out to see the mission through. Plus we found a diary entry in Julian's diary for a convention at Nuremberg this weekend, tomorrow actually. Eva has more details."

"I've spoken to the venue and they are calling it a personal development convention but my sources found the booking has been made by the NAO," Eva said.

"The same NAO as we have here?" Ellen asked.

"The very same—The New Aryan Order," Eva answered.

"We've seen photos from the last convention

they had here," Nick said. "You two need to be really careful. It was wall-to-wall Aryans and I'm not sure what the security was like but they'd be crazy not to have it locked down."

"Thanks," Mitch said. "We're yet to work out our strategy."

"Will you get that through to me tonight?" John asked.

"Sure," Mitch agreed. "Adam will be back on Sunday as well but we might have it wrapped up by then if we can tag Julian and Benjamin today and follow through with the convention tomorrow to see if there's any connection. What's happening there?"

Ellen began. "Thorsten Schmid made a move on me at the meeting the other night and there is no doubt that there's tension between him and his brother, Dirk. I think Thorsten is sick of being in the shadows."

"What do you mean, he made a move?" Mitch asked.

"He invited me to leave the group and sit somewhere outside. I think he will want more next meeting."

Nick agreed. "I think he wants Ellen to be an incubator. The atmosphere in the room was bizarre. I could have got laid half a dozen times. Ah sorry, Eva."

"You apologize to Eva and not me?" Ellen said.

"Yeah but I know you know me and won't be offended," Nick answered.

Mitch looked at Eva and shook his head. "See what I have to put up with. And you wonder why I chose to come to Germany."

Eva laughed. "Thank you Nick, but like Ellen, I am not easily offended."

"Ellie, you're at definite risk of attracting the wrong attention right now. Have we any info on the members or maternity rates as yet?"

"Not yet, you only authorized it yesterday," Ellen said.

"Was it? Mm, seems ages ago. So when can we get it?" Mitch asked.

"We're going to see if while I charm Thorsten Schmid, Nick can download the contents of his laptop. He's the financial controller, he's bound to have reports of that nature and more," Ellen said.

"I don't doubt you can charm him but make sure there's no way Nick can get caught in the act. It will shut down the whole operation and we can't afford to do that just yet," Mitch said.

"Mitch is right. Only if there's a clean window to do it," John agreed.

"Right, next NAO meeting, Ellie ... when is it?" Mitch asked.

"Tomorrow afternoon," she answered.

"I think it is best that you're pregnant, okay? You

did dramatic arts at college, turn it on—tears of joy, hand holding with Nick, long happy stares, make sure you share the news with everyone you can at the NAO meeting. Clear?" Mitch said.

"Done," Ellen said.

"And Nick, then we've got you to worry about. Since you're clearly capable of impregnating, you may be called on to do so again," Mitch said. "We're going to have to move faster so we can get you both into the higher echelons and with luck the birth announcement might help. We need to know if they are just a club or if there's a more involved strategy and if so, who are their connections."

"Leave it with us," Ellen said. "We'll see where tomorrow leads."

"Hold up," Mitch said, thinking out loud. "If you're going to announce you're pregnant tomorrow, that's probably going to be the end of Thorsten's affections towards you, at least for nine months or more. So try and distract him before the announcement so Nick can get the data."

"You're right it will be a turnoff, especially if I'm glowing and clearly in love," Ellen said. "Hold the love, get the data first!"

"Moving on," John steered the meeting, "we've got the DNA results from Eli's items before he went to the camp; the items Dieter Bäcker gave to Adam. As your photo confirmed, Mitch, the real Eli Hoefer never left Germany and never immigrated here to the States. The man who raised Benjamin Hoefer was the Nazi guard Hans Schmid, father of Franz, grandfather of Dirk and Thorsten Schmid."

"I don't understand why Dirk and Thorsten would want to draw attention to Benjamin Hoefer and his book by staging all those stunts to scare him from having the book launches," Ellen said. "All they did was raise his profile and surely as key players in the NAO, why draw attention to the fact that their grandfather fled and disowned the Nazi Party?"

"That's the big question," Mitch agreed.

"Maybe they thought the scare tactics would shut Benjamin down and he'd go away but he didn't," Nick said.

"And if Benjamin had no idea who his father was, then maybe those threats would make you more determined to get your father's message of persecution and survival out there," Eva said.

"I agree," John said. "But there's money involved as well. Eli Hoefer, or rather Hans Schmid, left his fortune to Benjamin, and even though the funds were probably from Jewish gain and rightfully Benjamin's anyway, I imagine Dirk and Thorsten feel they are the rightful heirs and owners."

"We've got to go," Mitch said. "The garage door has just opened, someone is on the move."

"Mitch, talk to me tonight before you finalize any plans for the convention tomorrow," John ordered.

"Will do." Mitch hung up and Eva started the car, ready to follow the vehicle that was slowly backing out of the Schmids' driveway. In the front seat they could make out two people.

"That's both of them," Mitch confirmed. "Where are they off to?"

"My guess, I think they are off to meet someone who knew the real Eli Hoefer."

43

EVA STAYED FAR ENOUGH BEHIND JULIAN SCHMID AND his passenger not to be seen, and Mitch watched intently.

"Do you know this area?" he asked her.

"Sure," she said, skillfully tracking the car in front. After a while she glanced at him. "Are you missing your team?"

Mitch looked briefly at Eva and back to the road. "I hadn't thought about it to be honest. Is that bad?"

Eva laughed. "No. But it's early days. I bet you will miss them soon. It's nice to have a team around you. I'm always on projects with different groups, but that suits me. I like to work alone."

"Yeah, I suspect Adam does too but he seems to be coping," Mitch said. "He was my translator until he upped and left!"

"See, you did need me after all," she said, smiling.

They followed Schmid's car for another few blocks before he indicated and went down a residential street. Eva pulled over and they watched the vehicle. Halfway down the street, it turned into a driveway. Eva followed, stopping at a safe distance. The two men alighted and walked into a large residential village. Eva waited until they were out of sight and parked nearby.

"What does it say?" Mitch asked about the small sign out the front of the building, next to the letterbox.

"Meadepark Aged Care Community," Eva read. "Three levels—independent retirees, supported and dementia care."

Mitch's phone rang. "John?" he answered. They spoke for a few minutes while Eva watched the building.

Mitch hung up. "We can't move in."

"Why?" she asked, surprised.

"John's just confirmed that Julian Schmid has an active role in the convention, the one that is in his diary. We need him to go there, I don't know why exactly but orders from above." Mitch sighed.

"So if they come out together?" Eva asked.

"We continue to follow them. Somehow I doubt they'll come out together."

"He can't kill Benjamin here, surely," Eva said.

"No, but if he has what he wants, he can leave him here. Clearly Benjamin's not looking to call the police on Julian," Mitch said, rubbing the lump on the back of his head.

They waited. Thirty minutes later, Julian came out alone.

"We'll wait until he leaves and then go in and find Benjamin. No point following Julian, we know he's likely to be at the convention tomorrow and we can take our next step then," Mitch said.

Eva nodded.

As soon as Julian Schmid drove out of sight, the two agents left the car and entered the aged care center. At the main desk, Eva showed her badge and introduced Mitch. He nodded, not understanding a word she said but recognizing the introduction.

The middle-aged German nurse spoke to Eva for a minute, looked at a file, then pointed to a room down the hall. Eva thanked her and beckoned Mitch outside. She moved to an area in the garden where they could not be seen.

"They're here to see Mrs. Marion Kaminsky, she's sixty-five years of age, in good health and living in the independent retirees' section of the facility."

"What did you ask her to look up?" Mitch asked.

"Her maiden name. It's Hoefer. I think the real Eli Hoefer, Benjamin Hoefer's father, had another child or maybe more after the war and this is one of his daughters."

"So she'll have a claim on his will. But why would the real Eli give up his son to Hans Schmid and then carry on his life here and have more children?"

"I don't know, but maybe Mrs. Kaminsky will."

"Let's go hear their story. We can probably drop the assault charges on Benjamin," Mitch said.

"That's nice of you Mitchell, especially as your head is still sore," Eva said.

Mitch grunted and walked beside Eva as they entered the hallway and searched for Mrs. Kaminsky's room. Eva knocked on the door that was slightly ajar. The neat, thin, gray-haired woman looked up and smiled. Beside her sat Benjamin Hoefer. There was some family resemblance. Mitch appeared beside Eva and Benjamin Hoefer jumped up from his seat.

"Mr. Parker, I am sorry, so sorry, I had no choice, you must believe me, I've never harmed anyone in my life, ever, but this is my half-sister and if I hadn't struck you...he told me my real father was still alive and dying and he would take me to him but—" he ranted.

Mitch entered the room and held his hands up in a surrender. "It's okay, I understand, please sit down."

Benjamin took a deep breath, looked to his half-sister and lowered himself into his seat. He spoke to her in German. Eva translated to Mitch that he was explaining who Mitch was and what had happened.

Mrs. Kaminsky invited them to sit and rose to get chairs. Again Mitch and Eva organized the room. Eventually they all sat. Mrs. Kaminsky dabbed her eyes with her handkerchief and said something in German.

"It's been a shock," Eva translated.

Mitch focused on Benjamin. "Your father, biological father?"

"He died many years ago, my half-sister tells me. Telling me he was alive was a trap to get me here," Benjamin said.

"What did you give Julian Schmid, what did it cost you?" Mitch asked

Benjamin looked to his half-sister. "It's a long story."

"I will translate for your sister," Eva said.

Benjamin nodded and began. "My father was always very, very private about his past and he went to great length to avoid talking about it, staying in touch with anyone from the old country or joining any support networks. I on the other hand, being a teacher, was curious and wanted to write his story. He wouldn't speak of it. It was only when I started to do research that he agreed to tell me."

"So you could hear his version and not find out the truth," Mitch said.

"So it would seem," Benjamin said. He sat back in the chair and Mitch noted he looked aged.

"He made me promise not to release his story while he was alive; he said he couldn't bear to relive it. I understood this. His tale was very sad and typical—taken with his wife on a truck, the young son smuggled to the neighbors who raised me until his return and never seeing his wife again. He spoke of doing what was required to stay alive, starving, being cold and never taking for granted anything ever again.

"He said he was ashamed when he was finally liberated to show himself to the people I was with—Gynther and Antje Bäcker. My father said they had all been friends, young and ambitious and now he was broken emotionally and physically with no wife and no life plans. He came by, took me and left, never to return." Benjamin Hoefer stopped and waited for Eva to finish translating his sentence to his half-sister.

Eva nodded and Benjamin continued. "When he died, I worked with the Holocaust Memorial Museum to release his story. They organized the launch night and exhibition. That was when I was first threatened to stop the tour and pull the book from circulation. I couldn't understand why and I assumed it was anti-Jewish feeling. Then Julian Schmid arrived and threatened me. He told me my father was a Nazi and if I didn't pull out of the tour they would expose me. Well I couldn't pull out, I was committed and I had to make a certain number of book sales to meet the publishing costs. I also did not believe him." He shook his head with resignation.

"And that's when they started trying to scare you by writing the Nazi messages at your book launches and desecrating the film and banners," Mitch said.

Benjamin nodded. Mrs. Kaminsky reached for his hand and the two elderly people consoled one another. Eva asked would they like tea and they agreed. They waited while Eva organized it and returned.

Benjamin continued. "I was frightened and when you started investigating I couldn't tell you what I knew Mr. Parker—"

"Mitch," Mitch interrupted him.

"Mitch, because he threatened that he would not only expose my father as a Nazi but that he would never tell me who my real father or siblings were. I didn't know if any of it was true and if it was, if my real father went by some other name."

"What did he want?" Eva asked.

"My father was a very wealthy man and he left it all to me. He wanted that money," Benjamin said.

"And he wanted the book closed down, as they didn't want publicity."

The tea arrived and Mrs. Kaminsky and Eva took the tray from the staff member and served.

"So you know that the man who claimed to be your father was actually Hans Schmid, a German Auschwitz concentration camp guard, and his real son is still alive and living here in Berlin—Franz Schmid?"

"Yes," Benjamin said, "Julian told me, he's in his late seventies."

"That's right," Mitch agreed. "Hans Schmid abandoned Franz after the war to take safe passage to the US, masquerading as your father and avoiding any sentence he might have incurred. He also has two grandsons, Dirk and Thorsten, who live in the States and are in their forties."

"Plus Julian is a nephew," Benjamin said. "Hans, my father, had a brother."

"Correct," Mitch said.

"But did Eli—the man pretending to be your father—amass that wealth or was it Jewish wealth from the war that belonged to the real Eli?" Eva asked.

"Both," Benjamin Hoefer answered. "But I happily signed it away to them for a chance to know who my real father was and to meet my siblings." He squeezed Mrs. Kaminsky's hand.

"Don't worry, we'll get back what is yours in due course, but now we have to play it carefully just for a little bit longer. Has he released you?" Mitch asked.

"Yes, I've signed it over, so we both got what we wanted."

Mrs. Kaminsky clapped her hands together, remembering something. "But I have something for you," she said to Benjamin. "Our father left a letter in his will marked 'To Benjamin'. We were directed not to open it and told that a long-lost soul from the war might one day make contact. He never said you were his son. It was only to be opened if a man by the name of Benjamin sought him out. There was no last name and no one has opened it," she said. "I will call the solicitor and get it for you."

44

ELLEN SAT BESIDE HER MOTHER, CARLA, ON A LARGE navy couch, her feet tucked up under her as she looked through an old photo album. Her mother was a carbon copy of Ellen—small, neat, tidy with a stylish haircut to shoulder length. Unlike Ellen, Carla's hair—which was once dark—now shone platinum gray. Carla's hands were wrapped around a fine china tea cup as Ellen traced her finger over the old black and white photos on the yellowing pages. Sheets of plastic held the photos in the albums.

"I always hoped you would take an interest in the family history, but why now?" Carla asked.

"It's a case I'm working on," Ellen said. She leaned over to pick up her teacup and sip from it. "A book launch at the Holocaust Museum."

"Ah yes, I read there had been some trouble. I'm guessing you can't talk about it?" her mother asked.

"Not really, but it made me think about our ancestors. I understand war, but I can't understand how any person could round up the elderly, females and children and not feel some compassion," Ellen said.

"The propaganda machine was in full swing, the Jewish people were blamed for the state of the German economy, so they were the enemy." Carla looked over Ellen's shoulder. "I love this photo of my grandmother—your great-grandmother. She was a twin but her sister died from typhus in one of the camps. My grandmother never got over it. She lost three of her siblings, but losing her twin was the hardest to bear."

"And who is this?" Ellen asked, showing Carla the photo of the handsome young man in his school uniform.

"That was your great uncle, Frederick—your great grandmother's youngest brother. He survived until liberation and died from complications several months later."

"That's horrendous." Ellen looked up at her mother and back at his photo. "He survived all those years of war just to die when he was free."

"I remember as a very young child hearing my grandmother speak of it and she would say that he showed them he would not be beaten, and he did, I suppose. He made it through—it gave her strength to think of it that way," Carla said. "Another tea?" she asked, reaching for the pot.

"Yes, please," Ellen said, coming to the end of the album. "Imagine what their lives might have been if there had been no war."

Carla topped up their tea cups and put the pot down.

"But that was their life, Ellen," she said. "That was the life they were born to have. I've always believed that. And this is the life we are meant to have."

"Then I need to do more with it," Ellen said, turning side-on to face her mother. "I'm single, no family and my work is my life."

"But that's okay if that is what you want," Carla said. "I'm not saying I wouldn't like to see you settled down and giving me some grandchildren, but I would rather you were happy."

"You say that like someone who regrets not having a career," Ellen said.

"Yes and no," Carla answered. "I had choices—contraception, education, career options, husbands, lovers; anything I wanted—my generation was modern. But my mother was old-fashioned and pressured me to settle down, start a family, and that's what I did. You, on the other hand, have a mother who prefers that you do what makes you happy."

Ellen nodded and sat deep in thought.

"Don't let history weigh you down my love." Carla patted Ellen's hand. "You know the saying, 'never forget the past, but keep your sights forward'."

Ellen frowned. "No, I don't know that saying. Who said that?"

"Me just now," Carla said.

Ellen laughed and shook her head. "You're good therapy."

"Well then, brighten my day. Is there anyone on the scene that you are interested in?"

Ellen rolled her eyes. "I knew it was coming."

"It's my job. Tell me about these men you work with—is there a potential son-in-law amongst them?"

———

Dirk Schmid disconnected the call and slipped his phone into his coat pocket. He walked down the hallway of the NAO offices and opened the door to the afternoon meeting. The large gathering was mingling before they discussed the topic of future leadership—a lecture Dirk Schmid had given many times. Looking in from the doorway, he saw his brother talking with Ellen Bauer again; there was no doubt he was infatuated with that woman.

Throw him a bone and let him have her first, he heard his conscience say. *Maybe. But I want her more.* He looked around for Ellen's husband; he was never too far away. Dirk couldn't see him in the room. Suddenly he felt someone at his shoulder and turned.

Nick Everett stood there, he extended his hand. "Nicholas Bauer, we haven't had a chance to meet in person."

Dirk Schmid stepped back and shook hands. The two men were similar heights and they stood appraising each other. Both in dark suits, blond and confident; Dirk admired the man opposite him.

"It's great to have you and your lovely wife in our organization." Dirk said the party line.

"Well about that, Dirk," Nicholas said, "we're pleased to be here too, but you'll forgive me if I say it's a bit tame for us."

Dirk laughed. "I think I know what you are saying. Shall we sit? I've got a few minutes until I have to give this afternoon's lecture."

He indicated the chairs in the quiet area where Ellen and his brother had sat last meeting. Nick followed him and both men sat opposite each other.

"You want to make more of a contribution and

I'm not talking financial?" Dirk Schmid led the conversation.

"Yes." Nick sat back, placing his arm along the top of the chair. "If I want to meet and do fundraising and social work, I'll join Rotary."

Dirk Schmid laughed again. "I love a direct person."

"I want to make what you have here the blueprint for the society we are living in. What does it take, Dirk? What do we—Ellen and I—have to do now?" Nick asked.

Dirk's eyes widened in surprise. "Okay, well we may have underestimated the ambition you both felt."

"You have no idea," Nick said. "And now my wife is pregnant, so it is more important to us than ever to get this right."

"Ah, congratulations!" Dirk realized his problems with his brother and Ellen were solved but Nicholas Bauer was still available to do more breeding.

"Thank you. So are there other challenges for us?" Nick asked, "or is there another organization more suited to our needs?"

"Oh no, I think you are just what we need," Dirk said. "After the lecture, why don't you both come and see me. My office is down the hallway, last room on the right. We'll work out how the Bauers and the

organization can both benefit. Now, I best go in."
Dirk nodded towards the room.

"Of course," Nick said.

The two men rose and Dirk Schmid led the way.
As they entered the room, Ellen rejoined Nick. Dirk
congratulated her as he walked past. He took his
brother's elbow and whispered as they walked to the
stage, "Julian's called. He has everything signed and
handed over by Benjamin and all is on track for the
convention tomorrow."

Thorsten Schmid nodded. "That's a relief."

"And I guess you heard that Mrs. Bauer is pregnant. You'll have to wait a year or so now for that
bounty, little brother." Dirk Schmid smiled at
Thorsten as they took the couple of stairs up to the
stage.

———

Ellen pulled Nick aside at the back of the room.
"How did it go?"

"Fine. He wants to talk with us after the lecture;
I think we're advancing," Nick said. "He seemed
pleased with our enthusiasm."

"Good, but how do we get the stats? We're not
going to get a chance for one of us to be alone to
download the data."

"You know what Ellie?" Nick whispered. "We're

members wanting to contribute to those stats. We could just ask."

Ellen smiled. "Ah yeah, that's so simple it actually might work."

"I'll ask, you record his answer."

Ellen nodded. "Let's see how forthcoming he is."

"Oh I think they like to boast," Nick said.

45

"I'm starving." Eva, said eyeing the pizza that the waiter was delivering to her. She inhaled appreciatively. The waiter put a steak sandwich in front of Mitch and he nodded his thanks. Eva began to eat immediately.

"You don't eat enough for a man of your size," Eva told Mitch.

"I get busy, you know how it is," Mitch said.

"No, I never forget to eat," Eva said.

Mitch looked towards the waiter. "When he next passes, can you order me another coffee please translator?"

Eva nodded. She waved down the waiter and ordered two more coffees. She continued to eat with robust enjoyment, all the time studying Mitch.

"Why are you looking at me like ... like you're up to something?" he asked.

"I think we have to dye your hair blond," Eva said, looking intently at Mitch.

"Why? Not every German is blond; the Führer wasn't for starters." Mitch sat back, picking on the chips at the side of his sandwich.

"Because, if the convention is anything like the gatherings your two agents are going to, you will be in a room full of blonds and if you are the only dark-haired German, don't you think you might stand out?" she asked.

"Hmm, I guess so. I've never really seen myself as a blond; it won't help my tall, dark and handsome image," he joked.

"That's true, you are that," she said matter-of-factly. "I'll organize it."

"You sound too enthusiastic," he said suspiciously. "You can't just use a bottle of bleach, it'll be obvious."

Eva rolled her eyes. "I know that Mitchell. I have a friend who is a hairdresser. I'll get her to come over tonight and dye it blond for you. She'll need to do your eyebrows too."

"Great."

She reached for a chip on his plate.

"Have a chip," he invited her after she took it.

"Try a slice of pizza, it's good." She pushed the

pizza platter towards him. Mitch looked tempted but went back to his steak sandwich.

"Maybe later."

Eva reached for her phone and rang her friend. She had a quick conversation in German which Mitch did not understand except for the occasional mention of his name and the time and she hung up.

"Lena is coming around to my place at six tonight and she'll do it for you." Eva began to search for a site online on her phone.

"What are you doing?" Mitch asked.

"Lena said there's a color chart online if you want to pick your preferred blond color and she'll pick up the dye. Do you want to?" Eva found the page and looked up at Mitch.

"What do you think?" he said, and smiled.

"Okay, I'll pick for you," she said, "but don't complain after if you wanted a different shade."

"I'm bound to," he said.

"The blond will look good; it will really bring out your eyes," Eva said with a smile.

"That's what I was hoping," he agreed drily.

Later that evening, Mitch took a taxi from Eva's place, leaving her drinking wine with her hairdresser friend, Lena. He returned to the hotel room alone and blond. He showered and then made a coffee. Grabbing his notes, he waited for the conference call from his team; nine p.m. in Berlin, three p.m. in Washington D.C. He sent a text to Adam Forster to check if he was okay and to ask after Astrid and then his phone rang.

"Hey John," Mitch answered.

"Hi Mitch, while I think of it I've emailed you an e-ticket for Benjamin Hoefer so he can return home. Maybe Eva can print it out. I'm putting you on speaker phone now."

Mitch greeted his team. "So are congratulations in order? Are you pregnant, Ellie?"

Ellen laughed. "I am, and glowing."

"I've never seen her more beautiful," Nick agreed. "Although I think Thorsten Schmid was a little upset."

"What happened?" Mitch asked.

Ellen gave him an update. "Then after the meeting, Nick scored us a one-on-one with Dirk."

"I basically said we were more ambitious than the organization and if we couldn't get to make a difference we were going to join Rotary."

Mitch laughed. "I hear Rotary is pretty selective."

"Yeah thanks," Nick continued. "Anyway, we met afterwards and we were invited to progress to the next level or levels as need be. We were invited to endorse the NAO's party candidate for the next election."

Mitch inhaled. "Now we're talking; was it Ulric Adler?"

"It was indeed," Ellen confirmed.

Mitch let out a low whistle. "This is very dangerous."

"Let's just say the dots have been connected," John agreed. "I've informed upstairs."

Nick continued, "And given Ellen's been knocked up, so to speak, I was invited to contribute to the NAO's *Fountain of Life* 2 program—the re-born program once launched by the Nazi Party. So I've got to go shag some blue-eyed, blond Nordic girl for the good of the cause."

"Tough gig," Ellen said.

"This may come as a surprise to you," Nick said, "but hell will freeze over before I bring anything into the world that supports that ideology, as gorgeous as that kid might be."

"That's okay, Nick, we're not expecting you to lay down your values for the job, so to speak," John assured him.

"We got the maternity rate stats too," Ellen said.

"Good work. How?" Mitch asked.

"It was Nick's idea," Ellen said. "Since we were about to enter the program we wanted to know what we were contributing to."

"So we just asked," Nick said, "and they gave them up; they love boasting about their success."

"So what are the results?" Mitch asked.

"Of the just over two thousand local members, twelve hundred are female and five hundred have been pregnant or given birth in the last two years," Ellen said.

"You're kidding me?" Mitch said. "No one could see that as normal, surely?"

"Make that five hundred and one," Nick said.

"That's unbelievable."

"I've started the report," Ellen said. "I'll send it through to you to sign-off in an hour or so, Mitch, then John can pass it up the line."

"Thanks, Ellie," Mitch said.

"Mitch, what's happening there?" John asked.

Mitch filled the team in on Benjamin signing over his fortune, Julian Schmid having a letter from the real Eli Hoefer that was with the Will and going blond for tomorrow's rally.

"We're going to have to play that by ear," John said. "You might look the part Mitch, but if you have to talk to anyone you're in big trouble. This is when we needed Adam on the ground."

"I know. Eva and I decided I'm going to be hoarse from combined flu and yelling at a football game, so she'll talk on my behalf and I'll do my best strong, silent impression. I'm also going to take cigarettes so if anyone wants to draw me into a conversation, I can wave the packet at them and make an exit, and hope they won't smoke too. We've got a few tricks up our sleeve but it's going to be risky," Mitch agreed.

"Don't stay the whole time, just get the lay of the land and get out of there," John said.

"As long as that doesn't attract attention to us," Mitch agreed. "As Julian Schmid has it marked in his diary, I'm guessing he'll be there. Can we grab him yet?"

"We haven't got clearance to do that yet," John said. "Just mind yourself there and keep me updated."

46

EVA TURNED HER EYES AWAY FROM MITCH AND BACK to the road. The traffic was heavy for a Saturday morning.

"What is it?" he asked her.

"I know you find me very direct." She said.

"And so you are going to be again ... go ahead," he said.

"You look so different with your hair blond. Your face looks more angular, your eyes really stand out, and I think you look a bit sinister," she said.

"I scared myself this morning," he agreed. "But that was just from the dark circles under my eyes from lack of sleep," he said. "Sinister is good isn't it?"

"You look like you don't want to be messed with. Why aren't you sleeping?" she asked.

"I am, I was just joking."

"But you don't sleep. I know because you send me emails very late and very early and you look like you need to eat and take a week off," Eva declared.

"Great, thanks. You on the other hand look healthy and glowing," he said.

"Thank you, Mitchell." She smiled. "Are you still taking the pills?"

"If I need them," he said.

"Why do you need them? Are you in pain?"

"Did John call you and give you a set of questions to ask?" He turned side-on to face her.

"No."

"Don't go all Florence Nightingale on me okay? We're on a job."

"I know her, she was a nurse who saved a lot of people just by recognizing the need for fresh air, sunshine and sanitary measures in the hospitals during World War I. We read about her at school," Eva said.

"Here in Germany?" Mitch sounded surprised.

"No. I went to school here, and in England and in the USA for a while. That's how I could apply to become a legat for the US on German soil. Dad was an architect but my mother was a diplomat." She put the car indicator on and turned off, following a line of other cars. "I bet they are all going to the convention too," she said.

"You have an interesting family," Mitch said.

"What did your parents do?" Eva asked.

Mitch looked out the window. "My mother was a teacher and Dad was an idiot."

Eva laughed.

Mitch changed the subject. "What is it with Nuremberg that attracts the Nazis?" he asked as he sat looking uncomfortable in the passenger seat of Eva's Volkswagen Golf. She turned as the Navigator told her to take the second exit at the roundabout.

"Its position in the center of Germany," Eva shrugged, "and its history. The Nazi Party chose it I believe because of Nuremberg's relevance to the Holy Roman Empire. It was sort of the unofficial capital, courts used to meet at Nuremberg Castle. Then the Nazis used Nuremberg as the location for their rallies and there was a lot of military production here. The saddest part is that so many of the old historic buildings were destroyed in WWII. Devastating." She shook her head.

"I wouldn't have picked you for a history buff and lover of architecture," Mitch said.

"I might look very modern or as they say, hip, Mitchell, but I'm a classic at heart. As I said, my father was an architect and many of my school holidays were spent roaming around Germany admiring buildings. Nuremberg really distresses him."

"I can imagine," Mitch said. "I thought neo-Nazi groups were banned in Germany?"

"Our Office for the Protection of the Constitution has banned several right-wing groups in the last few years," Eva said, "and the Office is often criticized for not being more vigilant. Let's just say the problem has not gone away."

Mitch's phone rang and John's name came up on the screen. He answered it, spoke for a minute and hung up.

"John said our NAO candidate for Presidency, Ulric Adler, left the country last night on a flight for Germany. He arrived in Berlin this morning."

"You think that he is coming to the convention?" Eva asked.

"I think yes," Mitch imitated her. He sat thinking through the consequences and Eva did not interrupt him.

Eva drove into the convention center parking lot and pulled up beside a Mercedes C-Class. She cut the ignition.

"Nice," she said, admiring it.

"Yeah, but I like the Audi better."

They stared out of the front windscreen and studied the area. There were wall-to-wall cars covering the oval and parking lot of the major stadium; the same stadium that usually housed all the big concert bands that came to the city.

"Ready?" Eva asked.

"As ready as I'll ever be as a blond in a room full of people speaking German," Mitch shrugged.

"I'll try and translate when I can," she said.

"No, don't do anything to draw attention to us," Mitch warned. "I'm happy just to observe while you listen. We can swap notes later."

"Understood," she answered, checking herself in the car rear view mirror.

"You look fine. Do I look all right?" Mitch teased.

Eva laughed. "Like the perfect specimen of Aryan manhood." She winked at him.

They alighted and Eva locked the car. They were parked a good half a mile from the exhibition center and the area was full of cars and buses.

"I don't believe this." Mitch lowered his voice.

"You think the number of cars here is frightening; I can't imagine what we are going to see inside," she agreed.

They casually walked in. Eva linked her arm through Mitch's and they joined the flow of people entering the venue. Security guards stood at the door but they didn't stop anyone or check identifications. Eva and Mitch confidently walked in with a look that said they belonged. They followed the group through the hallway and into the huge indoor stadium area.

Mitch's heart raced. The entire room was

crowded with the freakiest sight he had ever seen—wall to wall blond men and women. He had to control his expression to look comfortable and at home when his insides were screaming 'get out'. From every pillar in the room hung huge swastika banners; and on the far wall was a projected larger than life image of Adolf Hitler. A stage had been set up in the round so that every person in the hall could see the stage and the person who would be speaking.

Eva freed her arm from Mitch's and instead took his hand. She turned to smile at him and he reciprocated, faking confidence that he wasn't feeling.

Okay for her, at least she can understand what they're saying. He nodded a greeting to a few people who addressed him and Eva answered on his behalf. She explained, touching her throat as a signal to Mitch, that he had a cold already but he finished his voice off shouting at a football game last night. The other couples laughed. Mitch made a point of trying to clear his throat and she shook her head and rolled her eyes.

Mitch looked around. *Thank God it is cold and I can get away with the scarf and sore throat.* He had to admit he was truly freaked out. This was like nothing he had ever seen. Suddenly a stain of German music rang out and everyone turned to the stage. Shouts of Heil Hitler arose and the room erupted into applause. Eva joined in and Mitch followed suit. If Mitch was surprised before, now he was flabbergasted. The man introduced as the CEO of the German NAO, Sebastian Graf, walked on stage flanked by a tall security guard, and following him with more security posted around, was German politician, Leon Voigt. Mitch heard Eva inhale sharply.

He's obviously important. Mitch made a note to ask her who Leon Voigt was. A moment later he worked it out, as the man beside him came into view —American independent Presidential candidate, Ulric Adler. These two men were to be the future leaders; one of Germany, one of the United States. Mitch scanned the stage area for Julian Schmid and found him in the wing area with a clipboard, standing next to what appeared to be a stage manager.

The crowds were invited to sit, or at least that's what Mitch assumed when Eva led him to a chair and everyone began to take a seat. As the orator spoke, Mitch avoided making eye contact with Julian Schmid who would have done well to pick him as a blond in a crowd after only a brief encounter before knocking him out—but still it was not worth the risk, Mitch reasoned. He subtly studied everyone in the stage area and worked his way back. Frightening he thought, *absolutely, positively alarming.*

As the speakers each took turns, Mitch followed Eva's lead—standing, clapping and sitting in turn. After ninety minutes the speakers finished and convention-goers rose and began to mingle. Drinks and food came out on trays and people lined up to meet the speakers. Eva grabbed them both a drink from a passing waiter and Mitch flashed his cigarettes at her. She nodded and they headed outside.

Making sure there was no one in earshot, Mitch lit their cigarettes.

"Do you smoke?" Eva asked.

"Nope, you?"

"Never."

"Right, well that'll be convincing." He held the cigarette. "We've got to get backstage. When they come off, I need to know what happens next—where they are staying and what they are doing. Will Adler just return now to the US or is there a bigger plan while he's here?"

"You're serious?" Eva studied his face.

"Of course, we can't miss this opportunity."

"You don't speak German, but you want to somehow sneak past guards and thousands of cheering neo-Nazis to hide in their meeting room and hear what they say next?" she clarified.

Mitch nodded. "They'll be speaking English, or they'll have a translator there; Adler has little or no German."

"How do you know?" Eva asked.

"Because I know, I'm a spy," he rolled his eyes. "I've checked it out!"

Eva laughed. "Okay, point taken. Sorry."

Mitch grinned and shook his head. "Our Hate Crime Investigation Team has been watching him for months and I get their reports. He's American-born, but has German ancestors. He studied German in high school, but didn't get good marks and his German is as good as my high school Spanish and French—trust me, you wouldn't want to rely on that."

A couple came out, passed by and greeted them. Eva replied and Mitch nodded. They moved on.

"Can we get backstage now? They might have some files we can go through," Mitch said, looking through the doors at the worked-up crowd.

"You're insane," she said.

"There are caterers backstage, they're all in black with those aprons on...but Julian Schmid is a little too close to the stage too for my liking."

"You think he'll recognize you as a blond?" Eva asked.

"Maybe not. There's got to be a sizeable industrial kitchen here for the caterers; let's find it and see if we can lift a tray and a few aprons."

"Then what?" Eva asked.

"Not big on being impulsive hey?" he asked her.

"Then we'll grab some bottles of water and soda to deliver, head backstage, see if we can find their main meeting area—where they've dumped bags and briefcases—check out the security there and where to hide while we deliver the drinks and work out the next step from there."

"And if anyone speaks to you?" Eva asked.

"I've got a sore throat, so you'll have to stick close and answer for me. Got your phone?"

"Yes." She withdrew it from her pocket.

"Can you look up the website for the venue, see if they have a function room layout?"

Eva called up the convention center. "Rooms and spaces," she said, opening the tab. "Here we go...at the back of the main convention space, where the function is now, is the industrial kitchen. On the next level up are meeting rooms and on the top level is the Sky Room which is subdivided as need-be for your size function," she read.

"Let's go." Mitch started walking outside the convention center to the back of the venue where catering staff and waiters were lingering and smoking. Eva raced to catch up.

47

"WHAT HAVE YOU GOT FOR ME?" NICHOLAS EVERETT asked as he lobbed in front of Amy Callaghan's desk in the FBI library.

"Is it not enough that we are housemates without having to see each other during the day?" she teased.

"I figured you would be missing me since I've been playing house after hours with Ellie."

"How's that going?" Amy asked. "Are you the father?"

"Very funny." Nick grinned. He slid down into a chair in front of her desk.

"I've got some more information for you on the *Fountain of Life* program or *Lebensborn,* just so you know what you might be in for, Dad."

"Are you talking about the original program in

Hitler's time or their new one *Fountain of Life 2*?"
Nick asked.

"Both," Amy answered, putting a blond strand
behind her ear as she read from the screen. "What
do you want first?"

"Give me the gist of the original program first."
Nick sat back.

Amy nodded. "Lebensborn means 'wellspring of
life' or 'fountain or life' and was the creation of
Heinrich Himmler in December 1935. Himmler put
the program into place because Germany's birthrate
was decreasing."

"And he wanted to increase the Aryan population," Nick added.

"Correct. He encouraged SS and Wermacht officers to have children with Aryan women with the
belief that those children would obviously grow up
to be the future leaders of a perfect Nazi-Aryan
nation."

Amy stopped to answer the phone and Nick
closed his eyes and waited. She hung up.

"What's up? Tired?" she asked.

"Just getting my head around this whole case.
The time difference with Berlin makes it tricky too. I
was on the phone to Mitch at four this morning."

"What time was that for him?" Amy asked.

"About ten in the morning."

"How is he?"

"Good, wired, like he always is in the middle of a case. Wondered how long it would take you to ask," Nick teased her.

"Shut up." She smiled. "Want to hear this or not because I'm a very busy and important person."

Nick laughed. "You are. Yes, go ahead, thanks."

"I could just print it out for you, like I do for everyone else," she suggested.

Nick shook his head. "No, if you can spare the time tell me. It gives me a break from the office and reading," he said.

Amy nodded. "Okay, so we covered Himmler's objectives. Now, the mission of the program was to give 'racially pure' women the chance to give birth in secret and then the SS organization looked after the child's education and adoption. Both mother and father needed to pass a 'racial purity' test—you know, blond hair and blue eyes with family lineage traceable for at least three generations. Only forty per cent of women who applied were actually 'worthy'."

"You mean women actually applied and were not forced into it?" Nick asked.

"Oh yes, it was an honor to serve the Fatherland, supposedly. About ten Lebensborn homes were established in Germany, nine in Norway, two in Austria, and one each in Belgium, Holland, France, Luxembourg and Denmark. And you'll be pleased to know that any of the children born on Himmler's birthday were considered extra special."

"Good grief." Nick exhaled.

"It gets worse," Amy said.

"It can't," Nick said.

"Yeah, it can. They also kidnapped children from their parents if they matched the Nazis' racial criteria of blond hair and blue or green eyes. Up to 100,000 children may have been stolen from Poland alone. But the saddest thing of all is of the thousands of children sent to Lebensborn centers to be 'Germanized', many were taught that they were abandoned by their parents. In the end, many were transferred to concentration camps and died. Some were adopted by SS families."

Amy stopped and reached for her glass of water.

"Are you okay?" Nick asked.

"Yes, no, I don't know how anyone could do it, those poor little kids."

"Want to print me out the report and I'll get out of here?" Nick asked.

"No I'm okay. In 1945, a day after Hitler's death when our American troops moved into Germany, several hundred children aged between six months to six years were found abandoned. Of these, most were adopted or returned to the birth families if they could be found. A report says that many were too Germanic to fit in. I don't even know what that means or what became of them," Amy said.

"Any idea how many children were born into the program?" Nick asked.

"Roughly ten thousand were actually born from the breeding program," Amy said. "You have the data we've managed to access from the current New Aryan Order—the number of births here to date has been five hundred and seven to be exact."

"And if they believe Ellie and me, five hundred and eight," Nick said.

Mitch moved quickly and with authority as though he belonged. Following a young female waiter, he entered the large industrial kitchen at the back of the convention center taking in as much as he could.

"Aprons," Eva hissed near his ear.

He turned to see a stand of equipment. They moved behind it, selected two aprons and put them on. Momentarily out of sight, Mitch studied what was going on. The kitchen was full of cooks, easily twenty or more busily filling plates with hors d'oeuvres. To the side he saw two chefs working on a more formal meal. About ten plates were set aside and vegetables were being prepared.

"I think there might be a VIP meal being served

and the rest of this is going out to the masses," Mitch whispered.

"So in theory that will be in the Sky Room if it is the most prestigious room ... and you want to be in that room?" Eva frowned.

"You got it. But I want to go to the meeting rooms first in case they've got their notes and bags stashed there."

"That's the next level," Eva said.

"There are some trays over there," Mitch indicated to his left. "I can't see any water."

"Industrial-sized fridge near the exit," Eva said. "Are you sure about this?"

"Yeah," Mitch said. He moved away from her, grabbed two trays, handed Eva one and opened the fridge to place a half dozen bottles of water on both of their trays.

Mitch moved towards the stairs, acknowledging a male waiter who passed them on the way. He entered a new level with a hallway featuring four large doors.

"They're all meeting rooms," Eva said.

"The door to the middle one is open and closest to the stairwell," Mitch observed.

Outside the room stood a security guard. Mitch moved towards him, said a standard greeting in German and entered the room fully expecting to be stopped. He breathed a sigh of relief on getting past.

Eva stopped at the door, greeted the guard and offered him a bottle of water. He accepted and she distracted him with small talk.

Mitch studied the area. It was set up with a round table in the middle, and blank writing pads, pens and mints were placed on the table. A laptop in its case, a briefcase and compendium sat on the table, all sealed and closed. *Damn, unless I take the guard out, I won't have time to look at any of these without drawing attention.*

He noticed the guard glance in and in response Mitch removed the opened bottles of water on the table and replaced them with fresh water. Eva entered, grabbed a cloth from a bar in the corner and made a show of wiping down the table.

Think, quick. Mitch glanced to the windows which were sealed from inside; no throwing anything outside. He looked up at the screen which showed what was going on live in the main hall.

"I need to remove the laptop and then bring it back shortly," he whispered to Eva. "Follow me out and let him know we'll be back shortly with..."

"Clean napkins?" Eva suggested.

"Perfect."

Eva's eyes widened as Mitch reached for the laptop, placed it under his empty tray, pressed both against his body and walked to the door. She followed him out and told the guard they would be back shortly.

Mitch headed down the stairs and outside. He moved to the back of the building, looked around for security cameras and made sure the area was clear. It was six in the morning in Washington D.C., but he placed a call to the I.T. division and Marcus answered.

"I knew you would be on call," Mitch said, relieved. He slid down into a squatting position and turned the computer on. "I've got a laptop with a password on the document files area," he said, looking at the screen that prompted him to enter the right word. "I need to get into it, put in a code so ..."

"Spy code," Marcus finished his sentence. "Like the way you think. Okay, here's what we're going to do. Open the emails and tell me the email address for that computer."

Mitch did as directed.

Marcus continued. "Now I'm going to email you a file to that laptop, click on it, download it and run it."

Eva stood on guard, looking around nervously while Mitch followed the instructions Marcus dictated down the line. A couple came around the side of the building holding hands and, seeing Eva and

Mitch, turned back the other way. Eva rolled her eyes at Mitch.

"Is it working?" Mitch asked.

"It will be in a minute," Marcus confirmed. "Okay, I'm in. Now you need to remove all evidence that you were there and then I'll start going through it from here."

Mitch did as Marcus told him and once finished, shut the laptop down.

"Thanks for that, Marcus, top security clearance only," Mitch said. "Talk later." He hung up. "Eva, let's get this laptop back in position."

48

MITCH PLACED THE LAPTOP FLAT UNDER THE TRAY and pressed both flat to his body. They retraced their steps, Eva inconspicuously grabbing some clean napkins from the shelves as they passed through. Heading up the stairs, Mitch saw the guard was gone.

"He must be in the room," he whispered to Eva. As they neared, Mitch saw on the screen that the speeches were over and the stage was clear. *Shit.*

"I think they're in the room," he turned and passed the laptop hidden by the tray to Eva. She turned it sideways and stacked the napkins on top.

"I can't risk going in just in case Julian Schmid is in there or they ask me something in German. Will you be okay?"

"Of course," she said.

"Hurry before they realize."

"If they haven't already." Eva raced past him into the room. Mitch moved farther along the hall, nearby but not visible, and waited. He hated not to be in control.

Within a minute she was back out and walking down the hall towards him. He looked at her and she nodded. Mitch took the stairs to the next level and, finding an empty meeting room, pulled her in.

"Okay?" he asked.

"Fine. Just in time. They were taking drinks from the refrigerator; I don't think they had been back more than a few minutes. I blocked their view of the table, put the laptop and tray down, dumped the napkins in the middle, picked up the tray and got out. That was very risky, Mitchell."

"Where was the guard? Did he see anything?"

"I don't think so, he was with them," Eva answered.

Mitch thought about her answer for a moment. "I'm not sure we should risk going to the Sky Room now. If they have the same guard and if he is at all suspicious, we're screwed."

"Are you saying that for my benefit?" Eva asked. "Would you go if I wasn't here?"

Mitch hesitated.

"Right, we go," she said.

"Subject to us being able to find a suitable place to lie low," Mitch said.

"Deal."

Mitch opened the door of the room they were in and looked up and down the hall.

"Clear," he said. He could hear chanting and cheering from the convention area. He glanced to a screen at the far end of the hall but could not make out the cause of the cheering. Staying close to the edge, Mitch moved along the hallway until he found a room with a table formally set, ready for its guests. He looked in, no-one was inside. Mitch slid in and Eva followed.

"This must be the Sky Room; it's the best view in the house." Mitch noted the rectangular dining table was placed next to the glazed glass and looked down on the convention floor. He could see the thousands of neo-Nazi supporters there but they could not see in from the floor level. Quickly they looked around the room for a suitable spot.

"There's nothing, the room has no blind spots." Eva looked around.

"Let's try the room next door." Mitch moved to the door. "Two waiters coming." They glanced around again but were stuck. "We'll just have to bluff it."

They moved out of the room, meeting the male and female waiters at the door. The male waiter said something and Eva answered. The waiters moved past Mitch and Eva and entered the room. Mitch went as far as the next room and slipped in. Eva followed. Mitch closed and locked the door.

"What did he say?" Mitch asked.

"He asked if the room was ready," Eva said. "I said 'almost'. How do I know?" She shrugged.

"Good answer."

"Well, keeps you out of trouble. Besides I'm a perfectionist, there's always something that could be added."

Mitch moved to the edge of the room where the adjoining wall had been pulled in place to create smaller rooms. There were no gaps and no chance of seeing. Mitch listened. He could barely hear the conversation from the two waiters.

"This is not going to work. We can't bug the room, I can't hear their conversation through these walls and I'll be surprised if they don't check these rooms again before the group gathers." Mitch sighed. "We're going to have to pass on this and hope the laptop reveals something about their next step."

Eva agreed. "Can we get out of here?"

"Let's go." Mitch strode to the door.

He waited until they heard the waiters pass by and unlocked the door, then motioned for Eva to follow him. They hurried down the hall and stairway, removed their aprons and headed out via the kitchen.

They made their way to the parking lot. Thousands of cars were still there as people stayed on inside. Mitch looked around; no one seemed to care if they came or went.

"I really wanted to hear that conversation in the Sky Room." He sighed.

Eva patted him on the back and he flinched.

She noticed, but uncharacteristically let it slide.

49

On the drive back, Mitch rang John and put the call on speaker. It was seven a.m. Saturday morning in D.C. He told John that Marcus now had access to one of the laptops from the group and to reissue the level of security warnings.

"Adler was there," Mitch added.

"So was Leon Voigt," Eva said. "That's two politicians running for the top jobs in two countries with the financial support and numbers to win."

They spoke about the rest of the rally and Eva confirmed the messages were the same as those being espoused by the American NAO.

"John, we have to expose Voigt and Adler now, there's no other way. What are we waiting for?"

"Orders. Let me come back to you after taking it higher. Eva, we're talking to your superiors too but they may call you in to debrief them on today's convention," John said.

"Of course," she said.

"Sit tight, both of you. I'll be back to you as soon as I can." John hung up.

"Are you all right?" Eva asked Mitch.

"Sure. I've seen some shit over the years, but that was positively weird. You know what the scariest thing was?" Mitch said, still in disbelief.

"The sheer numbers?" Eva guessed.

"No. Everyone was bordering on beautiful," Mitch said. "Tall, blond, fit, strong. There was no one who wasn't striking in some way or had an air about them or a presence. No one that was, I guess you could say, inferior."

"I think that is the whole idea. When you passed the guard at the door he whispered 'schöner'. That means beautiful," Eva said.

Mitch shuddered. "That's creepy. He was probably talking about you or the woman behind me," Mitch said.

"No he actually said 'schöner mann', beautiful man," she translated. "There is nothing wrong with admiring a beautiful specimen of human nature. I can appreciate that. Where to now?"

Mitch looked at his watch. "I'm working you all weekend, sorry."

"That's my job. When you go home, I'll get a day off again luckily," she teased him.

"Let me make a call." Mitch called Benjamin Hoefer's phone and he answered with hesitation.

"It's just me, Mr. Hoefer," Mitch introduced himself. "I've got an airline ticket for you, so you can return home if you are ready. We'll act on Julian Schmid soon, we're just watching him, but it's safe for you to go home. Just don't do any publicity until we tell you it's okay to do so."

Mitch listened to the elderly man.

"We'd love to. Now is good, see you there." Mitch hung up. "Can we print out this e-ticket and go back to the aged care center? Benjamin's dropping in on Marion Kaminsky this afternoon to collect the letter from the solicitor. He'd like us to be there."

———

Mitch and Eva returned to the Meadepark Aged Care Community Center to meet with Benjamin Hoefer and his half-sister Marion Kaminsky. Mitch had the airline ticket printed and transfer arranged for Benjamin's safe passage home.

Mitch and Eva met them in a private sitting area this time and tea was already prepared.

"You were kind to drop the charges, Mitch," Benjamin Hoefer said.

"I'm sure it was out of character," Mitch said.

"Completely, I assure you." He accepted the airline ticket and transfer documents. "Thank you. I can't tell you what a relief it is to be going home, for it all to be over."

"Have you had some quality time together?" Eva asked Marion Kaminsky in German.

"We have indeed dear, it's been an amazing and heart-wrenching time," Mrs. Kaminsky said and Benjamin nodded his agreement. Eva translated for Mitch.

"Although my German is very rusty, Marion has been most patient," Benjamin said in German. "I was taught it as a child and through school, but I don't use it very often."

"It came back to you," Mrs. Kaminsky said in German.

"Marion has read the letter, and she translated it for me. But I want to share my father—my real father's, letter with you," Benjamin said, reaching into his coat pocket for the translated version.

"You don't have to do that," Mitch assured him.

"But I would like to; if you would like to hear it?"

"Of course," Mitch said.

"It helps me to understand why he let me go to the States with the man I thought was my father." Benjamin Hoefer opened the letter and donned his reading glasses which hung on a chain around his neck. He nodded to his half-sister and began to read.

"*My son, should you ever receive this letter, I hope you will forgive me and understand why I had to do what I did and why you have spent your life estranged from your real family. Your mother and I were taken away by the Nazis and from my research I discovered your mother died three years after we arrived at the camp. I am overwhelmed with her fighting strength; to have survived so long in such conditions, I can only imagine she fought every day to return to you, my boy. She was twenty-two when she died at Auschwitz.*"

Benjamin Hoefer stopped to wipe his eyes before continuing to read:

"*I didn't think I would make it; I was so thin, tired and weak, and like your mother I imagine, the only thing that got me up every day and standing was the hope that one day I might return to you both. During my time at the camp, the guard in my section was a man by the name of Hans Schmid; he was an evil man who took joy in his position of power. He was a brute, a mechanic before the war and he wielded incredible strength. I was very unlucky one day to see him stealing and he was close to killing me when he decided he could use me instead. I didn't understand why he spared me but he reminded me that one day he would call in the favor. I didn't know the war was coming to an end but he must have heard stories of the Allies advancing. He knew I*" *had a wife and son; he knew the stories of several of us that worked under his command and he used us as he needed us.*

"One morning when we stumbled out to the morning patrol, the gates were open. We were frightened and the guards were randomly shooting prisoners in the yard. I felt myself being yanked into a room and Hans Schmid was there. He told me he was calling in the favor and he was going to be me. He took my photo of you and your mother, made me reveal where you were and told me that if I told anyone, you would never be safe while he was alive, war or no war. I thought I had been through hell but it was beginning all over again. He said to forget ever seeing you again, he was now me and I was some dirty Jew with no name."

Benjamin took large gulps of air and cried. Mitch placed his hand on the man's shoulder while Marion held his hand. He regained his composure and continued reading.

"Benjamin, I was very frightened. I sent a friend in pretending to be a relative to see Gynther and Antje Bäcker but they confirmed that the man posing as me had come and taken you away and had left no forwarding address. They said they didn't even see him, they just got a note. I received information not long after that your mother had died. But I didn't let it go. I thought I could prove he wasn't me, get him on criminal charges and get you back, but after the war no one

wanted to touch the case. Some even said he might kill you and escape under another alias if he thought he was being hunted.

"For years I looked for you in every face I saw and a thousand times I thought I saw you. But it is hard to imagine what sort of man might evolve from a little boy and you were so very young when I left. Eventually I remarried and was blessed with a son and daughter, but you have always been in my heart, my son.

"If you are reading this, I know you have found me and we will meet on the other side. What a reunion we will have. Know that I love you. Your only father."

Benjamin removed his glasses and folded the letter carefully.

"I'm so very sorry, Mr. Hoefer," Mitch said.

He nodded his thanks. "My poor father, what anguish he suffered. And yet, it is so hard to hate the only man I have ever known as my father."

50

Mitch read a text to Eva from John Windsor. "He'll be back to us by tomorrow at the latest with our orders and we're to sit tight until then."

"That's as good as a night off," Eva said. She walked around Mitch's hotel suite while he made coffee. Mitch studied her; she was agile for a big-boned woman, he thought. Her short cropped blond hair suited her and she had something about her that made you look twice, even if she could crush you to death in a bear hug.

"Have a look around if you like," Mitch teased.

"Thanks. I am. It's nice, very nice. I remember it before the renovation; they've done a good job. When is Adam returning?" She joined Mitch and sat on a stool opposite the kitchen bench.

"Any time in the next few days. If he doesn't get

back by then he can head straight back home," Mitch said. "But I'd like him here if something is going to go down, not that I don't appreciate your help." He pushed the coffee towards her and offered the sugar and a spoon.

"You're a handsome man, Mitchell Parker. Why aren't you married?"

Mitch smiled. "I love that you're so direct. No beating around the bush."

"I want to know so I ask."

"Right." He moved to the lounge. "Coming over?"

She picked up her coffee and followed, sitting in the chair opposite.

"I just broke up with someone not long ago and I guess with the job and the hours we do, I haven't found anyone or found time to get hitched," Mitch answered.

"I'm surprised a woman hasn't just organized you down the aisle. I would have if I lived in the same city."

Mitch smiled and shook his head. "I can see that happening. You're not wearing a ring either? Why haven't you goose stepped someone down the aisle?"

"Ha, amusing Mitchell. I have, twice, but I'm resting in between men at the moment. You know the goose step was a Prussian invention, not German?"

"Of course," Mitch said. "Who doesn't know that?"

"Ah, now I think you are teasing me. You think German women don't have a sense of humor or we should have blond plaits and be wearing a little dirndl dress."

"Is that the dress the wenches wear when pouring beer at Oktoberfest?" Mitch stirred her.

Eva rolled her eyes. "Yes. Or perhaps we should all look like our German models. You know some of our German exports—Heidi Klum, Claudia Schiffer or that actress, Sandra Bullock, you know her mother is German," Eva said. "You must have been disappointed when you were assigned me."

"Wow, you've nailed me," Mitch said. "I was really hoping for a blond model agent."

"Okay I may have made a few assumptions," she acknowledged.

"Only a few? I don't know which men you have been hanging around but first of all I don't know any German women personally so I assume like American women, some German women are funny, some are not?"

"I suspect so," Eva agreed.

"As for what you look like, it is irrelevant really. But it's probably good you aren't identical to Heidi

Klum or Sandra Bullock or that other one you mentioned. Adam is very easily distracted. Personally, if we're stuck in a dark alley, I'd rather you could handle yourself, manage a gun and have my back than look like a skinny supermodel."

"Very diplomatic, Mitchell."

"Thanks." He smiled.

They finished their coffee. He glanced at his watch; it was nearing ten p.m.

"Long day," he said.

"I can stay the night," Eva said. "Shall we have sex?"

Mitch's eyes widened in surprise.

"Unless you don't like sex or you like it with men?" Eva asked.

Mitch laughed.

"What? You find me funny not sexy?"

"I find you funny and sexy," he declared.

"That's a good thing." She smiled.

Mitch rose, and extended his hand to her. Eva accepted it and he pulled her up and led her to the bedroom.

"Wait," she said.

Mitch turned to face her. "We don't have to if you've changed your mind."

"No, I haven't changed my mind. But I am seducing you, it was my invitation."

"Oh, that was foreplay in the lounge room?" Mitch asked.

"No." She pulled him towards her sharply. She was the same height and she looked into his eyes. "American woman like you to lead?"

"Most prefer I'm the man in the bedroom."

"This time I will seduce you, and that will make me more memorable than your American girls when you get home," Eva said, pulling his sweat-shirt up and off.

"Oh don't worry, you were memorable before the seduction."

She smiled. "Thank you, Mitchell."

Undressed and in bed, she straddled him. Mitch admired her; she was solid, strong but well-proportioned with not an ounce of fat; her body was pure muscle.

She took his hands and pinned him. It took all of Mitch's self-control not to flip her over and take charge and he knew she sensed it.

"You have a good body, Mitchell." She admired him.

She ran her tongue down his body, her eyes flicking to his face every now and then to watch him. She moved around his groin, licking, sucking and finally taking him in her mouth.

Mitch inhaled sharply, enjoying the ride. She

took him to the brink, then stopped, moving her tongue back up his body to his lips.

"You can't enter me yet," she said. "I'll tell you when. I want to see how much control you have."

"I'm going to lose control soon, if you don't hurry up," he panted.

She laughed. He moved to flip her over and enter her, but she stopped him, grabbing his jaw with one hand, while using her other hand to stroke him rhythmically. She stared down at him.

"No, you said I could seduce you, Mitchell Parker. I'm in charge."

He stopped, closed his eyes and regained control. Finally she lowered herself onto him and he shuddered.

"Thank Christ," he sighed, feeling himself moving into her.

Eva laughed. "We have ways ..."

"That you do." He opened his eyes to look at her.

"Don't you come yet," she threatened him.

"You're a control freak."

She smiled, moved faster, enjoying watching him, enjoying the momentum and the rush. Her hips, her breasts and thrusts moved to a rhythm.

"Eva!" he yelled.

"Okay, now."

Mitch came, feeling it power through him into

her. He gripped her hands, his eyes closed, breathing fast.

"Holy fuck." He lay back, spent.

She stayed on him but lowered herself to lay her head beside him as he breathed quickly. With his now-released hands, he stroked her back and hair.

"That was ... unbelievable," Mitch said.

Eva smiled. "And that's what I call a debriefing."

Mitch laughed. "I'll never hear that word again without thinking of you."

They lay quietly for a while, listening to the sound of the night traffic outside the hotel.

"Want a drink?" she asked.

"Not so fast," Mitch said. "Your turn."

Before she had time to dictate, he pulled her under him and with one knee between her legs, her arms pinned to the bed, he grazed her nipple with his teeth.

She groaned with pleasure.

"I don't want you to control yourself at all," he directed and she let go. Loud and lively, she begged him to move from her breasts to lower and when he did and she orgasmed, Mitch was sure there was no faking that.

They lay beside each other, breathing heavily.

"Sometimes I wish I smoked," he said.

Eva laughed. "I know exactly what you mean. Do you have any beer?"

"Sure." He began to rise but she pushed him down.

"I'll go, I'm closer to the door."

He watched her walk naked and comfortable in her own skin to the door. He grabbed the pillows off the floor and stacked them along the bed head. She returned with two beers and allowed him to take the top off for her. They leaned back on the pillows and clinked the bottles.

"Cheers," Mitch said.

"Prost," she responded in German.

"I'm glad you stayed," he said.

"Thank you, Mitchell. Me too."

They drank in silence.

"You have some interesting scars on your chest and I felt some on your back too. Are they all from work?" she asked.

"Some are," he said.

"Ah that was a bad draw," she sighed.

Mitch looked over at her. "What do you mean?"

"You were a street kid or child abused maybe? That is a bad draw to get."

Mitch looked confused. "I'm not sure what you mean by bad draw."

"It's my theory," she said, pulling the sheet up.

"Are you cold?" Mitch reached down for the quilt and pulled it up before she answered.

"Thank you."

"Tell me your theory," he said, lying on his side to look at her.

"Well I see life as a lucky dip. You know, everything goes into two buckets—one good, one not so good—and you put your hand into each and draw out different things. We all get a mixture of good and bad. You drew a not-so good card early on. I drew a bad-at-marriage card later in life."

"Hmm, interesting theory," Mitch said. "I like to think we all get a mixture of life lessons and that was one of mine."

"That's too sensible," Eva said.

Mitch laughed. "Sorry, I thought that would be right up your alley. Can I ask you something about your family history?"

"Yes, if you tell me first where the scars came from?" She looked at him.

"My father," Mitch said.

"Ah, I am sorry. Is he still in your life?"

"No."

"Is he dead?" Eva asked.

"I don't know."

"Can I see them?"

Mitch frowned. He turned on his other side so his back faced her.

She touched an indented scar on his back and he flinched.

"You are still not very trusting," she said.

"Just prepared," he answered.

Eva moved her hand along his back. After a minute, she pulled him around to face her.

"Ask your question. It's going to be about the Nazis isn't it?"

"Is that okay? I want to know your family's story during World War II."

Eva finished her beer, put it on the coaster on the drawer next to her side of the bed and slipped down under the quilt cover. Mitch did the same. She turned side-on to face him.

"My great grandfather, who has long since passed away, held the position of SS-Scharführer, or I guess the equivalent of a staff sergeant in your military. He was responsible for atrocities that don't need to be repeated; no one is a stranger to what happened."

Mitch nodded, watching her intently.

Eva continued, "He was sentenced after the war and died in prison. My grandfather, who is also dead now, was in the Hitler Youth. My father never could come to terms with their involvement—no, that's not correct. He understood how they were swept up in it, but he could never understand how proud they were of being involved even after the war ended."

"Amazing," Mitch said. "I'm always blown away

by the fact that it is history but still so alive and recent, if you know what I mean?"

"I know. What would you have done?" Eva asked.

"I've thought a lot about that," Mitch said. He ran his hand over her bare shoulders. "I don't know. I hope I would have rallied against it, I hope I would have helped Jewish people by getting them out of the country or hiding them, but I don't know. I might have feared for repercussions on my own family or got caught up in the propaganda or ambition. It's easy to say from the sidelines, but I know what sort of person I would have wanted to be."

"Yes, me too."

"There's been a lot written about the collective guilt of the next generations. Do you feel it?" Mitch asked.

Eva shook her head. "No. It was before I was born. It is a terrible history but I have no power to change or contribute to it any more than you can change your country's history. But my father suffered. He did humanitarian work all his life trying to make up for the sins and attitude of his father and grandfather."

Mitch drew her closer and began to kiss her. She responded warmly and willingly.

After a few minutes, she opened her eyes and looked at him.

"Want to go again, handsome man?" she teased.

Mitch grinned. "Yes, and as mind-blowing as it was last time, this time I'm in charge." He pulled her down farther into the bed and lowered himself on top of her.

51

MITCH HEARD THE DOOR TO HIS HOTEL SUITE OPEN; his own bedroom door was ajar. He saw Adam Forster enter and throw his duffel bag on the couch. Mitch glanced to the clock beside the bed; it was five a.m. Eva stirred beside him.

Adam stuck his head in. "Oh shit, sorry." He pulled the door closed behind him.

"He's back," Eva mumbled. She ran her hand over Mitch's chest and began moving down his body.

He grabbed her hand.

"What? You don't want sex in the daylight?" she asked as they lay side by side staring at each other.

"It's not that. If you can be a lot quieter than last night we could go again, but is that possible?" Mitch raised an eyebrow.

She smiled and wriggled her hand free from his, resuming her travels over his body. "No. Not possible. Can we do it anyway?"

Mitch laughed. Before he could answer, he realized he had no choice.

———

Showered and shaved, Mitch went to the kitchen and made breakfast from the few supplies they had stocked in their kitchenette. Adam joined him.

"I'm liking the blond look," Adam said.

"Give me a break," Mitch said. "Will Astrid be okay?"

"She'll get back on her feet, I hope," Adam said. "She came back with me and her family met us this morning at the airport. I'm sorry about leaving like that."

"You had to. I'm glad you're back though, we should be getting new orders today and your German skills would be handy."

"You've missed me! And uh, apologies for walking in on you and Eva. I thought I had the wrong room with your blond hair and Eva in bed with you."

"Yeah sorry about that, if I'd known you were coming ... I would have locked the door."

Adam laughed. "But still done it." He leaned

against the kitchenette wall and folded his arms. "So Mitch, tell me, how is that any different from me having Samantha in London?"

"She was on a job."

"So are you," Adam shot back.

"And she was on my team," Mitch said.

"So are you ... on my team."

"Samantha should have been focusing, not doing the attaché," he tried again.

"Yes, so should you."

Mitch stopped beating the eggs and looked up at him. "I don't know, fine, it's the same. Leave it with me and I'll come up with something."

Adam laughed again.

"I've got it!" Mitch exclaimed. "Samantha was part of a team, working as a team and she should have been focused. I'm here by myself so any distraction is only going to impact on me. How's that?"

Adam shook his head. "Yeah, not bad. Don't worry about it, I'm glad you got laid but I didn't think she'd be your type."

"Shh," Mitch warned him, looking into the room where Eva was showering. "She's not, but that's what makes it interesting."

"I'll make you a deal," Adam said, "I won't mention it to anyone if you cut me a break next time I need one."

"Didn't I just do that? Where have you been for the last few days?" Mitch resumed his egg beating.

"Not that kind of favor. The kind that might need discretion at some point in time," Adam said.

"Why, what are planning on doing?"

"Nothing," Adam assured him, "I'm just saying if I need a favor."

Mitch thought about it. "Deal. Especially not a word to Sam."

"Agreed," Adam said.

Mitch nodded toward the drawer. "Make yourself useful and put some cutlery out."

Eva entered the room dressed in her jeans and pullover from the night before. Mitch introduced the two agents.

"Adam, it is good to have you here. We can debrief over breakfast," she said with a glance and smile to Mitch.

"Eva, good to meet you," Adam smiled. "So did you have a good time last night?"

"Oh yes, he has great control," Eva said.

Mitch wheeled around. "Seriously, you two."

"See Mitch, I told you last night if you want to know something you ask," Eva said to Mitch. "Adam lived here for a number of years, he's learnt the direct German way."

"Garbage," Mitch said, handing her a plate of

toast. "Butter those, Adam pour the juice and both of you cut it out. Honestly, is nothing sacred?"

"It's not like I asked were you any good," Adam said.

"He was great," Eva answered.

Mitch leaned over, grabbed the television remote and turned the volume of the German news on loud.

52

MITCH'S PHONE RANG AND MARCUS' NAME CAME UP. With a glance to his watch, Mitch noted it was eight a.m. local time, and two a.m. in Washington D.C.

"Marcus, what are you doing up?"

"We have something major. I finished the laptop sweep last night, then I set an alarm to alert me if anything new came in. A file just came in now. A file called *The Fourth Reich* and I've only read the first page but this is top security."

"Can you ring John, then both of you call me back on a conference line?"

"Done," Marcus said, and hung up.

A few minutes later the phone rang again. Mitch answered.

"John, Marcus, I'm putting you on speaker

phone, we're in a secure area and I've got Adam and Eva with me."

"Morning everyone," John said. "Marcus has just got this file in. I'll go through the contents with you and then we'll need to act. Mitch, I will accelerate this after our meeting but I need a plan from you on how you would like to handle it on the ground. How soon can you do that?"

"Thirty minutes," Mitch said.

"You couldn't have picked a better laptop to lift yesterday," John said. "The laptop belongs to Ulrich Adler. A file was received at seven a.m. your time called *The Fourth Reich*. It appears to be the agreed and signed-off plan from yesterday's convention meeting. I'm sending it to you now Mitch. You know the security clearance number."

Mitch picked up his phone and went to his emails. "Got it," he confirmed.

"The document confirms that in both the USA and in Germany, two men are ready to accede to the role of President and Chancellor. They have the numbers and they have the funding. In exactly three days' time, there will be in both countries a repeat of the 'Night of Broken Glass'."

"Kristallnacht," Adam said.

"Is the date significant?" Mitch asked.

"Yes, 9th of November, the anniversary of the original Kristallnacht in 1938," John said. "It is planned for two areas: the third district in D.C., an area rich in ethnic and cultural diversity and statistically high in crime; and Kreuzberg in Berlin. Eva?"

"Yes this is an area with a significant portion of migrants, poor education maybe and a history of violence," she confirmed.

"So what's their plan?" Mitch said.

"Think of it as the official launch of their campaigns for the top job. Both candidates will take 'followers'—their term not mine—and walk through these areas. Unlike the first 'Night of Broken Glass', they will not break shop windows and burn synagogues. Instead they will carry glass lanterns on the march as a symbolic measure and call for immigrants and the descendants of immigrants to leave the country," John said. "At some point in time they will stop and the two leaders, Adler here in D.C. and Voigt in Berlin, will deliver their campaign speech, call for support, reinforce American and Germany for the pure and begin their run for the top. Remember, they have the numbers and funds to run for President and Chancellor."

"Can they lawfully protest like that in D.C. and Berlin?" Adam asked.

"Yes and no," John answered. "The message is not illegal, and a peaceful march is legal, but if like the original 'Night of Broken Glass' violence breaks out, then they're breaking the law. Otherwise, they can espouse their views and values, we're democratic societies."

"Do they need a permit?" Eva asked.

"The Washington D.C. Metropolitan Police Department prefers groups get a permit, but they can protest as a group in the street without a permit as long as they stay in a single lane and it is non-violent and orderly," John said.

"That's unlikely given the emotions they will evoke," Mitch said. "And isn't there a catch-22 here? Any illegal immigrant who is seen to join in could be deported."

"Yes, that's an interesting spin," John agreed. "Just reading from the notes here—according to local law, a group that acts violently causing grave danger of injury or property damage can be fined up to $1000 and/or sentenced to 180 days in jail. If anyone is harmed or if more than $5000 in damage occurs, those inciting the riot can receive up to ten years in prison and/or a $10,000 fine. Scaled down, charges for unlawful assembly, profane and indecent language amount to about a $250 fine or ninety days in jail."

"And in Berlin?" Mitch asked.

"It's not dissimilar," John said. "Peaceful protests are permitted, but will be closed down and arrests made should violence escalate. Correct Eva?"

"That's my understanding," she agreed.

"So it needs to be violent in order to shut them down," Mitch started thinking out loud.

"And if we want to ensure that there is no mistaking what they stand for, we need to ensure all of their campaign messages about an Aryan society and the work of the *Fountain of Life 2* program are outed," Adam said.

"Lebensborn!" Eva exclaimed. "They have resurrected Lebensborn?"

"Yes, didn't I mention that?" Mitch asked her.

She rolled her eyes. "No, and I would say that is a major concern," she said.

"It's happening in the U.S., so I'm assuming it is happening here," Mitch said.

"How do you know it is happening?" she asked.

"Two of my team are undercover and in the program as we speak," Mitch confirmed.

Eva dropped back on the couch, her eyes wide with shock.

"Mitch, I'll leave you to finish reading *The Fourth Reich* document with your team there. I'm going to make some calls, wake up a few people and move this up the line now. You'll have something to me in thirty minutes then?" John said.

"I will," Mitch confirmed.

"Resources and budget won't be a problem, so factor that in," John said. "Great work getting that laptop Mitch and Eva, and excellent work Marcus on monitoring incoming information." John hung up.

Mitch looked at his team. "Right, let's finish reading *The Fourth Reich* and then we've got our own army to form ... or not."

53

JOHN WINDSOR RETURNED FROM THE HIGH-LEVEL meeting that had been called. He summoned Nick and Ellen into his office. It was five a.m. in Washington D.C., and eleven a.m. in Berlin. As promised, Mitch had sent the bones of a plan to John several hours earlier. John called Mitch and on answering, Mitch put the call on speaker.

"Mitch, the powers-that-be agree with your plan, as radical as it may seem," John said. "To allow a peaceful protest of this nature to take place does not bode well for history or the future. The anniversary will bring out more radicals and we can't have a threat to democracy and equality in either country. We cannot allow these men to accede to governing."

Mitch stepped in. "So to close them down we need to make it a violent protest. But more than that, we need to ensure that Adler and Voigt are seen to be violent—endorsing and enacting that. There needs to be charges laid and there needs to be information exposed about their extreme strategies ASAP."

"There's a level of personal risk here," Ellen said.

John agreed. "There's no use glossing over it. If you are going to be the initiators of trouble, we know you'll be at risk. But we'll try and get enough of our own people in amongst you to recognize and support you. Mitch, do you want to detail the plan?"

"Sure. Over the next two days, we will make the march known to as many local neo-Nazi sympathizer groups as possible in Berlin and D.C. We can ensure some grassroot passion there. Nick and Ellie, you've already got a head start with those groups at home, given we saw a few. Eva will have to guide us here. Ellie, you need to brief however many officers are available to us on how the march is to be handled. We'll do the same here through Eva. As well as ourselves, we need a group of officers to act as agitators. I'm thinking twenty or so would do it, John?"

"I agree," John said. "It won't take much for people to get fired up. We will have some way of identifying each other as officers. I'll let you know what that sign will be."

Mitch continued, "We need to decide at what time during the rally is the best time to start the aggression and if we're lucky, it will happen naturally. I imagine the rally will draw some angry protestors especially given they are staging these in communities with a heavy immigrant population. We will need to agitate, whether it's starting a fight with another protestor, picking on a group of immigrants to get a riot going or breaking shop windows and creating our own Kristallnacht."

"This could get very dangerous," Eva said.

"Yes, but the consequences of allowing it to start and finish as a peaceful protest are more dangerous," Mitch said. "The media is going to play a major part in this and our communication teams in both Berlin and D.C. are crucial. They need to be ready to send out the parties' statements about the immediate banning of immigration and returning of immigrants and their children to their country of origin. They need to put out information about the *Fountain of Life* 2 program—that has to horrify anyone, immigrant or not. Plus we need as many violent images during the protest distributed immediately."

"We're working on that with the communications team now," John confirmed.

"John will you send me the details of who the authorizing officer is here and Eva can make contact? Ellie, will you take charge of that from your end?'

"I'm onto it," she confirmed.

"I suggest we talk again later today...about three p.m. our time," John said.

"That's fine." Mitch calculated that would be nine p.m. in Berlin. "We'll be back here by then. Just remember to keep it as controlled as possible. The neo-Nazi groups will be easy enough to manage; they won't want to miss the chance to participate and will understand the need to keep it under the radar, but we have to control all other outbreaks, especially media at this stage. That will be the hardest part. It will be on Twitter and Facebook before you know it."

"We have to ensure in our word-of-mouth message that people know it will be closed down if it is not kept below the radar. The neo-Nazi radicals won't want to miss their chance to parade," Eva said.

"We'll call you this afternoon unless there's anything breaking," John said and hung up.

———

Mitch looked from Adam to Eva. "Do you think this is nuts?"

Adam nodded. "Absolutely, but clever too."

"You know regardless of whether the march is violent or not, because the area has a history of outbreaks, our riot police will be present," Eva said.

"I'm counting on it," Mitch said. "Regardless of

our actions, I'm sure this rally will attract a lot of negative attention."

"The challenge is to ensure we're not shot by any of the German police mistaking us for instigators," Adam said.

Mitch sat tapping his foot and thinking.

"What's going through your head?" Eva asked.

"I'm thinking about the teams ... if I've got the right mix in the right locations. You know, whether I need to be here or in D.C., or if Ellen and Nick are in the right place," Mitch said.

"Why?" Adam asked. "What are your concerns re D.C.?"

"I'm just thinking about infiltrating other groups to create the stir we need ... Nick and Ellie can't do the ground work with the other neo-Nazi groups. It's too risky when they're Mr. and Mrs. Bauer—members of the NAO—in case they're seen. No one here has seen you Adam, so you can spread the word in the right areas, with Eva helping out. It also makes sense to have you here as a German speaker."

Adam followed Mitch's train of thought. "You can't talk with the other neo-Nazi groups at home because you've already interrogated them about Benjamin Hoefer, even if you are blond now. So has Nick."

"I know, but it depends who we talk with. We don't have to go through the neo-Nazi leaders, we can find a few grassroots members, spread the word and let them pass it up the line and be heroes," Mitch said. His phone beeped as a text message arrived. He looked at it and rose.

"Let me think on our structure." He refrained from mentioning that while he knew Adam could run the show in Germany, Mitch still wasn't sure that Ellen's leadership wouldn't be better. He could manage the Washington D.C. rally with Nick who was good at following orders and providing back up.

Mitch read the text message. "It's from John, it's the name of the person we need to meet in your organization, Eva. Can you set it up for the next hour?" Mitch passed over his phone with the name and number.

54

"I THINK YOU SHOULD GO TO THE CANTEEN AND GET your wife a banana smoothie," Ellen said to Nick. "The morning sickness, you know how it is."

"Good Lord, is this an insight to what you'd be like if you were really pregnant? Would I have to get up at two a.m. to make you toast with a side serve of eggplant?"

Ellen grimaced. "I'm sure my cravings would be really normal."

"It's six a.m. Let's go for breakfast somewhere. Work will still be here in an hour and we can work on our next steps then."

"Good idea. I'll see if John wants to join us." Ellen turned back to John's office.

Nick returned to his desk, logged in and checked his messages. He checked the false account set up under his NAO membership name Nicholas Bauer. There was an email from the NAO. Nick opened it. It was an invitation to lunch with Thorsten Schmid and just for himself, not with his lovely Aryan wife.

This will be interesting. Nick typed back an acceptance. *I suspect I'm about to join the breeding program.*

He logged out and while waiting for John and Ellen, he sent Mitch a text.

"Okay there, Major?" he referred to Mitch's old Air Force title and hit send on the phone. *Good to check he's not over-thinking everything or pacing himself into oblivion.* Nick rose as he saw Ellen beckon from the stairs. A few seconds later, his phone beeped and he opened the return text from Mitch.

"Could do with a beer and a curry, Captain."

Nick grinned and texted back. "You'll have to settle for sauerkraut."

Mitch, Eva and Adam met with three specially trained agents from the Criminal Investigation Department at the Berlin headquarters of the Bundeskriminalamt (BKA)—the German equivalent of the FBI. To Mitch's relief they could speak English and the lead agent had received a full brief at the same time as John Windsor had provided it to the American counterparts. He asked Mitch to run him through it again and Mitch began from the start explaining how Benjamin Hoefer attracted their interest and how it rolled out from there.

When Mitch finished he waited while they absorbed it. The BKA lead agent excused himself to Mitch, asking Eva to translate while he lapsed back into German. Eva advised they were discussing who else at what level needed to understand the implications.

"We are not short on strong leadership here," Eva told Mitch and Adam. "Our Chancellor has been voted the most powerful woman in the world by your media organization, Forbes. I don't think she'll put up with this."

Mitch nodded, watching the faces of the men talking. The lead agent returned his attention to Mitch.

"What do you suggest now?" he asked.

"I suggest we map out a plan. If we can get a scale map of the route of the march, work out where we can position agents and police. We'll need to be very clear where we intend to begin and create the first act of aggression and ensure the police know this, assuming no acts break out before this not by our hand."

The men around the table nodded their understanding.

Mitch continued. "Then we'll decide how far we carry the act; we can probably safely assume the other neo-Nazi groups will perpetuate it once it begins to roll out. Most importantly, we need to understand where to put your media and communications team to get the appropriate images of aggression from Voigt, along with his party's key messages, to distribute immediately to your national media. The same plan will be put in place in Washington D.C. We lock it in, everyone understands their role and then it is a waiting game until we can enact it."

"Excellent," the lead agent nodded. He turned to his men and spoke in German.

Adam translated. "He's asking them to get whoever in their own teams is trusted and authorized to make this happen, bring them back into this room in one hour and clear their diaries for the day."

Eva nodded her agreement.

"Good," Mitch said. "Let's talk about our team," he said, pulling them away from the other group. Mitch continued. "I'm getting Ellen over here to manage hierarchy—working with Eva to liaise with the police, our counterparts, any media—and report back; Adam, that leaves you free to run rally management on the ground with Eva for support. You need to have Ellen's back and work closely with Eva."

"Understood," Adam said.

"You know the risk?" Mitch clarified.

"Yep, I get it."

Mitch continued. "Get it all locked down here today; don't let them leave until the map, staffing and rally points are in place. Then later tonight and tomorrow, visit the neo-Nazi groups and any dissidents and spread the word that there's a march planned."

Adam nodded.

"When Ellen arrives tomorrow, walk the area. Then day three, you're on. Understood?"

"Yep, agreed," Adam said.

"I've got a plane to catch."

"I'll get you to the airport." Eva rose. "Adam, will you be right here until I return?"

"Sure Eva, no problem. Mitch, I'll talk with you when you land."

"Thanks Adam, keep it under control," he said with a glance to the other three men at the table.

"I hear you."

Mitch rang John, then Ellen and Nick separately to discuss plans with them. Ellen was pleased; Mitch couldn't tell if it was because she was keen to go to Berlin or keen to stop acting like she was pregnant or Nick's wife. He filed that away to rib Nick later. Eva waited while he threw his gear back into his black duffel bag. He gave his key to Eva to give to Ellen and they headed to the airport.

"I was hoping we had time for farewell sex," she

said as she took the international airport turn-off and pulled up outside the terminal.

Mitch smiled. "Eva, what's the German word for incorrigible?"

"Incorrigible," she answered.

"That's you." Mitch leaned over and kissed her. He pulled away. "Thanks for the ride. Take care."

"You too, Mitchell Parker. If you ever want a German holiday, you know where to come," she said. "There are many sights I could show you."

"I may just take you up on that," he teased her and with a wave, he exited the car and joined the flow of people heading into the airport.

55

NICHOLAS EVERETT GLANCED AROUND AND FOUND Thorsten Schmid sitting at a table against the rear wall of the restaurant Thorsten had selected. It was a dark interior, but a plush venue with private tables placed well apart from each other and plenty of wait staff hovering. Nick indicated to the waiter that he knew where he was going and headed towards Thorsten Schmid's table.

Thorsten, in a pale gray suit, crisp white shirt and red patterned tie, rose and extended his hand, the men shook and Nick took a seat.

"I've ordered a gin and tonic. What would you like?" Thorsten asked.

"Scotch neat, thanks," Nick said.

Thorsten indicated to the waiter and ordered.

Nick studied Thorsten. He was a weak version of

his brother; half the charisma, half the charm, slight but shrewd.

"So why do I have the pleasure of this invitation?" Nick asked.

Thorsten laughed. "Cut to the chase, hey?"

Nick smiled and nodded.

"Congratulations by the way on your wife's pregnancy."

"Thank you, a lovely planned surprise if there's such a thing. Got to keep the ladies happy haven't we?" Nick said.

"Indeed, which is why I wanted to meet with you."

Thorsten stopped and waited while the waiter placed Nick's drink in front of him.

"Are you ready to order, sirs?" the waiter asked.

"Not quite, my guest hasn't seen the menu yet," Thorsten said.

"What do you recommend?" Nick asked. Let's wrap this up and get out of here, Nick thought.

"I always have the rabbit or duck. Today I'm going to have the rabbit," Thorsten said.

"Then duck for me." Nick nodded at the waiter.

"Very good sirs," he said and departed.

"I love game food," Thorsten said.

"I love the hunt." Nick smiled. He sat back, looking confident and in charge in a dark navy suit.

"My brother told me that you were frustrated in

the little league, so to speak," Thorsten started, "and were keen to make more of a contribution."

Nick sipped his scotch and nodded his agreement.

"You've already achieved one of our major milestones with the starting of a new generation of perfect Aryan children and knowing you and Ellen, I've no doubt that child will be beautiful."

"Thank you," Nick raised his glass, "more so if he, or she, takes after Ellen."

Thorsten nodded, his envy obvious. "I wanted to talk with you about your willingness to contribute more in this area. We have a program which was started by the Führer himself. It's a program we're very proud to continue, the *Fountain of Life 2*. I'm hoping you might be ready to play a part."

———

Mitch knew he had crossed time zones, but was still surprised to get off a morning flight in Berlin to arrive almost eleven hours later but mid-afternoon in Washington D.C. He turned his watch back. Ellen was on her flight and would arrive in the early hours in Berlin. By then, Adam and Eva would have a completed plan to present to her and have started stirring in the bowels of the district.

He felt better about the placement of his team;

his experience and Adam's were too much alike and they would be doing the same role if he stayed with Adam in Berlin. But Ellen would manage the agents and politicians without offending, leaving Adam to focus on the ground-work. They would be well-matched to get the job done. Mitch was confident that he and Nick could manage in D.C. He walked past the passengers waiting for luggage; his own bag slung over his shoulder and able to fit on board as hand luggage. As he walked towards the taxi rank, he spotted Nick waiting. Mitch walked right up to him before Nick saw him.

"Holy crap," Nick said.

"What?" Mitch asked, surprised. "Hey, thanks for picking me up."

"You're blond."

Mitch grinned. "Ha, I completely forgot about that."

"Yeah, well I prefer you as a brunet," Nick teased.

"Since you're married these days and expecting a child, that counts for nothing." Mitch followed him out of the terminal and they crossed to the parking lot. "I didn't know you knew what time I was coming in," Mitch said as he threw his bag in the back seat of the car pool vehicle and climbed into the passenger seat next to Nick.

"John sent me a text. I had lunch with my good

friend Thorsten Schmid which just finished, so I thought I'd pick you up on the way back to the office. You must be wiped out?"

"Yeah, long flight and I've gained an extra eight hours or similar." Mitch yawned at the thought.

Nick started the car and pulled out into the traffic exiting the airport.

"You could have warned me you were blond. I would have held up a sign with your name on it in case I missed you. It's a little freaky, makes you look tougher."

"Yeah, that's what Eva said." Mitch shrugged.

"What was Eva like?" Nick asked. "Claudia Schiffer?"

"More like a blond Amazon warrior—big boned, solid and sharp. A great agent." Mitch smiled, thinking of her.

Nick glanced at him, raised an eyebrow and turned his eyes back to the road.

"How's Thorsten? Was it what we expected?' Mitch asked.

"Of course, look at me," Nick said, maneuvering out of traffic. "He wants me to donate my sperm to other NAO women."

Mitch shook his head. "Lord help us. When?"

"He wanted me to start right away, but I've stalled him," Nick said. "I said that Ellie was going to Berlin to visit her family while she could still fly, before she got too big, and that my cousin was coming over ... that's you. So after expressing my enthusiasm for the mission, we agreed I would start when Ellie came back."

"And by then it will all be over, with luck," Mitch said. "Good excuses, well done!"

"Tell me what happened with Benjamin Hoefer," Nick said.

Mitch brought him up to speed on Benjamin, his real father and the role of the Schmids. As they came to the FBI building, Mitch calculated the time difference and put in a quick call to Adam.

"Okay there?" he asked.

"All fine. We've got the plan finalized. Eva is scanning it and emailing it to you as we speak, so you should have it in seconds. Everyone played nicely together."

"Great," Mitch said, "thanks. We'll use a similar model here. Any major concerns emerge while working it out?"

"Just keeping it under wraps for a few days will be a challenge," Adam said.

"Yeah, but the rumor mill in the right areas won't hurt us. Ellie's flight got away on time, so will you be right to collect her?" Mitch asked.

"Yeah, that's fine. Eva gave me your hotel key. We're going to walk the proposed protest area tonight and we'll start our word-of-mouth campaign," Adam said.

"Be careful. Tomorrow afternoon your time we'll have a conference call. I'll text you to confirm. Thanks Adam," Mitch said. "It's great to have you back on deck."

"Sure, all's under control," Adam assured him.

Mitch hung up as Nick pulled into a parking lot in the basement of the building and cut the ignition. They headed up the elevators. Mitch arrived on his floor, oblivious to the second glances he was attracting with the blond hair. He threw his bag into his office and saw John was in his. He walked past Nick's desk.

"Thanks again for picking me up, Nick. C'mon, let's catch John while we can." He rapped on John's door and entered.

"For chrissake, I thought it was the German police force." John held his hand to his heart.

"What? Oh the hair, yeah. I've just got the plan from Berlin." Mitch waved his phone.

John held up his hand and motioned for Nick to enter and close the door.

"Mitch ..."

"Yeah?" Mitch took a seat.

"Hello, how are you? Welcome home," John said. "Take a deep breath."

Nick laughed. "It's like he never left."

Mitch looked sheepish. "Sorry. I'm a bit absorbed in the case."

"How are you?" John asked.

"Good, yep good."

John nodded. Mitch shuffled with impatience, waiting for the niceties to finish.

"Good flight?"

"As good as you can have when you're not flying the plane," Mitch said. "Everything all right here?"

"Yes, Nick's probably given you an update."

"Sure. Since we're all good, can we start now?" Mitch asked.

John smiled and shook his head. "Let's get to it."

Mitch leaned forward. "I've got the plan from Berlin and I want to emulate it here, so I need the key people from each area—police, our guys, media and communications—together for a few hours ASAP."

John nodded. "We're ready to roll, everyone is on standby. We'll meet in the boardroom in an hour."

56

WITH AN HOUR TO SPARE BEFORE THE MAJOR briefing, Mitch rang Adam and Eva and, talking on speaker phone, went over the final Berlin plan and the issues raised in the meeting so he could be forewarned before the local briefing. After the call, he printed a dozen copies of the Berlin model and saved it to his laptop from his email to project it on the boardroom screen. He glanced at his watch—twenty minutes left. He had time to visit Henri.

Taking the stairs two at a time, Mitch headed for Henri's lab area. Henri's two young assistants were both at their benches.

"Yeah, love the hair," Jared said as Mitch entered.

"Sinister," Tom agreed.

Mitch grinned. "Thanks. Not planning on keeping it though."

"I would," Jared said.

"Yeah but you'd do anything to stand out," Tom baited him. "Like the time you had it all blue."

Mitch left them to continue their verbal sparring.

"Henri." He entered the professor's office.

Henri looked up and for a split second did not recognize Mitch.

"You're back and ran into a bottle of bleach." Henri rose and went to give Mitch a hug. Mitch braced and Henri, reading the body language, gripped Mitch's shoulder instead.

"Welcome back. Is this part of the German disguise?" Henri asked, returning to his desk.

"I would have stood out at a convention without it. How are you?" Mitch asked, lowering himself onto a stool on the opposite side of Henri's workbench.

"I'm very well son, more importantly how are you?" Henri asked. "When did you get back?"

"An hour ago," Mitch said. "Got a meeting in fifteen minutes so got to run."

"Well I appreciate you dropping in. Did you want to come around for a good meal tonight? You know Ann likes to see you eating when you're on a case."

"Thanks," Mitch said, "but I'm exhausted, it was a long flight. I'm going home to my own bed and to make sure Lyn hasn't rented out my room to someone else. Can I ask you something? Did Nick seem okay in my absence?"

Henri frowned. "Yes. Why do you ask?"

Mitch looked around before speaking. "Dan, the counselor, seems to think Nick's a bit lost at the moment and that my sending him in undercover to the NAO might not be good for him. I figure no one would probably notice a change in him except you, given our history."

Henri nodded. "Nick and I had a coffee late last week when he dropped in. He seemed fine, was asking after you actually. Nick's very anti the NAO, so I think you can rest easy there."

"Good. Thanks Henri." Mitch rose and with a wave, he was gone. As he headed up the stairs, Dan Tarrow was coming down.

"Mitch, when did you get back?" Dan asked.

"An hour ago," Mitch said. "Got to run."

"Hold up. You owe me a second counseling session and you know how it works, the sooner the better. Counseling is more effective if consistent," Dan said.

"Yeah Dan, really busy this week. The case is about to come to a head."

"Tomorrow for an hour?"

"Can it wait until next week?" Mitch frowned.

"And what will come up next week?" Dan asked.

"I can't talk about this now, I've got a meeting in five minutes," Mitch said.

"Just commit to a time then. Ten a.m. tomorrow?" Dan continued to push.

"For chrissake Dan, seriously I'm really busy." Mitch realized Dan would be watching his reactions. He drew a deep breath. "I'll come back to you."

"Thanks Mitch, sometime tomorrow then." Dan smiled and continued down the stairs.

Mitch wanted to punch Dan Tarrow or the wall. He turned and continued upstairs to the boardroom. He saw a number of heavies entering, went to his office, grabbed his diary and files and followed them in. John Windsor was the last to enter, closing the door and thanking everyone for their attendance.

The next five hours were spent locked in the boardroom plotting out a similar plan to that established in Berlin. Mitch and Nick, along with leaders from the SWAT team and key police leaders, marked where the first outbreak of trouble would begin, how it would be initiated and carried through, and where agents would be, blended undercover in the rally.

Mitch and Nick discussed their pending work

visiting a few underground neo-Nazi organizations to get word out. The media and communications team took the NAO's key messages from Mitch to release to the media with the appropriate photos to be captured as the rally heated up. The potential issues were flagged out and crisis plans put in place. By the end of the session, all parties were clear and a plan had been drawn up.

———

Mitch knocked before he walked in to his new home and called out. Lyn emerged from the kitchen with a grin and raced towards him. She surprised Mitch with a hug.

"Welcome home, you don't have to knock, you live here!" She let him go and stood back.

Mitch grinned, looking embarrassed. "I've been away a week, I thought you might have found a new housemate."

"Seems longer, but thanks for letting me know you were coming home tonight. Wow, blond!" She studied him. "I like the dark you better."

"Yeah, me too," he agreed.

"I've cooked dinner so we can catch up and then you can hit the hay early, I bet you're tired," Lyn led the way into the kitchen. "Get changed if you like."

"I'll be tired when I stop, you know how it is."

Mitch stopped off at his room and threw his bag onto the bed. He slipped off his suit jacket and tie, hung it up, removed his watch and then joined her in the kitchen. Mitch watched her at the oven, dressed in jeans, a baggy jumper and an apron covered in bright sunflowers.

"What can I do?" he asked.

"Why don't you pour us both a drink? I've got a few good bottles of red there or you've got beer in the fridge still."

"Red, yeah?" Mitch said.

"Perfect."

"Thanks for cooking, you didn't have to do that." Mitch inhaled the aroma.

"I wanted to catch up, plus, it's not often we're both home and home alone. I've done a beef and zucchini lasagna with a ginger vegetable side." She grabbed two plates ready to serve.

"Wow, that beats the bowl of cereal I had last night." He offered her the glass of red and they clinked glasses. "How's Sandy?"

"She's great. I'm in love." Lyn grinned. She raised her glass, sipped and turned back to the oven. "Mitch, I know you've just walked in, but I do have something I need to talk with you about and it can't wait."

Uh oh, sounds like a partner is moving in and I'm moving out.

"Did I leave my socks in the lounge?" he teased.

Lyn smiled. "No." She bit her lip. "I've thought a lot about whether to bring this up or mind my own business. I really like you, Mitch."

Mitch nodded. "I like you too, Lyn. But ... you've cooked dinner and organized a night at home to soften the blow. What's the blow?" He willed her to cut to the chase.

"I don't like to be judgmental but we all have things we believe in or have to stand up for. You know what I mean?"

"Sure," Mitch said.

"For me it's animal cruelty, I can't bear it and—"

"Lynnie, spit it out," Mitch cut her off.

She turned and looked at him, then reached into her pocket and pulled out a badge. She walked towards him and put it on the counter between them.

Mitch recognized it. It was The New Aryan Order badge; he had purchased half a dozen for his team to wear before he left for Germany, just in case they needed to blend in.

"Where did you find this?" he asked.

She picked it up again and studied it. "When you left for the airport, you must have dropped it. It was near the front door. Mitch, I can't condone that, I can't live with someone who supports what the Nazis did. I'm sorry."

Mitch smiled. "You were very brave to confront me with this."

Lyn stepped back.

Mitch held up his hands. "Sorry, no, I'm not threatening you, I didn't mean that." Mitch rose to assure her and she stepped back again.

He sat back down. "It's okay, I'm not going to hurt you, Lynnie. Do you know where I work?"

"You're an investigator," she said.

"Yes, for the FBI."

She mouthed the word FBI. "How do I know that's the truth?"

Mitch motioned for her to stay put. He went to his room, grabbed his badge from his jacket and returned. Lyn stood farther away, this time holding a knife.

Mitch sighed and sat back down. He passed over his I.D. She moved closer and grabbed it.

"I'm in the middle of a confidential case." He waited while she studied his identification.

He extended his hand for the badge and she gave both back to him. "This neo-Nazi badge is part of the case. That's why I've been in Germany."

"That's why you're blond and look Aryan. You're not a member?" she confirmed.

"Hell would freeze over first, and even then I wouldn't be a member," he said.

Lyn groaned. "Thank God. I didn't know what to do. Sorry Mitch, but I had to ask."

Mitch smiled. "So can I stay now?"

"You bet! You're the best housemate I've ever had," she assured him.

"Because I'm never home?" He took a mouthful of wine.

"Well partly because you do have your own life and because I feel safe with you here, when you're not a Nazi that is." She returned to the stove and checked the lasagna. "I'm really sorry, Mitch, I feel like an idiot now."

"I'm not sorry you asked, but sorry you pulled the knife maybe," he teased her, "especially if you knew how easy it would have been to overpower you and use it against you."

"Really?" She frowned.

"Really," he assured her. "You're just handing the villain a weapon."

She narrowed her eyes. "I might have got a few good stabs and slashes in."

"You think? Okay then, arm yourself with a butter knife, something that won't do me any damage, and give it your best shot."

Lyn grinned. "You're on. You'll see it is better than being unarmed."

"I doubt that," Mitch said. He waited for her to

get the knife and return to the same position, brandishing it near the stove.

Mitch rose from the kitchen stool. "Ready."

She nodded.

In three quick strides he was beside her. Her arms were pinned to the wall, he pressed hard against her and the knife toppled to the ground.

"Oh my God!" she exclaimed. She tried to fight him off. "I can't move."

"That's right." He moved off her.

"You gave me a fright." She put her hand on her heart and breathed fast.

"And you know me and knew what I was going to do. You all right?" Mitch bent down, picked up the knife and put it in the sink.

"I think so. It's been a night for high drama," she said.

"Warrants a wine top-up," he agreed. He filled their glasses. "Lynnie, I think you are a very principled person and as I said, very brave to bring up the Nazi membership. What are you going to tell Sandy now? I'm guessing you told her."

Lyn nodded. "I asked her advice. I'll just tell her the truth, but you don't want me to reveal what you are working on or where you work I'm guessing?" Lyn said.

"Maybe just say it was research to do with my work. Will that work?"

"Works for me," she sighed and smiled. "I'm so glad you're not a Nazi."

Mitch smiled and shook his head. "You and me both."

"Want me to dye your hair brown again?"

57

THE DAY BEFORE THE RALLY IN BOTH COUNTRIES, Mitch arrived at the office early, his head running through a thousand scenarios. He had an hour of quiet time before John Windsor was due to arrive at his usual time at seven a.m., except today he arrived at six-fifteen.

"Coffee?" John asked sticking his head in the door.

"Are you making or buying?" Mitch asked.

"Buying. Let's walk across the road."

Mitch rose and followed John out of the office. John looked pressed and fresh. Mitch increased his pace to keep up.

"You're looking drawn," John said.

Mitch grunted. "It's the blond hair, washes me out according to my housemate," he joked. "I'll be better in a day or so when I hope it'll all be wrapped up."

They entered the coffee shop and John ordered their regular take-away coffees.

"Anything to eat?" he asked.

"No thanks," Mitch said.

"When did you last eat?"

Mitch rolled his eyes. "Lyn made me lasagna last night, Dad."

John chuckled. "Good." He handed over a ten dollar note and on receiving the change, threw it into a tipping jar. They moved aside to wait for their order.

"What's the feeling upstairs?" Mitch asked.

"They're keen to shut it down with an emphasis on shutting it down for good," John said. "There's a couple of agendas running there."

"No doubt. Politics and humanity, gee which would win?" Mitch asked.

John took the two coffees, thanked the staff and handed one to Mitch.

"Thanks," Mitch said.

They walked across the road, dodging traffic.

"Dan tells me he's booked you in for an hour at eight this morning for your second counseling session and that you weren't happy about it," John said. He led the way up the stairs to their floor.

"I just asked him to wait until next week when

the case should be closed all going well, but he wouldn't. I don't think that's too much to ask," Mitch said, stopping at his office. "We're flat out at the moment and a few days isn't going to make much difference to him."

John exhaled. "It wouldn't be a problem for anyone else Mitch, but you can't blame him. With your avoidance record, you're the boy who cried wolf. See you for a catch-up at nine-thirty."

———

Ellen slept well on the plane; she made a note to tell Mitch and rub that in. Arriving in Berlin, she passed through customs and navigated her way to the exit lounge where she caught sight of Adam Forster, sitting and reading messages on his phone. He looked up as though sensing her and saw her. Adam rose, waved and came towards her. A number of women glanced at the tall man with the tied-back hair and confident air.

"Ellie, *willkommen in Berlin*," he said.

"Thank you Adam, nice to be here, even if it is late and cold and I want to go to bed."

He took her bag from her shoulder and threw it over his own.

"C'mon, the car's this way." He put his arm around her in a protective manner and moved her through the crowds milling around waiting to pick up luggage. "You'll like our hotel and yes, we have separate rooms and bathrooms."

"Great, that especially applies to the bathrooms." She smiled. "Any news?"

"Nothing that won't wait," Adam said. "I'll make you a tea when we get there, then you can hit the sack. We hit the ground running tomorrow and we've got a conference call in the afternoon our time, morning in Washington."

"And I get to meet Eva," Ellen said, following him into the airport parking lot.

He motioned towards a white sedan and unlocked the doors of the hire car. Adam opened her door before putting her bag in the back seat and going around to get into the driver's seat.

"When did you get this?" she asked of the hire car.

"Mitch rented it for us on the day he left so we could get out to the suburbs and do some stirring and pick you up. Now I've just got to find my way back to the hotel," he said, turning up the heat and concentrating as he moved the car towards the parking exit.

58

"GOOD TO HAVE YOU BACK IN COUNSELING, MITCH," Dan Tarrow said, locking his office door and coming over to join Mitch on the couch opposite.

"Yeah, great to be back, Dan," Mitch said.

Dan laughed. "Now try that with sincerity."

"Second and last counseling session," Mitch reminded him.

Dan sat back and put his arms along the back of the chair. "So this really does not help you one bit?"

Mitch sighed. "Dan why do you ask me questions when you know the answer and you make me insult you by saying it?"

Dan shrugged. "I was hoping you might surprise me."

Mitch didn't answer.

"Okay then." Dan opened Mitch's file. He

glanced up at him and back down. "Don't worry Mitch, I'm not going back there."

"You're dying to though." Mitch leaned forward and clasped his hands between his legs. "All of you —psychologists, psychiatrists, counselors, whatever —you all want to go there for research gathering, a chance to study someone. But afterwards you hope that by talking about it, your patients will leave feeling much better, so then you can feel good about yourselves too. But as far as I'm concerned talking about it makes no difference. It's still there the next day, the next week, the next year. Filing it away and getting on with it makes it better. That's what they did in the past, after the wars and the depression; they didn't sit around analyzing their lives or if they were happy." Mitch sat back. "They just got on with it. Well, that's the world according to me."

Dan looked surprised. He took a deep breath and studied Mitch before answering. "Wow, Mitch. I bet that's the most you've ever said on a counselor's couch."

Mitch raised his eyebrows in thought. "Probably."

"Does that mean I have permission to talk about your childhood then, for my own research purposes?" Dan asked.

"No."

"Right then. Tell me about your team. I want to

understand your relationship to them, their strengths and how you see them," Dan continued. "Start with Nicholas. That's a complex relationship."

"Can I ask the relevance?" Mitch said.

"I'm looking at your support networks: who you trust, how you cope, who has your back, and it helps me build a picture of you. But Mitch, just so we're clear here—for the hour you are assigned to me, it's my job to make sure you are balanced and coping, to analyze you whether you like it or not. So how about you lower your guard a bit and work with me here?" Dan said.

Mitch took a deep breath and started. "Nick contributes skills that I don't have; he's a great navigator, a whiz at math, he's orderly in the way he sees a case, he's disciplined but that comes from his military background—"

Dan held up his hand and Mitch stopped.

"Who is he to you?" Dan asked.

"I don't get the question," Mitch said.

"Yes you do, but let me spell it out. You've given me a list of Nicholas' skills, but why do you trust him?"

"You've read my history, you know we go way back."

"When you were boys, were you the leader?" he asked and watched Mitch's eyes narrow as he thought about the question and the significance of it.

"Nick was the elder so he took charge a lot of the time," Mitch said.

"And because you had to step up at home, I imagine it was a relief to have someone look out for you out of the home. Did he defend you?" Dan asked.

Mitch rose and walked to the window. "You're finding a back door. Why don't you just ask what you want to ask?"

Dan changed tack. "Tell me about your first meeting with Ellen."

Mitch turned back around to face Dan. He leaned against the windowsill and crossed his arms. "She came for an interview for the role as an agent in my new team. John had narrowed down the applicants and I got to interview them. I had J.J. at that stage—that's a former officer not with our team anymore—and I was yet to interview Samantha. But Ellen was impressive."

"How?" Dan asked.

"She was this little powerhouse; so composed and intelligent. I could hear her brain ticking," Mitch said.

Dan watched him; *Mitch is relaxed talking about Ellen, because he isn't talking about himself and he thinks it doesn't come back to him. But it does.*

Mitch continued. "She had topped her class in law, forensic science, leadership, even firearms and she was fluent in French. Her whole demeanor challenged me not to take her at face value."

"And you've had feelings for her since day one?" Dan asked.

Mitch snapped to look at Dan. "What?"

"You're denying it?" Dan asked.

Mitch returned to sit opposite him. "Why are you asking me this?"

"I told you, I'm looking at who you have around you and who you trust."

"And you think that if I had feelings for Ellie I could go off the rails on the job?" Mitch asked.

"No, I think it would be good for you," Dan said.

Mitch shook his head and looked to the clock.

"Mitch, you are so repressed."

Mitch laughed. "I'm repressed now?"

"Yes," Dan challenged him. "It's a well-known defense mechanism, keeps information that you don't want to acknowledge out of your conscious awareness. But let me tell you something, repressing memories or feelings doesn't make them disappear. Sure you've got them all filed away neatly, but they will influence your behavior."

Mitch's jaw locked as he listened without reacting.

Dan continued. "Let me give you an example. A

person who has repressed memories of child abuse for example, might find it difficult to form relationships."

Mitch crossed his arms across his body, then unfolded them again knowing Dan would be reading his body language.

"So what's the cure, doc?" he asked.

"There's work you can do on that, but you don't want to hear that and you don't want to do that. You're happy going along surrounding yourself with a boss who protects you and teammates who would put themselves on the line for you."

Mitch scoffed. "Give me a break. Clearly you weren't around last week when John told me to pull my head in or I'd be answering to Ellen." Anger flashed across his face. "Anyway, I'd put myself on the line for them too in a heartbeat."

Dan nodded. "Yes I'm guessing you would. Mitch, I'll do you a deal. I'll give you an early mark if you do something for me."

"What?"

"Give me one honest and sincere feeling. I know it won't be easy for you, but tell me one genuine thing you are feeling other than frustrated about being here. Please. Then you can mark your second session off as completed."

Dan watched as Mitch held his gaze and then dropped his eyes. He was thinking. Dan waited.

After a few minutes he prompted Mitch. "Any feeling ... sad, lonely, nervous, in love, excited, hopeful, anything? One feeling? Anything at all?"

He's even struggling with this, Dan thought. He waited and watched Mitch in silence.

Mitch inhaled and began, looking Dan in the eyes. "I'm feeling grateful that Henri came into my life and showed me what a father could be like. I wish he was my biological father. I'm feeling grateful for this job because not only does it challenge me and I'm doing something that is good, but it is a great distraction to get me through my recent break up which has left me feeling flat; I'm feeling like I really don't want to start another relationship again unless it's a sure thing; I'm feeling happy that Nick is back in my life and I've helped him get on his feet like he's helped me; I've had feelings for Ellen since the first day I set eyes on her but I won't cross that line in case it's not mutual and she thinks it puts her job in jeopardy; and I'm feeling like you should back off and give me some credit for not feeling, because sometimes that's the best way to get through."

Mitch looked at the clock and turned back to Dan. "Deal then? Session two done." He rose, unlocked the door and departed.

Dan slid down on the couch and looked up at the ceiling. "Holy shit."

———

Mitch headed out of Dan's office and down the stairs to see Henri. The counseling session had taken fifteen minutes all up. He was relieved to find Henri's two assistants not in. He could see Henri with his glasses on, reading a document on his screen. Mitch walked in.

"Got a minute?" he asked and closed the office door.

"Of course." Henri took off his glasses and frowned. "What's up son?"

"Nothing."

He began to pace from one end of the office to the other.

"Right. You've just had your second counseling session with Dan, haven't you?" Henri looked at the clock and frowned. "Wasn't it at eight?"

"Why does everyone know that?" Mitch stopped pacing. He pulled up a stool at the bench opposite Henri. "Second and last session."

"So what happened?"

Mitch rubbed his hands over his face. "I said too much."

"Well can I suggest that is what Dan's there for and you're supposed to bare your soul a bit? It won't go any further than him," Henri reminded him.

"He'll be writing notes as we speak." Mitch rose

and began to pace again. "For chrissake, he just baited me until I wanted to prove something to him. I can't believe he got me."

"Mitch, look at me."

Mitch turned to face him.

"Dan is there to help you. Perhaps what you said might make him think you're perfectly, well, normal," Henri said. "He deals in emotions all day. It's foreign to you, not him."

Mitch considered this.

"Sit down for a minute," Henri ordered.

Mitch returned and sat opposite Henri.

"You don't have to tell me, but think of what you told him. Is there anything he didn't already know or couldn't assume?"

Mitch thought back over his comments. *He guessed about Ellen, knows about Nick and my history, won't be surprised I value Henri and wish he was my real father and that the breakup of my last relationship would make me or anyone normal unhappy.*

"Probably not," Mitch said.

"So it's just the fact that you verbalized those thoughts, because that's way out of your comfort zone. Fair call?" Henri asked.

Mitch nodded.

Henri continued. "He's a professional. He won't repeat what you said and I bet if you saw Dan again right now, he'd be delighted with the session; he's

425

probably over the moon feeling like he really helped you get in touch with your emotions and express them."

Mitch scoffed. "Yeah I did mention that I thought in his profession it was more about the study and win, than the patient."

Henri picked up the phone, dialed a number and indicated for Mitch to wait. He put it on speaker phone and put the handset down. Dan Tarrow answered.

"Hi Dan, I know your session with Mitch was confidential, but I just wanted to check he was okay?"

"It was a great session, Henri, I feel we made real progress. Good of you to check on him," Dan said. "He's lucky to have the support network he does, I told him that."

"Thanks Dan, good to know." Henri hung up.

Mitch exhaled.

"Trust me, it's a big deal to you Mitch, but Dan will have his next patient in there within the hour, willingly revealing more than you've said, I imagine."

Mitch nodded.

"Anyway, well done, son." Henri smiled at him. "At this rate, can I expect a hug on my birthday?"

"Didn't we shake hands last year?" Mitch smiled. "You expect too much."

Henri laughed.

———

John Windsor passed Dan Tarrow in the hallway later that day.

"Hey Dan, all okay with today's session? Did he show up?" John asked after Mitch.

"We had a breakthrough," Dan said.

John looked surprised. "Really?"

"Really, a huge, surprising breakthrough." Dan tapped John on the shoulder and walked away.

59

ADAM FORSTER WAS UP AT FIVE A.M. ON THE DAY OF
the rally in Berlin. He made a coffee and, sitting in
front of the window in his hotel room, watched and
waited for the sunrise. He glanced at his watch—it
was eleven p.m. in Washington D.C. He stood,
grabbed his phone and returned to the window.
Adam dialed Mitch.

"Hey Adam," Mitch answered.

"I didn't wake you obviously," Adam said
speaking in a low voice so as not to wake Ellen.

"No, I was waiting up to give you a call after six
your time to make sure you were feeling okay about
it all," Mitch said. "I'm just watching a re-run of the
Redskins game from last week."

"The Cardinals will still win," Adam said.

Mitch laughed. "Spoiler. So are you under control?"

Adam exhaled. "Sure. But you know how it is before these things ... you've run through every scenario in your head except the one that will happen. Remember in London with Hackett in the Underground? Who would have thought he'd pull that prank at the last minute."

"Who would have seen that coming?" Mitch agreed.

"Yeah. I've been thinking about The New Aryan Order, thinking about how desperate they might be to win. We've counted on them having significant security in place themselves, but..." He stopped mid-thought.

"So you think that despite the fact they want the top jobs—Chancellor and President—they would be prepared to take those jobs at any cost?"

"That's what I'm thinking."

"Nothing in any of their notes or transcripts indicated that they intend to go that way," Mitch said, "but we're prepared for that. The SWAT teams are ready."

"Fine, just wanted to flag it again," Adam said. He finished his coffee.

"How are Eve and Ellie going working together?" Mitch asked.

"Chalk and cheese but thick as thieves," Adam said.

"Only two idioms, that's slack of you."

Adam laughed. "Well it's early here. Ellie's up, I can hear her moving around. Want to talk with her?"

"If she comes out of her room. Do your best to keep me posted throughout. It's a blueprint for here."

"Are you going to stay up all night?" Adam asked.

"I'll get a few hours' sleep now and get up about three-thirty. If the rally is at ten a.m. in Berlin, that's four a.m. here," Mitch calculated. "I need to know how it plays out. It should be all over by noon, which is six a.m. our time and then it will be all over the international media."

"What time does your march start?" Adam asked.

"Seven, and I suspect they started it early for that reason. By the time the USA is waking up to the international news of the neo-Nazi march in Berlin, it will begin to stir on our own streets," Mitch said. "It will be interesting to see how that works here, but I'm guessing D.C. will attract more dissenters on the back of the European news."

"Agreed," Adam said. "Here she is, I'll put Ellie on."

"Be careful Adam."

"Yeah, sure. Talk during the morning. Ellie ... it's Mitch." Adam passed the phone over to her. "Nice pajamas by the way." He admired her leopard print flannelette shirt and pants.

"Thanks." She took the phone. "Hi Mitch."

"Are you wearing the leopard-print pajamas again?" Mitch asked.

"It's cold. There is nothing wrong with my leopard PJs. I'm going to get everyone in the team a different pair to reflect your personalities, like an FBI zoo."

"I'm not even going to ask ... so, are you feeling okay about today?" Mitch asked.

Ellen nodded as Adam held up a coffee cup to her.

"I'm fine. I couldn't sleep for thinking about it, but I think we've covered everything that is in our control. If you like, I can wear my phone earpiece and call you. You can hear it all."

"No, but thanks. As much as I'd love that, I want you to be one hundred per cent in the moment paying attention. Just call me when you can. Now Ellie..."

"Is this when you give me the 'be careful' lecture or the 'don't sleep with Adam' lecture?" She rolled her eyes at Adam.

"Well if you don't want it ..." Mitch said with a hint of dejection in his voice.

Ellen laughed. "No give it to me. I know you'll feel better afterwards."

"Good. Don't take any risks, Ellie, you know that. It's not worth it. Make sure our security guys and the Berlin police have eyeballed you before the march begins and know who all three of you are. Watch each other's backs so at least we have our own cover and all the other things I regularly say about coming back safely, good luck and thanks. Got it?"

"Got it boss. You and Nick be careful today too."

"I'm always careful."

Ellen scoffed. "Yet somehow trouble finds you."

Adam and Ellen heard a soft knock on the door and Adam opened it to find Eva there, dressed in black and wearing a New Aryan Order badge.

"Eva's just arrived," Ellen told Mitch with a wave to Eva.

"Good, and Ellie, call me during the morning when you can." Mitch hung up.

"Speaking of not being able to sleep ..." Adam turned to Eva.

"Who sleeps before a mission?" She saw Ellen's coffee. "Yes please, a coffee would be great," she said to Adam.

"Right, I'm onto it."

"Was that Mitchell?" Eva asked.

"Yes, he's up late to check we're all coping. He's a worrier," Ellen said.

"I can imagine that. His head is always going, even when he's not using it," Eva said.

Ellen looked at her, surprised. "Wow, you read him well in a short space of time."

"Are you both feeling ready?" Adam butted in to steer the conversation away from Mitch.

"Absolutely," Ellen said. "It's a bit hard with the language barrier, but I suspect actions will speak louder today."

"They will," Eva agreed. "Plus Adam and I will be close by so if any orders are yelled that you need to know, we'll direct you. I have two NAO badges for you to wear so we can blend in with them." She removed them from her pocket and gave them each a badge.

Eva continued. "So we leave here at six-thirty, head to Kreuzberg, lie low, and have breakfast nearby where we can sit in the window of a café to watch the flow of people coming into the area. Then we can blend into the crowd after nine a.m., eyeball security and the police, ready for the ten o'clock start."

Adam agreed. "Then, we do our bit at around twenty-past-ten, unless someone starts the action for us sooner."

"We need to check out where the media and

communication team is as well, as we don't want to be on their footage. They've been told to keep to the perimeters for their shots but it helps if we keep it in mind," Ellen said.

The three sat in silence as the sun rose and filtered through the windows.

Eventually Eva spoke. "Are you two going in track gear and leopard pajamas or changing?"

Ellen laughed. "Yes ma'am, we're onto it."

She rose and headed for her room. Adam stayed behind.

"Can I ask a favor?" Adam asked.

"Of course, Adam," Eva said.

"Can you not tell Ellie that you and Mitch, you know ... slept together."

Eva looked towards Ellen's room. "Oh, are they together?"

"No! Definitely not, I didn't mean that."

"She likes him?"

Foster shrugged. "I don't know."

"He likes her?" Eva asked.

"I don't know."

Eva frowned.

"I'll go change," Adam said.

"Right. Good idea." Eva watched him leave the room.

60

Mitch hated not being there. He looked at the clock—eleven-thirty p.m.; time to get a few hours' sleep before he would head into work around three a.m. and monitor the calls and news feeds from Germany. He set the alarm on his phone, and put all his gear near the door so he could leave without waking Lyn.

No sooner had he laid down, than the alarm rang. He was surprised that he had fallen to sleep. Mitch dressed in the dark and quietly left the house. There was no quiet way to start a car and drive out of a garage at that hour of the morning.

Arriving at work, he waved to a surprised security guard who glanced at his watch and back up again at Mitch. He made his way upstairs to his office and turned on the television in his own office to

CNN and the two in John's office to BBC and Fox news. He positioned his chair so he could see all three screens and logged onto The Huffington Post website on his office PC and Yahoo! News on his laptop.

By three-thirty a.m. John and Nick had joined him. Mitch resisted calling Adam and Ellen. He put his watch on Berlin time and waited. It would start in thirty minutes.

———

Adam, Ellen and Eva blended in with the swelling crowds in Kreuzberg. For several hours they had waited; watching the numbers build. At nine a.m., they had made themselves known to the security and police team, and checked out the location of the communication team. They observed the early crowds were mainly New Aryan Order members; they amassed together looking polished and Aryan. They knew each other and wore the badges on their shirts. Many had signs supporting Leon Voigt for Chancellor.

It was easy to pick the agitators and neo-Nazis as they arrived—shaved heads, heavily tattooed, wearing swastikas and piercings. They were thin or overweight, unkempt and not fitting the perfect mold of the NAO. By nine-thirty, the streets were filling and too quickly.

"This is going to get ugly without any help from us," Ellen whispered to Adam as they began to mingle with the NAO members.

Adam looked at his watch. "Thirty minutes until it begins. I'm going to get in position." He squeezed Ellen's shoulder as he moved away. There were easily a thousand NAO supporters filling the area and Adam moved towards the outside boundaries where he could agitate as planned, if needed. His hand slid over his hip, feeling the small concealed gun that would allow him to break the shop window glass. The breaking glass would be enough to encourage any dissident who wanted to recreate Kristallnacht. And if it didn't, the sound would be enough to cause panic amongst the peaceful marchers. It should get the media the vision we need, he thought.

———

Ellen and Eva held the symbolic lantern that was given to them by the NAO organizers when they arrived. Eva listened to the discussion around her as they mingled and waited. She pulled Ellen towards her.

"They're worried about the number of nonmembers that have arrived. They are discussing how to handle it," she whispered.

"They won't call it off will they?" Ellen asked.

"It's one of the options they've flagged but I think that ship has sailed."

"We need this to go ahead to shut it down forever, if that makes sense." Ellen looked around her.

Eva nodded and continued listening to the NAO leaders' discussions beside her. It was 9.50 a.m., ten minutes before the march was to officially begin and the streets for blocks were filled with Nazi supporters.

Chants were beginning further down the street and as the crowds swelled, Ellen felt the people around her pressing in. She looked around and shuddered; the scene was frightening and the language jarring and foreign. She felt the panic rising within her and then felt Eva's hand on her arm.

"I'm here, don't forget," Eva said.

Ellen nodded. "Is it that obvious?"

Eva leaned close to her ear. "It's exciting or frightening. You and I fall into that category last."

Ellen understood what Eva meant. She strained to pick out the security officers and police—there was no chance that they could protect her, Eva or Adam. She strained to find Adam, but there was no hope of seeing him amongst the crowd.

From the sounds swelling from further down

the block, Kristallnacht was going to become Kristalltag—the daytime version. Ellen worried about the Berlin Jewish population; what would they be feeling: terror, trauma, disbelief? What would they tell their children?

61

MITCH, JOHN AND NICK WATCHED THE NEWS FEEDS. Mitch kept an eye on the time; he and Nick needed to be on the streets at six a.m. for their own rally starting at seven. His phone rang and Mitch grabbed it. Seeing Adam's number he put it on speaker phone.

"Adam, you're on speaker phone. John and Nick are with me. What's happening?" Mitch asked.

"It's out of control already." Adam fought to be heard above the noise.

Mitch could barely hear him.

"I can't see the girls or the cops. The noise coming from the next block is full-on and I've heard sirens down there so that's all over. Upfront, there's no violence yet, so I'm sticking to plan," Adam said.

"Be careful Adam, you don't know who is listening around you," Mitch reminded him. Adam changed his message slightly.

"Got it. There are thousands here, word not only spread but the NAO obviously has a huge following...there's thousands of us in our black and badges," he said, including himself for fear of being overhead.

Mitch could hear the tension in his voice. "Can you see Voigt?"

"Oh yeah, he's in place with his team around him," Adam said. "There's wall to wall signs with his image on them as well, being waved around. Ellie and Eva are up front near him."

"Adam, just do the deed early and get out of there," Mitch said. "All we need is for the media team to capture the worst for the feed and our work is done. You don't need to stick around; the locals can clean that up. Just set up the shot we need, get the girls and get out."

A loud noise like an explosion could be heard.

"What was that?" Adam asked. The line cut out.

"Shit," Mitch swore and rang him back. It went to message bank. He looked from John to Nick and back at the footage now on BBC of the rally.

"This is out of hand before it starts," Mitch said. He turned up the volume of the news report.

"Thousands have turned out for a rally in the suburb of Kreuzberg in Berlin; a suburb traditionally known for

immigrant unrest. Our correspondent Rosemary Mc-Quirk is on the scene."

Cross to journalist on the streets:

"Thank you Andrew. Yes, the organized rally location seems a strange choice for the launch of candidate Leon Voigt's run for the seat of Chancellor. Supporting him are thousands of people wearing badges for The New Aryan Order and carrying campaign signs. Voigt is at the front of the march which extends down several blocks. It seems to have attracted hundreds of neo-Nazi supporters who, by the looks of their attire, are not members of The New Aryan Order."

The newsreader cut to an interview with a beautiful blond male, tall and chiseled. Underneath him a caption read: *Sebastian Graf, CEO of The New Aryan Order German Chapter.* He spoke in English, directly to camera.

"The New Aryan Order is the party that will return Germany to Germans. Leon Voigt will be Chancellor and the glory of Germany—its history and its culture—will be restored."

The news piece cut to the thousands marching and carrying lanterns before returning to the reporter.

"Andrew, you'll notice the use of lanterns. A NAO member told me that the glass of the lanterns signifies the anniversary of the original Kristallnacht on this day in 1938 when windows of synagogues, homes, and Jew-

ish-owned businesses were smashed during a violent outburst. Then German officials responded that it was an act of public sentiment in response to the assassination of German embassy official Ernst vom Rath by a seventeen-year-old Polish Jew. It is noteworthy that Kristallnacht marked the first instance in which the Nazis incarcerated Jews on the basis of their ethnicity. It is an interesting anniversary to mark for a party supposedly launching a peaceful campaign.

The reporter steadied herself after being shoved by the crowd and continued.

"I am told this is meant to be a peaceful campaign launch but it is very frightening here. A New Aryan Order spokesperson said they weren't expecting a crowd like this. The swell is pushing and crushing people along the streets."

The news feed cut to crowds protesting and cheering as they marched along the streets. Hundreds of people were pressed against shop windows or jostling for position on footpaths to watch.

"I contacted the head of the Jewish Central Council based in Berlin who said they had no knowledge of the rally and expect the government and police to act to shut it down immediately."

———

Ellen felt the crowd pressing against her. It was hard to breathe, hard to hear, but she could hear her heart thumping a hundred miles an hour. She attempted to move to the sidewalk out of the crowd, but throngs of people were pushing into the parade and filling up the paths. She felt Eva take her hand and pull her through the crowds. The front of the rally was chanting "Voigt for Chancellor, Germany for Germans". Camera crews were everywhere and the communication team from Germany's BKA— the German equivalent of the FBI—was waiting for that one shot to capture Voigt in a moment of violence.

Ellen knew the aggression had to start at the front as soon as possible to get the footage needed; the media was moving to the back streets where the sirens were blaring. Ellen and Eva had passed the point at which they agreed Adam would break the glass, which meant Adam would almost be parallel to it.

C'mon Adam, it's now or never, Ellen thought.

————

Adam realized the timing of his shot would have to be moved forward. He moved as close as he could to several shop windows to put his plan in place and as he reached for the gun to shoot a pellet through the glass, a loud roar went up from behind him, turning heads away.

Perfect, he thought. As he went to take the shot, a young man in a black leather jacket with a red swastika on the back, threw a rock through a window, shattering the glass. People nearby began to scream and yell. Many dropped to the ground. Caught up in the excitement, three young men followed suit, throwing their lanterns at more windows and shattering them as they'd predicted.

"Bloody hell," Adam muttered, "Job done." He hid his gun and moved through the crowd, away to the meeting point Eva and Ellen had selected.

Further up the line, Ellen flinched at the sound of breaking glass. NAO members around her began to get excited. Arms were raised and cries of *Heil Hitler* filled the air. She saw Voigt; he was yelling, his face red, the image could be misconstrued as anger or support. His campaign signs waved around him and members of the NAO did the Nazi salute in support. *Got you,* she smiled. She allowed Eva to continue to navigate their way through the crowd to the meeting spot.

———

Mitch, John and Nick watched it unfolding. They saw the vision of the glass window breaking and a man in a leather jacket running away. They saw the crowd erupting in fear and trying to disperse. Leon Voigt was yelling amidst a sea of signage and Nazi salutes.

"Someone's done Adam's job for him," Mitch said. He rocked on the balls of his feet as he watched. He glanced at his watch, his phone and back to the screen. "Get out now," Mitch said, talking to himself and willing his Berlin team to safety. The rally was getting more violent, reaching fever pitch.

They turned to the CNN footage. A middle-aged man was reporting the news, a subtitle carried his name: Chris Townsend.

"A neo-Nazi rally organized to launch the campaign of Chancellor-candidate Leon Voigt on the anniversary of Kristallnacht has sent shock waves through the city of Berlin. Kasey Donolly is on the ground."

Kasey, backed up against a shop window on the sidewalk near the rally, yelled above the noise: *"Chris, it is a frightening turnout for what was supposed to be a peaceful campaign launch. I don't think anyone expected the campaign message to be neo-Nazi; now the protest has erupted in violence. We spoke to the candidate, Leon Voigt earlier."*

Leon Voigt: *"This is a peaceful rally to show the superiority of the Aryan race and to announce that if I am* elected Chancellor, my team and I will make Germany the superior country that it is entitled to be."

Kasey continued to yell: "*Officials are saying the choice of location in an area known for multiculturalism and civil unrest was counter intuitive for a peaceful rally and an irresponsible choice by the New Aryan Order. Police and the riot squad have made hundreds of arrests and at this stage the violence is not abating.*"

A roar of noise erupted behind her and the camera panned to catch Voigt and his party as they searched for cover. Near the reporter several cars were rolled and set on fire and the front windows of a row of shops shattered. Kasey ducked as an object was hurled past her, smashing into the glass window next to her. A cheer went up.

She dropped the microphone as the crowd surged towards her. The camera operator was shoved with her, the camera continued to roll. Kasey began to scream, pressed against the glass of the one remaining pane in the shop front where she stood.

"Get back, you're going to break the glass," she said gasping, the glass pane bent in. "I can't breathe, get back". Her voice could barely be heard over the noise of the crowd. The vision continued to roll.

———

Adam Forster could see the young reporter and a group of other people being crushed against the window. He moved towards them, yelling for people to clear the area. He could see she was gasping, her chest was caving in with the pressure, the glass dangerously bowing behind her. People next to and around Kasey were screaming. Adam was yelling "move back, move back."

The glass window shattered; a large piece above acting as a guillotine. Kasey and a dozen other people pressed against the glass fell into the shop. Adam watched as her body was cut in two from the shoulders up.

———

The CNN presenter's voice could be heard. "Kasey can you...we need to come back to the studio." The camera stayed on Kasey. CNN went to an emergency black screen. The rally had its first fatalities. Mitch covered his face.

"Fuck." He dropped his hands. "John, we need to make the call upstairs and call the plan off—we don't need to agitate; the party by the nature of their message has done that themselves. Let's focus on just managing the march safely. There should be enough bad publicity now from Berlin to make our case here."

"I can tell you what the response will be now," John said. "There's politics at play here."

Mitch shook his head. He and Nick watched the news as John returned to his own office to make the call. He returned moments later.

"They're not convinced that enough people will see or care what is happening on a global stage. Our orders are to continue as planned," John said.

Mitch nodded and turned to Nick. "Let's go."

62

"YOU'RE KIDDING ME," MITCH HISSED. ALREADY IN the streets of Washington D.C., ninety minutes before the start of the rally, hundreds and hundreds of NAO members had gathered. Dressed in black, wearing their gold badges, a sea of blond heads filled the streets. Mitch looked as far as he could see and saw nothing but people.

Blending in with their blond hair and NAO badges, Mitch and Nick slipped into the gathering masses. NAO members were distributing campaign signs of Presidential candidate Ulric Adler and rolling posters of his campaign onto street posts.

They weaved their way to the front of the crowd and Nick saw Thorsten Schmid organizing the workers. He was scanning the crowds and his eyes found Nick's. He raised his hand in a wave. Nick reciprocated. He saw Thorsten's eyes flicker to Mitch but he didn't appear to make the connection between the tall, blond man beside Nick and the man who came in to interrogate him several weeks before. Dirk Schmid was nowhere in sight yet.

Mitch leaned closer to Nick. "Will you go help out, see what they're saying about the Berlin rally? And remember I'm your cousin if anyone asks. Can I have your phone?"

"Sure. What are you going to do?" Nick asked.

"I just want to see the CNN footage on yours while I try and reach Adam or Ellie on mine." Mitch moved away out of the gathering masses and made his way to the edge of the street. He rang Ellen. As he expected the phone went to voicemail. He watched the vision of the Berlin riot police moving in. The camera caught ambulances loading victims. Along the bottom of the screen a tally ran: four confirmed dead, hundreds injured.

"Christ," Mitch cursed as Adam's phone went to message bank. He tried Eva's phone and she answered. Relief swept over him. "Eva, it's Mitch. Are you all safe?"

"Mitchell, we can't find Adam, but Ellen and I are fine," she shouted above the noise. "We went to the meeting spot but we couldn't get close to it. We're heading to the second liaison now."

"Thanks Eva," Mitch said. "If he's not there, get

out, head back to the hotel. He might do the same. Tell him to call me as soon as you find him."

Mitch hung up. He watched the footage for a few minutes more and glanced over at Nick. He was handing out badges, mingling in. He made eye contact with Mitch and looked worried. Mitch gave him the thumbs up and saw him visibly exhale.

Mitch hung up and began to walk away from Nick. The rally was growing in size; he wanted to see the extent. He walked for a block past hundreds of NAO members arriving, easily as many as in Berlin. There were very few ring-ins as yet, but it was still forty minutes until the official start of the rally. As he turned the corner, Mitch's eyes widened. He stepped back out of sight to observe, his pulse racing. Several hundred skinheads, all wearing black leather jackets with red Nazi swastikas emblazoned on the sides and backs of their jackets, filled the square in the street behind that which was designated for the rally.

"Shit," he muttered, "the trouble's here." Mitch called John.

"John, just spoke with Eva. She and Ellen are out, but no sign of Adam yet."

"Right," John said. "Thanks, keep me posted."

"Hold on, we've got a bigger problem." Mitch explained what he was seeing. "New plan—we have to disperse the rally right back at The German-American Friendship Garden; send the police to turn away anyone that's arriving now. The march is not only filling 17th Street but 15th as well. H Street is filling up and Lafayette Square is almost over-crowded to the point of not being safe. Nick and I will stick to the plan, cause trouble early, let the communications unit get the shots they need and close it down early. But the riot squad and police have to stop the crowds farther back and start dis-persing them now. That way there's no damage and no crushing of the crowd. It's the only way to avoid what happened in Berlin."

"I'm onto it. Anything else?" John asked.

"No, thanks, but can you confirm they've under-stood the plan?" Mitch hung up without waiting for an answer.

He turned and scanned the crowd in the other direction. It was a sea of black everywhere. The rally had expanded over two streets. He felt a little of the anxiety that must have been felt on that dark night in Berlin when the windows were broken and Jewish people were threatened in No-vember 1938. Mitch took to the sidewalk, edging his way back towards Nick, glancing at the two phones—Nick's for the vision, his own for Adam's call. The rally images of Ulric Adler were every-where. Further up towards Nick, Mitch heard a cheer as the crowd erupted. He saw the crowds part for a black limousine crawling along H Street; it stopped and Ulric Adler alighted to more cheering. He walked a very short distance in the crowd before heading towards the rally point in Lafayette Square.

Mitch was beginning to feel the crush of people around him. He avoided the sidewalk for fear of being crushed against the windows and waded through the crowds. He tried to look enthusiastic, greeting fellow NAO members as he moved, their eyes were bright with excitement. Eventually he reached Nick and they moved ahead of the rally starting point where the crowd would eventually march.

"What's NAO management saying?" Mitch asked.

"It's going ahead but they're going to start shortly, fifteen minutes early, to ease the congestion. Then when they get to the stage for speeches, Adler will call for calm and ask people to put down their lanterns and heed the message."

"Yeah, good luck with that," Mitch said. "We'll be sticking to plan. I've called John to get the rally dispersed now back at the starting point near the German-American Friendship Garden and to clear 15th Street. With luck that will stop the surge and avoid any more moving forward. The SWAT team and police have already closed off entry via New

York Avenue. We'll do our bit at the start for publicity but it won't reach the masses."

"Good idea," Nick said, looking around. "Any news on Adam?"

"Not yet." He handed Nick back his phone. "Thanks. There's a freaky scene around the corner, at least a couple of hundred neo-Nazi skinheads ready for action." He looked around before continuing to speak. "Given the rally is starting early and what's happening in Berlin, I think we should start our action five or so minutes earlier as well, get it contained sooner. Thoughts?"

Nick looked around. "Agreed. We should get in position."

"You remember where we're meeting?" Mitch checked.

"Got it."

Mitch nodded and turned.

"Mitch ..."

Mitch turned. "Yeah?"

"How bad is it down there?" He nodded towards the end of the street.

Mitch grimaced. "Bad."

"Be careful, I don't want to have to save your ass again," Nick said with a nervous smile. Mitch grinned and watched him walk away, swallowed by the crowds.

Mitch's phone rang and he grabbed it. "Adam?"

"We're all out and okay," Adam said.

Mitch breathed out. "Thanks." He felt a huge weight lift off his shoulders.

Adam continued, "But Mitch, there are now seven dead, and the injuries are in the hundreds. They picked the wrong area, stupid fucking idea to have it in an area that is already hostile."

"Adam ..." Mitch interrupted him.

"Why do that unless you want trouble? They were asking for it and innocents have paid the price," Adam continued. "They knew what they were doing; they knew it would incite a riot and I bet they planned to make the immigrants the scapegoats, just like they did with the Jews."

"Okay, listen Adam—"

"People have been crushed to death," Adam was ranting, his voice rising above the noise, "there's glass injuries everywhere; we didn't need a plan, it was always going to be a disaster."

"Adam!" Mitch interrupted him.

"It wasn't just the other neo-Nazi groups, it was refugees, students, anyone who had a bone to pick with authority in the end. Jesus, I saw a girl guillotined by a glass window. It's—"

"Adam, stop!"

Adam stopped talking.

"Put Ellen on," Mitch ordered. He waited.

"Mitch?" It was Ellen.

"Ellen get him out of there now!" Mitch ordered and hung up.

He shook his head, exhaled and called John.

"John, all three are safe, but Adam's lost it. Can you call Ellie back in five minutes and check on them?"

"What do you mean, he's lost it?" John asked.

"He's freaking out—I get why he was stood down from action for a while," Mitch said. "He's out of danger, and we've got bigger problems here at the moment. Nick's been up the front with NAO management and they're going ahead with it. Are the police dispensing those neo-Nazi groups at the other end?"

"Yes, happening as we speak. After the Berlin situation, we've put the city on alert, and we've got the army coming in too," John said.

"Thanks. I don't know that we're going to need to do our part now, given the situation in Berlin, but we'll see. I'll bring it forward and we'll do it in the first ten minutes so it doesn't bubble over down the line."

"Yes, good idea, then we can shut it down with any luck before it reaches the masses. I'll alert the security team on the ground to pass the word and let the media and communication team know," John said.

"Thanks." Mitch hung up.

He turned to find the street awash with an Aryan race. A cheer went up and the rally began. Mitch felt for his concealed weapon as he walked along on the fringe of the parade. He searched for Nick; not seeing him but hoping he was far enough ahead to be out of harm's way and out of the media and communication team's photos.

63

ELLEN GRABBED ADAM'S ARM AND INDICATED FOR EVA to take the other. She tried to focus him.

"Adam, lead us back to the car, you know the way."

He looked at her, his eyes darting from Ellen to the crowds.

"Yeah, it's this way," he said, stepping up at Ellen's request. He pulled the two girls through the crowds, many fleeing now to avoid the police and crushing.

Ellen gripped tightly to him. She felt battered; Adam and Eva were easily a foot taller and wider than her and had more physical presence in the crowd. Finally she could see the break and they moved into it and away into the back streets.

She sighed with relief. Eva visibly slumped.

"I never saw that coming," Eva said. "I thought we were spreading the word to a few select people, but the NAO people are their own worst enemy."

"There's so many of them," Ellen agreed. "Let Eva drive, hey Adam? She'll know the best way out."

Adam nodded. His jaw locked, eyes squinted as he continued to watch for every action and movement. He handed the keys to Eva. The women exchanged looks.

"Let's go back to our hotel and we'll debrief," Ellen suggested. As they pulled away from the curb, going the opposite direction to the crowds and damage, Ellen's phone rang and John's name flashed on the screen.

"John," she answered, "we're all in the car and leaving the scene now. We're heading back to the hotel to debrief."

"Be subtle, but how is he?" John asked after Adam.

"Intense."

"Focused?" John asked.

"No. Distracted."

"Get Eva to organize an agency medic to come to the apartment urgently. Just do your best to calm him down. Don't let him leave the hotel room if you can," John said.

"Understood. Is everything okay there?" Ellen asked.

"The march has just started. Mitch and Nick are in it but there are all the same problems. Thousands upon thousands have turned out and there's a huge group of skinheads at the end of the parade. Our teams are on hand to shut it down half-way," John said. "Call me back as soon as the medic arrives."

"Will do." Ellen hung up. "Eva, I think I should drive and you navigate and make some calls to management with updates." She gave Adam a focus. "Adam, keep your eyes open to help us get through the traffic."

"Yeah, I'm doing that," he said, casing the area intently.

Eva read between the lines and pulled over. The two women swapped places. Outside the car Ellen whispered in passing, "Can you get an agency medic to the hotel urgently?"

Eva nodded and slipped into the back seat next to Adam. Ellen checked him out in the rear view mirror. His skin was pale and clammy, his eyes glazed. She drove on.

———

In Washington D.C., a sea of people in black, many waving placards, swarmed through the streets. The noise of the chanting could be heard for blocks. Helicopters hovered overhead. The crowd was pouring into the German-American Friendship Garden on the National Mall and down 17th Street towards H Street and Lafayette Square, lanterns swinging by their sides. Mitch could feel the swell and while the crush had not started, it was almost impossible to move in, out or sideways from the flow of the crowds. He glanced at his watch and kept as close to the edge as he could. A huge double-glassed shop window would prove the perfect starting point.

Mitch heard a gunshot. People in front of him screamed and fell to the ground. A solo figure stood with his hand on his chest near the stage set up in Lafayette Square—Ulric Adler. Mitch could see the blood appearing on his white business shirt.

Mitch glanced around. A man ran from the tight pack of NAO officers around Adler. The SWAT team moved in, bellowing orders. Crowds were streaming away from the scene; screaming and yelling over the wail of sirens, pushing and running through the streets.

Mitch kept his eyes on the figure and waded through the crowd. He tried to follow him as best he could as the man disappeared through the crowds and around the side of the building. He moved quickly away from the scene and down 16th Street, away from the masses, taking advantage of the panic to escape. Mitch was getting closer, pushing against a stream of people. He cleared them and increased his pace. The figure moved around the corner of another building and Mitch kept up.

He stopped, unable to see him. Then he saw movement again out of the corner of his eyes. The figure was heading to a car. Mitch stepped up the pace. The man unlocked the car, threw something on the floor and leapt in. Mitch slid across the bonnet to the driver's door, pulled it open and grabbed the figure from the car. After throwing him to the ground, Mitch restrained him and looked into the car; on the floor of the passenger's seat was a gun, the gun that just shot Ulric Adler.

Mitch pressed his knees into the man's back as he grabbed his phone and called John.

"Mitch, where are you?"

"I've got the shooter. I'm not moving with him, send someone to us." Mitch gave the location. "Adler?"

"He's dead," John reported.

Mitch hung up and waited for the collector. He looked down at Thorsten Schmid.

"Is he dead?" Thorsten asked.

"Yes."

Thorsten exhaled. "It's over then."

"All that time, you played along—or did you just want the top job for yourself or your brother?" Mitch asked.

"I was never one of them." Thorsten spat the

words out. "I did this for my country today and I'm very proud of my actions. I'm a patriot."

Mitch nodded. "Except for the murder, can't say I disagree with the sentiment."

Mitch pushed Thorsten Schmid upright against the car. Thorsten exhaled, his body slumped.

"If you had the chance to kill Adolf Hitler knowing what he was capable of, would you take it?" Thorsten asked.

"Knowing what we know now, I'd finish him with one clean shot."

Thorsten smiled.

"Tell me something," Mitch said, "why did you go for Benjamin Hoefer? Why attract attention to yourself when you had this other mission?"

"I didn't want to," Thorsten said, "you're right, we didn't need the distraction or attention. But Dirk hated Eli Hoefer—our grandfather—hated him with a passion. He knew he was alive and living here and he had this unhealthy obsession about it. But once Benjamin released the book, it was too much for him. He had to act."

Mitch saw two SWAT team members at the corner and motioned to them. He took Thorsten's arm, pulled him up and handed him over.

Mitch sat on the sidewalk and watched them take Thorsten Schmid away.

· · ·

FROM CNN:

"It was a day of violence and disillusionment on the streets of Washington D.C. Presidential candidate Ulric Adler was shot and pronounced dead at 7.15 this morning at a political rally to launch his campaign to be President. Adler declared his party policies and allegiance to a neo-Nazi group, The New Aryan Order. Ashleigh Maymen is on the scene.

"Good afternoon, Simon. Order has been restored to the streets with the dispersing of several thousand rally members. Adler was declared dead by paramedics at 7.15 this morning, allegedly shot by a member of his own party, identified as Thorsten Schmid. Paramedics treated several hundred people for shock and minor injuries.

Thorsten Schmid and his brother Dirk Schmid, a respected anesthetist, were senior members of The New Aryan Order. Dirk Schmid is denying all knowledge of his brother's actions but Thorsten Schmid had prepared a post that appeared at ten a.m. on his Facebook page saying he was a patriot who did this for his country. He said if a brave German had assassinated Adolph Hitler when the opportunity presented itself, the world would have been a better place. The party leaders have been taken in for questioning and I'm sure we will hear a lot more about the march and The New Aryan Order over the next few days, Simon. Back to you."

64

IT WAS JUST AFTER ONE A.M. MITCH LAY AWAKE thinking back over the case. He calculated it was seven a.m. in Berlin. He had left it a day before calling, rolled over, picked up his phone and dialed Adam Forster's phone. Adam answered on the second ring.

"You're up late," Adam answered.

"You know how it is. How are you? I didn't wake you?" Mitch asked.

"No, I've been up for a while. I'm better, embarrassed ..." Adam said.

"There's no need to be. Really," Mitch assured him.

"I've been under worse pressure than that, Mitch," Adam said. "You know I've seen a lot worse; I don't know why ..." his voice trailed off.

Mitch sat up and leaned against his bed head. "It accumulates, all that stuff. But sometimes it's the unexpected that trips you up."

There were a few moments of silence before Adam answered.

"Yeah. I saw her guillotined. I've seen men shot down in battle, but that was just ... I couldn't reach her." He choked.

"Have you got someone to lean on?" Mitch asked.

"Yeah, I've got plenty of people lining up to read my head," Adam said.

"I bet you have."

"Astrid has been great. We're going to try and work it out. Two nutters together," he laughed.

"That could work," Mitch agreed. "I'm sorry Adam, for my part in it."

"You did nothing wrong Mitch. Nothing. But thanks for calling."

"Sure," Mitch said. "Call if you need to. Any time."

"Thanks."

Mitch hung up, put the phone down and slipped back down under the sheets. He suddenly felt very alone.

———

The next day, Mitch, his boss John and his team members Nick and Ellen sat around in his office late in the afternoon. Ellen had returned on her flight after midday and Mitch was yet to finish his report.

"I'm sorry to report that Adam will be staying in Germany for a while. He's been stood down and is getting some help," John informed the team.

"And he's spending a bit of time with his wife, ex-wife, Astrid, seeing if they can work things out," Mitch added.

Mitch closed the file on his lap. "Thorsten Schmid comes before the court next Wednesday. There is a petition online calling for his release and calling him a hero."

"It's a fine line," Ellen said, "I feel like he is in a way, but he did take a life."

"If we were at war he'd get a medal," Nick agreed.

"He's definitely more attractive to me now than before." She nudged Nick. "If I'd known when we were undercover ..."

"You still would have married me," he assured her.

Mitch looked from Ellen to Nick and then, ignoring them, continued. "His brother Dirk has been charged with ... well you name it, it's on the rap sheet—spreading anti-Semitic and xenophobic messages, terrorizing and organizing attacks on

Benjamin Hoefer, blackmail, incitement to hatred and glorification of war crimes, etc., etc."

"The party has been decimated," John said. "Adler is dead, the images we captured of Voigt in Berlin inciting violence shut down any hope he has of becoming Chancellor, and Sebastian Graf CEO of The New Aryan Order in Berlin is under investigation. It will be a lengthy procedure; they'll work through the top party members here and in Germany in due course."

"What happens to the *Fountain of Life 2* children?" Ellen asked.

"They're all loved and wanted aren't they? Like our love child would have been." Nick winked at her. "And unlike the original *Fountain of Life* children. The only drama will be explaining to the kids when they get older about their family genetics, if they do explain."

"What a mess." Ellen shook her head.

"You did a great job, team, thank you," Mitch said. "I'm sorry about what happened to Adam. I should have been more vigilant, seen it coming."

John shook his head. "He coped well on the London assignment. Something in the march that day was a trigger. He'll get the help he needs. Mitch, I need to talk to you about a replacement, so if we've finished here?"

Mitch nodded.

"We're going for a quick round at the bar across the road. Well maybe a few rounds," Ellen said. "Come over when you're done."

"Both of you," Nick said with a look to Mitch. "The report can wait, can't it John?"

John agreed. "Yes, tomorrow will do."

Ellen and Nick left Mitch's office.

"Got someone in mind?" Mitch asked. He rose and went behind his desk to log out.

"Samantha came to see me this morning."

Mitch looked up at John and frowned.

"I know what you're thinking, but she asked me to put in a good word for her and consider her application to return to the team," John said, rising. "I'm going to leave it to you to decide if you can rein her in but give her a hearing at least. She's at her desk downstairs if you want to call her up."

Mitch stood to full height with his hands on his hips. "It would be easy to have her slot back in but ..."

"I'll tell her to come up and see you now and we'll see you across the road in fifteen minutes or so. You don't have to make any decisions tonight but I'll support your decision either way," John said, and departed.

After closing down his laptop, Mitch grabbed his coat jacket and put it on. Minutes later he turned to find Samantha Moore at his door. She smiled nervously. Tall, dark-haired, slim and fit, Samantha had been patiently waiting for her chance to return to his team; to prove herself.

"Sam." Mitch smiled. "It's good to see you."

"Isn't it?" she teased. "Haven't you missed me just a bit?"

"Missed saving your ass you mean?" he teased back.

"Missed my enthusiasm, my ability to break in to any system, my support, my sparkling personality?" Samantha said.

Mitch laughed. "Gee, now that you mention it."

She moved towards him and handed him three pieces of paper.

"What's this?" he asked, taking the sheets.

"The first one is my swimming qualification that you wanted me to do. I've done it. The second is my shooting record; I've been keeping it up and I've improved—especially in a sniper capacity. The final one is a statement showing for the last six months I've been a part-time Army Reserve officer. One weekend per month for the last six months I've been in training and for my two weeks' annual leave I did their Annual Training program."

Mitch looked up, surprised.

"Well, you said I wasn't disciplined and couldn't follow orders, especially under pressure. You also said or maybe muttered that some military training would help the way I think and approach situations. So I've been learning how to fall into line. I've improved, Mitch, I really have."

Mitch sat down on the edge of the desk and looked through the certificates and statements.

"I'm impressed, Sam."

She moved closer to him. "Please Mitch, let me rejoin your team. I know I've made promises before, but I've taken on board what you said, so let me prove myself."

Mitch nodded. "Okay, Sam."

"Okay? Really?" Her eyes lit up. "As in okay I can come back?"

"Yes, okay, really. Welcome back."

Samantha closed her eyes for a moment, exhaled, opened her eyes, and thanked him in a controlled and professional manner. Mitch looked surprised. The old Samantha would have run at him and enthusiastically hugged him and ran out of the room in excitement.

"We've just finished a job and are having a drink across the road. Come and rejoin the team."

"I'll grab my gear and meet you there," she said. "Thank you Mitch."

"It will be good to have you back."

She clapped her hands together and then impulsively hugged him. Mitch winced, and seconds later she was gone.

He turned to get his phone before heading to the bar. Nick and Ellen stopped by.

"I thought you'd be there ordering me a beer by now," Mitch said.

"We're on our way. I see she's back then, by the look of that," Nick nodded towards a smiling Sam as she headed down the stairs.

"Yeah, what's with the hugging?" Mitch frowned. "Everyone's hugging these days. Women either want to hug me or dye my hair."

"Lucky you," Ellen said. "Did you invite Sam for a drink?"

"I did. She's meeting us there. Ellie, can I have five minutes with you?"

"Uh oh," Ellen said.

"I'll go invite Amy then hold up the bar," Nick said. "Don't be all night."

"You didn't have to come into the office this afternoon," Mitch said as Ellen walked further into his office.

"I know, but you know what it's like. I landed just after midday, then I was wired. You don't want to sleep because you'll be out of sync, so it's best to keep going." She shrugged.

Mitch rose from sitting on the corner of his desk. "Can you close the door for a minute?"

"Sure," Ellen said, surprised. There were only a

few people left on the floor but she closed the door as requested. She turned to face him.

Mitch put his hands in his pockets and rocked.

"Ellie, I know about your history—your Jewish ancestry."

Ellen's eyes widened in surprise. She put her bag and jacket down on the chair near the door. "My history. How?"

"It doesn't matter. Why didn't you tell me?" he asked, keeping his voice low.

She bit her lip but didn't answer.

"Out of everyone in the team, you were the one who I thought would be upfront about that. You've gone undercover with a vested interest, a dangerous one, and don't tell me it was because we were short-staffed and we needed a female on the job. That won't cut it. You should have declared your family history and that it might have compromised your objectivity." Mitch stepped back and sat on the edge of his desk again while Ellen paced.

"If I had told you, you wouldn't have let me do it," she said.

"That's right," Mitch agreed.

"After working with me for two years, don't you think that I can judge my limits? It's ancient history, Mitch. Yes, my relatives on my mother's side were murdered by the Nazis and yes, I was disgusted being amongst the NAO, but it wasn't emotional."

"What was it then? A history lesson?" Mitch asked.

"Yes, in a way. But it was more than that," she said. "What I mean is that I am deeply saddened by my family's history but I didn't know those family members personally to be overly emotional, I'm just ..."

"Angry, revengeful?" Mitch helped her.

Ellen stopped pacing and looked directly at him. She crossed her arms across her chest and thought before answering.

"No, stop putting words in my mouth. I wanted to right a wrong," she said. "I don't expect you to understand that, but I was honored to have the chance to do this and to use my job and my skills to possibly shut down something that should never have started again. Imagine if I could have done that in 1939."

Mitch thought about what she said. They stared at each other, neither speaking for a few moments.

"Okay, I hear all that," Mitch said, "but what about you? You can't tell me that you weren't hearing their plans and it wasn't making you sick?"

"Sure. But no more than it made you or Nick angry or revolted. Mitch, if you could go undercover and catch someone who did something to your grandmother, wouldn't you give it your best performance ever?"

"And you couldn't trust me with any of that before I sent you in?" he said.

"Trust works both ways, Mitch."

"What does that mean?"

She stopped pacing and turned to face him. "When we were on our last case, do you remember when you had to return to the scene where you were tortured?"

Mitch looked away.

"You had a panic attack," she continued. "I was the team medic and you sent me from the room to get Nick to help you. You couldn't trust me enough to get you through that. You had to play the macho guy or whatever that was."

He looked back at her. "It's not comparable. My actions didn't put you at risk but you withheld information that could have affected you on the case."

She continued. "In the two years we've worked together, your housemate Lyn is the first person in your life I've ever met." She held up her hand to stop him protesting. "I know, I sound like your ex, but you met my ex last year, you've met my mum when she came to visit on holidays, you've come to my place for coffee ... you keep all elements of your life compartmentalized. So you can't be surprised when I choose what to tell you and what to trust you with." She began to pace again. "We work on some level, but I don't know what it is and I'm following your lead."

Mitch's eyes narrowed in anger; he bit his tongue and looked at the floor, thinking before responding. After a few minutes, he spoke. "You're probably right Ellie, about all that. I accept the medic comment, fair enough, and everything you've said I'm guilty of, but this is not you talking. You've never really wanted to invade my life, you're as private as I am. You're just trying to justify your actions in your head."

He stood. "The buck stops with me, Ellie, and if you get hurt, I'm responsible. If I get hurt, you're not. Try me next time, I might just surprise you." He shrugged. "But probably not since my entire team seems to think I'm anal, compartmentalized, too uptight or whatever you all want to call it when you have to do it my way." He opened the door for her to leave. "I'm going to finish this report. You go join the team. You did a great job Ellie, thanks, despite the risk," he said.

Ellen nodded and walked out of his office.

No tears, no emotion, she was cool and calm and maybe she was capable of making that decision.

He turned to look out the window at the dusk. He sighed, leaning on the windowsill, letting her comments run through his head. For the second time that day he felt very alone. Mitch ran a hand over his short blond hair, wincing at the pain from the blow to the back of his head.

He heard his office door close again and turned to find Ellen standing there. She had tears in her eyes.

"I'm sorry Mitch, you are right, I should have told you." She swallowed. "But there was so much at stake for me and I didn't want you to remove me from it. You do have my support, one hundred per cent support around the clock."

"Ellie." He sighed.

"You do, honestly, and I don't think you're anal. I think you're brilliant and tactical and you are right, I don't care about our private lives, I was just justifying it in my head, as you said." She wiped her eyes with a tissue she pulled from her sleeve, then turned to leave.

Mitch moved quickly to the door and grabbed her arm. "Ellie, wait. Thanks for saying that. I will take on board what you said. I'll work on it ... where I can."

She smiled. "I feel like an idiot for crying."

"I'm so relieved you're a girl," Mitch teased her.

She hit him on the arm. "Shut up."

Mitch grinned. "Want me to hug you?"

"No, definitely not," she said. "Weren't you just complaining that everyone wants to hug all of a sudden?"

Mitch held up his hands in a surrender. "Just offering since it seems to be the done thing."

Ellen moved towards him and, slipping her arms under his jacket, wrapped them around him.

He smiled, closed his eyes and held her. He lowered his chin to the top of her head and wished.

65

Mitch and Ellen entered the bar and found Nick and John amongst the crowd of after-work drinkers.

"So?" John asked.

"Sam's back," Mitch told him.

John nodded. "Good, I think given her new focus and the self-improvement she's been doing that it will work out fine."

Ellen smiled. "It will be like old times."

"I'll get this round," Mitch said, heading to the bar.

"Here she is." Nick looked around Mitch to Samantha entering.

She raced in and embraced Ellen, John and Nick. She began to tell them about her new certificates.

"Don't mention it again when Mitch comes back in case he makes me do that parachuting course I haven't done yet," Ellen said. She looked at John. "Damn, did I just say that?"

John laughed. "Your secret's safe with me Ellie, for now."

As Mitch returned with drinks, Samantha embraced him again.

"Again with the hugging!" Mitch frowned.

Nick put his arm around Mitch's shoulder. "I know, it's nice isn't it?"

Mitch shrugged him off. "No. Here, drink this." He pushed a drink into Nick's hand.

John raised his glass. "Welcome back, Sam. To the team."

"To the team." They clinked their glasses.

Behind them, Nick's housemate Amy entered the bar. She turned a few heads with her fitted red dress and blond hair. Nick waved her over. Mitch rose, moving over to make room for her in their circle. He offered her a drink.

"Don't hug him," Nick warned her. "It's a blond thing."

"It's not a blond thing ... it's ... never mind," Mitch said.

"Want me to dye your hair brown again?" Amy asked.

Mitch shook his head. "The world's gone mad."

THE END

Dear reader,

We hope you enjoyed reading *The Fourth Reich*. Please take a moment to leave a review, even if it's a short one. Your opinion is important to us.

Discover more books by Helen Goltz at

https://www.nextchapter.pub/authors/helen-goltz

Want to know when one of our books is free or discounted? Join the newsletter at

http://eepurl.com/bqqB3H

Best regards,

Helen Goltz and the Next Chapter Team

You might also like:
Ophelia Adrift by Helen Goltz

To read the first chapter for free, head to:
https://www.nextchapter.pub/books/ophelia-adrift

Mastermind

An ambitious plan to switch two planes in mid-air began as an online game ... but now it is more, much more. It is a plan to mastermind the perfect crime. Will Special Agent Mitchell Parker and his team discover the plot before it is too late? If you love it when a plan comes together, hold on, because nothing is about to go right!

Graveyard of the Atlantic:

Below the surface of the ocean, off the shores of Cape Hatteras, lie the bodies of many ships that never made it to shore and something more ... silent and sinister. It's a rough and violent ride for Mitch and his team against the ocean and the clock.

ACKNOWLEDGMENTS

My sincere thanks to:

Rachel Quilligan for her subbing prowess;

Sally Odgers and Chris Adams for proofreading and feedback;

And most importantly Atlas B. Goltz - my beloved writing partner.

ABOUT THE AUTHOR

After studying English Literature and Communications at universities in Queensland, Australia, Helen Goltz has worked as a journalist and marketer in print, TV, radio and public relations. She was born in Toowoomba and has made her home in Brisbane.

Visit her website at: www.helengoltz.com

Or Facebook at:
www.facebook.com/HelenGoltz.Author

Follow on Twitter at: @helengoltz

The Fourth Reich
ISBN: 978-4-86752-364-3
Large Print

Published by
Next Chapter
1-60-20 Minami-Otsuka
170-0005 Toshima-Ku, Tokyo
+818035793528

26th July 2021

CPSIA information can be obtained
at www.ICGtesting.com
Printed in the USA
BVHW030739160223
658640BV00002BA/12